The queen spoke again, almost softly.

"Captain, I command you: clear the bridge!"

"Lady. . . ."

No man could have done anything then except obey. But only the wolf of Dohann would have obeyed with a laugh. It was the last thing Kiri expected, that soft growl of a laugh, like the triumphant sound of an animal unleashed.

"Lady, the bridge is yours!"

Everything changed then, with a throat-tightening swiftness. Names were shouted out, ranks fell into place; all around her Kiri could hear and see the Kamil fighters checking their weapons and their harnesses and the calmness of their hands, making small gestures towards their gods. A shawm joined the chant, harsh and wailing, and the men began to bang their shields. The drum beat quickened.

"So." Whatever outcome Prince Held might have imagined he could achieve, it was clear to him now that only one outcome had ever been possible. "You are a false and bloody people," he said grimly. "I wonder why I ever sought your friendship. When this day is over I will never seek it again. As for you, mongrel of Belengar—now I make you an oath."

He drew his sword and held it high, as men did when they swore before the lord of all the gods.

"It's two hundred leagues of mountain road from here to Aralev, and if I live, I will take you back with me, dragged by your feet behind the fetlocks of my horse. And what is left of you when we come there, I will throw to my dogs."

"You won't live," Shadrak said.

The words were not spoken as a threat, but as a fact, a thing already written: *From the mountains of Kamilan, enemies do not return. . . .*

High
Kamilan

For Elona,

High Kamilan

A Novel by
Marie Jakober

*with best wishes,
and hopes that the
world may once
again be different!*

Marie

GULLVEIG BOOKS
CALGARY, CANADA

Printed in Canada by McAra Printing Limited
Cover illustration by Michelle Zarb

Gullveig Books
Box 66023
University of Calgary Post Office
Calgary, Alberta
Canada T2N 4T7

Canadian Cataloguing in Publication Data

Jakober, Marie.
High Kamilan

ISBN 0-9697631-0-7

I. Title.
PS8569.A42H5 1993   C813'.54   C93-091896-7
PR9199.3.J34H5 1993

For Donna,
who liked it so much.

Acknowledgements

I would like to thank everyone who has helped to make this book possible, especially the following:

—Donna Smith, for editing assistance;

—Cate Vail, for proofreading;

—Michelle Zarb, for the splendid art work;

—and most of all, Gale Comin, for her amazing dedication, energy, and expertise in the launching of Gullveig Books.

I wish also to express my sincere thanks for financial assistance received, during the writing of this novel, from the Alberta Foundation for the Literary Arts.

Characters of the Novel

Kamils:

Marwen, queen of Kamilan
Medwina, her aunt, high priestess of the goddess Jana
Shadrak, captain of the border post of Belengar
Cassian and Tamon, his friends, soldiers in the border guard

The Kamil High Council:
—Angmar the Wise, chief of Council
—Borosar, warlord of Kamilan, commander of the Kamil army
—Landis, lord of Maene
—Crayfe, seneschal of the royal city
—Theron, high priest of the god Mohr
—Favian, lord of Tamri

Oswin, war-leader of Tamri
Ranir, war-leader of Maene
Caithland, captain of the queen's guard
Malia, the queen's chief cook
Harad, her steward
Luned, a servant

Dravians:

Held, crown prince of Dravia
Berend, his younger brother
Algard, their aged and dying father, king of Dravia
Erland the Red, a Dravian war-captain
Telhiron, legendary conqueror and ancestor of the Dravian kings

Caravaners:

Kiri of Vanthala, a minstrel and caravan guard
Mercanio of Sardas, a merchant
Clodis, friend of Kiri
Mara, his beloved
Tharn, Parel, Gareth, hostlers on the caravan

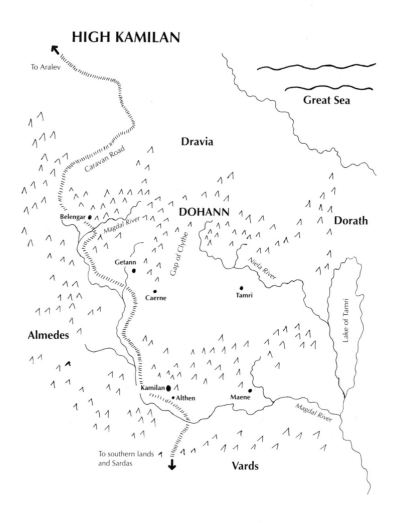

HIGH KAMILAN

To Aralev

Caravan Road

Dravia

Great Sea

Belengar

Magdal River

DOHANN

Dorath

Getann

Gap of Clythe

Niela River

Caerne

Tamri

Almedes

Lake of Tamri

Kamilan • Althen

Maene

Magdal River

To southern lands
and Sardas

Vards

Book One. The Captive

In the seventeenth year of the reign of Algard of Dravia, his firstborn son Held crossed the mountains into High Kamilan, and carried back the queen of that country for his wife. From this deed came much bloodshed, and all the misery which fell on Dravia in the years to follow.

The Chronicles of Larandau

Now as for the carrying off of women, it is the deed, they say, of a rogue; but to make a stir about such as are carried off, argues a man a fool. Men of sense care nothing for such women, since it is plain that without their own consent they would never be forced away.

Herodotus

Ten thousand clouds and mountains
Bar my road home. . . .
Men here are as savage as giant vipers
And strut about in armour, snapping their bows.

Ts'ai Yen

1. Marwen

It was a night of full moon and wolves. They came out of the high reaches of Dohann where, although it was summer, the day's rain had fallen laced with snow. They came black and silver in the cold light, circling into the valleys where hardy peasants slept uneasy and small things did not sleep at all. From pinnacle to high pinnacle they signalled their packs, and the cries reached even into the heart of Aralev, a fierce and melancholy howling that rose and fell with the wind.

But in the royal greathouse, secure within the stout wooden walls of the city, the prince of Dravia slept well. He lay on his bed naked, his light blanket gradually shoved away until it was only a tangle around his feet. He slept as he always did, with the grace of a boy and the absolute confidence of a man who would be king.

The woman who was called his wife did not sleep, but waited. It would come, as it had the first time. The pain, and then the quick spill of blood. The erasing of a life in the same manner as it had been made—without words, by darkness and by violence.

She sat on the floor not far from the window. She was afraid, but she did not have much consciousness of fear; it was too old, too blunt from use. The crying of the wolves was so close that sometimes she felt sure they must be just outside, in the broad square where the traders gathered, where next week the great caravan from Sardas would camp. *You may choose a gift,* the prince had promised her, *one gift, anything you wish, no matter how costly. I will buy it for you.* He was troubled now by her hollow eyes, by her thin body which would set neither flesh nor seed.

Give me a fast horse, Prince Held, and a road without a gate until I come to Belengar. Give me that, or speak no more of gifts.

A sharp cramp convulsed her, but she made no sound. Sweat ran down her armpits and spilled over her face. A large drop coursed suddenly into the crevice of her lips, and she licked it, tasting salt. She glanced hungrily at the blanket the prince had cast aside, but she made no move to take it.

She watched him for a time, reassured by his deep, steady breathing. He was, she supposed, quite beautiful. Other women certainly thought so. He was a splendid bear of a man with a great mass of red hair, a powerful voice which had a remarkable talent for song—and yes, that extraordinary confidence, that sense of himself as a king among men, moving through the world as though he owned it. His weapons were laid carefully on the wooden table beside his bed: sword, shield and bow in easy reach because he could not imagine being anywhere without them.

And he slept peacefully, as if he did not know that the woman who shared his chamber had those same weapons in the same easy reach, and more cause to use them than any man would ever have.

What did it feel like, she wondered, to be that sure, not merely of one's own rank and power, but of its absolute inviolability? To have that certainty as a birthright? She could not imagine it.

What is it you believe of me, Held of Dravia? That I am too weak to lift your sword? Or too weak to bring it down? I have already killed two of your children, and you sleep there like a boy. . . .

She bent over the sharp pain in her belly, clasping her knees. She did not know when the wolf came. She looked up and it was simply there, moving slowly across the room in a spill of moonlight as brilliant as day, its body rippling with strength, its face and its forepaws covered with blood.

She went rigid with terror. Only Held's presence kept her from screaming—his presence, and the silence she had taught herself in the face of almost any peril. Then, very deliberately, she closed her eyes. It was the potion she had taken; it had to be. The city was encased in walls, the palace sturdy and well guarded, the window shut tight against the mountain wind. No wolf could pass unchallenged through the heart of Aralev, to the very bedchamber of the prince. It was only the potion, dear goddess, and she had almost cried out, she had almost wakened him. . . !

She heard a soft sound, the sound Held's dogs made when they collapsed on the stone floor in the hall. She looked up. The wolf was still there. It had settled in the centre of the room and was licking the blood from its feet. Its fur was a smokey gray, tipped with black; its body was lean and beautiful. Was it real, then? She could not tell, and now it did not seem to matter. The animal clearly meant her no harm. It only wanted to rest, and to rid itself of those bright stains which never diminished, no matter how methodically it licked them, over and over. Once it looked directly at her, as if to question her, to ask her perhaps what it meant, why there was no end to all this blood.

She felt sorry for it. Had she been less weary she might have walked over to it, and knelt to stroke its smooth back. Surely it was a wolf from Kamilan, from her own mountains; surely it had come to her because of that?

A great lassitude closed over her, dissolving the boundaries of time and identity. From its depths she seemed to share the creature's thoughts.

—*Are you a messenger from Jana, Wolf? Is that why you're here?*

—*I am from Jana as all things are.*

—*But she sent you to me? She sent you here?*

—*I've come on my own errand. If it's your errand also, that will be for you to judge. When the time comes. When you're a queen again.*

—You've come to fetch me, then? You'll take me home?

—No. You must make your own way.

—I'm surrounded by enemies.

—There are many who will help you. You need only to seek them out.

—Even in Dravia, Wolf?

—Even in Dravia. Don't judge the land by its lords.

—Who are you?

There was no answer, and after a moment the woman questioned again:

—What are you?

The wolf got to its feet, as bloodied as before.

—I've searched long for one such as you, Marwen of Kamilan. We will meet again.

It moved without a sound towards the window and leapt into the night.

Some time later the woman rose, and carried from her chamber a bundle of darkly stained rags, and put them into the hands of a gnarled slave, along with three bright coins.

The moon was almost set.

2. Kiri of Vanthala

The caravan of the Sardas trader Mercanio the One-eyed camped the night of the full moon in a valley sixty leagues from the Dravian royal city of Aralev. They camped in good spirits, having come without harm through the most dangerous part of their journey: the borderlands between Dravia and Kamilan, the terrible mountains of Dohann. In the fifteen hundred leagues of their journey, from the sun-drenched vineyards of Sardas where they had begun to Vianon where they would end, no territory was more feared than Dohann. The border war between Dravia and Kamilan gave license to every kind of banditry. Robbers preyed on even well-armed caravans. And fighting bands from both armies, though they did not slaughter travellers as the robbers did, regularly demanded tribute for the right to pass. Many caravaners came out of Dohann with little left except their wagons and their lives. Some never came out again at all.

So every league of the fertile plateaus of central Dravia seemed beautiful to them. Aralev itself would mean feasting and dancing and wine. Aralev would mean coin in their hands, and pleasures to spend it on. Aralev would mean a great exchange of wealth and lust and stories.

"I'll be glad enough to get off the road," Parel said, "but let's not pretend we're in Vianon. Compared to the cities of Larandau, these mountain towns are nothing but barbarian camps, really."

Ah, Kiri thought, that was Parel, strutting and preening again. He had caravaned for five years, and every year he grew more insufferable. He was Dravian, just as she was, and he considered that a tragedy. For Parel, the only birthplace a man could be truly proud of was the empire of Larandau.

Kiri shifted her crossbow on her shoulder and paced a little. Safe though they probably were here, Mercanio left nothing to chance. The wagons were camped in a circle, with three perimeters of armed guards. From her post on the inside perimeter Kiri could not see Parel's group of hostlers, but she could hear nearly everything they said. There were seven or eight of them, gathered to gossip and play counters in the shifting light.

They spoke Dravian because Parel dominated the group, and caravaners learned quickly to be comfortable with many tongues. They spoke it, however, with many strange accents, the strangest of all being Sardas. People from the south had a habit of saying everything backwards.

Sometimes, with a group like this, Kiri would be fascinated by the mix of nationalities and ways of speech and thought. At other times the variations seemed utterly superficial, transcended by an overwhelming likeness: the likeness of male to male.

Except for Parel, who sometimes insulted her and other times tried to seduce her, she disliked none of these men. Often, with one or two of them alone, she had wonderful conversations, and thought of them as friends. But when men came together in a group they became different. And she could never decide which was real: the selves they showed to women, or the selves they showed to each other when women were not there.

—*I'll say one thing for Aralev; the whores are as good there as in Vianon, and a lot cheaper.*

—*Trust Parel. That's the first thing he thinks of.*

—*The first, and the second, and the last.*

—*What have you got there, Gareth? Let me see.*

—*Meal cakes. I traded old Hadge that buckle he's been wanting.*

—*The Thyrsian buckle? It's worth ten times as much as those meal cakes. You're a fool.*

—*I was hungry.*

—*Well, don't be a pig, lad. Give us some. There'll be plenty of good food in Aralev.*

—*There'll be plenty of everything in Aralev.*

—*I wonder if we'll get to have a look at this famous stolen queen.*

—*You'll be disappointed, Lafe. They say she's skinny, and plain as a stick.*

—*Perhaps. But with a royal crown tucked between her legs, even an ugly woman must have a certain charm.*

—*What I don't understand is why they're still fighting. I thought this marriage was supposed to end the war.*

—*It wasn't the sort of ending the Kams had in mind.*

—*Well, I dare say they brought it on themselves. They wouldn't marry the wench for quarreling among themselves who should have her: Landis of Maene on one side and Borosar the warlord on the other, and a half dozen more in between, every one of them with a son or a cousin suddenly fancying how he could be a king.*

—*It's incredible old Adelmar didn't settle it before he died.*

—*May be it he thinks he shuts his eyes and waits long enough, his girl child changes into a boy.*

—*A man could die two or three times waiting for that.*

—*Who knows? That one with the crossbow might manage it yet.*

—*Kiri? You could be right there.*

—*Is all right Kiri.*

—*You know, I've heard there's an island in the Middle Sea where the people have both. Maybe she's one of them.*

—*Both?*

—*Breasts and balls.*

—*Naw. She doesn't have balls.*

—*You know that for a fact, Parel, do you?*

—*He knows not, he will not say. He knows, he is dead. Either way, nothing you will get from him.*

—*Move your counter and shut up, Tharn.*

19

—*These meal cakes are worse than dry straw. Gods, just think, in a week we'll be eating in Aralev. Roast pig. Roast pheasant. Puddings dripping with honey. Barrels and barrels of wine. . . .*

—*Aye. Our own wine. Seventeen wagonloads of it, and we have to drag it eight hundred leagues, and then pay before we can drink it.*

—*Then become a merchant, and buy your own.*

—*Don't laugh. I will one day.*

—*And I'll become a prince, and carry off the queen of Kamilan. And I won't even bother asking first, like Held did.*

—*He asked for her? I didn't know that.*

—*Of course he asked. He's a prince, not a brigand. And he's no fool, either; he could see readily enough that an alliance with Kamilan would make him the greatest lord east of Larandau. He sent couriers with fine gifts to the High Council of Kamilan, to ask for the Lady Marwen in marriage.*

—*And they rejected him?*

—*They were outraged.*

—*You're exaggerating, Parel. They didn't take it seriously enough to be outraged. They made fun of the couriers to their faces. Did the prince of Dravia imagine that he could win with his prick what all the warriors of Dravia couldn't win in seventy years with all their swords? So the prince of Dravia took twenty men, dressed plain and travelling by night, and rode into the heart of Kamilan, and did exactly that.*

—*Now* that's *what I call courage.*

—*There's no bolder man alive. Or more utterly magnificent. They say he's nearly seven feet tall, but I only ever saw him mounted, so I can't say.*

—*Still, it was a great insult to Kamilan. I can understand why they almost killed you just for admitting you were Dravian.*

—*They'll get over it, when they see what they have in the manner of a king.*

—*It's an old hatred, Lafe.*

—*Do you think the Kamils will try to steal her back?*

—*You don't have an ounce of brains, lad. Steal her back with what? Dravia has ten armed men for every fighter in Kamilan. Better weapons. Five times the wealth to sustain a war. And a prince who has no equal as a warrior anywhere in the world. Who do you think they will send for her? That band of barbarians who took tribute from us at Belengar?*

—*I thought their captain seemed formidable enough.*

—*He has a black enough look. But what is he? I'll wager he's not even a lord of Kamilan, but a foreigner in their pay.*

—*Actually, Mercanio told me something interesting about that. Mercanio says he's Thyrsian, and a freedman.*

—*What does Mercanio know?*

—*On the caravan road, Mercanio knows everything.*

—*Well, if it is true, it just proves my point. What is Kamilan reduced to, if Borosar is placing strategic posts like Belengar into the hands of brigands and slaves? The Thyrsians are the worst savages in the world. Your move, Tharn.*

—*I am thinking.*

—*He's thinking. I'll have grandchildren by the time he's finished thinking.*

I wasn't born here, Kiri thought. *There are cracks in the world, and I fell through one of them, and landed here by mistake. . . .*

It was bottomless, that feeling of not belonging here, of not belonging anywhere at all. The world these men lived in caught her endlessly off guard, created repeated dislocations which never lost their edge, their sense of pained bewilderment. Had she joined the discussion tonight, the questions she would have asked would have made them laugh. Did Marwen of Kamilan *want* to marry the Dravian prince, and if she did not, what kind of life would she have, and what would become of her? What did it mean to be the greatest lord, and why did it matter to be one? And why did it matter if the captain at Belengar was slaveborn or not—why should anyone care?

They would have been amused. More than that, they would have been reassured: clearly, women understood nothing of the world.

A figure emerged from the circle of wagons, approaching with a step so easy it seemed almost to be a dance. Clodis. Tharn's beautiful brother, with the sun of Sardas in his blood.

"Hello, Kiri. Notice, please. Again I am not late."

"That's twice. When it's ten times, I will notice."

"Is quiet everything?"

"Yes. Except for the wolves."

"No danger the wolves. They are far away."

"You're very happy tonight."

"In the dark you see, Kiri."

"In the dark you glow, Clodis."

He laughed. "I will see her tonight. Has late watch the old man on the outside perimeter. When I finish here. . . ." He smiled, and left the rest unsaid.

"You'll be caught one day, Clodis."

"May be better so. We would marry then; he must let us, no? I do not understand. Only caravaners we are anyway—all of us. In the end he must give her to someone just like me."

"I know." Kiri had nothing new to say to him; they had this conversation over and over. Matu the leathermaker was unyielding. His daughter was not to marry, was not to have admirers, was not to hang about and fool with men. She was too young.

"She is fifteen," Clodis said. "Was fifteen my mother when I was born."

"I know."

"There is a reason, yes? It must be there is a reason."

No, Kiri thought, it did not have to be that way at all. Men imagined there was a reason for everything, and half the things they did had no reason at all. They just did them because they could.

She went back into the camp. Parel and his friends were still clustered, grown tense and quiet as the game neared its finish, growling at each other now and then: *Here, you moved twice! No, I didn't! You cursed Dravians will never learn how to count. . . !*

She went to her wagon, or rather, what she thought of as her wagon. It was one of Mercanio's three finest, covered with hides to shut the rain and the dust away from his fine silks. She found it amusing sometimes to think of herself, grubby and sunburned in her boots and rugged tunics, sleeping every night surrounded by these mountains of silks.

She took her lyre and played for a long time. Even at night no one ever minded. Mercanio said it was like rain, that lyre; it softened the bones of the world. In twenty years that was the only poetic thing Mercanio had ever been heard to say.

But tonight the bones of the world would not soften. The wolves kept up their long, melancholy cries, and in the last chilly hour of darkness a hand scratched clumsily at the flap of her wagon and a muted voice pulled her from a drugged sleep.

"Kiri! Kiri, are you there?"

Parel again, she thought dazedly. *May the gods forgive me, I'll kill him. I've had enough. I'll kill the little toad. . . !*

"Kiri, please?"

It was not Parel's voice. Parel would never whisper that way, never sob like a hurt animal. She bolted upright, suddenly awake.

"Clodis!"

She jerked open the flap and half dragged him into the wagon. There was a wetness like that of blood on his hands and on his tunic. She groped quickly to find his wounds, but there were none. He was gasping something in Sardas, a language she could understand well only if it was spoken slowly. But she understood the word for death, repeated and repeated.

"Clodis!" She gripped his shoulders hard, almost shaking him. "Clodis, what happened?"

He straightened then, clutching at the wall, and steadied himself.

"Is over my life, Kiri. Is over everything. He is killed."

"Killed? Who is killed?"

"Matu. Mara's father. He came back. It must be he knew. With a great knife he comes at me. I fight. For my life I fight, Kiri, not to kill him. I did not mean . . . I did not wish. . . ." He fell silent and wiped his face. "Already they look for me. Please. Two gold ells I have which Tharn keeps for me, and many silver pieces. Whatever you can give me, he will pay you back."

"Where will you go?" she whispered.

"Back. The way we come. They will welcome in Kamilan anyone who flees from Dravia."

She rummaged for the pouch which she had laid beneath her pillow, and handed it to him. He took it almost absently.

"Mara weeps," he said. "I think never she will forgive me. Please. Tell her I grieve. Never would I touch him, because he is her father. Never."

"I will tell her."

23

"Is heavy this pouch. Shall I leave some of it?"

"No. It's mostly small coins. Seven ells, maybe. Take it all, you'll need it. And take this."

Quickly, because it was painful, she handed him her crossbow and quiver.

"Your bow I cannot take," he protested. "How will you work?"

"You can't feed yourself in the wilderness with a sword. I'll be all right. I'll buy another in Aralev."

"A beautiful friend you are to me, Kiri. Never will it be possible to pay you back. But I will try."

"In Kamilan," she said. "When the caravan comes back next summer, have a feast for us."

He laughed softly, a laugh which was almost a sob. "A splendid feast, yes, with all the wine we can drink . . . oh, gods, how easily is one man undone!"

"Go now. You've no time to lose. Go west, as fast as you can, until there are no more farms. Follow the edge of the forest into Dohann. After that . . . after that you're in the hands of the gods, Clodis. May they keep you well!"

She gave him a farewell embrace, and sat in her wagon until the clamour slowly building in the camp reached and engulfed her, knowing that her prayer was an empty prayer. The gods of men were dark and jealous gods. She would make her offering for Clodis in the temple in Aralev, the same as she bowed her head to kings and walked carefully around armed men in the streets. And her doing so would make an equal difference to anything they did.

Kiri did not try to hide her sympathy for Clodis, since everyone knew they were friends. But she lamented openly the loss of her crossbow. He had borrowed it from her, she said, late in the night—when he came off sentry duty, she supposed—because he said there was a wolf prowling around the camp.

"And you did not go yourself to investigate?" Mercanio demanded.

"I thought he was imagining things. I gave him the bow and went back to sleep."

He studied her thoughtfully but did not respond. The people of Sardas tended to be short—graceful as cats if they were slender, solid as bulldogs if they were stout. Mercanio, tall as the average Kamil, was an exception, and Kiri always thought he looked a little stretched. Physically he was all but indestructible; a man did not caravan this road for twenty years if he were less than that. He joked sometimes that the gods had made him out of salt, rawhide, and yew: he would never spoil, never give up, and always bend rather than break.

He knew the world well, and many times it seemed to Kiri that he saw more with one eye than most men saw with two. His long silence made it clear that he did not believe her.

"And you will tell me, perhaps, of what use to me is a caravan guard without a weapon?" he asked finally.

"I will buy another in Aralev."

"We are a week from Aralev."

She waited. She knew what was coming next. He had trusted her. He had judged her conscience and her loyalties to be of a certain kind, and he had been proven wrong. He would never trust her again.

"You will work with the hostlers until we reach Aralev. Lafe will take your place in the guard. In Aralev. . . ." He paused. "In Aralev we will speak again."

No doubt they would speak again. And no doubt he would remind her that he had gone against the advice of many sensible people when he hired a woman for a guard. He had gone against such advice, too, when he allowed into his caravan nomad traders who travelled with their families, like Matu. Mercanio would sit long and thoughtfully by his fire for many nights, reflecting on the many pieces of good advice he had not taken.

They buried Matu quietly by the side of the road and prepared to leave. Mara was dragged shrieking from his grave, pouring earth from the mound over her hair and her face. Thereafter she sat in her father's wagon, more and more silent as the days passed, scarcely eating, sending away the women who tried to comfort her. She did not want comfort. She had sinned a terrible sin against Mohr the Father, against all the gods, and she would wait for them to pass their judgment. Of Clodis she would not speak at all. When others did, she did not want to listen.

"He has destroyed me," she whispered dully.

"I think," Kiri said, "it was your father who destroyed you both."

It was as though she had not spoken. Mara went on staring at a place somewhere just beyond Kiri's shoulder, where a man still loomed over her with a great knife in his hand.

3. The Queen's Minstrel

A magnificent chaos ruled in Aralev. The caravan of Mercanio the One-eyed filled the central square and spilled out from it in all directions. The streets were jammed, and from everywhere came the harsh voices of hawkers selling wine and silk and fine knives; selling healing potions and aphrodisiacs and amulets and rings; selling hides from the splendid cattle of Kamilan, and figs from the sultry valleys of Sardas; selling longbows from Larandau, pottery from Dorath, embroidered belts and tunics from Thyrsis; and hundreds of other things, each more wonderful than the last. There were entertainers, too: soothsayers and jugglers and wantonly-clad women who beckoned and smiled. There was music everywhere. The soft sounds of Kiri's lyre were almost lost amidst it all.

Women minstrels were no longer common in Dravia—or indeed anywhere else—and people gathered around her as much out of curiosity as for any other reason. She was a sturdy woman. Her age was difficult to guess, but mostly they guessed it at twenty-five or so. Her hair was short and cut straight all around, in the fashion of the south. Her hands were large, and they handled the supple instrument with ease. It was necessary to stand close to hear her well, but they did so, and were often reluctant to move on.

Her voice was not exceptional, and the songs she sang were mostly common ones, stories told simply and without pretense: tales of kings and tales of beggars, chaff that blew away and would have blown away forever except that someone, a storyteller, remembered.

There was a noise down the street, a noise she had long ago learned to recognize as the kind which followed important men in public places. People were shouting and pushing, some trying to get out of the way, others trying to get closer for a better look. Then harsh, commanding voices began to rise over the clamour: *Make way, there, make way! The prince is coming!*

Held of Dravia was moving in a leisurely fashion through the great caravan, surrounded by armed guards, and followed by a cluster of slaves. He was clearly enjoying himself, pausing here and there to admire things, and to share jokes with the traders. On his far left was his younger brother, Berend. Between the two men was Marwen of Kamilan.

Kiri never forgot her first sight of the queen, though she could not then nor ever after have described the queen's clothing, except for a green cloak; nor her jewellery, nor anything else she wore. All Kiri saw was the woman herself. Her hair was the pale, dusty colour of a field of ripened oats, and very long. Her eyes were large as a child's, but watchful, with a carefully honed watchfulness such as children rarely had. The Dravians all agreed that she was not pretty; even those who admired her would only speak of promise. The lean body, they said, might yet fill out, the small breasts flower, the thin unsmiling face take on a bit of flesh and softness. She would never be beautiful, they said, but in time she would be regal. That was all true, Kiri thought, but it was less than the truth; the queen was regal now. She was poised and quite tall for a woman, as tall as many of the soldiers, and she carried herself with great dignity.

Kiri bowed and greeted them, and offered to sing.

"You are Dravian," the prince said.

"Yes, lord."

He was pleased, and threw a coin into her bowl. "Sing."

She plucked her lyre, aware of the fact that the queen was watching her carefully. It did not take a subtle eye to see that Marwen was unhappy. She did not pout, but a cold reserve lay over her expression and her gestures, almost a defiance: *I will not laugh in Aralev. You will never make me laugh in Aralev. . .!*

That coldness was widely noticed. Kiri had heard many comments about it along the road, in the villages through which they passed, and especially here in the royal city itself. Who did she think she was, they said—this scrawny little barbarian queenling, whose mother could not breed a single son, and who herself could not breed at all? Who did she think she was to be so icy, and look down her pale Kamil nose at all of them? She had everything she could want: soft beds, fine clothes, slaves to do the scrubbing and the grinding and the carrying; and she valued none of it, least of all the royal husband who had given it to her. Clearly, it was time he took more wives, good Dravian women who would teach her what it meant to be married to their prince.

Even women spoke of her thus, sometimes, and there was no doubt she must have known it, yet she did not seem to care.

Kiri had seen captives enough on the caravan road: many men, mostly captured soldiers destined for tin mines and galleys; but more women, women with roped hands or necks, trudging in the dust behind regiments of soldiers; women in great wagons with barred sides, staring out like caged birds, destined for faraway cities, for sculleries and stables and carding rooms—and always, if they were young, for the brothels or the bedrooms of their conquerors. Had Marwen seemed to her only another like them, Kiri would not have kept looking at her; she would have looked away. She had already seen too many.

But Marwen, captive that she clearly was, dwarfed by these two great princes who stood beside her, had nonetheless a quality in her face which Kiri saw very rarely in the faces of captives, and that was power—power shifting and half hidden and bewildered, power turning this way and that way against its restraints, unsure of its possibilities and perhaps even of its own existence, but there, present—so savagely present that only the boldest of men would have failed to notice it.

29

The mood of the lyre changed, grew at once darker and stronger.

In Kamilan long ago
In the days of Alyth, queen of the hill people,
There came warriors from the north,
Warriors who passed across the sea. . . .

Warriors who came like waves, with new weapons and new gods, and changed the face of the mountain lands forever. But for one lifetime, the lifetime of Alyth, the last of the hill queens, neither their weapons nor their gods were powerful enough. Then even Telhiron, the greatest of all the warriors who ever lived, went down in defeat, for the earth itself rose up against him. Lightning burned his camps, and flooded rivers drowned his men, and Alyth at the head of a fierce and ragged army drove him back across the mountains into Dravia. For one lifetime the Kamils stood alone against the dying of a world.

It was the darkest, proudest song she knew, and she sang it all, every verse until the end. When she looked up to an uncertain applause and saw the prince's face, she knew that she had dared too much.

"The glories of the past are but shadows of the future, lord," she said quickly. "Even more splendidly will Dravia and Kamilan, now united, resist all their enemies."

Held's face softened. Berend's did not. He looked much like his brother, although he was not as big a man, nor as handsome. He had the same ruddy complexion and flaming hair, the same blue and piercing eye, the same looming, bear-like stride. But there all likeness ended. Berend at twenty-two was already known throughout Dravia as an irresponsible and dissolute man, fawning towards the representatives of empire who came from Larandau and arrogant towards everyone else. Even in Dravia, with its singular history of violence, he was considered a man too fond of blood.

"You speak of enemies, minstrel," he said harshly. "Do you refer to Larandau?"

"I don't refer to any land, lord. But the world is dangerous."

"Nothing is dangerous to Dravia."

"Indeed not, lord. That was the meaning of my song."

When the queen spoke, both men looked at her in surprise. "What is your name, minstrel?" she asked.

"Kiri of Vanthala, lady."

"Tell me, Kiri of Vanthala, what I should pay you to serve me for a year. I know what we would offer in Kamilan, but perhaps here that would not be enough. What is fair?"

Kiri faltered, and looked about. Her fellow caravaners were no help; their mouths were all hanging open.

"I don't know, lady. I've never served a queen."

"Would you accept twenty ells, then?"

Kiri swallowed. It was a splendid sum, and at this moment she might have followed Marwen of Kamilan for a loaf and a bowl of soup.

"Yes, lady. I would be very honoured."

"Prince Held," the queen said, "you've insisted that I choose a gift today, anything I might want from this caravan. I would like the services of this minstrel for one year."

Berend raised his eyes to the gods, as if he could not decide which of them was more stupid: the prince for making such a reckless promise, or the queen for making such a trivial request.

"That's what you want, lady?" Held asked, bewildered.

"That's what I want."

"Well, then you shall have it."

"Twenty ells is far too much," Berend told his brother bluntly.

"I would have spent a great deal more on a jewel."

"It's too much for a minstrel. Give her ten."

"The bargain is made. I'm not going to make a liar of the queen."

"I see no reason why you shouldn't. You've already made a fool of the crown prince." With that, the young man stalked away.

Held shouted after him, but Berend paid no attention. Held's face darkened with anger; his enjoyment of the market was now utterly gone.

"I've had enough of this bear-pit," he said harshly. "Come, lady!"

They swept away in a clatter of metal and dust, and were lost in the clamour of Aralev so quickly that Kiri could not quite believe they had ever been real.

She slung the lyre over her shoulder and elbowed her way through the street until she found a wine-seller. The cool liquid slaked her thirst, but it did nothing for her confusion. Everyone was dizzy with excitement over what had happened except herself. She was appalled.

Dear gods, what have I done?

She could not think; she could not play. She was terrified that the whole affair would be forgotten by the time the princes returned to the palace, and her own life would go on exactly as before—her own unpromising life, half gone already and so little to show for it, and Mercanio waiting to scuttle her before they left Aralev: *You will tell me please, Kiri, what use to me is a caravan guard without a weapon?* She had bought a new crossbow, a very fine one, but she doubted that it would matter. The damage was done.

What if the queen changed her mind, and it was all a dream?

And more frightening still: what if she did not?

Two soldiers came about an hour later, members of the royal guard, with the mailed fist of Dravia on their breastplates, and long bright swords on their belts. With them were two slaves to carry her belongings.

"The queen awaits you."

Well, she thought, *I have done it now. . . .*

"I would like to take my leave of Mercanio."

"You may do so."

Mercanio was, to her great amazement, sad. "I will miss you, Kiri. Few I have had in my service as capable as you, and none better. I wish you fortune."

"You would have kept me on?" she whispered.

"Of course." He smiled. "You think not so? Because of Clodis?" He shook his head. "One does reckless things when one is young. I had a friend once, back in Sardas. With another youth he quarrelled, during a game of dice, and in anger he pulled his knife and killed him. I gave him help to get away. I would not do it a second time. Nor, I think, would you."

She wanted to embrace him for his friendship, and to strangle him for his blindness. Did he think the two quarrels were at all alike?

"I'll miss you, too, Mercanio. We've been through a lot together." She paused. "Will you take care of Mara? She has no one now."

"I will see that she gets back to Sardas. Beyond that, nothing I can promise."

She wanted very much to see Mara again, to see Tharn, to see all of them, in fact, except Parel. But they were scattered about the caravan and the city, hawking wares, or buying them; or drinking and feasting. She prayed the queen would give her leave, later, to search them out and say good-bye.

She went back to the silk wagon and packed her things into a large satchel. They were few things, but she treasured them. Good clothing, mostly from Larandau, where people with a bit of gold could buy some of the finest things in the world. A few pieces of jewellery, valueless but striking. An amulet Clodis had given her. The crossbow and quiver; and her dagger, which she could not wear openly in the house of a king. Last of all she fetched her gold. There were several false compartments in Mercanio's wagons, and from one of these she plucked out a small hoard of coins: seventy-three ells—no fortune, but a very respectable sum, her savings from six years on the caravan.

She stepped into the sun-drenched clamour of Aralev, and paused, squinting against the light. The slaves reached as one for her bundle and she surrendered it mutely, feeling foolish; she did not need any help to carry that. But her lyre she kept in her own hand, like a talisman.

Once, after they had left the market and begun the long climb to the greathouse, she looked back in disbelief. None of this, she thought, could possibly be real.

Thus did Kiri of Vanthala enter the service of Marwen, queen of Kamilan, in whose service she remained until she died.

4. In the Royal House of Aralev

The king's house was in the centre of the city, on a knoll overlooking the main market square. Guards in full battle dress guarded its entrance and patrolled its walls. The dwelling was huge by Dravian standards. There was a great hall, used only for banquets, ceremonies, and the business of the state. There were storage sheds and granaries; a huge kennel for the princes' dogs and a stable for their horses; an entire wing of slaves' quarters, another of ovens and pantries, and a third which was a barracks for the guards. Very little space was left to live in. Kiri was lodged in a room tinier than Mercanio's silk wagon, without a window. She was close enough to the slaves' quarters that she could hear the children whimper in their sleep.

She did not sleep well that night, or for many nights thereafter. Under its façade of princely comforts, the greathouse of Aralev was a harsh and violent place. Berend quarrelled with everyone. His three wives liked him well enough, perhaps, but the rest of the household breathed a collective sigh of relief every time he leapt on his horse to go hunting or philandering or causing trouble somewhere else.

His father, the old king Algard, was a sadder figure in the royal household, but no less difficult to live with. He was mortally sick, and he cried out often in the darkness, for fear or pain or the reliving of old battles. Then there would be a great running about of servants, and sometimes the tramping boots of his sons. On her second night in the palace, Kiri was summoned in the hope that music would soothe him. She crept into the room, frightened and uncertain as to what might be expected of her. The king lay on his bed, wrapped in damp and tangled sheets. He was sunken and terrible, skinny as a child, without hair or teeth or much remembering. He did not want music; he wanted certain prisoners beheaded, and no one could convince him they were already dead for sixteen years.

Gratefully, Kiri was allowed to creep away again. She noticed then and in the days which followed that his sons never stayed long by his bedside. It was for the women of the house to deal as best they could with his long dying—all the women except Marwen. Marwen was Kamil, and the old king hated her.

Sometimes at night, when everyone had been shouted out of their sleep and even Berend's dogs had set up a royal howling, Kiri remembered the camps of Mercanio's caravan with longing. But she would not have gone back to them for anything—not alone. Not without Marwen.

There was nothing slow or subtle about their friendship. It leapt into life like a summer storm and grew like thorns on a barrow. Years later, when everything which was to happen to them had become history, Marwen would speak of fate and the will of Jana. But to Kiri it was always a simpler and earthier thing: shared pleasures, shared loneliness, and most of all shared perceptions of the world. It was those moments when her mind would leap out in astonishment and delight, watching the unfolding thought of another, crying *Yes, yes, yes, I have thought that, too! Exactly that!* It was those moments of knowing before a word was spoken what the word would be, because she knew the speaker so well. It began with their first cup of wine, and continued through the lengthening summer afternoons, when the princes were usually gone and the old king slept. At first they talked of very safe things: places Kiri had been, and people she had known.

"Is it true," the queen asked, "that Thyrsian women mate with animals, so they will bear more powerful young?"

"I've never been to Thyrsis, lady. But I don't believe it. I think it's a tale invented by their enemies. They're a fierce people, and although they're admired for it, they aren't much loved."

"And what of Larandau? Is Vianon as great and rich a city as they say? I've heard that all of Aralev would fit into a tiny corner of it."

"It's the richest city in the world—and the poorest. The chief lords of Larandau would think this greathouse no better than a granary. The emperor has three palaces. One of them, which he built for his queen, is built entirely on water."

"How could that be possible?"

"They made a lake. Some say it took a million slaves, some say three or four times as many. They dug out the earth and carried it away, and built the palace, and then, so it could be ready for the queen's birthday, they didn't wait for the rains to fill the lake, but carried back the water. Time was short by then, and those who fell were not even taken off the line and cast aside to die; they were trampled under. The emperor calls it the Lake of the Gods, but in the slave pits it's called the Lake of Bones."

"That's a tale for Berend," the queen said thoughtfully. "Perhaps if he heard it he would have less praise for Larandau's fine ships and glorious armies."

"I doubt it, lady, if you will forgive my saying so."

Their eyes met. It was the first of a million understandings.

The second was discovering that, although the queen did not share the Larandav royalty's passion for luxury and excess, she liked certain pleasures very well, and they were the same pleasures Kiri liked—music, warm fires, good wine, and fine things to eat.

"If anyone had told me," she said, "that the great and powerful kings of Dravia lived in a place as dismal as this, I would never have believed it. Algard must be the only king in all the world to rule for twenty years with no bard in his court, no rituals, no dancing—dear goddess, nothing but brawling men and hunting dogs and war. And they call us Kamils barbarians!

They don't even know anything about making food. They throw a few haunches of venison over a fire until they're charred black, and call that a feast."

She sighed. Her resentment had dissolved into genuine longing. "I would give a solid gold ell for a stew like Malia made, full of roots and herbs and cream. . . ."

It took a week or so for them to edge into dangerous questions, and finally that most dangerous question of all: what was happening in Kamilan?

"I hear only what Prince Held wants me to hear," the queen said. "You've just come from there, Kiri. Do you know? What are they going to do? It's been twenty months now. What are they going to do?"

For the first time there was fear in the queen's voice—a fear which Kiri sensed went deeper than any simple physical fear of Held or of the Dravians. It was fear for her country itself, and for what might become of it.

"Lady," she began carefully. "I can only tell you what's being said in the streets. I've never been—"

"What's said in the streets is often truer than what's said in the palace. Tell me what they say. And Kiri," she added sharply, "don't try to spare my feelings. Tell me the truth!"

"As best I know it, lady. The Council is divided. It's said that Borosar the warlord would raise a great army and invade, and except for Angmar, many think he would prevail. Angmar, they say, sits with his elbows on the table, and looks at no one, and says: 'We haven't the strength. Let's be sane men, and debate only what is possible.' "

The queen turned away bitterly, staring at the high walls which surrounded their small garden. Beyond them, distant as the houses of the gods, lay the wild mountains of Dohann.

Stricken, Kiri said no more.

When Marwen spoke again her eyes were wet and hollow as pools. "He's right," she said softly. "I've been lying to myself. Dreaming empty dreams. Sometimes when we were all in the great hall and some messenger could be heard riding up to the gates, I would picture him running across the hall and throwing himself at the prince's feet, all dishevelled and sobbing: *Forgive me, lord, forgive me! The pass from Belengar is lost, and twenty thousand Kamil warriors are riding to Aralev. . . !*"

She shook her head. "They don't call him Angmar the Wise for nothing. He is right. He doesn't love me much, but he loves Kamilan, and he is right. They can't invade Dravia; they don't have the strength.

"So. . . ." She broke a dead branch from a tree, and began to snap it into tinier and tinier pieces. "They won't fetch me home. What will they do instead? Name a regent?"

"There is talk of that. But they can't choose one, no more than they could choose you a husband, and for the same reason. They can't agree who it should be."

"That was just as well. Goddess of the world, Kiri, if I ever marry I will choose my own husband!"

"There's one other thing you should know, lady. The Kamils are angry at what was done to you, and it's a terrible anger. Stolen, you belong to them as you never did before. I'm not sure why, and I'm not sure I would respect the reason if I knew it. But it's true, and it's a powerful thing."

"People told you this?"

"Yes, lady. In different ways—in the markets, on the road, in the taverns. And above all at Belengar. We were stopped there by a company of soldiers, armed to the teeth, with a captain whom I would have taken for a bandit except for his flags. He said his name was Shadrak, which is no Kamil name I've ever heard—"

"Shadrak is at Belengar?"

"Do you know him?"

"I met him once. I'll tell you the story. But go on. What happened at Belengar?"

"He took a heavy tribute from Mercanio, but he was fair. He told us a great deal about the conditions of the pass, the road, the weather; and every scrap of information he gave us was correct. He knows Dohann, I think, like the palm of his hand.

"When we asked him about bandits he laughed. It was a laugh I would rather not hear again. Across the mountains, he said, there were thousands of bandits, and the greatest of them lived in the palace and called himself a prince. And then he said this: 'You may give him a message, if you dare. Tell him he won't cross this border a second time and live. Tell him we will have back our queen!'

"And then he raised his sword, and shouted out your name, and every man of them took it up in a great chant. And it echoed, lady, it echoed from mountain to mountain; we crossed into Dravia with the sound of it still running through our bones."

Kiri paused, and concluded: "I don't know what sort of man he is, lady, but I think you have a captain there who would follow you through anything."

For a time the queen seemed lost in thought. "I don't know what sort of man he is, either," she said quietly. "But it's strange you should have encountered him just now. He won a splendid victory for us four years ago. It was a small victory, but it came when we needed one most.

"It was a dark time for Kamilan. My father had just died, and the Council considered us leaderless. There was only one tragedy worse for a country, Angmar said, than to be left with a half-grown king, and that was to be left with a half-grown queen.

"It was then, I think, that I learned to live with fear. The Dravians crossed the borders almost as they pleased. For months we expected daily to be overrun. Medwina ordered a tunnel dug from the palace, and hiding places were readied for us in the forest. I came to dread the sight of messengers. And then one day one of them came riding as madly as the others, babbling of victory.

"It happened near a place called Medra. A thousand or so Dravians came upon a small number of our men, just a few hundred, already battered from a previous fight. The invaders drove them into a ravine, and it seemed our men would be utterly wiped out. A young freedman, quite young and just a common soldier, went to his captain and said he'd found a cave; he asked for a hundred men and permission to try a plan he had. He took all the best archers, and all the shawms and drums, and hid them in the cave. The others fell back, and the Dravians followed."

"And he attacked them from the rear," Kiri said.

"Yes. With a terrible noise and a demonic rain of arrows, so they must have thought the whole of Kamilan was at their backs. They broke. Many were killed there, and many scattered into the countryside and were killed after, or surrendered. So I think except for a handful they were all destroyed.

"We could scarcely believe it. We had been battered into the ground so many times that even a small victory made us drunk. There were bonfires all over the city, and offerings in all the temples. And when the company returned, the High Council decided that this new hero should receive the personal gratitude of the queen."

"At least they judged you useful for that," Kiri said dryly.

"Any girl can smile and hang a wreath around a man's neck," Marwen said. "But it wasn't much of a day for glory. In normal times, even in war, we would have had a feast for the men, and an evening of talk and singing. But we couldn't even do that. We were living ourselves like rabbits in a warren, and the troop was leaving again the same day. They had marched since daybreak in pouring rain, and it was still raining when they brought Shadrak to the palace. He left a trail of water with every step he took. I don't remember much of what he looked like, except that he was dark and shaggy and wet, like a half-drowned wolf.

"He looked so . . . he looked so *hungry*, Kiri. And I couldn't help thinking that perhaps he didn't want the personal gratitude of the queen nearly as much as he wanted some warm food and a dry bed. So I ordered the servants to take him to the kitchen and give him anything and everything he wanted to eat, and food to take with him as well.

"Medwina said it proved I was a queen. Angmar said it proved I was a child."

"How old were you then?"

"Thirteen."

"Perhaps they were both right."

Marwen smiled, just a little, and then grew thoughtful again. "So Shadrak is a captain now. I'm glad of that. I sometimes wondered what became of him."

The sun was low. In the distance, faintly, they could hear the sound of drums. It reminded them, as nothing else could, of where and who they were.

"You are Dravian, Kiri," the queen said, very quietly.

"Yes, lady."

"Will the day come when that will matter?"

"It came and passed six years ago."

"I don't understand."

"When I joined the caravan. It wasn't simply for adventure, or for pay. It was because I saw no world I wanted to belong to—neither my own, nor any other." She paused. "Until now."

"Do you mean that?"

"Yes, lady. With all my heart."

The drums were closing, vibrant and menacing. They could see members of the household and the guard gathering on the wall, and they climbed up also to see.

It was a company of returning soldiers, the princes riding with them. In litters at the rear they carried a half dozen or so dead and wounded. In the middle were eight prisoners, naked to the waist, tied backwards by twos on their horses, their arms pinioned behind them.

There was shouting back and forth between those on the ground and those on the wall, half lost in the tramp of horses.

"Did you understand them?" the queen asked.

"Something about bandits," Kiri said.

The troop moved into the square directly below them, and she could see the prisoners quite clearly.

One of them was Clodis.

Oh, gods, he had said, *how easily is one man undone!*

The killing of Matu had been talked about in Aralev, of course, and condemned; but the affairs of the caravan were not the affairs of the Dravian state. No one in authority really cared if Clodis were captured or not, and he had travelled safely for almost two weeks. And then on a hot and dusty afternoon he stopped by a stream in a small clearing and lay down for a drink of water. The woods which might have swallowed him were forty feet away.

"He looks up," the Dravian captain said, "and there was thirty filthy bandits grinning down at him. Or at least, that's how he tells it. He says they gave him two choices: to join them or to die. He says he went with them only to stay alive, hoping he'd have a chance to escape."

"It may be true," Held said. "Justice has many ways of finding men. And Mohr can use even bandits for his purposes."

Indeed, Kiri thought. Bandits would suit a god like Mohr very well. . . .

She rarely spoke at their gatherings unless they spoke to her, but this question she could not restrain. "What will become of him, lord?" she asked.

"What becomes of all murderers in Dravia," Held said. "They're hung from the walls and left until they fall and are carried off as carrion." He looked up suddenly from his food. "Did you know the villain? I suppose you must have."

"He was my friend, lord."

"I'm sorry for that."

"Brother," Berend said, "if you'll forgive my saying so, it's a long time since a company of Dravian warriors was content to come home with a few bandits for prisoners."

"Bandits can be as perilous as any other kind of enemy," Held said. "Don't provoke me, Berend. I'm getting tired of it."

Berend was silent then, but not for long. The meal was drawn out and exhausting, sparked with small snarlings between the crown prince and his brother. Berend's wives spoke little, mostly about the king: he was better; the doctors thought he still might live. Marwen said nothing at all.

Kiri played her lyre, grateful to be apart from it.

It was very late when the captain begged to take his leave, and Berend, more than a little drunk, said a blunt good night, and took his wives back to their own wing of the house.

Held did not return to his seat. The hall was suddenly very empty, very still. In the shifting light the queen, alone at the end of the long table, seemed melancholy and perhaps to him quite beautiful. His voice was surprisingly soft.

"Come, lady. I am weary."

"I would speak with you, lord, just for a moment, if I might."

"You would speak with me?" His voice held an edge of both mockery and warmth. He motioned a servant to give him more wine and sat down. "Very well. Leave us, minstrel."

"There's no need for her to go, lord, for this concerns her."

"Speak then."

"The prisoner, the runaway from the caravan. He's very young, and the harm he did was forced on him. You're praised in Dravia as the most just of all the princes the land has ever had. I appeal to your justice, Held. Pardon the boy. He's not evil."

"You appeal to my justice?" Held said, very quietly.

"Or to your mercy, then, if you can't see it as just. It's a small thing, a kindness easily given, from a great lord to a man without power. Let him go."

"You appeal to all my virtues, lady, but not to me. You're still too proud to ask for anything from me."

The queen lowered her face almost to her hands, and then lifted it again, her eyes glistening.

"I do ask you, lord. I beg you. Let the boy go free."

"To please you?"

"Yes. To please me."

"Your eyes lie, Marwen of Kamilan. You don't know how to beg— though I marvel that you would make such a good effort at it over this. I would like to please you, as you know, but in this I can't. Think a moment. The borderlands are cursed by these bandits. They prey on everyone, and they kill like wild dogs. And I should let one of them go just because he says he didn't join them willingly? Probably they would all say that. He was already a murderer. What about the man he killed? What justice or order will we have if a man may be cut down like a dog in his own house for defending his family? When we go back to Kamilan, will you hang those of your household guards who shot arrows at me as we fled?"

He paused, and laughed softly. "On second thought, perhaps you *should* hang them. They were the most incompetent guards I've ever seen. You will be better protected here, lady, I promise you that."

"You mock me," the queen said with a terrible calmness.

"No, I don't. You mock *me*, pleading for a cutthroat." He seized his cup, drank deeply, and glared at her. "For nearly two years you've been my wife—"

"I'm not your wife."

"For two years," he repeated, grinding out the words, "you've been my wife. And you've given me nothing. Never once before tonight did you ask to sit at this table with me and talk. Never once did you smile at me, or come to me for anything. Never once was anything I had—any gold, any power, any justice, anything at all—good enough for you. And now suddenly it is. Now, suddenly, you find something worth asking for—a Sardas gypsy with blood on his hands, who first dishonours a woman and then murders her father!"

"And what of the woman you dishonoured, Held of Dravia?"

Everything stopped utterly still: the music, Kiri's breath, Held's goblet of wine poised halfway to his mouth. For a moment he could not believe what he had heard, and Marwen flung back her chair and continued savagely:

"What of the blood on your hands? If you hang murderers from the walls of Aralev, prince, start with the captains of your armies, and then your brothers and yourself! You speak of us going back to Kamilan? Don't hold your breath! I'll die before I give you to my people as a king. You have a slave, prince, and that's all you have, so don't ask her to smile. You have not even one handsbreadth of Kamilan, *and you have no wife!*"

He will kill her, Kiri thought numbly. *He will swing around the table in one great lunge and break her into pieces. . . .*

But he did not. He picked up his cup, drained it, smashed it down with a force that bent the stem in half, and wiped the back of his hand across his mouth.

"As you wish, lady. It's your choice. I will have a wife, or I will have a slave. For a long time it mattered to me which. It matters less and less.

"If Arden of Kamilan had been a Thyrsian, I might understand where she bred such a cold and snarling bitch as you— in the woods, among dogs and jackals."

"Better there than in the palace of Aralev."

Oh, Marwen, Kiri pleaded silently, *Marwen,* stop!

"I'll remember that, lady. It may be I will leave you in the woods one day." He stood up. "Now you will come to my bed, in whichever fashion you prefer: you may walk there as a wife, or be dragged there as a slave."

Marwen turned without a word. She did not even glance at Kiri. Held had forgotten the minstrel's presence; she would not remind him. She walked towards the door and disappeared into the darkness beyond.

5. To Bargain with Princes

Kiri would not have agreed with the lords of Larandau that the greathouse of Aralev was fit only to be a granary. But after her many years of freedom, she found its closed and always crowded spaces oppressive and sometimes frightening. The princes went out every day, but the women rarely did, and then only with guards and servants—so they were never alone, neither inside their home nor out of it. Kiri could not help wondering what it did to a woman's soul never to be alone with herself, or what it did to her body to have lost, by the age of twenty, any desire to run through a field of grass or feel the wind play in her hair.

She liked Berend's wives; they were skilled and beautiful women. (The prince, she supposed, would never marry any woman unless she was beautiful.) Although their slaves did all the hard domestic tasks, they nonetheless had plenty of work. They made their own clothing and their splendid head-dresses. They stitched the mailed fist of Dravia onto all the princes' pennants and flags. They made their kinsmen's tunics and leggings and soft woollen shirts. They supervised the gathering and preparing of herbs; they made the sleeping draughts and the poultices for wounds. And always, with a determination and ingenuity which astonished Kiri, they kept themselves fresh and scented and glittering with bangles; they wrapped their hair in ever more elaborate designs, and found endlessly new and clever ways to draw attention to their bodies. They were splendidly sensual women, and Kiri admired their sensuality as she admired their competence.

Yet it was their gifts, in the end, which so utterly saddened her: so many gifts directed without question to a life of absolute submission. They were not ignorant or insensitive women. They must have felt, in a thousand ways, the sharp limitations of their lives. They must have ached sometimes with longing, watching the princes mount their horses and ride wherever they wished into the morning sun, leaving their wives behind. They must have wept sometimes after yet another outburst of Berend's casual cruelty. They would weep more as they grew older and less exquisite, and found themselves replaced by always younger and prettier women.

Yet they accepted. They accepted so completely that Kiri felt sometimes as alien among them as she had felt among Parel's hostlers. There was something terrifying about that kind of surrender; it reached beyond their own marriages, and indeed beyond marriage itself, to an acceptance of every kind of structured power. Kiri doubted that any of these women would ever challenge—or indeed ever really notice—Berend's profoundly vicious nature, except as it sometimes touched upon themselves. The words "He is my husband" closed forever any discussion of a man's moral faults—as did the words "He is my king."

They had made their bargain with power, and having made it, they were prepared to pay the costs and gather up the rewards.

Marwen's failure to do the same bewildered them. Sometimes they were sympathetic; she was after all a woman like themselves, and very young. Sometimes they were resentful, seeing that she was permitted things for which they would have been beaten. But more than anything else they were bewildered. How could she fail to see the honour Held offered her, the glory he would bring to her savage little country? How could she fail to see how well he loved her, how generous he was, and how handsome?

And Kiri asked them—bolder than she should have been—suppose you went one day to visit an aging kinswoman, and while you sat with her outside her house, armed men came out of the forest, killing everyone who tried to stop them, and took you away to another country, to be the wife of an ancient enemy?

They would weep, they said, and put ashes in their hair, for whether they lived or died then, their lives would be over. But Marwen had not been married, they added, so it was not the same thing at all. And the youngest, with a wry smile, added: *Had I been queen of Kamilan, I would have strayed into the woods every chance I had, if I thought so fine a prince was waiting to carry me off!*

Held was a splendid man, they told her, a great prince who would be a magnificent king. He could fell an ox with one blow of his fist, and lift grown men in armour on the palms of his hands. He could ride whole days and nights without tiring. No warrior in all the world could defeat him in equal combat. And the haughty mistress of Kamilan scorned such a man, and turned away from him, like a spoiled, unmanageable child who would not eat, and who bashed her own face against the walls for spite.

They shook their heads. Well, what could one expect? The Kamils were all barbarians. This one called herself a queen, yet she would not even tie her hair up, or wear a gown to hide her bony knees. Instead she went about with the mane of a horse, and dressed herself in leggings and garish tunics, and wore as her favourite piece of jewellery a bronze ring with runes on it, more fit for a gypsy than for a queen.

They sighed. The gods had already shown their displeasure by keeping the woman barren. One day the prince would say *Enough!* and turn against her, too. And then she would be utterly undone. She would end her days in bitterness and regret—or worse, in an iron cage.

Why could she not see?

"That's what they think?" Marwen brooded. "That I don't see?"

"Aye, lady."

It was very late, and they were alone. Prince Held had gone to visit his cousin Edgard in the valley town of Heydren. Edgard, as Berend explained pointedly at dinner, had a very beautiful daughter, one of the loveliest young women in all of Dravia. No doubt Berend was pleased with himself when the queen fled to her own quarters as soon as the meal was decently finished. Perhaps he shared a knowing look with his wives: *Aha! the queen has a rival now, and she doesn't like it!*

What would he have thought, Kiri wondered, if someone told him that all Marwen wanted was the rare and precious pleasure of an evening to herself?

They made a roaring fire in the hearth in the prince's bedchamber, and sat before it on the floor, like children.

"He laughs at me," the queen said, "for wanting a fire in the summertime."

"Well, then. While he's gone we'll burn up all the wood in Aralev."

The changing light glinted in the queen's hair. She had lovely pale hair, without a trace of red; it was not the sun which shimmered in it, but rather the moon. Hair made for wind, Kiri thought, for wind and the hungering of a lover's hands, not for braids and the dead weight of Dravian bindings.

You must leave here, lady, somehow, I don't know how, but you must go free. . . .

They were silent for a time. The previous evening's violence was heavy on their minds, but it was not easy to begin to speak about it.

"I failed you," Marwen said at last. "I tried to help your friend, and all I did was make things worse. I'm sorry, Kiri. I'm so sorry."

"You did as much as anyone could have done."

"No. I did what was possible for me. But for anyone? No, Kiri. Any soft-eyed concubine with a smile and a hand on his thigh could have had a pardon for a common prisoner. I might even have tried that myself, except that he knows me too well. He would have laughed. At first he would have laughed, and then he would have been just as angry."

"Do you never fear that anger?" Kiri whispered, and then added, quickly: "I know that in a way you do—you must. But . . . but in a way it seems to me you don't."

"What you say is true, Kiri. I've never feared him as I should, because he's never seen me as I am. He can't. His whole sense of the world prevents it. In that, he's like Berend's wives. He thinks I'm simply young or reckless or maybe just Kamil, and that he can train me somehow, like a wild horse. And if in the end I can't be trained, well, it will be too bad, he'll kill me, finally, but he will try. He'll try quite hard, I think."

"And if he takes another wife?"

"I pray that he does. No matter what risk there may be in it for me, I pray that he'll marry someone else, and let me be."

"You hate him beyond telling, then."

"Yes." Marwen picked at her sleeve, where a bit of embroidery had come undone. "I hate him, but it's not a simple thing. In many ways he's a splendid man. He might have had everything he wanted. He was right to want an alliance with Kamilan, to try to end the war and strengthen us both against the threat of Larandau. He's honourable in most things. The people consider him the best lord they've had since their country fell to Telhiron.

"That's the worst of it, Kiri. That it might all have been different. I might have married him willingly, if he had come to me. If he had asked. If he'd asked at the beginning, when it mattered. He asks now. He asks in a hundred ways which once would have been more than good enough, but now it's too late. There are places from which no return is possible."

She paused, finding words. "It's not even a question of forgiveness. In time almost anything can be forgiven. It's simply that there's no way back.

"The first camp we made, he forced me. In the woods where he said my mother got me—among dogs and jackals, wasn't that how he put it?—there he would have bred his own sons, his own future kings of Dravia. Strange how men's words come back to echo them. . . .

"We were both utterly exhausted. It made no difference— no difference to his lust, no difference to my rage. A bridal bed in a windswept pass, he said, was no different from any other bridal bed, and in that he spoke the truth. A woman chooses to lay with a man, or she doesn't. The rest is ritual.

"But it was ugly, Kiri; there are no words to tell you how ugly. He cared nothing for me then; I was only booty. He shoved me down among the rocks and the roots, with his twenty men gathered all around us, listening to every sound of our struggles. I was silent because of them. I fought him, but I was silent. Afterwards, when at last he slept, I could hear them whispering. Laughing and whispering. Admiring his prowess, I suppose; making wagers on how quickly I would breed, how quickly I would be brought to heel.

"Now he brings me gifts, and wonders why I don't love him."

They watched the fire leap and fall.

"I would hate him till I died," Kiri said at last. "And then my ghost would haunt the world, hating him still."

"You grow tired of hate," Marwen said. "It's like a wound; you can't help finally wanting it to heal. I know that if I ever had his child it would be the end of me. I couldn't look into its little face day after day and tell myself: I hate your father.

"I would give up. I would shut away everything except my will to live, and to see my children live. Perhaps in time I'd even come to love him, out of despair and loneliness. And so I'd be swallowed up, and Kamilan with me, for we have no treaty, no guarantees for my people, nothing. There would be only his power and my acquiescence.

"I bait him sometimes, Kiri, to make him hate me. Do you believe that? So I will not yield."

Kiri stared at her, unable to speak. She would write songs all her life, she thought, and still she would find no words to paint her queen, to describe that thin, angular face whose rare smiles showed gapped and uneven teeth, whose eyes had no more colour than a Kamil sky in winter; that face which compelled not by form but by substance, and so called into question every given standard of beauty.

I adore her, Kiri thought. *Already I adore her, and princes will follow me in that, and warriors, and poets. Because of who she is they will say that she is beautiful, for there is no other word they know to name the power of a woman.*

"Do you know," Marwen went on bitterly, "what was the greatest wrong Prince Held did me? He destroyed the future. He destroyed the peace we might have made, the honour in which we might have held each other. It is that, above all, for which I hate him."

"Lady. . . ." Kiri hesitated, trusting neither her voice nor her judgment. She delayed by picking out small pieces of wood and stuffing them into the fire. "Lady, why don't you run away?"

It was said. She stopped, wiped off her hands, and faced the queen. "You can't stay here. They're going to destroy you if you stay. There must be a way to leave this place!"

"I've thought about it," Marwen said. "Many times. Only . . . only it's a bit like suicide, Kiri. If one does it, one had better do it well, and not be left maimed and still alive."

"We have to find a way," Kiri said. "That's all. We simply have to find a way."

6. The Making of the World

From The Book of Beginnings, an apocryphal religious text of the Chronicles of Larandau:

In the beginning was the sea. It rolled and tossed in an endless tumult, and Jana rose immortal from its depths; she was the first of all that ever lived. Jana took mud from the bottom of the sea, and mixed it with her blood, and made the land, and the mountains, and the sky. But the world she made was dark and cold, and no creatures could live in it, so Jana kindled a great fire in her hearth, and threw it into the sky to make the sun; and from the small coals which were left she made the moon and all the stars.

One day Jana lay down in pain, and all day and all night small creatures ran from her legs: mice and hares and birds and snakes and cats and fishes; and then larger creatures: goats and pigs and wolves and deer; then with a great cry Jana gave forth horses and oxen and at last the elephants; and then she waited to see if there would be more, but there were no more, for these were the greatest creatures that would walk upon the earth.

Jana had many sons and daughters, who went everywhere across the world, finding places where they wished to live. Only Mohr, the eldest of her children, could find no place which contented him. For everywhere he went he asked if death had been there before him, and always the answer was yes. So he wandered many years until he came to a desert where death had never been, where no creature had ever been except a blind and ancient sage. The sage said to him: "The world is bent; that is why everything dies. You must straighten it." And Mohr asked: "How can I do that?" The sage said: "You must become strong. You must become strong enough to take up the world in your hands, and bend it back."

And then the sage said: "I will make you stronger than the wind," and made him a coat; "I will make you stronger than the sun," and made him a house; "I will make you stronger than the tiger," and made him a bow.

"Now," the sage said, "there is only one thing in the world you must fear, and that is Jana—for it is her world, and she would not have it changed."

And Mohr passed through the world the strongest of all beings, and came again to Jana, who found him pleasing and wished to lie with him. But, remembering the sage's words, he went away, and crossed the mountains into Vianon.

There he came upon Leya of Amaran, who was the loveliest of all the women in the world, and the swiftest. Mohr was seized with desire for her, and pursued her, but always she fled faster. So Mohr dug a great pit, and spread it with grass and flowers, and beyond it he planted beautiful trees laden with ripe fruit. It took him many years to build this pit, for it filled all of the valley of Amaran. In time Leya returned from her long flight, and saw the beautiful things in the valley, and wished to pluck them. She fell into the pit and could not escape again, and so she was made Mohr's wife. And of this union were born three daughters, who are the givers of the arts, and who stir men's souls with beauty. Thus did music come into the world, and poetry, and the making of pictures.

But every night Leya wept to Jana her mother, and after many years her cries changed into falcons, and flew away to Jana's home in Dohann, and fell with great sorrow at her feet. Only one of them yet lived, and Jana picked it up, and warmed it with her spit, and cast it into the sky, saying: "You shall now live forever, as long as there are men upon the world." And so was born vengeance, which outlives all men, and all their sons.

Then Jana crossed in a great storm into Vianon, and smashed the pit which Mohr had made, and flung the pieces into every corner of the sky. Mohr himself she seized by his feet and threw into the sea, where he was swallowed by a fish and carried to safety on a distant island. There he lived for many years, recovering from his wounds, until the time came for his great battle.

Then he went in search of the sage, who gave him much good counsel. "You must make a spear," the sage said, "using the bones of every animal in the world. Only thus can you destroy her. And when she is dead you must take care to burn her body. You must burn every bit of it, or all the evil she has brought into the world will return."

Mohr fought Jana for many days, and great caverns were torn into the earth, and mountains were smashed down. But at last the young god seized hold of two thunderbolts, and with them he put out her eyes. And then, when she could not see, he cried out to her in the voices of her daughters, first from one place and then from another, so that she knew not which way to turn, and thus he crept towards her, and with the spear he had made of the bones of every animal, he pierced her through the heart.

Mohr called then for all the people of that place to make a fire. They cut trees for seven weeks, and burned her, but they were careless, and as they dragged her to the fire some of her hair snagged on the mountain tops, and her hand was torn off by a rock, and all her blood was lost. And her hair blew everywhere across the world, giving birth to chaos. And her hand rolled into the sea, from which come all storms and winds and shipwreck. And from her blood grew discord and envy, and the hatred of race against race.

For three days the heavens were black with Jana's burning; neither sun nor stars were seen. When it was done Mohr took the ashes and placed them in golden urns, and took them into his house, and from each urn sprang forth a goddess: Marath, the goddess of motherhood, Ariana, the goddess of grain, and Jola, the goddess of love. Mohr lay with Marath, and so were born the gods of the sea and the wind, the god of hunting, and the goddess of the hearth. He lay with Ariana, and so were

*born the gods of the underworld. He lay with Jola, and so was
born Harash, the god of war, who was the father of the immortal
hero Telhiron.*

"Jana is not dead," Marwen said. "Even the priests of Mohr
know that, or they wouldn't fear her as they do. She is worshipped everywhere in Kamilan."

"But not since your father closed the temples?" Kiri said. "I
still remember that—I was nine or ten, I think, though I suppose
the news was old before it got to our village. It was the first
time my father ever said anything good about the Kamils. He
approved of closing the temples; he said it would be the end
of Jana."

"It didn't turn out the way your father expected—or mine.
The priests of Mohr wanted to burn the temples and put the
priestesses to death. But hardly anyone else was ready to go
that far. The high priestess was a sister of the queen; and even
ordinary priestesses were revered. They could heal and tell the
future. They kept the histories and the genealogies. They
understood the weather and the ways of the rivers and the
winds, and they gave advice in planting and in warfare. They
were even called into the Tribunals sometimes to guide a
judgment, for it was believed that they could see the truth
when no one else could.

"On the surface, all of that is gone now. Even before my
father closed the temples, he stripped them of all their outward
powers. The high priestess Medwina was barred from Council,
and afterwards accused of sorcery when my mother bore no
sons. And yet, driven to silence, they are still mighty, as Jana
is. Mohr rules, but he rules looking over his shoulder for the
goddess who threw him into the sea."

Kiri fell silent, remembering the first time she saw the abandoned temple of Jana in the royal city of Kamilan. It was closed
round with a great fence made by King Adelmar's soldiers.
Wild cats howled through the empty chambers; weeds grew
high from cracks in the stone steps; leaves and broken branches
rattled across the courtyard. She wondered why they did not
simply tear it down, or put it to some other use. Each year, as
the caravan came through and she rode past it again, it seemed
to grow more desolate, and yet also more permanent and more
imposing. It was as though, bereft of human care, the goddess's

temple was sinking roots into the Kamil rock, becoming part of the mountain itself.

"So the people worship her in secret, then?" she asked.

"Not in secret, exactly," the queen said. "It's not forbidden—not yet—though a man who wishes to keep his place in the world makes his offerings in the woods. And many do, even some of the highest rank, who would still rather risk a brother's wrath than a mother's abandonment. They come to the new temple and bring their gifts to Mohr, and listen patiently to his oracles, and then they go to a clearing or a stream and build an altar to Jana.

"But at midsummer nothing can stop us. At midsummer Kamilan is alive with flutes and drums and fires. At midsummer all of Kamilan is a temple to Jana. And the priests of Mohr grind their teeth and howl about his punishments, and we laugh. We laugh and dance and lie together in the grass, and everything is made again. And Mohr can do nothing, for he made none of it."

"He made these walls, lady."

Something close to joy had flashed across the queen's face as she spoke of the Kamil summer. It vanished, and Kiri wished she could take back her words.

"Yes," Marwen said. "He made these walls, and he fathered the people of Telhiron who are devouring the world. But there is one thing I'm sure of, Kiri. No matter what he does, he will never have the mastery he craves. He can destroy the world, but he can never make himself into the god of all things, the god who never had a mother."

7. Leaving Aralev

From the moment Kiri told the queen they must somehow find a way to flee, many thoughts crossed her mind, including the thought that they were both mad. But the one thought which did not occur to her was to give up, to say: *Alas, there is no way, the prince is not so bad; make your peace with him. . . .*

No. In the end, even Marwen might come to that before she would.

But what way was there out of Aralev?

Once acknowledged, the hope of freedom was like lust. It blinded them to the world. It shut out every care and every other passion. Alone, they talked of very little else. Their first plans were complex and were abandoned as unworkable, one by one. They came to realize that there was no wonderfully clever way to do this. They had no allies except the terrified slave Thesa, who procured abortion potions for her mistress in return for the gold which might one day buy her children free. There was, Marwen insisted, no one else.

"I have no ties here, no kin, nothing. I am Kamil."

"Surely among the servants—?"

"No."

"The palace guard? The grooms? There must be someone who can be bought!"

"Perhaps. But I don't know them. What hope do I have of knowing them, with Held and Berend and Berend's wives and all of Aralev watching everything I do?"

Kiri sighed, unable to decide if Marwen was exaggerating the extent of her isolation. Perhaps she was, but it hardly mattered. They dared not trust anyone in the prince's household unless they could trust them absolutely. And without help, all of their early elaborate plans fell one by one along the wayside. More and more it seemed to Kiri that they would simply have to prepare themselves, find a reasonably suitable moment, take a deep breath, and run.

She never thought of herself as a person with a talent for conspiracy. Yet every few days she snatched up something which would serve them, and none of it was noticed. Later in the summer, when Prince Held announced his intention to take a second wife, the greathouse was scrubbed and refurbished from top to bottom for the celebrations. Stores came in by the wagonload, and old things were discarded for the servants to use. Gradually everything they needed was found: ropes, a water bag, pieces of flint, two pairs of high-laced mountain shoes, a hatchet and a pick, and two good knives. In Aralev she bought figs and other dried food, and arrows for her bow. *(I hunt partridges, sir, for the princesses.)* She acquired a waterproof satchel which a man less desperate than herself had used to keep gaming cards and trinkets for his mistress.

She took three servants and went to hunt the partridges she had promised, refreshing her memory of the land. They returned to the city by the western gate. A rainstorm had gathered in the east, and against its clouds the watchtowers were outlined in stark relief. All along the wall, silent and black with flies, the bodies of hanged men turned and twisted in in the sun.

"New ones," the servant whispered. "Don't stare at them, minstrel. Unburied, they do not rest. Please, let's go by quickly."

One of the dead was smaller than the others, and very dark. Probably it was Clodis, but she was not sure; the face was too destroyed to ever tell.

Inside the walls, she sent the servants back to the greathouse with the partridges and their gear, and escaped from the city's clamour into the darkness of an old inn.

The caravan was in Larandau now, where it would stay until the new year, where they would dance and feast and revel, and make bargains, and make love. *Clodis, ah Clodis, you should be with them! What did you ever do to die like this? You never had a chance. . . .*

Tears ran down her face, spattering onto her hands and onto the rough, wooden table. She did not care. If weeping was a sin, it was in the best of company; love was also a sin, and so was freedom.

She grieved for a long time, half aware that her grief was wrapped about with hatred. It was not hatred of any person, not even of the prince whose command had taken Clodis's life. It went beyond that, past the stone walls of Aralev with the mailed fist flying from all its watchtowers, past the men who kept those walls, past Matu with his knife in his hand, past the caravan roads tramped east and west with conquerors and slaves, past all of it, to the power that underpinned it all: the power of men to break the world, and the power of gods to smile on them for doing it.

It was dark when she left the inn. There were no other women on the streets. She walked with her hand on her dagger, and she would have used it that night without any hesitation. No one bothered her. Perhaps they knew.

She went quietly to her bed, but she did not sleep at all. She thought endlessly of Clodis, and of the queen. Clodis had not escaped through those terrible mountains. What hope had she and Marwen of doing so?

They might get away from the king's house, and even from the city. But the world beyond was a very different matter. Where might they run to, when every soldier in the land would count it his sacred duty to hunt them down, when peasants and woodcutters and idle travellers would all, except for a handful, nod eagerly and point: *Yes, lord, I saw them just this morning, heading southeast they was, lord. . . .*

If they fled to the wilderness, where Held's men might not find them, perhaps bandits would—bandits first, and then wolves, when the bandits were done with them. Such men might give another man his life in exchange for his loyalty, but any woman who fell into their hands they would use until she was dead. What else could she expect, having left behind her home and her rightful protectors?

And beyond, in the deeps of the mountains, where even bandits did not go, it was whispered that there were other creatures. Creatures who looked human but were something else, something strange and unnatural. Creatures who ate foul things out of the earth, and human flesh, too, when they could get it. . . .

Few captives ever fled, and they had reason to hesitate. Kiri might well accomplish nothing except to lead her queen to her death.

She buried her face in her pillow and sobbed for hours.

In the days of the Dravian clans, minstrels had been cherished; they had been ranked among the people second only to priestesses and chiefs. Empire had changed that—first the coming of Telhiron, and now the spreading influence of Larandau, where histories were recorded in scrolls by men who no longer answered to the memories of the people. Minstrels were entertainers now, and nothing more. Kiri's task in the court of Aralev was mostly to please: to soothe the old king's dying hours, to flatter the princes with songs of Dravian glory, and to mellow the long and quarrelsome evenings with a bit of pleasure.

From the beginning she was careful to remember her place, to be deferential to the lords of Dravia and to anyone connected with them. It was difficult sometimes, but her bond with Marwen was dearer to her than any satisfaction she would have gained from defiance. It helped that the crown prince was, as Marwen had said, honourable in most things, and that he liked to sing. Many evenings, after they had eaten, he would insist that Kiri play to accompany him.

> *Arngard was a noble king;*
> *With the mailed fist on his breast*
> *And his sword in his hand*
> *He rode into Kamilan, he rode into Dorath.*
> *Telhiron slew thousands,*
> *Arngard slew tens of thousands. . . .*

Arngard, son of Telhiron, himself almost a legend, accomplished what his sire had not: he conquered Kamilan. He was murdered by his brothers in Dravia, whereupon the Kamils rebelled and his own warrior captains fought among themselves for his crown. Out of this struggle was founded, finally, the royal house of Adelmar, who made peace in Kamilan by marrying the last of the hill queens, the granddaughter of Alyth. Kamilan was changed forever by Telhiron, but the conqueror's blood did not flow in the veins of its kings. The house of Aralev would never be content until it did.

"I wonder," Berend said to his brother, "what songs they will make of you."

Berend's face was flushed with wine. He had quarrelled that morning with his eldest wife—the only one who would dare to quarrel with him at all. And that afternoon he had lost three dogs in a hunt. He was in a darker mood than usual.

"Perhaps they will sing thus," he went on; "what an unusual man was Held, who was the king of two lands and the lord of none."

"If you think I'm not lord here, Berend, press me a little farther. Brother or not, I will enlighten you."

"I wonder about that. You haven't even taught your Kamil wench not to come to our table dressed like a savage."

Held glanced briefly at Marwen, and then at his brother.

"That troubles you, Berend? Then I pray to Mohr that you'll never be king, for you have no wisdom at all. It's going to be hard enough for the Kamils to accept me; what will it profit me to turn her into a Dravian, so they won't accept her, either? You're a fool, brother."

"You may call me a fool, but will you also call your father one? He was well enough to eat with us tonight, but he refused. Ask my wives if you don't believe me. 'I won't sit with that creature,' he said. 'Her mother was a sorceress, and so is she.' That's what he said. Why do you suppose King Adelmar fathered no sons, and no children at all after this one? No children, brother, none—not on whores, not on slaves, not on any female he mounted. For thirteen years, until he died, gelded like an ox."

"Do you think me gelded, Berend?" Held asked calmly, but with an edge to his voice that made Kiri's stomach knot.

Berend had the good sense to laugh. "No. I've seen evidence enough that you're not. But perhaps you should try and explain to our father why you haven't claimed your rights in Kamilan.

He keeps asking me, and gods know I can't give him any answer. The better he feels, the more he wonders about you. Crowns are won on battlefields, he says, not under blankets."

"Crowns are won where they are won," Held said. "Our good father left more men dead in Kamilan than any lord since Telhiron, and won nothing for the effort. I see no reason to do the same."

A small ripple of shock went around the table. Berend's wives looked at each other in the manner of people who had witnessed a sacrilege.

"You dare to dishonour him thus?" Berend said harshly.

The crown prince put his cup down and put his elbows on the table, as though he were about to explain something very complicated to a child.

"I'm not dishonouring the king by saying he tried valiantly to accomplish something and did not succeed. I'm merely stating a fact. It seems to me that a man with a bit of intelligence looks at such facts honestly, and looks to see if there might be another way."

And a man with a conscience to match his intelligence, Kiri added silently, *might not seek any way at all, but live his own life, and rule his own land, and let the Kamils be. . . .*

"And while you look for other ways," Berend said, "the Kamils build their defenses, you grow old without sons, the world shakes its head, and your father thinks you're bewitched."

"I will have sons soon enough." Held hesitated, looking at Marwen almost apologetically, and then plunged on. "On the feast of Ariana I will marry Edgard's daughter Leanthe. Make me a wager, Berend, if you think I'm unmanned and bewitched: twenty gold ells for every time I mount her before the sun comes up. Will you risk that much?"

Berend laughed. "Yes, by the gods! And I'll lose happily. I didn't think you'd ever do it."

"I am not a fool," Held said.

Kiri knew that he was speaking not only to Berend, but to Marwen as well, and to all the world. *Don't push me too far. Don't misjudge my good sense for weakness.*

Don't imagine that I will ever give up my power!

The feast of Ariana the grain goddess fell late in the summer, a few weeks before the equinox, when the harvests ripened for gathering and the fruit hung heavy on the trees. A fortnight earlier, Prince Held of Dravia rode out of Aralev in great pomp and splendour, with an escort of two hundred warriors dressed in gold and crimson, their standards flying in the wind and the sound of their drums ringing through the hills. Seven wagons followed behind him, loaded with gifts for the highborn Edgard and his daughter. It would take them two days to reach Heydren, and they would remain there two or three days more before bringing everyone back to Aralev for the wedding.

Kiri and Marwen watched the procession until the last lingering coil of dust dissolved behind it.

"Well," Kiri said, with a lightheartedness she did not feel, "if we have a bit of luck, that's the last we'll ever see of Held of Dravia."

"Kiri." The queen took her earnestly by the shoulders. "It's not too late to change your mind. If we fail, he may still forgive me. But you he will put to death."

"I know that." *He will hang me from the city walls like he hanged Clodis.*

She did not fear death itself; death was simply dissolution. But the loss of life was a bitter loss: to never see the sun again, or taste a peach; to never make another song; to never see a new city or cherish a new friend. She had lived so little. She did not want that living to be over.

Yet to live was finally to act, to do all the things one could that were worth doing. And what could she ever hope to do that was worthier than this? She would not risk death for many things, but she would risk it to be able to say one day: *With Marwen of Kamilan I came out of Dravia, to glory and to freedom.*

And by a similar logic, she reflected, men were led by tens of thousands into battle. The object was different, the personal motives were much alike.

It's all come round again. I sat year after year at my window, watching the riders pass by night towards Kamilan, and now at last I will follow them. It is all changed, and it is all the same.

That night, in the hearth of the prince of Dravia's chamber, the queen made a tiny altar, and placed on it her offerings for the journey: grain, so they might not lack for food; an arrow, so they might be safe from enemies; flowers, so they might find friends; and a lock of her own hair—the only thing she still possessed which was entirely Kamil—so they might find their way through the mountains and come home.

"Wise One, mother of the world, forgive me that I worship you in so unholy a place as this, where you are scorned and all your laws are broken. I beg you to help us. Hide us from our enemies, and guide us home. I swear to you, Great Mother, if we come safe again to Kamilan, I will open your temples, I will give back your priestesses, I will restore your place of honour in the land. This I swear.

"This I swear.

"This I swear!"

The next day's sun dawned hot and brilliant. It was splendid harvest weather, dry and clear. As far as the eye could see, carts and horses were on the roads, and men and women were in the fields, cutting and piling and gathering their riches. The air had a hazy sweetness of dry heat and smoke.

"For a pair of honest travellers," Kiri said, "I could think of no better time to be on the road. For us, I could think of no worse."

The queen's gaze was restless and distant; she did not answer.

"He will reach Heydren tonight, lady," Kiri went on. "They will feast and drink. It's as good a time as any for us to go."

Marwen shook her head. "No. We'll wait. It will rain soon."

"Rain? Forgive me, lady, but look at that sky. It won't rain for days—perhaps for weeks."

"It will rain."

Kiri faltered. This was not something she had expected. They were ready. Held was far away. Every hour they waited was an hour in which something might go wrong.

She studied the sky. There was a heavy sultriness in the air, and the birds were swarming. She had caravaned for years; she knew that might mean rain. It might also mean nothing much at all. The sultry build-up to a thunderstorm often lasted for days, and the birds always swarmed over fresh-cut fields. Was the queen foretelling rain, or merely wishing for it?

They waited. The next day was the same, and Marwen would not yield. They would wait, she said.

She's afraid, Kiri thought. *She's afraid and she will wait until it's too late, and all our plans will be for nothing.*

"Lady," she pleaded. "We can't go on waiting. The prince may well be back in your bed before it rains."

"And if he were," Marwen said darkly, "what would it matter? He has slept through much already."

There was a hardness in the queen's eyes which seemed new to Kiri. Or perhaps it had always been there, and was merely heightened by that brilliant and burning sun. Marwen was not waiting because she was afraid. She was much less afraid than Kiri herself, and that was *why* she could wait.

She's dangerous, Kiri thought. *Why does that surprise me? I would have taken it for granted in so strong-willed a man.*

By the next afternoon, everyone in Aralev knew that it would rain. The sky was black with birds, the palace cats would not go outside, and in the fields beyond the city, peasants were loading their wagons on the run, watching the southwestern sky. Over the heights of Dohann, clouds rolled heavy and dark, coiling with thunder.

Kiri played for their supper, her music half drowned out by the pounding of rain on the palace roof. Sheets of lightning consumed the sky, brightening the room like day and turning their flaring torches pale. With every crash of thunder Berend's youngest wife cringed. When she began to cry, he slapped her for a whimpering fool.

Marwen stood up. "Storms make me unwell," she said. "If you will pardon me, I will bid you all good-night."

"What is there in all the world, lady," Berend said scornfully, "that you women are not afraid of?"

A glance passed between the queen and Berend's wife, a glance not precisely of understanding, but of empathy. Then Marwen turned a cool and level eye on Berend.

"We fear least what you fear most, Berend: the existence of things we cannot master and do not possess."

It hurt to cut off Marwen's lovely hair and see it crumble in the fire.

"It'll grow back, Kiri, never mind. In Jana's name, hurry!"

"You were the one who kept saying wait, lady," Kiri reminded her dryly.

The queen, she thought, made a tolerable man, or rather a tolerable youth, tall and gangly, and young enough to still be beardless. Kiri herself was harder to disguise, but a false beard made of horsehair and a sheath wrapped over her breasts did a creditable job—at least in the light of Thesa's one weak lamp. She had made up more than one clown and travelling actor on the caravan. Indeed, she reflected, she had learned more useful things there than she ever suspected at the time.

The slave watched them in bewildered fascination, as she might have watched the incomprehensible behaviour of gods or barbarians. Then she led them through the warren of storerooms to the little door where the slaves took out the rubbish and the chamber pots, and carried back the wood from rows of sheds.

"No," Marwen said to her, "don't come outside. Better you don't have to explain to anyone why you're wet. Farewell, Thesa. You've served me well. May the gods be with you."

The slave took the coins Marwen gave her and bowed. She was too afraid to speak.

The rain hit them with astonishing force, drenching them in seconds. Kiri climbed onto the roof of a woodshed and from there tossed a rope over the palisade and climbed up, raising her head carefully over the top to reconnoitre.

There were many guards by the entrance, but along this wall only two sentries paced, hunched and miserable, their lanterns serving for little more than comfort in the blinding rain. She hitched the second rope and dropped it down to Marwen, motioning her to climb.

The queen was young and healthy, but she had never climbed a rope before, and her progress was painfully slow. *My arms will fall off,* Kiri thought, *before she gets here. . . .* But when Marwen finally reached her, gasping, she realized that the climb had been the easy part; getting her mistress over the spiked top unharmed was a good deal harder and suddenly very perilous, for no matter how slowly and unhappily the sentries paced, eventually they would pass directly beneath.

Eventually they did, with Marwen hanging over the palisade like a sack of meal, Kiri holding her with one arm and trying to wield her crossbow with the other, cursing through her teeth a world which refused to teach girl children anything except how to dress and flirt and sew.

The sentries passed, feeling no desire to look up into that cold and hammering rain. A third try got Marwen safely over, with a great rent in her trouser leg and badly bruised ribs. Kiri dropped their satchels, unhooked Marwen's rope, and skimmed down. Then they were in the streets. Kiri hid her crossbow beneath her cloak, and they walked through Aralev barely noticed and quite unmolested, two country lads heading home after a late evening in the tavern, stumbling down the last hill to the sentry post at the southern gate. They had to bang three times on the door before one of the guards came out, grumbling first at his comrades, then at the rain, and finally at them.

"You be pure fools," he said to Kiri. "Spirits be out on nights like these."

Kiri reeled a little and thanked him, obviously too drunk to tell live men from spirits in any case.

The gate clattered shut behind them, and the wish to bolt like uncaged animals was almost more than they could bear.

8. The Mountains

The rain continued unabated; the roads turned to rivers, and the fields to plains of mud. They tramped on doggedly, league after league, their eurphoria giving way to grim determination and finally to exhaustion. Although the world was still drenched in blackness, Kiri began to sense that sunrise was dangerously close. They were in open country, in the heart of Dravia's beautiful farmlands.

"We should hide soon, lady," she said.

"But it's still dark!"

"When it's light, it will already be too late."

"But where can we hide here? I don't think we should risk using granaries or sheds. Those are the first places they will look."

"We'll hide right in the middle of the field."

"Please don't make jokes; I'm too weary for it."

"I'm not making jokes. Look."

She led the queen to a large coil of cut grain, lifted away several armfuls to make a hole, placed one of the packs there, and covered it again.

"There are thousands of coils like this one, and they all look the same. After we've eaten, we'll crawl under like a pair of mice, and stay till it's dark again. A half hour of rain will wash out any sign that anything has been touched."

She spoke cheerfully, unwilling to admit how terrifying it would be to simply lie there defenseless, shielded by nothing but a bit of straw. It would be so much easier to just run. Run and run and run until they dropped. . . .

Beneath the coil the ground was dry. In a very short time they were warm and drowsy, half aware of the small, squeaky protests of the mice, who did not care at all for their large and uninvited guests.

"Kiri," Marwen whispered.

"Aye, lady?"

"There may not be another chance to say this, so I will say it now. I've never loved anyone as I love you. Medwina raised me, and she is the noblest woman born, but you are my dearest friend, and I don't think there will ever be another like you."

Kiri swallowed tears. Unable to find words, she reached an arm around Marwen's neck, and held her so until they slept.

They woke to the sound of horses and the shouts of men, and a baying in the distance which they knew was Berend's hounds. The hunt had begun then, and it would be pitiless. The prince's men would not care what ruin they left behind them, storming into houses and granaries and barns, trampling and slashing through woodlands and uncut crops, bullying bewildered peasants who did not even know what the trouble was about—what had they to do with queens?

The riders came nearer. She could hear the splatter of their hooves in the mud, the jingle of their harnesses. They stopped, and Kiri's heart stopped with them. *They have seen something, it's all over. . . !*

But no, they were waiting. Another group of riders approached from a different direction. She heard them shout. One of the voices belonged to Berend, a voice so raw with anger that, just for a moment, she wished it were Held's voice instead. With him came the dogs, howling and snarling. Would he turn them loose, she wondered, if he found his prey?

For a moment she listened hard, trying to understand their words against the rain and the restlessness of the horses. And then she forgot the men entirely.

One of Berend's hounds was sniffling and pawing at the coil, whimpering with eagerness. Beside her, it seemed to Kiri that Marwen had stopped breathing. She pressed her face into her arm and waited for the coil to be torn apart, for voices to cry out in the triumph of discovery. She rarely prayed—but now, for the first time in her life, she prayed to Marwen's goddess.

A shout followed, the splattering of hooves, and then a howl of pain as a boot crashed into the dog's ribs.

"This is no time to be chasing mice, you useless cur! Let's go!"

They rode on. One of them tore a great piece of the coil away with his stirrup as he passed; he never looked back.

It rained almost continually for days, and when it did not rain the clouds hung black and sodden, low enough to touch. It was a rain which the Dravians would forever after remember as unnatural, as an act of sorcery worked by the Kamil queen. How could she have chosen the moment of her flight so well, they would ask, except by having caused the storm herself? Even Kiri, tramping night after night through the mud, wondered at those remorselessly sheltering skies.

They slept three days under roofs of grain. The fourth day found them in the first wooded reaches of the hills below Dohann.

From this point onward they ate as little as possible from their stores of food, foraging instead for seeds and roots and berries. When Kiri judged them deep enough in the wilderness, she began to hunt grouse each morning for their breakfast, and showed the queen how to pack them in mud and bake them in tiny, smokeless fires.

"How did you learn all this?" Marwen asked. "All these things—you know so many things, and they don't seem to have much to do with minstrelsy or caravans."

"I learned them from the young men of Vanthala. My village."

"But villagers are peasants and foresters. They may hunt and cook grouse, but why would they make smokeless fires, or learn how to scale walls?"

Kiri did not meet the queen's eyes. "They were border folk, lady."

There was a long silence.

"They were raiders, then," the queen said at last.

"Aye, lady."

"Did you ever . . . go with them? Into Kamilan?"

"I wanted to—more than anything in the world. They wouldn't let me. They said I couldn't come because I was a girl; girls were too small and too weak to fight. Their own leader was a skinny rat only a little taller than I was, and ten pounds lighter. He was very brave, and he could figure his way out of any kind of mess. That was good enough; he didn't have to be the biggest or the strongest. But when I couldn't run as fast as some of them, or draw a bigger longbow, or lift as big a stone, they smiled and said: See, we told you, girls just can't do what men can do; stay home.

"I was determined to join them, just the same. I dreamt of it all the time. I made up stories in my head about how it would happen. Every time they went, I promised myself: next time I'll be riding with them. Once, I remember, they had some boys along whose parents didn't want to let them go, and so they all sneaked off before daybreak. I lay in my cot and listened to them pass, and cried my heart out. The boys they took were thirteen and twelve; I could have dragged them both from their horses and beaten them silly. But they were men.

"In the end, I think they would have yielded; I would have made them. Only by then I didn't want to go any more."

"Why?" Marwen asked softly.

"A raiding party came back one summer. They had over a hundred horses, and many cattle. The whole village turned out to celebrate. There were bonfires everywhere, and huge crocks of beer, and bagpipes, and everyone telling stories at once. By the fire were maybe a dozen piles of plunder that would be given out—bags of corn, hammers and axes and pots and pans, fine Kamil tunics, god-offerings, satchels of coin—it was quite magnificent. And right by the fire was a young man dancing, with a bright red Kamil sash around his neck, keeping time to his own feet with a captured whistle.

"Sometimes it isn't good to be a story-maker, lady. You see what you might have wished not to see. It came without warning, and I couldn't shut it out. I looked at our fires and all at once I saw other fires, I saw a child reaching for that whistle, I saw the sash torn from a young woman's tunic . . . and all I could think of then was to wonder what had become of them, what had become of all of them, all the people who had owned the corn and the pots and pans and the coins. And I knew—I can't tell you how it was possible, but I knew that the woman and the child were dead, that many others were dead beside them. And I knew that I would never ride with my kinsmen and my friends to Kamilan.

"I left the village a month later, and I left Dravia before the year was gone."

If there had been anywhere else to go, I would have left the world. . . .

"And you joined the caravan," Marwen said.

"Yes," Kiri said.

And the caravan went everywhere, and everywhere it went it crossed the paths of armies, and every path was another Kamil borderland. She saw more and more clearly the terrible meaninglessness of it which was so evil, finally, less because it was cruel than because it was meaningless. All the armies tramping back and forth across the world were nothing more than plunderers who would be trampled and robbed in their turn. The empire of Larandau was a Dravian raiding party writ large, carrying home legions of slaves as well as pots and pans, slaves to swell the armies to conquer more slaves.

It's not for this, she had cried silently. *All our skill, our strength, our splendid ships, our magnificent horses, our courage, our hunger for glory. It's not for this!*

And then she had asked herself, as many a man had asked her: *If not for this, for what?*

She did not know. She could never forgive the men who fought those endless wars, and she could never stop admiring their courage. The stories were still splendid. The songs still made her blood race. The sound of horses passing in the night still made her long for something she could not name, for the name it once had could no longer be endured. And so it never went away, that yearning from her earliest youth, that force inside her which seemed sometimes to be no more than force itself: pure energy, pressing outwards and recognizing itself in everything else which was in motion. It never went away, and it never came to terms with itself or with the world.

She looked up, and was glad to see that Marwen's face held neither bitterness nor anger.

"I'm not squeamish, lady," she went on. "I killed bandits on the caravan, and I will kill now if I must, to bring us safely to Kamilan. But I will not kill for plunder, or for glory, or for the joy of it, for the sake of seeing something dead.

"There is . . . I don't know how to say this, lady, but it seems to me there is an order . . . a pattern . . . in everything, even in violence. There are times when it's right to kill. But what we've done—I mean the world—we've made violence a pattern by itself, and lost sight of all the other patterns. And now we live in blood."

"The patterns you speak of are Jana's," Marwen said. "They are what we lost when she was driven into exile."

"But those who follow Mohr claim it was he who brought order into the world."

"And so he did, after a fashion. He brought slavery. He brought the silencing of women, and the chaining of passion and desire. He brought empire. A few rule now, and everyone else obeys. Where is there better order, after all, than on a galley ship? A hundred men row as one, and the ship flies without wind, wherever it is sent, at a mere word. That's much more orderly than raising sails and praying for wind. Mohr's destiny is to straighten the world, Kiri."

"By breaking it?"

"There's no other way. Only dead things can be ordered as he wishes."

"He has so many dead things, you'd think he would be satisfied by now."

"He will never be satisfied," the queen said darkly. "Medwina has dreams sometimes, about the future, and they are dark dreams. She's lost everything she valued in her youth, and she is bitter, but I don't think that has made her visions false; it has only made her more willing to speak of them. And she fears Mohr."

"As I do, lady."

"But Jana does not. He can unmake the world, but he can't unmake her. She will be here when he's gone, and make another."

"That's small comfort to us."

"Yes. Very small comfort. So we'll live on what comfort we have: two baked grouse and a sky without walls."

As the landscape grew rougher, it became necessary to travel by day. Another week brought them to the edges of Dohann, and there Kiri's courage faltered. Ahead was only savage forest, reaching always upward until at last it faded into thinning scrub. Beyond was bare gray rock, as old as the bones of the world, silent, the highest reaches wrapped in eternal snow. They could wander for months, she realized, and never find a pass. And the summer was nearly gone. The nights had grown steadily colder as they climbed; Kiri knew they would grow colder still. In the highest passes even bandits and warriors wrapped themselves completely in skins, like the people of the steppes, so that nothing could be seen of them except their eyes.

They made a cheerless camp in the lee of a cliff and watched the last light go down. They ate the nuts they had gathered along the way; like the fruits and the berries, these were becoming scarcer now; the forest creatures were claiming them first.

Marwen was sitting on a rock, exhausted, tying strips of rag around her shoes. A week of rain and mud had all but destroyed their footwear. Every day as they walked Marwen gathered herbs to make poultices for their feet. That eased the pain and sucked away the poisons, but even the queen's healing skills would be no match for the brutal walk ahead.

"There isn't much chance, is there?" Marwen brooded. "There never was, I suppose."

"We could turn east," Kiri said, unwillingly; "and try for the caravan road."

They both knew the risk in that. Marwen pressed her face into her palms. When she looked up again, Kiri saw the raw anguish of indecision in her eyes.

"You know this country, Kiri; you know the roads. Tell me what you think."

"If we turn east, lady, we will probably be taken—either by Held's men, or by bandits." She paused, and forced herself to continue. "If we continue this way, we will probably die in the mountains. I know of no way through, and there isn't much chance that we'll find one on our own. Even a late winter is less than two moonturns away. And we can't live through it without shelter."

There was one thing more which needed to be said. "Held won't kill you, lady. You're still the queen of Kamilan. Even bandits, if they have some wits, will try to ransom you rather than destroy you."

"And what of you, Kiri?"

Neither answered. Neither had to. Marwen spoke again. "Held won't kill me, no. He'll put me in a cage."

She looked up at the sheer wall of rock above them. As the night fell the mountains became even more bleak and terrible. The thought of dying here was so frightening that any world of living people seemed merciful; one's instincts reached out blindly for food and voices and fire. One might well run, waving with eagerness, into a bandit camp, thankful only that they were men, and not wolves.

"So we will die in Jana's hands, or in Mohr's," Marwen murmured. "Whose are more cruel, in the end?"

Aye, Kiri thought, that was indeed the question. For however bitterly they might die in Dohann, they would still die with a measure of dignity. It was not wolves but men who made slaves, and hung flayed bodies from their battlements, and staked women out by their fires to rape until they were dead.

"Are you willing to go on, Kiri? This way?"

"For myself, I'd much rather go this way. I thought only for your sake, perhaps. . . ?"

"I am not going back to Aralev."

They huddled together, and ate a bit of cold food, and said nothing more of turning east. That night, for the first time on their journey, they heard the cries of wolves.

They slept poorly from the cold, and rose exhausted to a day gloomy with cloud. They climbed on. The forest was still beautiful, but they could no longer take any pleasure in its beauty. It seemed made of nothing but wet branches slapping at their faces, rocks gashing their feet, roots tripping them and dragging them down. And shadows—shadows which had about them an increasing sense of menace.

Twice Kiri would have sworn that she saw someone—or something—moving in the trees, but each time she paused and focussed her eyes, there was nothing there. At noon they rested briefly by a creek to eat and drink. Marwen said, without any warning at all:

"We're being watched, Kiri. I'm sure of it."

"You saw it too, then," Kiri said, half appalled and half relieved.

"I don't know if I saw anything or not. I *feel* them. But I don't know who they are."

By late afternoon they were stumbling over shadows and leaves, hanging on to each other sometimes out of blind exhaustion. Between climbing through gulleys and around foothills, they had covered hardly any real distance at all. They made camp early, knowing that to do so was a first small admission of defeat. For a palace-raised woman, Marwen's endurance had been exceptional, but it was failing rapidly, and they both knew it.

The queen sat limp against a tree while Kiri unwrapped her feet. They were badly cut, and so swollen they no longer seemed human. Perhaps some of Kiri's despair showed on her face, for the queen said calmly, without bitterness:

"I haven't been good for much, have I, my friend?"

"Don't say such things, lady. You were the one who knew that it would rain." *Or the one who made it rain,* she added silently.

"I am the heir to a hundred generations of such knowledge," Marwen said. "I would be much to blame if I had lost it all." She laid her head back against the tree. "If Medwina were here. . . ." She sighed faintly. "If Medwina were here, you'd see how little I know. She used to shake her head at me, over and over. 'You have such potential, child,' she would say, 'but you're so *clumsy!*' "

Clumsy? Kiri thought scornfully. Marwen's lean body was anything but clumsy. And then she realized that Medwina would have been speaking of something else—of Marwen's role as seer and priestess and witch, as interpreter of signs and fashioner of magic. If Marwen was clumsy, Kiri wondered, what must Medwina be able to do?

They could no longer risk the luxury of sleeping the night through, Kiri told the queen, but instead would have to take turns standing guard. It was a decision she judged necessary, although she knew it would hasten their complete exhaustion. Each night thereafter, when they camped, she felt certain that Marwen would not be able to walk another day. Yet the queen persevered, and sometimes even seemed to grow stronger, as though she were drawing on a last inner resource, which even she had not known she possessed.

The certainty that they were being followed did not diminish, and all the terrors of legend crept out of the back of Kiri's mind, the stories of people who were said to live in the darkest reaches of Dohann, who had been there since the beginning of the world, people who were not really people at all. Some said they were ghosts who had taken on new bodies; some said they were demons. Kiri never really believed the stories. No one she spoke to had ever seen these people. It was always a dead grandmother who had seen them, or a long-vanished stranger, or a friend from another town. Such stories were everywhere. All along the caravan roads she had heard similar ones, and listened to them all with fascination, and shrugged them aside in the clear light of morning with a smile.

Now, it was less easy to smile. They were almost certainly being followed. And yet after days of knowing it, they had seen no one and nothing, not even a brief glimpse of someone in the trees. The only comfort they could take in the situation was to feel sure that, whoever it was, it was no one connected with the Dravian prince.

"Perhaps they're fugitives like ourselves," she mused to the queen, "and they're following us because they think we know the way."

Poor devils, she added silently, *if that is the case.*

She took the first watch that night, as she always did. Her years on the caravan had made her an alert and disciplined sentry, but she saw nothing different that night, only a cold sickle moon. She heard nothing different, only the wind in the trees and the distant, melancholy wolves. She woke Marwen sometime after midnight and sank into a chilly, troubled sleep. She woke again to the sound of her name, spoken in a flat, edged voice which she only slowly realized was the queen's.

She sat up. In the thin light of daybreak she could see figures gathered in a half circle, closing herself and Marwen against the rock wall where they had sheltered. She reached for her crossbow, and heard the soft sound of many arrows being notched against their strings. She laid the bow down again, gently.

"I swear I didn't fall asleep, Kiri," the queen whispered. "It's as though they came out of the earth or the bodies of the trees."

They were small people with dark, weathered faces. They were dressed in skins, and they spoke to each other in quiet, sibilant whispers which sounded much like the rustlings of plants. Kiri tried every tongue she had learned between Sardas and Vianon. *Who are you? Why are you following us? What do you want?* They clearly did not understand, but the attempt to communicate seemed to reassure them.

One of them stepped forward from the others: a man already aging, lacking most of his teeth, with a gnarled look to his face and his body. He touched his forehead, then his stomach; then he made a gesture towards the sky.

"Friends?" Kiri wondered.

"We can only hope so," Marwen said, and returned the gesture.

The man smiled and launched into a tirade of signs.

"I think," Kiri said unhappily, "you've just told him you understand his language."

He signed for a long time, then appeared to repeat the message. His face darkened as Marwen made helpless gestures of bewilderment. Finally he made a sign no one could possibly misunderstand. He took the knife he wore on his belt and drew it across his throat; then he waved at them to follow him.

"We go with them," Kiri said, "or we die."

"Wait," Marwen said.

She bowed very low and then knelt on the ground, motioning them to gather around. Using sticks and leaves, she began to draw her history. Mountains. A place on the other side of the mountains. A place very far away—she waved to the southeast. She folded her hands and laid her face upon them and closed her eyes as if in sleep. Home. She pointed to herself again, and again across the mountains, to be sure they understood. She sat back on her haunches and pounded her thighs with her palms. The galloping of horses. She mimed herself as a prisoner, wrists bound; she slapped her face and bowed her head, and traced the path back across the mountains. She stood up, waving to the north. Aralev. Piles of sticks, with neat sticks laid all around them. A walled city. She bowed her head again, showing herself as a prisoner. She picked up leaves and blew them away. One year. Blew them away again. Two years. She pointed at Kiri and touched her heart. Friend. She took Kiri's hand and crouched, miming flight, ducking, hiding, running, climbing, falling. Searching. Searching and searching. No way across the mountains. No way at all. She knelt again, reached out one hand with the palm upraised. Please?

All the while she was telling her story the tree people—for that was what Kiri called them in her mind—the tree people watched, at first with distrust, and then with growing understanding. Galloping horses they recognized at once, and the image of the walled city created among them a deep stir of fear. They knew of Aralev.

When Marwen finished there was a long rush of talk among them. One of the women seemed to be arguing with the leader. He turned back to Marwen finally, pointed angrily to the walled city, then to her, then to his people.

Marwen shook her head emphatically. *No! We were not sent to look for you. We mean you no harm.* She pointed across the mountains, laid her face on her hands again. *Home. We want to go home.*

The leader considered that. Then he unlaced the shapeless skin garment which hung from his shoulders and bared his chest, indicating that she should do the same.

"Marwen, don't. . . !" Kiri whispered helplessly.

The queen did not hesitate. She pulled off her tunic and opened her shirt, standing before them unashamed. The woman who had argued with the chief gave him a frank look of triumph. *You see? I was right!* There was another rush of talk, softer this time, almost awed. The leader of the tree people bent and drew a line through Marwen's small pile of mountains. He pointed to himself and his followers, pointed to Marwen, and traced a path halfway down the line that he had drawn. He pointed to her, and traced the line onward; he pointed to himself, and traced the line back.

Marwen smiled the loveliest smile Kiri had ever seen on her face, and held out her hand.

They were perhaps the most ancient race in all of the mountain countries. To them the Dravian tribes whom Telhiron conquered were themselves recent invaders; before them had been others. Each fresh wave of enemies drove them higher and higher into the reaches of Dohann, until only a few hundreds still survived, living in caves. They had no divinities.

They worshipped the forest, and although they would hunt animals for food and skins, they would make fires only inside of caves, and they would not cut even one leaf from a living tree. They knew nothing of Kamilan, but they hated the Dravians. Using signs and picture histories like those Marwen had used, they told of incursions by hunters and warriors, raids which went back for many generations. They told of people carried off as slaves to a walled city from which only a handful escaped, of women passed around among bands of men, of children taken from their mothers and never seen again. Most of it, Kiri concluded, had happened a long time ago. Now there were so few of them left that the Dravians had almost forgotten them, except as creatures of legend, as stories to frighten children. The tree people were younger than they had seemed. Their gnarled looks were the fruit of terrible hardships, and a lifespan which now was less than forty years. The toothless chieftain had two small children. One of them, he explained to them sadly, had just been born. Autumn was not a good time for children to be born.

They moved like deer in the woods; even with undamaged feet Kiri and Marwen could not have matched their pace. So for long stretches they simply lifted the two women onto their shoulders and carried them. They often travelled well into the night. Even when they camped they did not seem to sleep much, but rather sat in clusters, talking among themselves in their soft and rustling voices.

They headed east for such a long time that Kiri was certain they had lost or forgotten their way, and would crash out onto the caravan road at any moment. But finally they turned south again, following a narrow valley which seemed to climb towards the highest peaks of Dohann. For two days they followed it, and Kiri began to hope that they had finally entered a pass which would lead them into Kamilan.

The third morning Kiri slept longer than usual. It was fully light when she woke. The first thing she became aware of was silence. There were birds and wind, but nothing else; no human footsteps, no soft, rustling voices. She leapt to her feet. Only herself and Marwen remained in the camp.

"Where are they, do you think?" she whispered to the queen. "Are they planning some treachery?"

Marwen shook her head. She liked those soft-voiced, alien people. "Perhaps it's a ritual," she said. "Something they have to do, without any strangers in their midst."

But she spoke as though she did not believe her own words. They made a small fire and ate, and then waited until the sun was high. None of the tree people returned. And Kiri knew they were not going to return. They had not gone to carry out some secret ritual of their clan. They had fled. They had simply fled, into the gray wilderness, silent, like startled foxes speeding for their caves.

"Why did they go like that?" Kiri wondered sadly. "Without saying good-bye? Without giving us a chance to say good-bye, or even to thank them properly?"

Marwen's eyes followed the valley back as far as it was possible to see, as though she believed they were somehow still there, and would suddenly step lightly out of the trees with their bark-like skin and soft eyes.

"They're afraid, I think," she said.

"Not of us?"

"Of everything, Kiri. Of absolutely everything."

It was true autumn now; the days were brilliant and warm, but increasingly short, and the nights were bitter cold. Rested, with their feet somewhat healed, they made excellent progress for the first few days. Then the valley levelled into a plateau and they were utterly surrounded by mountains. It took them a week to find a passage which did not lead to a wall of gray rock. By that time they were once again footraw and exhausted and hungry, and it had begun to rain. The food they had brought with them was all gone. They could hunt, but it was too wet to make a fire. They huddled in the dismal shelter of an immense, groaning pine and cut two dead birds apart and skinned them and looked at them for a long time, weak with longing and revulsion.

Kiri cut off a small piece of flesh and put it in her mouth. It tasted raw, bloody. She could not bear the thought of chewing it. Quickly, she swallowed it whole. The second piece was easier.

"Is it awful?" Marwen asked.

"Not really," she lied. "Try a little."

Bit by bit they ate one bird, and then the other, and slept.

They woke again, and walked. Days faded into each other with numbing weariness. They had no sense of time or distance left, and no idea where they were. They had no options now except to follow where the land led them, and hope. The only thing they could take courage from was the fact that they were, most of the time, descending. A downward passage, unlike an upward one, was rarely a dead end. But it could lead them anywhere—even, for all they knew, back into Dravia. The border, like the mountains, twisted and coiled like a snake.

The weather cleared. For two days they tramped through woodlands which grew thicker and more tangled as they descended. The third day was almost like summer. The sun was hot, and there was a brilliant clarity to the light which made the forest dazzling in its colours. Lost and hurting though they were, they could not help being happy: it was so splendid a morning.

Perhaps because of that they were less alert than usual, or perhaps the men who stalked them were as silent as panthers. But there was no warning at all of danger. It simply struck. Something moved in the trees to Kiri's left, and she saw what seemed to be, incredibly, the neck and shoulders of a horse. From that instant onward, everything was chaos.

An arrow whapped into the tree beside her. As she whirled, raising her bow, a huge arm closed savagely around her neck, and a rough male voice hissed against her ear:

"That be the end, ye swill-eatin' Drav! Let go the bow!"

She drove her elbow into his stomach with all her strength. On the caravan roads she had felled more than one man with such a blow; this man grunted a little, that was all. His knife came up fast and sharp against her throat.

"That be *now!*"

She let the crossbow slide from her hands. His language was so harsh, so ill-bred that it took a moment for her to recognize it.

"You're Kamil!" she gasped.

He laughed brutally. "They's bright, these Dravs," he said to another like himself, emerging armed from the forest. "He thinks we be Kamil. I bet he thinks these be trees."

The other laughed, and picked up Kiri's bow. He was rough-hewn and ugly, dressed like a forester or a bandit. Kiri struggled, trying to turn her head, and saw Marwen being twisted to her knees by still another of these savages.

"Listen to me!" she cried. "We're not—"

The arm tightened around her throat, cutting off her breath. *Oh, gods*, she prayed, *whatever gods there be, don't let it end like this! Not like this—not when we've come so far. . . !*

The second man began methodically to search her for weapons, and then stopped, stepping back with an oath.

"We got us a she-Drav, Tamon," he said.

"You be joking!" Perhaps the one called Tamon would have determined the matter for himself, but the sound of Marwen's voice rooted them both where they stood: an undisguised woman's voice, with a clear ring of mastery in it, speaking what even they would surely recognize as perfect, palace-bred Kamil:

"Do you have a captain, soldier, or do you run about in the woods attacking poor travellers on your own authority?"

"By the balls of Harash," Tamon whispered. "They be both womens." Then he laughed, looking towards the queen. "We got captain, Drav. When you sees, you sorry you asks."

His companion drew a horn from his belt and blew two quick signals. Within minutes a half dozen mounted men crashed through the trees. At their head was a dark and barbaric figure, dressed in a mail shirt and menacingly armed. Had Kiri not recognized him, with a drenching flood of relief, she might well have taken Tamon's threat very seriously: *you sorry you asks.* A ragged fox pelt hung over his shoulders. Wild shapes Kiri could not identify were carved into his helmet. His bright red shield was decorated with runes and painted with the sharp, upraised profile of a wolf.

He sprang lightly from his horse and approached them. He carried, along with the usual weapons of the borderlands, a bow and quiver. It was a kind of bow rarely seen in the mountain countries, short and curved, ideal for use on horseback. Its bolts could pierce light armour, but it took a very powerful man to draw one.

"Who are these ragamuffins?" he demanded.

"Be Drav spies, captain. And women spies, at that."

"Drav spies." The captain looked at Kiri, then at Marwen who, despite her captors, managed to face him with a measure of dignity.

"You are Shadrak," she said.

83

He stood utterly still. "And you?" he asked warily.

"I gave you a hero's supper in the palace kitchens after the battle of Medra. You haven't changed much since then, but I suppose I have." She paused, as if expecting him to answer, and then said desperately: "Will you not welcome home your queen?"

"Lady. . . ." It was little more than a whisper, but all of them could hear it. The arm around Kiri's throat eased its grip considerably as Tamon turned, open-mouthed, watching his perilous captain pull off his helmet and drop to one knee.

"Forgive me, lady, I didn't know you. . . . None of us . . . they're poor soldiers, lady, and couldn't possibly have guessed. I beg you to forgive us."

"There's nothing to forgive, captain. But there will be, if your man doesn't release my minstrel before he strangles her."

Shadrak sprang to his feet. "Let the woman go, Tamon!"

"But this one be Drav, captain. An' she be armed!"

"Let her go!"

He released Kiri so quickly that she almost fell. She staggered, gulping for breath. The queen brushed past Shadrak and ran to her, grasping her by the shoulders.

"Are you all right?" she begged.

"Yes," Kiri said hoarsely. Her throat hurt, but that did not matter at all. They clutched at each other, understanding that they were safe, but not quite able to believe it.

"We're in Kamilan," Marwen whispered.

"I know."

"We did it. *You* did it. Oh, Kiri. . . ." The queen bit her lip, but it was too late. They had both begun to cry and giggle and say foolish, incoherent things: *Dravian spies, can you believe it, they thought we were Dravian spies. . . !*

When they had recovered a semblance of dignity, Shadrak asked:

"Where are the others, lady? We will fetch them."

"Others?"

"Your guides. Your escort."

"There's only us."

"They were killed?"

"There were no guides, captain. There were some who helped us along the way, but only Jana walked with us. She alone was our escort and our guide."

No one spoke for a moment. The men looked at each other.

"You came alone through Dohann? Just the two of you?"

"Yes."

"I honour you, lady," Shadrak said.

It was not a formality, but a frank admission of his thoughts. The captain was deeply moved.

9. Belengar

Belengar was a wild little outpost, rough-hewn but stout, built against a crag which towered over the caravan road. It was desolate even in summer. In winter, Kiri thought, it would seem to be on the very edges of the world. Yet it was, strategically, one of the most important garrisons in the country. No doubt Borosar the warlord had judged it the perfect command for the young hero of Medra, a man too valuable to waste and too powerless to grumble about the hardships.

Shadrak gave the queen and her minstrel his quarters: a small, bare room, with a smaller anteroom attached. It had a window, a table and chair, and two modest luxuries—the only things, except for food, which the two exhausted fugitives wanted—a hearth, and a great bear rug lying on a pile of straw. He had sent men ahead to prepare it; the fire already burned, and a huge basin had been dragged in to serve as a bath.

"I regret this is all I can offer you, lady," he said. "I've ordered water to be heated for you, and some food. It will take time to prepare the feast—"

"Feast?" the queen said, bewildered.

He flushed slightly. "A simple feast, lady, but if you would honour us by accepting, we would like to welcome you to Belengar."

"That would please me very much, captain," she said. "But let it be tomorrow. Tonight I would fall asleep with my head in my plate, and disgrace us both."

A young man appeared with a basket of bread, a roasted quail, and a flask of wine. He was thin and vaguely consumptive, but he carried himself like a warrior. This was Cassian: Shadrak's servant, aide, and sometime bodyguard. Also, judging by the easy, affectionate manner between them, he was also very much his captain's friend.

"If I'm not here," Shadrak said, "he will look after anything you might need."

They ate greedily, without speaking—barely civilized, Kiri thought, and not especially concerned about it. The bread was hard, the meat leathery, the wine harsh and sour. It was the loveliest food they had ever tasted.

Tired as they were, however, they still wanted to go on talking, as if telling their story were the only thing which could make it true. They told it all from the very beginning. When they had finished, Shadrak was thoughtful.

"Jana has shielded you from much, lady," he said, "not least the weapons of your friends. If you had come to harm from us. . . ." He shook his head. It was too dark a thought for any of them to bear.

Kiri woke early, and found that, no matter how hard she tried, she could not go back to sleep. Finally she gave up, leaving the queen sound asleep on the bear rug, and went in search of breakfast. The post was bustling with preparations for what was clearly going to be a splendid party. Shadrak was nowhere to be seen, but Cassian gave her food, and then told her that Tamon and his comrades—the three soldiers who had found them—had gone to make sacrifices of gratitude and penance.

"I'm not sure Tamon will ever recover," Cassian said. "They came within a breath of killing you, you know."

"What?" Kiri whispered.

"Tamon had an arrow aimed clean at the queen's heart. He waited a bit, he said, for a more certain shot, and that was when he noticed she was limping, and you were both so miserable and bedraggled that he said to himself—" Here Cassian imitated the soldier's rough speech so well that Kiri had to smile a bit, grim as the subject was: "We takes these ones alive, can be we finds out what these bloody Dravs be up to."

The bloody Dravs, Cassian went on to explain, were clearly up to something. There was more activity on the border in the last weeks than there had been since the days of King Algard's invasions.

"But hadn't you heard about the queen's flight? The news must have reached the farthest shores of Sardas by now!"

"Not a word, Kiri. I don't think it has ever been publicly acknowledged. The only word we could get out of Dravia was that Prince Held's marriage to Leanthe of Heydren had been inexplicably delayed, and that the prince was not in Aralev. The captain wasn't sleeping well, I can tell you that, and we were all jumping at shadows. Except that we saw no sign of troop movements, we would have expected war."

Kiri felt limp. The realization that they had almost been killed by their own people made her numb. Being thought of as Drav spies was no longer funny .

"Had we known of your lady's flight," Cassian said, "we would have been combing the mountains for you—on both sides of the border, whatever the consequences. I expect Held realized as much, and preferred to see you die there rather than let us find you first. I can think of no other reason for his silence."

But there *was* another reason, Kiri thought. Like the Kamils themselves, Held would never have imagined that Marwen and her minstrel would walk alone into the mountains of Dohann. He would take for granted an elaborate rescue, an armed escort, guides who knew the way. His silence had a different cause.

"You don't know him," Kiri said.

Cassian cocked an eyebrow at her, waiting.

"What a man doesn't speak of didn't happen," Kiri said. "He means to have her back."

Never had the small garrison of Belengar imagined such an hour of glory. They might have had a smaller and more formal banquet in the barracks hall, but the queen did not want that. They would celebrate, she said, as the Kamils had done in the time of the hill queens: under the open sky, with bonfires and music and a place for everyone.

Her hair was still short and ragged, and she wore shoes many times too large over her cut and swollen feet. But she had never looked more like a queen. Without Kiri's knowledge ("I knew you'd think it was foolish," she said) she had stuffed into the bottom of her satchel a splendid Kamil tunic she had made in Aralev. It was a beautiful garment of heavy blue silk, lavishly embroidered with many colours. Unbelted, it fell just to her knees, and it matched her colouring exquisitely. Then, late in the afternoon, three smiling young soldiers brought her a crown they had fashioned for her, made of branches and gold leaves.

"Well," she said to Kiri when they were dressed, "do I still look like a Drav spy?"

Kiri laughed. "No, lady. But I fear I do."

They went outside. The air was rich with smoke and the smell of roasting meats, and heady with music: the wild, unwalled music of war camps and caravans—not lyres and soft ballads, but shawms and throbbing drums, at once reckless and melancholy, soaring into the treetops and echoing against the crags, so that the whole valley must have quivered with the power of it.

"I will wager," Cassian said, "that they can hear us halfway to Aralev."

Hunters and cooks had been hard at work since the previous morning. It seemed to Kiri that she and Marwen had done nothing all day except eat, yet when the first beautifully roasted chunks of venison and rabbit and grouse were brought to them, with small loaves of fresh bread and bowls of stewed herbs and roots, they ate like wolves.

"A hero's supper, lady," Shadrak said. "Not as fine as the one you gave me, but I hope it pleases you."

She laughed from pure happiness. "It's a wonderful feast, captain. I will never forget it."

The queen was drunk on freedom, almost dangerously so. Her eyes were brilliant and never still. She laughed as Kiri had never known her to laugh, and she might almost as easily have wept. Safe now, she seemed suddenly, unbearably vulnerable. As the night closed deeper over Dohann, neither Kiri nor Shadrak moved further than an arm's reach from her side.

Kiri studied the captain of Belengar with considerable attention. It was easy to do so, for his own gaze rarely left the queen. Copper-skinned and black-haired, he resembled the men of Sardas a little, but only a little, for he was bearded and shaggy, with nothing of their cultured elegance. He was younger than he had seemed in armour, certainly no more than twenty-five. Even a Kamil would have noticed his taste for bright colours and darkly flamboyant ornament. His embroidered red tunic was belted with fur, and a claw necklace hung about his throat. He wore a lot of jewellery, bronze and gold—the gold, Kiri suspected, was probably battlefield plunder, for though it was very fine, none of it matched. The lords of Larandau and the worldly, cultured men of Sardas would both have dismissed him with a shrug: *barbarian.* He was a large man, but not exceptionally so; even in rest his body possessed the smooth, almost liquid power of the animals whose amulets he wore. She would not have called him beautiful; he had a hawk's nose which had been broken more than once, and a long scar slashing downwards from his temple, disappearing into his beard. And he had that savaged look she had seen so many times in fighting men: the look left by too much hunger and pain and fear. But although he was not beautiful, he was nonetheless compelling.

She wondered if the rumour were true that he was slave-born; it would perhaps explain the wariness in him. For all his martial daring and flamboyance, he seemed a man who wore his gifts with caution, and who touched them sometimes when no one was looking, to see if they were still there.

It did not surprise Kiri that he fell hopelessly in love with his queen. He possessed nothing in the world except his singular ability—no wealth, no clan, no rank save what he could carve for himself by bitter combat. To him Marwen must have seemed almost like a goddess, and at the same time a woman very much at risk, who needed desperately the one thing he had to offer her: the loyalty of his sword. Perhaps he remembered with affection the girl queen who chose to give an exhausted soldier food instead of platitudes. Perhaps, so close to that fierce and bloodied border, he had even dreamed of riding to Aralev to free her. To find her here, ragged and utterly heroic, in his wild little fortress, and in his care—no, Kiri thought, it was not surprising that he gave up his heart. It was only surprising that he did so—that any man would have done so—before the sun passed twice across the world.

The music had grown steadily wilder, and nearby, some of the men began to dance. Marwen watched for a time, hungrily. Had her feet been only a little less hurt, Kiri thought, the queen would have leapt up eagerly to join them.

"How good it is," she said softly to Kiri, "to be among men like these, and not have to hate them."

It grew late, and a bitter wind began to snarl down the passes. Marwen spoke briefly to the soldiers, and thanked them for their kindness. Then, with Shadrak, she and Kiri went back inside.

"There is one flagon of wine left in the whole of Belengar," the captain said. "Will you share it with me?"

Cassian had made a hearty fire in their quarters, and carried in some extra chairs; they sat and drank the wine with pleasure. In the first bit of silence that fell, Marwen said:

"The device you are wearing, Shadrak—the wolf—can you tell me what it means? I know such things are sometimes sacred, and if you'd rather not tell me, I won't insist. But I'm not asking merely out of idle curiosity."

"I've told Cassian," he said, "and no one else. But I will tell you. A wolf came into our camp a few nights before the battle at Medra. We'd been fighting all day, and I was exhausted, so I won't say for certain the wolf was there, for no one else saw it."

The queen's face was rigid with attention.

"I was about to take my bow and raise the alarm," the captain went on, "when I realized that neither was likely to be of much use against a creature who could pass unnoticed and unharmed through a hundred armed men, stepping over the feet of some of them as they talked.

"So I waited. The wolf came and sat near me, almost . . . I can't say, exactly . . . almost as if it had come to shield me. Yet there was a darkness in it, too, which made me fear it."

"Did it speak?" Marwen whispered.

"No. But after it was gone, I knew we'd fight again at Medra, and I knew I wouldn't die there.

"I believe it will come back, lady, though I don't know when. So I wear its image, and men look at that image and fear my strength; that, too, is part of its meaning. Already many call me the wolf of Dohann."

He watched the queen intently. She turned a ring round and round on her finger, lost in her own thoughts.

"I think, lady," he said, "this tale does not surprise you much."

She looked up. "The same wolf came to my chamber in Aralev—the same one, or one much like it. It told me I had to find my own way home, and that I would find friends among the Dravians." She paused, glancing fondly at Kiri. "I would have thought also that it was a vision, except that in the morning its tracks were on the floor."

Shadrak's sharply indrawn breath was almost a cry.

"But, lady," Kiri protested. "The floor of your chamber is stone. How could it have left tracks?"

"The tracks were blood."

No one spoke at all for a time.

"The prince assumed that somehow one of Berend's hunting dogs had gotten into our quarters," Marwen added at last, "though even he could not say how." She looked directly at Shadrak. "I don't know for certain what I saw, captain. But I know it wasn't one of Berend's dogs."

Shadrak's eyes brooded now on his hands, now on some shadow in the distance, but always only briefly, always returning to the queen.

He fears for her, Kiri thought, *and fearing for her, he will only love her more.*

10. At the Magdal Bridge

They stayed four days in Belengar, while Shadrak pulled in sufficient numbers of his soldiers to provide the queen with an escort to the city. There were about two hundred men posted there, too few for the long stretch of borderland they were expected to protect. But the more Shadrak explained his strategies in Dohann, the more apparent it became that he was doing very well with what he had. Unlike his predecessors, who generally sent out large patrols in some areas and left other areas unattended, Shadrak scattered small reconnaissance parties all over Dohann, and found astonishing ways to stay in touch with them. They used mirrors and horns; they used smoke; they used trained falcons. And when nothing faster was available, they used relays of couriers. By the night of the feast, he told Marwen, the warlord Borosar already knew of her escape. By the next night the word had reached Kamilan and the Council.

The weather turned hotter still, and they rode out of Belengar in a last stunning burst of summer. They travelled slowly at first, with a certain solemnity, but a few miles from

93

the outpost the caravan road stretched out for miles in a long, winding ribbon across the valley. The temptation was too much to resist on such a day. The queen's horse wanted to run and she let it go, joyfully, bent low over its neck. The lead escort looked back in alarm, but Shadrak waved them on. They rode like the wind, for the pure wild pleasure of it, until the valley was behind them and the road began to curve into a hill.

They drew up then, wind-haired and breathless.

"You ride like a warrior, lady," Shadrak said admiringly.

She was pleased. "It has never felt so good to be on a horse," she said. "To be free. You can't imagine what it means to have been a prisoner, and then be free."

"I think I can, lady."

She regarded him thoughtfully. "Is it true what they say, then—that you were a slave?"

A flicker of unease crossed his face, a question: *Will she think less of me when she knows?* But he did not look away.

"I have never denied it," he said. "My mother was bought off a slave caravan by a merchant in Tamri. I was born there." He paused, and added: "I am Kamil, whatever else they may say about me."

"How did you come to be free?"

"My mother did the master a great service. She saved his only child in a fire. So he let us go."

"I'm glad of that," Marwen said.

She smiled frankly at him, and turned her horse to ride on, the captain staring after her like a starving lad who had just been handed a peach.

Noon found them moving into the rugged valley of the Magdal River. Many leagues onward, it would spread into a broad and fertile plain, rich with farms and cattle. But here it was a harsh and splendid wilderness, torn by chasms. Even in autumn the river would be high. More travellers were ambushed by bandits at the Magdal bridge, Kiri supposed, than at any other spot between Sardas and Vianon.

She was not afraid of being ambushed now. Shadrak had brought some eighty hand-picked fighters to guard the queen. Their presence would discourage even the bravest bandits; and scouts rode rear and front to watch for other enemies.

They crested the last ridge before the river. The leaders halted very suddenly. As the queen's party came up behind them, Kiri saw armed and mounted men, perhaps forty or fifty of them, massed before the bridge. At their fore, flanked by the standards of the House of Aralev, was the looming figure of Prince Held.

Shadrak drew up sharply, snarling the foulest curse Kiri had ever heard. The guards closed ranks around the queen, drawing their swords.

"I'm sorry, lady," Shadrak said bitterly. "I should have prevented this."

"They've always found ways to cross," Marwen said. "Always, until the snow comes. You could not have prevented it."

"We could have ridden day and night, just as he did. Until you were safe in Kamilan."

Her face was pale. "I'm not going to be chased about in my own country like a rabbit."

Even as she spoke, her eyes were fixed on the prince with disbelief and bitterness, as though he were an apparition, or a jest of some obscenely humoured god. She said nothing, nor did she need to. Kiri knew her thoughts.

Here, too? Even here, in my own lands, on my own roads, you would hunt me down?

The ridge where the Kamils halted was about three hundred yards from the bridge. The landscape between sloped gently downward, levelling off into a clearing just before the river's edge. There was not much room for a pitched fight, if it came to that. Kiri's stomach knotted. There had been skirmishes with bandits on the caravan, sometimes fierce ones, but this, she knew, would be very different. The Kamils had the edge in numbers, and whatever brief advantage the high ground might give them at the start. The Dravians had Prince Held, whose magnificence as a warrior and ability to inspire men were legends, not merely in the mountain lands, but as far away as the sleepy vineyards of Sardas.

From the Dravian ranks a courier and standard bearer were now solemnly approaching.

Prince Held of Dravia, the courier said, extended safe conduct to the queen of Kamilan for a meeting, and requested the same.

"Granted," Marwen said, without emotion.

They watched as Held trotted forward, accompanied only by a single warrior. Halfway across the empty ground he halted. The queen nudged her horse, but with a soft, sharp gesture Shadrak stopped her.

"No! Let him come to us."

Held waited briefly, until it became clear that no one was leaving the Kamil ranks. "Shall we have a parley, then," he demanded, "or a shouting match?"

"You're the one who wishes to talk," Shadrak flung back. "You have safe conduct to approach. You will get nothing else."

"I see. Kamil courtesy grows worse and worse."

"It matches Dravian honour," Marwen said scornfully. "Ride on or ride back."

Held rode on—an action which stirred a ripple of alarm among his men which was visible even at this distance. Whatever else, the man had great courage.

He halted a mere ten feet or so from the queen.

"Greetings, lady." He barely glanced towards Shadrak, and not at all towards Kiri. "I have come to take you home."

"My home is in Kamilan."

"You're as proud as ever. Do you mean to drench both our lands in blood for the sake of your pride?"

"You asked for a meeting, Held," she said wearily. "What do you want?"

Even he, Kiri thought, must have heard the edge in her voice, and noticed that she no longer called him lord.

"To settle this—peacefully if possible. I could have ambushed all of you, as I ambushed your scouts. I see no reason for so much bloodshed. You have men here. Choose one of them. I will fight him with any weapon, by any honourable terms save only this: Let it be a fight to the death. If I win, you will return with me to Aralev, and be my lady and my queen. If I lose, you will be free. My men already have been sworn to that."

An easy oath, Kiri thought bitterly; one they would never have to keep. He was Held, the prince of warriors; he could not lose.

"Do you agree, lady?"

"No." The queen's reply was blunt and cold. "I'm not a piece of booty to be traded on the point of a sword. And neither is my country. If you want peace between our people as you say, this is your chance to have it. Gather up your men, and clear my bridge, and go back to Aralev."

"You ask for abject surrender, and call it peace?"

"Say whatever you like, prince; it doesn't matter! I swear to you I'm riding south, and I'll kill any Dravian who tries to stop me!"

Kiri never knew who did it first, whether it was Shadrak himself or one of his men, but someone shouted out the queen's name, and then they were all shouting it, over and over in a great, swelling roar, the soldiers banging on their shields as they chanted:

"Mar-wen! Mar-wen! Mar-wen!"

There, Prince of Dravia, is your answer: You may fight if you wish, but you will fight us all!

For a moment admiration was naked on Held's face—but only for a moment. It dissolved into anger, and then into something else, something Kiri had never seen in him before: pure hatred. It did not surprise her.

"Very well!" he cried bitterly. "It will be war then!"

He reined his horse around so fiercely that it reared. He was lost in his anger, and only half-paused at Shadrak's harsh words:

"The meeting isn't finished, Dravian."

"I have nothing to say to you."

"And I have nothing more to say to you," Shadrak flung back. "Except with my sword. Or with any other weapon, as you said, and by any honourable terms, save only that it be a fight to the death. Weren't those your words?"

Held glared at him. "Are you deaf or merely stupid? You heard the queen reject my terms."

"So you're nothing more than a bandit, as I thought. You fight only for plunder."

It was astonishing how silent four-score men, clattering with arms and horses, could suddenly become.

"I heard men say that the fort of Belengar was captained by a slave," Prince Held said grimly. "I didn't believe it." He spat, and wiped his arm across his face. "Now I believe it."

And a lord owed nothing to a slave. To offer or to accept combat, even out of the darkest hatred, was still a kind of recognition—a recognition no man of rank would give to a freedman.

No more than he would give it to a woman.

"I don't lower the royal sword of Aralev to fight rabble on the road," Held said scornfully.

"You may not refuse!" Marwen wrenched the reins of her horse from the grasp of an astonished soldier and swept forward to confront the prince. "The captain of Belengar is my champion. You may not refuse him!"

"Your champion?" Held said. Kiri wondered if ever—even after half a lifetime—he might come to look at Marwen with anything other than this look of absolute male ownership. "A slaveborn foreigner who doesn't even captain a hundred men? You mock me, lady."

"I am queen of Kamilan. I am your equal in rank, and I may choose any champion I wish. By your own rules of honour, you're bound to answer him!"

There was a brief, ugly silence. It seemed to Kiri that everything which occurred before this moment had been a ritual, a ritual hiding far more than it revealed. Little was hidden now.

The Dravian prince ignored Marwen long enough to contemplate his enemy, to see him—probably for the first time—as something other than the faceless and nameless and endlessly replaceable animals in armour who followed queens and princes through the world. To see him as the only other thing he therefore could be: a rival male.

Held's long, penetrating stare took careful note of Shadrak's dark flamboyance: the garishly painted helmet ringed with claws, the amulets, the red shield with its black and howling wolf. He looked again at Marwen, bitterly:

You prefer that *to me?*

Then, with the serenity which only a birthright of power could give a man, he relaxed, leaned back a little in his saddle, and smiled.

"You're right, Marwen. A queen may choose any champion she wishes. And so may a prince."

He gestured briefly, and the one warrior who had accompanied him moved to his side.

"Andor, I have need of a swordsman to deal with this snarling Kamil wolf. Will you serve me in the matter?"

"With great pleasure, lord."

It was a consummate stroke of mastery—deft, brutal, and absolutely unanswerable. Shadrak, unable to do anything else, cursed and reared his horse in fury. The man named Andor watched him with a dull and yet terrible fascination. Kiri pitied him. He had been sacrificed, and he knew it.

"Shadrak!" Marwen wheeled, turning her back on the Dravians to face the captain. She was livid, and close to losing control.

"Captain, you will deploy your men as you see fit and clear the road to Kamilan. *Now!*"

He was astonished. "Lady, I have offered a challenge. I can't withdraw it—"

"May the hounds of the underworld take your challenge! They're playing with us! They will play with us until we're dead and ground under their feet. It's enough! Goddess of the world, Shadrak, it's enough!"

She faltered. In that moment, all the terror and pain of her captivity were naked on her face. She steadied herself and spoke again, almost softly:

"Captain, I command you: clear the bridge!"

"Lady. . . ."

No man, half in love with her as Shadrak was, could have done anything then except obey. But only the wolf of Dohann would have obeyed with a laugh. It was the last thing Kiri expected, that soft growl of a laugh, like the triumphant sound of an animal unleashed.

"Lady, the bridge is yours!"

Everything changed then, with a throat-tightening swiftness. Names were shouted out, ranks fell into place; all around her Kiri could hear and see the Kamil fighters checking their weapons and their harnesses and the calmness of their hands, making small gestures towards their gods. Slowly, hypnotically, a drum began to beat:

> *In the mountains of Kamilan*
> *Enemies may come;*
> *From the mountains of Kamilan*
> *Enemies do not return.*
> *We are Kamil.*
> *We are afraid of nothing.*

A shawm joined the chant, harsh and wailing, and the men began to bang their shields. The drum beat quickened.

"So." Whatever outcome Prince Held might have imagined he could achieve, it was clear to him now that only one outcome had ever been possible. "You are a false and bloody people," he said grimly. "I wonder why I ever sought your friendship. When this day is over I will never seek it again. As for you, mongrel of Belengar—now I make you an oath."

He drew his sword and held it high, as men did when they swore before the lord of all the gods.

"It's two hundred leagues of mountain road from here to Aralev, and if I live, I will take you back with me, dragged by your feet behind the fetlocks of my horse. And what is left of you when we come there, I will throw to my dogs."

"You won't live," Shadrak said.

The words were not spoken as a threat, but as a fact, a thing already written: *From the mountains of Kamilan, enemies do not return. . . .*

The story of Held of Dravia, as recorded in the Third Book of Kingdoms of the Chronicles of Larandau:

In the seventeenth year of the reign of Algard of Dravia, his firstborn son Held crossed the mountains into High Kamilan, and carried back the queen of that country for his wife. From this deed came much bloodshed, and all the misery which fell on Dravia in the years to follow.

Held was in all things the noblest of men, and the greatest warrior of his time. But his wife would not accept him, and was loathe to share her power with an ancient enemy. By sorcery she caused a great storm to come upon the land, so that all the crops were destroyed, and under the cover of this storm she fled secretly back to Kamilan. There the prince, with a small company of men, pursued her to bring her back.

There was in Kamilan at that time a freedman who was called Shadrak, who had been made captain of a border troop in the region of Belengar. This freedman was a great warrior, but baseborn and without honour; it was believed that he was of the people of Thyrsis, who are nomads and unbelievers, and whose women defile themselves with animals.

When the queen reached Belengar, she set out with the freedman Shadrak and a hundred Kamil warriors for the high city of Kamilan. But Prince Held had skilfully slipped ahead of them, and held the bridge of the Magdal River against them.

It was the prince's wish that there should be no bloodshed, that his wife might return peacefully with him to Aralev. This the Kamils refused. He offered then to fight a duel of honour, but the queen, without regard to custom, said that she would not abide by the outcome. Her men outnumbered the Dravians, and they chose to resolve the matter in the field.

Of necessity the prince had outfitted his company more for speed than for hard fighting, and they were not heavily armoured. Shadrak took note of this, and would not order a charge, saying that he would make the Dravians come to him. He had many good archers among his men, preferring them to swordsmen, and these he deployed on high rocks and in the trees. The Dravians massed at the bridge, expecting a headlong assault. Instead, Shadrak unleashed on them a deadly rain of arrows, bringing down both horses and men. Thus many were killed before their swords ever touched an enemy, and many were left afterwards to fight on foot. The prince himself was unhorsed, and the Dravians were thrown into disarray.

But Held seized another mount and steadfastly rallied his men. Outnumbered though they were, they abandoned the bridge and flung themselves against the Kamils.

Few battles were ever more bravely fought. Shadrak left twenty of his best fighters to guard the queen; yet even without them he held the advantage both in numbers and in his knowledge of the land. The prince fought valiantly, holding off two and three of Kamilan's fighters at a time. At length his horse was felled and he was thrown. From his knees, with the sheer power of his arms, he brought Shadrak's mount down as well.

But no man, however great his courage, can prevail when the gods abandon him. The prince was struck in the leg with an arrow, and although he broke it off and continued to fight, his strength began to fail; and Shadrak manoevred him into thick woods, where the prince's great size and reach could help him less, and his enemy's speed and craft could help him more. Still Shadrak could not bring him down, until at last, exhausted, he stumbled over a tangle of roots and fell, and the slaveborn Kamil pierced him through the throat.

Thus died the greatest of all of Dravia's warriors. His body was stripped, beheaded, and left for carrion. His armour and *fine accoutrements Shadrak gave to his men, and the prince's magnificent sword, which was set with many jewels, he laid at the feet of his queen.*

No proper graves could be dug in the granite of Dohann, so the Kamil dead were laid side by side, within sight and sound of the river, and cairns were placed over them with many offerings. Seventeen had died of the men who feasted and danced in Belengar three nights before, and eight more were gravely wounded. The Dravian dead they did not count nor bury.

For hours they did little except tend their wounded. The queen's healing potions eased their pain somewhat, and so did her words, but some of them would die nonetheless, slowly, as the moon crept hour by hour across the sky. Tamon, half dead from loss of blood, babbled incoherently as they bound up the stump of his right arm. He asked the same question again and again: *Be she safe? Be she safe?* He could not hear her answer.

Though small, it had been a bitter struggle. Both sides had fought in the presence of their sovereigns, and that fact had made them desperate in their courage. Even after their cause was clearly lost, the Dravians would not give way. It took the sight of the prince's severed head to break the last of them, and end it.

Kiri, brooding for hours in the queen's tent, wondered how it had been for him, if his terrible arrogance had sustained him to the end. She thought of him fallen and afraid, scrambling to recover and realizing that he could not—realizing in those brief, eternal moments of closing death what it meant to be defenseless, what it meant to face an enemy to whom his rank meant nothing, nor his standards of conduct, nor his expectations of life or of the world. Did he recognize, in that moment, the violence which he had done to Marwen returned to him?

Did he ask himself, finally, what it had all been for?

Like so many other things she had encountered in her life, Kiri understood Held's actions perfectly, and she did not understand them at all. One could not call him an evil man, nor a fool, yet he had done this thing which was both wicked and mad, without regard to Marwen's rights, or those of Kamilan, or finally even those of Dravia—for now that he was fallen, Berend would be king, and she shuddered to think what sort of king he would be.

Why had the prince done it? Had he never imagined that he might fail? Or had failure not mattered? Had failure perhaps been defined differently—defined as the failure to pursue, to strike, to assert his mastery?

She sat for a long time, watching the candle burn out and the queen toss sleepless in her blankets. They called Held of Dravia the bravest, the strongest, the most kingly of men. His countrymen would mourn him, and no doubt come one day to avenge him, and never ask, never dream of asking why so many virtues led their lord to so much ruin.

11. Shadrak

The morning broke clear, shimmering with light. Except for their sentries, very little stirred at all in the Kamil encampment; the endpoint of battle, after triumph and gratitude and pain and revulsion had all been tasted, was always exhaustion.

Some hours after dawn Shadrak and Cassian left the place by the bridge with its smouldering fires, and went into the woods. The day was breathless, the forest radiant with changing light, and heavy with the smells of autumn. Dead leaves crunched everywhere beneath their feet. Others, golden and russet, drifted around them as they walked. Squirrels were everywhere, and the drumbeats of woodpeckers, and the pungency of moss and wet earth and heat.

From the earliest times this valley, the valley of the Magdal, had been sacred to Jana. The goddess moved as she pleased about the world, but her home was here, in Dohann, and from these mountains came all the waters that brought life to Kamilan. From here, too, came the storms and the sky fire, and the terrible winds that closed the passes, and all the swiftest and most deadly of the animals.

As she was the deity of all things, both the light and the dark, Jana was also the true deity of war. Not Harash, with the clattering shield and thundering voice, who was only a boy-god in armour. Harash tended men's weapons and strengthened the sinews of their arms. But it was Jana who spoke to their souls, and she asked first if it was wise to fight at all. She was the one who came in the darkness of combat and whispered panic in a warrior's ears, or courage. She sent the rains which flooded the Niela and broke the advance of Telhiron. She showed Shadrak the cave at Medra. And she reached out of the earth and closed her hand on the man who had trampled and caged her daughter, and brought him down.

"Wait for me," Shadrak said.

"Aye, captain. And whenever did I not?"

Shadrak smiled faintly and went on.

The forest was close here, and already hot; all around him the sharp, sweet cries of birds greeted the sun. He was weary, and he did not search long for a place which suited him. He chose a large oak, whose roots so filled the earth that the surface around it for many feet was dry and clear. Here he laid down the satchel he carried, and laid his weapons and his helmet beside it. Thus, unarmed, he cleared away the debris and droppings of animals, and spread branches to make a small platform. On this he formed a mat of dry twigs and a mound of leaves. Then, kneeling, he opened the satchel and placed on his altar the severed head of the prince of Dravia.

He struck a flint in the leaves; they were damp and the flame caught slowly. It was the darkest of omens if the flame went out, but he did not strike it again. It burned softly, barely visible except for a coil of smoke. Imperceptibly it grew; he felt its force against his hands and his face. The branches began to burn, and a sheet of fire leapt into the prince's hair.

Shadrak bowed his head.

"Wise and beautiful one, Goddess of Light and of the Dark to which we return, accept my gift. You who are older than Kamilan, keep safe its borders. You who are stronger than the swords of men, keep safe my queen. Shield me, Goddess of the world. Accept my gratitude, and give me strength."

He did not return at once to Cassian or to the camp. He was hot and thirsty, and the river was close by, crashing and singing. He made his way there, and came upon a small but splendid waterfall, which over the centuries had carved a small pool at its feet.

He knelt and cupped the water in his hands. It was icy but delicious. He drank again and then again. Finally he splashed some of it over his head, which only made him more conscious of how battered and dirty and foul-smelling he was.

He hesitated a moment, and then stripped and walked laughing into the waterfall. He would have preferred a lake, a deep, summer-warm lake where he could dive and swim, but the river was wild and clean. It took the weariness of battle from his body, and left him chilled but very much refreshed.

He climbed out, shaking water from his hair, and stood naked in the sun to dry, pleasurably aware of its burning heat, and of his own fine, supple body. He was shaggy as a wolf; thick black hair matted over his chest and his loins, and two broad sweeps of it crossed his shoulder blades and converged down his back. He did not look Kamil. *(You will never persuade anyone that you're anything but a dangerous barbarian,* Cassian once told him cheerfully. *And if the gods mean to leave you in Dohann forever, probably that's just as well.)* Shadrak had laughed at that. Kamil or not, he was splendidly made, and he knew it. In this, as in so many things, Jana had been generous to him.

He was very happy. He was alive. He had defeated a great enemy. The goddess had honoured his sacrifice. And Marwen, Marwen, Marwen whose name he spoke only in his blood, Marwen who seldom smiled in so dangerous a world, Marwen's eyes had sought him out, and she had smiled at him. She had spoken for him before the Dravian prince, and named him as her champion. For that alone he would willingly have died for her.

It would have been easy merely to believe that he was favoured, as his mother always said: that Jana had chosen him for reasons known only to herself, given him his powerful body and his subtle mind, given him his freedom, marked him out for some great destiny.

It would have been easy to believe that, but he was wary. It was too simple an explanation for the incomprehensible caprice of the world to say that the gods loved one, or that the gods did not.

He did not think of the scar on his shoulder until it began to burn. He did not think of it for days, for weeks at a time, and then suddenly there would be something to make him remember: the indrawn breath of a woman lying with him for the first time; the startled look of a comrade who had not been told who his captain was. Or simply the sun, fire remembering fire, the scar drawing heat like bent glass, reminding him of a wound that marked him forever.

He had been a child, six or seven perhaps, very young, but old enough already to climb over the walls of the master's yard, or to slip through an ill-closed gate, drawn to freedom like a bird to the sky. He was quick on his feet and quicker still of mind. People noticed that, and spoke of it as though it were something dangerous. He did not know why. Nor did he know why he had to stay inside the walls. They were worthless little walls; he could climb them with his eyes closed. And beyond was the whole city of Tamri: markets and inns and traders from everywhere and laughing soldiers on horseback; and beyond Tamri itself was the valley and the winding Niela and the roads running seven ways to all the world.

It was those beckoning roads which made him first understand the meaning of his enslavement—the slow, painful realization that those roads of caravans and hunting parties and Kamil legions shimmering with flags were closed to him forever. He could not leave the city walls to gather wood without someone watching over him.

He asked his mother once why they were slaves. They were born slaves, she said. Just as masters were born masters and kings were born kings. That was how it was.

They came for him at night, a bit later that same summer: the overseer and a man from the master's household. "It is time," the overseer said to Shadrak's mother. "Before the brat runs away for good."

The boy backed into the corner of the room, trying to dissolve into the shadows. He did not know what these men wanted with him, but he knew he was afraid of them. They moved as one to seize him, but his mother blocked their path.

"Wait! He's not an animal to be dragged away like that. He'll go with you. Wait."

She knelt, gripping his shoulders fiercely in her hands, and made him stand very still and listen.

"Go with them."

"Why?"

"Because you have to."

"What are they going to do?"

"They'll hurt you, but it can't be helped. I can't stop them, Shadrak. I can't do anything. You have to be brave. Go."

"Why?"

He was grown now; he knew why. For years he had believed there was some strange and secret reason for which the master hated him, but it was not so. He had not mattered enough to be hated. He was no different from a pig in a cage or a rabbit in a snare.

They took him into a room in the back of the slave's quarters, stripped off his tunic, pinned him face down against the floor, and took an iron which had been placed in the fire until it glowed, and pressed deep into his shoulder the mark of two crossed staves inside a circle, which was the device of his owner. When he stopped screaming and lay still in the pool of his own vomit, the man from his master's household held up a torch to examine him. It was fine, he said. Falan always did a good clean job. Then they let him go.

Before that day he had not thought much about being a slave. After, it was never far from his mind. Everything around him took its meaning from the fact that he was owned. In the market square in Tamri once he saw a slave who had been hanged by his feet and flogged until he was dead, for having stolen a peach. It was foolish, people said; a slave was worth more than a peach. But that was his master's choice.

Shadrak had stolen many things. He stood very quietly, watching the corpse turning in the wind. He could be that slave one day. Or one of those who were more unfortunate still, the ones who were taken in caravans to the tin mines of Getann, and never spoken of again.

He knew it might be possible to run away. Not by day, with soldiers at all the gates; not dressed like he was in the rough tunic of a slave, without ornaments or sleeves or shoes. But it might be possible by night, with stolen food and clothing, with a weapon and a bit of knowledge of the land, however he might come by either. He could scale the walls. He could run. He was strong and healthy.

He was also marked, and the reward for captured slaves was very generous. The punishment was Getann. There were no exceptions. He could run, but if they caught him he would be taken in a cage into the hills, and dragged into the hollows of the earth. And he would die there, chained to a rock. So, although he thought a great deal about running away, he never did so.

Then, when he was twelve, a spark from the ovens landed in a patch of straw, and Jana changed the world.

Suppose the spark had gone out? Suppose it had burned too quickly, and the master's sleeping child had died, and Shadrak's mother as well? What sort of world would have been his? Would he have accepted his place, as most of the others did? Found a mate among the slave girls, who were already hungry for love because a taste of love was the only beautiful thing they would ever have? Fathered children, and grown cautious for their sakes, as his mother had grown for his?

Would he have gone no more to the walls of the city, knowing that the roads beyond were not his and never could be, content to have his bread and no beatings, content to grow old as a good and faithful servant? Or would he perhaps have managed to escape, only to end his life as a bandit, a hunting and ever hunted animal, ragged and bloody and filled with hate?

Would he have dashed himself to death against his chains, or would he have yielded?

He wanted terribly to know—to discover if there were something which had shaped him, something which was inherently himself, beyond the caprices of men and the incomprehensible ways of gods. He felt that there must be, sometimes. And other times he felt that everything rested on the roll of a dice, the shift of a small breath of wind. So many things could have happened to him and most of them were bad, and there was a frightening kind of arrogance in believing he had escaped it all because he was worthier than those who had not.

It was luck.

But if it was luck, what then—and who—was Shadrak?

The crunch of a footstep brought him to his feet in alarm. Cassian was standing a few feet away, shaking his head in a mixture of amusement and dismay. Shadrak put away his sword, feeling foolish—not for his vigilance, but for his lack of it. He was half-dressed, his tunic still unlaced and his boots and leggings lying on the rock beside him.

"Suppose I'd been a Dravian?" Cassian said.

"Then you would be either a minstrel or a ghost."

"Shadrak." Cassian bent and picked up the captain's belongings, handing them to him one by one. "You're the sharpest, most cunning man I know. That only makes it more incomprehensible when you do something foolish."

"I'm weary, Cassian. I wanted some time to think."

"What's wrong with thinking in a tent?"

Shadrak laughed a little, and gripped his friend's shoulder in a brief, half-conscious caress.

"A tent shuts out the sun," he said, "and the sound of water, and the taste of wind. I think better here."

Cassian was silent a moment.

"Does she speak to you here?" he asked finally. "Your goddess?"

"Yes. Sometimes."

"Well, then. Will you ask her if we might go and eat, while there is still perhaps a scrap of something left on the fires?"

They headed back, and as they entered the camp they saw the queen and her minstrel walking from their tent towards the shelters of the wounded. The queen moved with an easy, swinging step, and with each motion her pale hair danced and glinted in the sun.

"She is splendid, isn't she?" Cassian said. "It's hard to believe she's so young."

"Yes. She is splendid."

Her breasts would taste of honey, Shadrak thought, *and her hands would be eager on a man's body, eager and sure. . . .*

"Don't even think about it, my friend," Cassian said.

Shadrak tore his gaze from the woman, and looked at Cassian with irritation. "You have eyes like a hawk."

"I do. But in this matter the eyes of a bat would have served me just as well. And I'm troubled by what I see."

"Don't be," Shadrak said. "You may think I'm foolish sometimes, but you have no reason to think I'm mad. I know she's out of reach." He paused, and added ruefully: "Do I look at her that much?"

"You look at very little else."

Aye, and what did it matter? Shadrak wondered. After a few more days she would be queen again, and he would be keeper of the pass at Belengar. He would take back to Dohann every memory of her that he could, and treasure them against the wind and the dark nights, and the unknown but certain hour of his death.

Book Two.
The Wolf of Dohann

From the hour of their birth, some are marked out for subjection, others for rule . . . the male is by nature superior, and the female inferior; the one rules and the other is ruled; this principle, of necessity, extends to all mankind . . . the lower sort are by nature slaves. . . .

Aristotle

But may I be dead and the heaped earth huddled over me, before I hear your cries as they come to drag you captive.

Homer

12. Return to Kamilan

Kamilan was fortress town, an eagle's nest of wind and rock and defiance, set on the pinnacle of a mountain like a jewel on a ring. The road spiralled up from the valley of the Magdal, four leagues long, narrow and pitilessly exposed. Since the half-forgotten days when the city had been built, no attacking enemy had ever made it to the top.

The queen rode to the high city in a blaze of glory. For two days, as she moved out of the crags of Dohann, peasants and villagers gathered along the roads, some to wave and cheer and wander home again, contented; others to fall in behind the soldiers, so that the procession grew with every league they travelled, like a pilgrimage. When they made their last camp at the crossroads beyond Althen Field, the spread of their fires might have belonged to a small army.

There they were greeted by a delegation from the city. And there Kiri met, for the first time, the men who ruled Kamilan. Angmar the Wise, chief lord of Council, bowed deeply as he knelt. He was nearly sixty, and gray, but he did not look frail. His face and body had a worn but solid vigour.

"Welcome, lady. I cannot tell you what happiness it brings me to see you home again, and safe."

Theron, high priest of Mohr, bowed even more deeply, perhaps to avoid her eyes, and thanked his father-god for answering their prayers. Borosar the warlord laid his sword at her feet, and then, with refreshing simplicity, grinned and flung a comradely arm around the captain of Belengar.

"By the great Harash," he said, "you haven't lost your knack for turning up where you're needed!"

At Angmar's side was his cousin, Landis of Maene, who had ridden in haste from his vast holdings in the lower reaches of the Magdal, with an impressive retinue of men and a magnificent gift for the queen: a pure white mare with silver trappings and a silver saddle, to bear her in splendour into Kamilan.

He was a tall man, deceptively slender, with very pale blonde hair and a thin, patrician face. The three who had preceeded him did so by virtue of age and honoured rank, but in terms of sheer power Landis was at least their equal. The house of Maene controlled the richest lands in Kamilan, and was acknowledged second only to that of the royal house itself.

The queen thanked him for his gift. "I know well that the finest horses in Kamilan come from your herds," she said. "I am honoured."

"Lady," he said, "the honour is mine. And I could wish for none greater than to have you back among us."

The last of the lords of Council to welcome the queen was Crayfe, seneschal of the royal city. He was a heavy, bull-necked fellow, with a mighty paunch for his years, and the ruddy look of a man who ate and drank too much. He seemed to Kiri an unpleasant man, even on this brief contact. Borosar's warmth towards the border captain he noted very carefully, with a quiet smile of distaste. Somehow, the expression still lingered as he bowed to his queen.

There were others to greet as well—lords and kinsmen and various members of the queen's household. Then, as soon as proper courtesy permitted, the Council wanted a report. Only the barest details of the queen's flight and the battle at the Magdal bridge had reached them. The full account would be taken up in Council, of course, but they wanted at least a summary right away.

A conference tent had already been prepared, Angmar said; if the captain of Belengar would kindly join them there. . . ? Harad, the chief steward, had brought everything necessary for the queen's comfort, and he would see to her quartering. Later, after she had rested, he himself and Lord Crayfe would discuss with her the plans for tomorrow's triumphal entry.

"Angmar." Marwen stepped forward, her oversize shoes slapping against her ankles.

"Lady?" The chief lord inclined his head faintly, patiently.

"I don't mean to disparage Shadrak of Belengar, who is a loyal and valiant captain. But surely you don't intend to discuss matters of state with him alone, without the presence of your queen?"

Angmar did not falter. "Lady, we thought only that you would be hungry and exhausted, and that while you rested the captain could give us a very quick report."

He was looking at her earnestly as he spoke, and Kiri knew exactly what he saw. King Adelmar's girl child. A bedraggled princess in sore need of a bath and some proper royal clothing. A trampled princess in need of comfort and protection, in need of men's sure and sheltering walls.

"We're all hungry and exhausted," she said, "the captain no less than I. But I'm sure you have brought food and wine; we can eat as we talk." She smiled. The smile was pleasant, but it had a chill in it. It was a smile they would all come to recognize. Perhaps Angmar, who had been her guardian, recognized it already.

"Certainly, lady," he said, and bowed, motioning her to precede them.

Crayfe looked very meaningfully at the lord of Maene. Landis ignored the look, his face a pleasant mask. Borosar fell in step beside Shadrak, a hand on the captain's shoulder.

"Is it true the Drav challenged you," he asked, "and you cut his head off with a single blow?"

The rest of the evening was a blur of faces, and an endless retelling of their adventure. Kiri found herself surrounded by people who, unable to reach the queen or her captain, demanded to know every detail from her, including details she could not possibly have known.

Eventually she found herself by a fire with several members of Marwen's household, who had made everything ready for the queen, and only waited for her to finish with the lords of Council. One of these was Luned, who had been Queen Arden's body servant and her favourite. She was a plump, efficient woman, though somewhat bossy.

"You *walked* from Aralev to Belengar?" she said, for the third or fourth time. "My poor lady! Why didn't you give her better shoes? Those look like soldier's boots she's wearing."

"They are. We got them at Belengar. Our own were in shreds."

"But what about the wild animals?" another of the servants asked, appalled.

"We never thought about them much," Kiri said. "They left us alone." That was true, and now, for the first time, she wondered why. They had heard wolves howling so many times, and slept in so many desolate, fireless camps.

"Well, the goddess walked with you, that is sure," Luned said.

The silence that closed on them came slowly, like an inverted ripple. Those farthest from the fire fell silent first, and then those who were closer, until at last Kiri and Luned were the only persons speaking. Luned, looking up, said "Ohh!" very softly, staring at something beyond Kiri's head.

She turned quickly. A figure on horseback was framed against the last failing light, a figure caped and hooded, so that the face was in shadow, and the body a stark, sweeping silhouette. With a sudden gesture the hood was flung back, and she saw long, windblown hair, the vague outlines of an ageless woman's face. The people around the fire scrambled to their feet; whispers passed from mouth to mouth, some reverent, a few darkly hostile. Twice Kiri caught the murmur: *sorceress!*

"Who is it?" she asked, bending towards Luned.

"The lady Medwina," Luned said. There was pride in her face, but there was also a shadow of unease.

Medwina. Banished high priestess of the goddess Jana. Sister of Arden, the dead queen. Witch of Kamilan, whose skills were acknowledged equally by her enemies and her friends.

"I seek Marwen of Kamilan, my sister-child," the priestess said. "Will you tell her I am here?"

No one had to. The flap of the conference tent opened, and Marwen stepped out, followed by the lords of Council and the captain of Belengar. Medwina's eyes rested on each of them in turn, very briefly, as though with a look she could read their souls.

Marwen moved quickly forward; her face in the firelight was eager and hungry. The robed arm of the high priest reached to restrain her, but she was already gone, unaware of Theron's gesture, unaware perhaps of anything except the dark figure of the priestess.

Medwina dismounted. For a moment they stood an arm's reach apart, not speaking.

"Greetings, wise one and mother," Marwen said.

"Greetings, sister-child and queen. I have been waiting for you. Long and bitterly I have been waiting for you."

They embraced. It seemed both of them cried, but in the darkness it was hard to be sure. Medwina turned then to Kiri, recognizing her without needing to be told.

"Kiri of Vanthala," she said. "I never thought I would owe so great a debt to someone born in Dravia. You're welcome among us, minstrel. Forever."

Kiri managed a bow, a murmured thank you, but she could think of nothing else to say. The woman awed her completely.

"You will ride into Kamilan with us tomorrow?" Marwen said eagerly to the priestess. "And join the feast?"

"No, Marwen. You know that I will not."

"I would cherish your company."

Medwina's eyes fell, bitterly. "And I yours, sister-child. But I will ride into Kamilan to take my place in the temple, or I will die outside its walls. I swore that oath, and I will keep it. But let's not speak of that now; I'm much too happy. Come, take me to your tent, and tell me everything."

She turned, and Kiri saw that she moved with difficulty, as though she was injured. The queen saw too, and stopped utterly still.

"Medwina, you're hurt!"

"A little. But I'm well now. Come, before yon squawking raven makes me angry, and I put a stone in his gullet."

It was Theron she spoke of, who stood by the conference tent, arguing with the rest of the Council. They were too far away to hear the men's words, but it was obvious the high priest was angry. He paced this way and that, throwing out his long robed arms in stormy gestures.

Priestess and queen disappeared into the tent, and the flap closed; what passed between them Kiri never learned, neither that night nor ever after.

Outside, the whispering began again.

—*She should never have come here! She had no right!*

—*She's the queen's closest blood kin. Who has a better right?*

"The queen will grieve to see her crippled as she is," Luned said. "Poor child. Medwina was like a mother to her."

"What happened to her? To Medwina?" Kiri asked.

"You don't know? No, of course, you were in Dravia. She tried to save the queen. When the villains took her, Medwina tried to save her, and all but died for it."

"She was there?" Kiri whispered. Marwen had never mentioned that.

"Goddess, no, she wasn't there. If she had been, she would have turned the Dravs to stone. She was seven leagues away. But she has sight. She saw them, and she knew why they had come."

Slowly, stressing every detail, Luned told her the story. There had been a great wind, and a black cloud swallowing the mountains, and in the face of that cloud Medwina had seen the Dravians, armed and terrible, crashing out of the forest. She had seen one of them bend, and drag the queen upon his horse. She heard cries, but the voice was not Marwen's, it was the voice of someone wounded to death; the Dravian swords were red with blood.

The priestess, Luned said, had a horse which could run like no other living thing, faster than any deer, faster than the hawks in the sky. And so she rode for Althen Garrison, three leagues away. Possibly, just possibly, she could gather enough fighting men in time. She rode like a madwoman, over gulleys and rocks and bracken, but brave as her horse was in the end he fell to his death. Her leg was crushed like a reed. It was dark when the foresters found her, and Held was laughing on the road to Dohann.

Luned finished her story, and for a time no one spoke. Kiri glanced towards the conference tent, where the lords of Council still clustered. Shadrak was not with them. No doubt like Kiri he had been instantly surrounded and dragged off to a fire:

Tell us what happened! Was there a great battle? Is it true the prince of Dravia is dead? What is going to happen now? Will they come to avenge him?

Luned, too, was watching the lords. Her eyes were not altogether friendly.

"It will be different now," she said.

Kiri waited for her to explain. When she did not, the minstrel asked: "What do you mean, different?"

She shrugged. She was a servant; she would say nothing very directly.

"Those five have been regents," she said; "them and Favian, the lord of Tamri. For four years now, since old King Adelmar died. The queen was just a girl. Sharp as a dagger she was, and brave too, but just a girl. They hardly paid any attention to her, except to try and marry her to this one or the other. Now they will have to pay attention."

The argument among the Council appeared to be over. Theron the high priest turned on his heel, called for his horse and his servants, and galloped out of the camp.

"He can't bear Medwina's presence," Luned whispered. "I'll wager that's why he's leaving."

"But what is it to him if Medwina comes to greet the queen?" Kiri demanded.

"Everything," Harad said. "To him she's the great witch and the great whore, and he lies awake at night trying to decide which he hates worse."

Kiri glanced discreetly around. A lively conversation had started up among the others at the fire; the two servants and the minstrel were temporarily ignored.

"Tell me about the rest," she suggested boldy. "Lord Crayfe—what's he like?"

There was a breath of silence.

"I would walk a circle around the seneschal," Harad said. "A large circle. He sees too much."

"He is cruel," Luned added. "He killed his wife some years back—his second wife. She was a stupid little thing, pretty as a bird and no sense at all, taking up with a stablehand right under her husband's nose. But he should have known better than to marry her in the first place. He was begging for trouble."

"And he made a mortal enemy of the warlord over it," Harad added. "Borosar wanted the girl for his son, and Crayfe outbid him. Then he killed her. They had not exactly been friends before that. Borosar, gods know, is a fighting man—"

"Borosar is a drunk," Luned cut in.

"—and he baited Crayfe a lot, and Crayfe had to take it. But since then they hate each other bitterly. It has not been good for Kamilan, all that hatred."

"Ach, they're both fools," Luned said. "The man to heed walks yonder."

Landis of Maene had left the group, heading for the edge of the camp, where a cluster of guards kept watch over the road.

"Twenty-seven he is, and still unmarried," Luned observed. "It's not hard to guess why."

Kiri watched him until he faded into the shadows. He moved with poise and grace. Although he wore garments of obvious richness, there was not a trace of the usual Kamil flamboyance in his dress; everything about him was restrained and precise. It was not a quality common among any of the mountain people, least of all his own.

"He seems. . . ." She hunted for a word. "Austere."

"That's Angmar's influence," Luned said. She sighed. "He's such a splendid man. It's a crime the Council blocked his marriage to our lady."

"Why did they do that?" Kiri asked, although she had a fair idea, recalling the hostlers on the caravan, and their long discussion about the queen of Kamilan:

They would not marry the wench for quarreling among themselves who should have her: Landis of Maene on one side and Borosar the warlord on the other, and a half dozen more in between, every one of them with a son or a cousin suddenly fancying how he could be a king!

"They all had their own candidates to put forward," Harad said. "That was part of it. And Landis is already too powerful. Married to the queen, he'd be as good as crowned. They would give her to anyone rather than to Landis."

"Well," Luned said. "It won't be up to them now. I expect Lady Marwen will choose for herself. And I will wager you a cask of good wine, Harad, she will marry the lord of Maene."

"Nonsense."

"What do you think, Kiri?" Luned asked. "Isn't he a fine looking man?"

"I think," Kiri said, "that the queen won't marry anyone just now."

They looked at her with blank, bewildered faces, as if she had said: *I think that rock over there will fly.* Even to these people, who were Marwen's followers and friends, the world was laid out according to certain patterns; nothing else was possible.

Welcome home, Marwen of Kamilan, she thought bitterly. *Welcome home!*

The march into Kamilan was glorious. The mountain walls echoed with the pounding of drums and the wailing of pipes. People lined the roads and climbed onto crags and ridges, all the way to the top, waving caps and swords, and flying banners every colour of the rainbow.

The queen rode with Kiri at her right hand and Shadrak at her left; even the lords of Council had to be content to follow second. They rode slowly, for the way was steep; and it was, for all three of them, the most perfect moment of their lives.

Few streets in the royal city were flat. They ran uphill or down, they twisted this way and that over the rugged brow of the mountain. Marwen's palace was at the highest point, a small pinnacle in itself, fiercely walled and towered.

But one place had been laid out flat and square, the rock itself cut away to make a place for it. This was the great temple of Mohr. It was made of gray stone, immense and imposing, but it was not beautiful. The Kamils were not talented builders; their dwellings were rough-hewn and functional. At best, fitted to the landscape, they could seem harshly splendid, as Marwen's palace did, looming over its cliffs. Mohr's house in contrast seemed alien here, forced upon the earth as the god himself had been, and ill at ease for all of its brute strength.

They passed there without stopping. That did not seem important to anyone at the moment. Of course the queen would go later, with rich offerings, and give honour to the god. Only when the procession reached the abandoned temple of Jana, close to the palace walls, did the significance of her action become clear.

The temple was old, and not large. It had been built without the help of slaves. But it had been built well. Years of neglect had spoiled only its outward look: weeds grew from cracks in the steps, refuse lay everywhere, birds nested in its roofs and ledges, and stray cats prowled its leaf-strewn court. But the huge timbers which barred its doors would rot, Kiri thought, and the temple would still be there.

The queen reined in her horse, dismounting before anyone could react, even to take the animal's bridle. She walked to the fence, Shadrak and Kiri following quickly. The guards and soldiers turned this way and that, looking at the lords of Council, at the queen, at the gods themselves, utterly at a loss for what to do. It was forbidden to set foot upon those stones.

The fence, built when the temple was closed, was barred as well. The queen tested the gate lightly, and turned to her captain.

"Can you open it?"

"It will take a dozen good horses, lady, or a battering ram."

She hesitated. All around them the wildly cheering crowd had fallen utterly still. Now, finally, Kiri understood why the Kamil rulers, all stern men of Mohr, had allowed this place to stand, walled it off and nailed it shut and flogged anyone who was caught inside, but nonetheless allowed it to stand.

They were afraid to do otherwise.

The queen hesitated. She longed to tear that fence to pieces and fling it down the cliffside, but the moment was not right. She took the garland of flowers which she wore around her neck and hung it over the gate. Then she knelt on the rough stone, bowing deeply. (By nightfall, Kiri learned later, the fence around Jana's temple was hung all around with garlands.)

No one moved. It seemed to Kiri that no one breathed, that the entire city stood breathless in awe, or in horror. Theron's face was pale with outrage, but it was Angmar the Wise who broke the spell, climbing with slow dignity from his horse and approaching her.

"Lady, if you will forgive me, this is not—"

He halted sharply. A half dozen of Shadrak's soldiers were moving into his path, and the seneschal's men, seeing them, were reaching for their swords. Wisely Angmar stood still and waited for the queen to get to her feet and mount her horse again.

They rode on. All the way to the palace, the streets were packed with triumphant Kamils, four and five rows deep in places, and wild with happiness. How lovely she looked, they said after in the shops and the taverns, how lovely with her pale, windblown hair. How black and fierce seemed the captain of Belengar. And that other, the Dravian . . . it was strange, they said, how a Dravian came to serve their lady. But they drank to her health, they drank to the wolf warrior of Dohann, and over and over again they drank to the queen. All night long the wooden walls of the city glittered with torchlight and rang with song. Pipes cried to the sickle moon, wooden floors shook with hammering feet, braziers crackled with roasting pig and venison and lamb. When a cold sun finally crept over the eastern peaks the city looked as it looked only after the year's three great festivals. Debris drifted through the streets, a few last stragglers stumbled home, and nothing else moved at all.

Kiri woke to that cold sun, and went out on the roofs to look at the city which was now her home. It was a much smaller city than Aralev, rougher and more warlike. Marwen's home was itself more a fortress than a palace, with sturdy walls and high ramparts. From its bastions a few well-supplied defenders could hold off half an army, so skilfully was it laid out, and so inaccessible.

Yet in the days which followed she was surprised to find how comfortable it was—far more so than the greathouse in Aralev. The royal hall was black-walled, smelling of smoke and leather and old straw; in harsh weather the wind shivered through a thousand cracks, guttering the torches and tasting of storm. But, although fuel was precious, the hearth always blazed with fires. Travellers came and went, sure of a welcome, sure at the very least of hot food and wine and an animal pelt to wrap themselves in at night. So there was always company, and stories, and song. And for Kiri there was a room in the queen's apartments, next to Marwen's own bedchamber, with a fire and hangings of wool to drape the walls, and a bed covered in fur.

She allowed herself to think that perhaps, finally, she had come home.

13. Angmar

"The queen must marry."

Angmar the Wise frowned, rubbing his forearm. Beneath the fine woollen sleeve was a jagged scar, given him twenty-eight years before by a Dravian with a war axe—a Dravian whom he had imagined was dead. The old wound still bothered him sometimes. But when he rubbed it, it was usually because he was deeply troubled about something else.

The queen must marry. One did not need an oracle to reach that conclusion. Two years ago, until the Dravian prince ended the discussion, they had talked the matter to death without resolving it. Now the queen was back; only five days ago they had shared her welcome feast in the royal hall, and it was all beginning again.

"You must arrange it, Wise One," Theron said.

The high priest stood close beside Angmar; his voice was low but stern. His face had lost every trace of youth, every hint of gentleness or delight in life. His hands on his wine cup were knotted like the talons of a hawk.

He is only forty-one, Angmar observed with disbelief, *and he looks twice as old as I.*

"I must arrange it?" he said. "That's asking a good deal."

"You are her guardian."

"I *was* her guardian. The child who went to Dravia did not come back, Theron; surely you've noticed that. We have a queen now, whether it pleases us or not."

Theron's head shot up in a brief, aimless toss of anger.

"She must marry, I tell you. And she must marry wisely, before she brings ruin on us all."

"I know that, Theron," Angmar said wearily. "Women don't have the strength to rule, and we can't expect it of them. I know."

"I'm not speaking only of political ruin," Theron said grimly. "You were there, Angmar; you saw. She hadn't shaken the dust off her cloak before the sorceress Medwina turned up in her camp. And then she paid homage at that harlot's temple, in front of all the people. . . ! Do you know there's already talk in the streets that she will open that evil place, and bring the sorceress Medwina back?"

"She can't do that," Angmar said. "No one will permit it."

"It shouldn't even be discussed. I counselled you years ago to burn the temple and put the priestess to death. If you had listened to me then, you would have less cause now to grieve."

Aye, Angmar thought, *that may be so. Everything would have been different. But if we had tried Medwina and condemned her, there would have been mutiny in the land. And simply to kill someone, in secret, on one's own authority—that is not easy, high priest, nor should it be. You, more than anyone, ought to know that.*

"She was the dead queen's sister," he said.

"She was a necromancer and a whore. And you and the king both shut your eyes to it, and let her come back, and gave her the run of the palace. Who taught the queen her folly, Angmar, tell me that?"

"We were wrong. Does it satisfy you to hear me say it? We did what had always been done. A dead mother's sister tends her children; it is the Kamil way, and we allowed it, and we were wrong."

"There are some who say you had reasons of your own," Theron said. "Personal reasons."

"And there are some who say things of you, Theron, that I will not demean myself by repeating. Shall we judge each other by gossip? You'll get the worst of the bargain if we do!"

He paused. They had raised their voices, and others of his guests were glancing in their direction.

"I didn't say it was true, Wise One," Theron responded sternly. "I say only that we've failed to act before, and every time we did so, we suffered for it. The queen must be married—and to a man who can be trusted. It would be best if she were married to a priest. We could deal a death blow to sorcery in Kamilan."

Aye, and to many other things, not least the rule of sense and reason. Gods of wisdom, when I had Medwina driven out of Council, I did not intend her to be replaced with you!

"Don't look at me like that, Angmar," Theron said. "I have no . . . no worldly desires in this matter. I have been long widowed. I would gladly stay that way. And she is too dishonoured."

The possibility of such desires had not entered Angmar's mind until the priest denied them. Now, ungenerously, he contemplated what it might mean to a man of Theron's driven passions to possess the woman whose power he wished so desperately to absorb and make his own.

"No worldly desires, Theron?" he questioned. "At the very least, you desire to be the father of a king. So do a hundred other men in Kamilan. But the decision is no longer ours. For good or ill, I think the queen will choose her own husband now."

"And children would no doubt choose their fathers, and slaves their masters, and peasants their kings—*if we let them!* Is there no authority left in Kamilan? Does the tilled field give orders to the farmer, or does he plant as he sees fit?"

Ah, Theron, Angmar brooded, *this is why I grow weary of holy men: you don't think, you merely imagine the world—in whatever shape it pleases you.*

"She has a measure of power, Theron; that's what kingship means. She may be female, but she is also lord. I will be the first to acknowledge the contradiction in that, but the contradiction can't be brushed aside as though it did not exist. She can be forced to marry only in the manner which the prince of Dravia used. Would you recommend that?"

"Are you baiting me, Angmar?"

"No."

"Well, it wouldn't matter if you were. I will speak frankly. Yes. If it became necessary, I would recommend it. And I'll tell you why. If she doesn't choose a worthy husband, she will soon be chosen by an unworthy one. I will not go as far as you and say that she is lord, but she is the gate to lordship, and that gate will not stay open long. She's a beacon for violence as a carcass is for wolves."

He paused, and then added: "I wished to see her married into the temple, but for the sake of peace and the house of Adelmar I will not demand it. Let her marry any honourable lord, even Landis; I won't say a word against it. But let her marry, Angmar. See that she marries. Or someone else will see to it."

Their eyes met and locked. For a long, charged moment neither would yield or look away.

"Come, lords," said a cool voice, "we have glowered enough in Council. Angmar brought us here to make us friends again."

They both turned—Angmar with relief; Theron with obvious irritation.

"Hello, Crayfe."

The seneschal had a rabbit haunch in one hand, and a large cup of wine in the other.

"Speaking of friends," he added, "I haven't seen Borosar. Was he too snarly to come?"

"He's dining with the queen," Theron said.

"Oh, my," Crayfe murmured, and laughed. "He's a brave man, our warlord. He may be dined upon himself before the night is over. She has the fangs for it."

"He'll risk it," Theron said. "He's even more ambitious than he is brave."

Crayfe drained his cup, and Angmar signalled at once for a servant to bring him another.

"Is she in his camp already, do you think?" Crayfe asked. "It wouldn't surprise me. Nothing impresses a woman like a man with a good stout lance."

"I don't think she is in any camp," Angmar said. He left Theron and Crayfe to pursue the matter, and edged away. He was weary. He had invited them all here, and now he wished they would all go away.

He looked around the room, taking a small measure of comfort from its cultured elegance. It was a large room, finely furnished, part of the great stone house he had built twenty-six years before, when Adelmar named him chief lord of Council. He had been thirty then, and full of hope. Adelmar was a strong king in the prime of his youth: a splendid warrior, a tough-minded ruler determined to establish control of his borders and order in his realm.

For reasons known only to themselves, the gods denied him. The years passed empty. He grew old, warred upon by Dravia; beset by the forces of unreason in his own land; disliked by his people (as much for his virtues as for his faults, Angmar believed;) bereft of sons; and finally, for twelve unrelenting years, unmanned, his sterility a brutal symbol of the absolute failure of his dreams. He died with his country on the brink of collapse, leaving a thirteen year old girl and a divided Council to somehow salvage what was left.

What had gone wrong?

Even now, looking back, his chief advisor could see no turning point which they had missed, no decision which, made differently, would have saved them. Forces beyond the edge of reason had denied the king his victory.

Priest and priestess both—Theron and Medwina—believed the rightful place and honour of their gods had been betrayed—Jana by her exile, Mohr by the goddess's continuing presence in the hearts of the people, and in their secret rituals. Each insisted that Kamilan would come to ruin if things were not made right. Sometimes, in spite of himself, Angmar wondered if one or the other of them spoke the truth. And sometimes, in the very darkest hours of all, he wondered if they both did.

He straightened, shaking himself a little. *You are growing old, sage,* he told himself. *You must watch yourself; you are surrounded by too many fools for some of it not to rub off, unless you are very careful.*

It troubled him a little to think that way. It was arrogant, and the gods always made men pay for arrogance. But he could not help it. He felt above his fellows on the Council—above all of them but one. He felt that he looked down on them from a great height, and with a terrible weariness of soul. They understood so little.

Borosar was a brilliant general, a man of much practical good sense, but he was blunt and vulgar. Battle plans he understood; the subtleties of politics were beyond him. Theron was obsessed with his god. Crayfe and Favian were boys, for all that they had wives and half-grown sons. There was only Landis of Maene who gave him hope. Only Landis could think beyond the moment's greed or anger, and see the patterns in the world, and plan for some kind of ordered future.

He called over one of the servants. "I'm going to the garden," he said. "Ask Lord Landis if he will join me there. And please . . . be discreet."

The night was bitter, the garden bare and still. It had rained most of the day; winter lay gray and waiting just beyond the edges of Dohann. He tucked his hands inside his sleeves to shield them from the wind, but the cold felt good, bracing and clean.

"You may talk reason and common sense forever, Angmar," said a voice, "but you have the ascetic soul of a priest."

The old man smiled and waited. Landis was only a slender silhouette in the darkness, but Angmar knew his face as well as he knew the faces of his sons. He could picture it perfectly in his mind: fair and thin, with a high forehead and pale blue eyes.

"You have no wine," Angmar observed. Even when troubled, he was a thoughtful host.

"I'll have some more later. What did Theron want?"

"The queen. It's my duty, it seems, to persuade her to marry him—him or one of his underlings." Angmar sighed. Religion and respect for the gods were the foundations of the state; that was clear to any thinking man. But it did not follow that priests should rule, and he dreaded the possibility. Kingship, like warfare, was a task for practical men, men who understood the difference between the desirable and the possible, between the world that should be and the world that was.

"Theron as king of Kamilan," he brooded. "Can you picture it, Landis? It makes me shudder."

"He would not rule long," Landis said, and did not flinch at Angmar's sharp glance.

"That kind of strife within our own ranks," Angmar said, "with the Dravians at our borders and Larandau not far beyond—that also makes me shudder. May the gods forgive us, what were we guilty of, that Mohr saw fit to deny us a king?"

"If she were a king I couldn't marry her."

"Don't jest, Landis. If you marry her it will be the best hope we have, but it won't make up for what should have been."

"A pointless comment, coming from a man who says we must always deal with the world as we find it."

A cobbled path wandered among the bare hedges and naked flowerbeds. They followed it slowly.

"And will you take the lady as you find her, Landis?" Angmar asked. "Theron considers her dishonoured."

"He would marry her nonetheless."

"So would thousands of men, because she wears a crown." He paused. "What happened was not her fault. I wouldn't wish to see it held against her."

Landis shrugged. "Why should I hold it against her? You're touchy tonight, cousin. Theron must have leaned on you harder than usual."

"I'm sorry," Angmar said. "I suppose I'm tired. And Adelmar did give me charge of her, you know. I would like to see her married well—to an honourable man."

And yes, he added silently, to a man who could be trusted; Theron had been right about that. To this man, if only the gods would let it be, this man who had so many gifts: youth, rank, great wealth—and, better than any of these, that subtle yet relentless intellect which set him apart from every other man Angmar knew. Once Landis's mind closed on an object it did not let go. It followed ideas every way they shifted, and cut through pretense and delusion like a sword through a spider's web.

He was the youngest member of Council, but even Angmar forgot that most of the time. There was no brashness in him, and no self-indulgence. He reached decisions slowly, but once he had made them he was unyielding, unaffected by friendship or lust or wine or fear of failure—those small but perilous lures which made other men more malleable. He was not malicious like Crayfe or outspoken like Borosar. He avoided making enemies and he had few friends. If he had a fault, Angmar reflected, it was perhaps a lack of passion; even people who liked him grumbled that he did not live his life, he mapped it.

"Angmar, truly," Landis said, "just between us: has Borosar a chance? Are they meeting to discuss a marriage with his son?"

"She doesn't confide in me, Landis. She confides in none of us. Council has met three times, and she has learned all our minds, and we have learned her mind on nothing. But if I had to guess, I would say no. I think she's met with him to talk about the war with Dravia."

"And that grizzled old war horse is going to discuss strategies of combat with girl?—for queen or no queen, she's just a girl. Come, Angmar, who is jesting now?"

"There is more to discuss than strategies of combat. She lived in Dravia for two years; she will have useful things to tell him. And she is not frivolous. She has a sense of responsibility beyond her years."

"That may be true. But I'm quite sure all Borosar wants to talk about is marrying his son. And the war will give him her ear."

Angmar bent, plucking a dead branch from the path and tossing it over the wall.

"There is someone else who has her ear who I'm a good deal more concerned about," he said.

"Medwina?"

"Aye. The queen has already returned to the cult of the sorceress in private."

"What of it? By the Great Mohr, Angmar, you've always been the one who told us to ignore all that! How can females rule the universe, when they can't even rule themselves? How can a goddess be a virgin and a mother and an old hag all at the same time—three goddesses at once, and yet still one? Only women would believe in things that were so irrational, you said. Let it be, it would die of its own weight. And so on and so on. Don't tell me now you've changed your mind!"

"Landis." Angmar shook his head. "Landis, I fear folly in anyone with power. Why do you think we must have true kings, and train them in wisdom, and pass on their blood and their power as carefully as jewels? I don't care what peasant women mumble in the dark. I care very much who gives counsel to our queen. She is not without gifts. Well guided, she could make a splendid queen. But these priestesses, brooding over their lost power—they'll only use her for their own ends. She is already surrounding herself with her mother's kin. She has made Caithland master of the palace guard. Caithland! In Mohr's name, Landis, should that have been done?"

"Well, he's safe enough," Landis said dryly. "No one will ever accuse her of bedding with a eunuch."

Angmar laughed. The calmness in Landis eased him a little. His cousin was always a bit less likely than himself to be disturbed by abstractions, by the *meanings* of things. Even more than Angmar, Landis was a pragmatist.

"Do you know what she said to me when I questioned her about it—when I asked if her she knew what they said about him—that he had been maimed in punishment, because he defiled himself with men? She said: 'He was maimed in battle,'—and dismissed the matter, as if the gods were absent from the fields of war, and made no judgments there!"

"She's a woman," Landis said. "And Caithland is her kinsman. No doubt that's all she cares about. You can't expect her to think like a man."

He hunched his shoulders slightly against a harsh gust of wind. "It's getting cold, Angmar. I will get my cloak, I think—unless you want to go in."

"Yes. Let's go in. The others will already think we have been plotting. But one thing I want to say first. . . ." He closed a firm hand on the younger man's shoulder. "There isn't much time, Landis. She must marry, and quickly. If she doesn't, Kamilan may be torn apart. I won't discourage her from any worthy suitor; it's too late for that. I will do my best for you, but if she chooses another . . . if she chooses another, you must accept it."

"I will not accept a priest of Mohr."

"Neither will the queen." Angmar reflected on his words, and smiled bitterly. "If Medwina did one thing in her life for which we have cause to thank her, it is that."

Long after his guests were gone Angmar wandered alone in his garden. He thought back over the evening, and over the Council meeting which had preceded it. The queen wanted to talk about Dravia; Council wanted to talk about the queen.

It was Crayfe who began the uproar by asking her: was it true that she was recruiting women—some of them even from her highborn kin—and training them in arms, to be shield women for her personal guard?

Yes, she said, it was true.

They were appalled, but more than anything else, they were embarassed. Only barbarians, who had no respect for anything, asked their women to bear arms, and face the perils of combat. The queen, however, would not be dissuaded. She had been kidnapped once, she said; she had not forgotten it. For her own sake, and her country's, it would not be allowed to happen again.

"You were kidnapped, lady," Theron said, "from a place where in all good sense you should not have gone."

The council room fell very still. All of them, no doubt, agreed in some measure with the high priest, but no one else would have been so brazen as to say it.

"And what place is there in Kamilan where the sovereign may not go?" Marwen asked, very calmly.

Till that moment Angmar had always thought of her as a girl. Just then, she did not even seem young. She had presence, he observed; and in one way that plain, ungentle face was a subtle asset. It could erase, however briefly, a man's awareness of her as female.

"The sovereign may go anywhere, of course," Theron said stiffly.

"I am glad to hear that, for I mean to do so. And unless you would have me bathe in the company of soldiers, and share my tent with them when I'm afield, and lodge them outside my chamber door, then I will have armed women at my side."

"Lady," Crayfe said, "we'll be the laughingstock of every tavern from Sardas to Larandau."

She did not bother to respond to him. She had already chosen the women, she said, and taken their oaths. Her kinsman Caithland, master of the palace guard, would train them. And that was that.

"She recruited twenty-four of them in three days, Crayfe, can you believe it?" Favian said afterwards. "Are so many women secretly so eager to fight?"

"I doubt they're eager to fight," Crayfe said. "But I'll wager they're eager to live among soldiers. I wonder how Caithland will like the competition."

Angmar pulled his collar up. Crayfe said the queen had fangs, and indeed she did. Why should that surprise anyone? People with more power than they could handle invariably had fangs; Crayfe's own were of the very best.

Old roots, he reflected, were sometimes the bane of good men. It was because of old roots—those essential patterns and traditions which made all things stable—it was because of them that the entire security and hope of Kamilan devolved upon this wilful, not very bright creature with fangs, who argued logically enough from positions which were true only because she made them so. Except for those ancient roots they could have had a king. They could have by-passed her utterly when Adelmar died, and chosen his nearest male relative. Only it happened that of all Adelmar's male relatives, there was not one who was also descended from the line of Alyth. And to all but a handful of Kamils, it was the line of Alyth which mattered.

Reason made no difference to them, nor good sense, nor justice. They had accepted the first king because he married Alyth's granddaughter, and they had accepted every king since, not because the paternal line was unbroken, but because the maternal line was. To have discarded Marwen would have been to invite civil war.

Men just imagined they were rational, Angmar thought. They imagined all the old barbarian ways were gone. But they were not. They were still alive and still abroad, whispering in the darkness, waiting like shadows in the bottom of a pool. Men built temples and led armies and devised elaborate codes of law—and then turned, and tumbled like children into the most incomprehensible mistakes. Even now, after generations of splendid kings, no king who was not born of Alyth would seem to them a king.

14. Dinner With Borosar

Kamilan, Kiri discovered, was a country in which new traditions and power structures had everywhere been grafted upon the old. Nowhere was this more true than in the Kamil army. Under the old clan system, which prevailed throughout the mountains before the coming of Telhiron, each clan had its own warband and warleader, and the decision to fight was always a local one.

The invaders broke the heart of the clan system. They destroyed its social and sexual ethic. They swallowed up the land to create personal dynasties, and replaced a society of relative equality with one of domination and control. Nonetheless they found some of the old structures useful. Most of them had their eyes on their neighbour's territories, and many had their eyes on the crown. They all found it singularly useful to maintain the tradition of local fighting forces answering only to a local chieftain.

The new Kamil kings, trying to maintain their power in a social order based on violence, needed something more substantial than the royal warbands which had served the hill queens for centuries. They needed to build a professional army, and the very changes they created in the land enabled them to do so. As the great families grew rich, the dispossessed turned to whatever might enable them to survive—banditry, servitude, prostitution, and soldiering.

Kamilan's army was now a strange mix of the highest born men in the land, and the lowest. The bulk of it, commanded by the warlord Borosar, served only the sovereign—or so the sovereign was compelled to hope. The rest, commanded by the warleaders of the great houses, gave formal loyalty to the warlord and the crown, but one or another of them had rebelled at least once in every king's lifetime.

Borosar was well over forty now; past his prime as a fighting man, perhaps, but acknowledged even by his enemies as a brilliant general. He belonged to a smaller but highly respected clan from Caerne, and he was careful to stay on good terms with the rival lordships of Maene and Tamri. He always gave their warleaders the highest authority next to his own, and it was assumed by most Kamils that one or the other would be his successor.

On the third night of Council, Borosar came as a guest to the queen's hall, with his wife and his second son. His wife was a thin, sad-looking, excessively jewelled woman. Surprisingly, he had only one. If he had not needed heirs, as did any man of rank, he might never have married at all; he had a soldier's appetite for casual couplings and casual farewells. Borosar, they said, had enough bastards to man a garrison.

The warlord also had a soldier's appetite for food and wine, Kiri noticed. He ate for a company and drank for a regiment, and was not much affected by either.

For a time he talked about his family. He wanted to be sure the queen understood how excellent his lineage was, and how nobly his son Gareth would be placed in the world, even though he was not the firstborn.

But Borosar had no real interest in domesticity at all, and he had gone on to talk for hours about the only thing which really did interest him: Kamilan's defenses in the coming war.

For war there surely would be. Berend—the man who would one day be remembered even in the scrolls of Larandau as Berend the Scourge—Berend was now both lord and king.

When the story of Prince Held's death was brought to Aralev, old Algard rose from his bed with a shriek of grief and rage, demanded his sword and armour, and fell dead. He was placed in his tomb with magnificent gifts, seated as though he were still alive, facing southeast, towards Kamilan. The same day Berend was crowned in the temple of Mohr, and from its steps he swore a sacred oath of vengeance. And only when it was fulfilled, he said, only when Algard saw his son return at the head of a victorious army, his sword raised high, bright with the blood of the dog of Belengar and his sorceress queen—then and only then would the old king have rest.

If one could judge by the accounts coming out of Dravia with travellers and traders, Berend meant to keep his vow, and raise an army such as the mountain lands had never seen. He was emptying Dravia's treasury to hire mercenaries, and buying slaves by the thousands to work in Dravia's fields and mines, so that her own men could fight. And he had sent an embassy to Larandau to ask for help.

"Will the emperor help him, do you think?" Caithland asked.

"No question," Borosar said. "He will loan Berend money at the very least, and probably he will send a few legions."

The queen's hall was crowded. Unlike the Dravians, who had adopted the imperial custom of private meals and private audiences, and used their great halls only for state occasions, the Kamils ate and worked and sometimes slept in theirs. Meals were a cheerfully disorderly affair, with people coming and going, guards changing shifts, people singing and telling stories. Everyone was made welcome, and expected to down at least one plate of food and one cup of wine. The queen spent very little time in her private chambers.

They sat at a long wooden table. Close enough to the queen to be part of the conversation were Borosar, his handsome son whom he had brought to woo the queen, his wife (who did not say a word after the subject turned to arms), Kiri, several members of the palace guard, and Caithland, their captain.

Caithland, Kiri thought, was a man about whom many stories could be told. He was fair, like most Kamils, and somewhat rough-hewn; he did not talk much. They called him a eunuch, but for someone like herself, who knew the customs of the south, the word was misleading. The mountain people did not castrate boys, or captives, or indeed any men at all; in this the barbarians were infinitely more civilized than their urbane neighbours. Caithland was not a eunuch in that sense, but he had been maimed. It was not this, however, which caused his disrepute among some Kamils. It was the fact that he was believed to share his bed with men.

Highborn, protected by his rank and his close ties to the queen's maternal family, he was out of reach, and he seemed to look upon the world and its judgments with a melancholy disdain, as though they saddened him yet were not worth his sadness. He took the queen's trust in him as a clear vindication. No one—not even Theron—had ever questioned his courage.

The Council believed Marwen was foolish to give him command of the guard. None of them seemed to notice that she was quietly gathering around herself a core of people who would have every reason in the world to be loyal to her, and no reason at all to be loyal to them.

"Lord Borosar," the queen said, "there is a matter I wished to raise with you before, but we've had so many pressing things to talk about. On my journey here from Dohann I spoke with the captain of Belengar—"

"Shadrak," Borosar interrupted. "And what do you think of him?"

"He seems to me both valiant and capable. Exceptionally so."

Borosar smiled faintly, like a man who had heard what he wanted to hear, and was a little too tipsy to conceal it.

"He has interesting ideas," the queen went on. "He told me he has discussed with you some small changes in Kamil strategy."

"Small changes?" Borosar laughed. "Either he was being cautious, lady, or you are. Come, tell me, what did he really say? Never mind, I'll tell you. He said we're wasting our best weapons by giving them to ill-trained foot soldiers, and wasting our best men by giving them weapons good for nothing but a drunken brawl. He said we use bows for sport and swords for combat, and if we had any wits at all we'd do the opposite. I know exactly what he said, lady. I've heard it a hundred times."

"And what is your view, warlord?"

"He's right," Borosar said bluntly. "In theory he's right—if all you consider is the field. War is more complicated than that. Can you see the lords of Kamilan as anything but captains of cavalry? A man is a warrior, lady, and a warrior is a man with a horse and a sword." He turned to Caithland as the next most senior warrior present. "Don't you agree, captain?"

"Entirely," Caithland said. It was impossible to tell if he meant it or not.

"Shadrak is right, you say, if all we consider is the field." The queen looked thoughtfully into her wine cup. "If King Berend raises the army he plans to raise, I don't think we will be allowed to consider anything else."

Borosar grunted.

There was a breath of silence, suddenly broken by the stammering voice of his son: "We have never beaten . . . I mean been beaten. . . . No Dravian has ever beaten us."

He fell silent, flushing. Everyone ignored him. Even at his best he was probably not very bright. Now, dragged out for the queen's inspection like a prime stallion, he was almost witless. Kiri felt sorry for him.

The queen spoke again: "Shadrak told me he would ask you to relieve him of the command in Belengar, and let him recruit and train a special force of archers. To fight the Dravians his way, he said, to harry them day and night, and attack them from rocks and shadows and trees."

"And," Borosar said, "he also asked you to please have a word with the warlord, didn't he?"

"Yes," Marwen said frankly. "But I wouldn't have done so unless I thought he was right. I saw what happened at the Magdal bridge, Borosar. Prince Held's men were defeated before one of them crossed a blade with ours."

"I believe that," the warlord said. He held out his cup to a servant who filled it with rich, golden wine. He drank deeply, thought a moment, and drank again. "It's a good theory Shadrak has," he said. "But I don't think it would be well received."

"Have you given him an answer?"

"I told him I'd think about it." His eyes were heavy-lidded, watching the queen with a kind of amused bewilderment, as though he did not quite understand how he had come to have this conversation. He was supposed to be pursuing her.

"Are you commanding me in this, lady?" he asked. For the first time, there was an edge to his voice.

"No," the queen said. "I'm not commanding you. But when Berend brings his army down, it will not be just another war. It will be a fight for absolute survival. I think we might be wise to give the captain his head, and see what he can do."

Borosar said nothing for a time. He had spent a lifetime fighting the Dravians, and at unexpected moments he seemed weary, as though he knew that the bitterest of his battles was still ahead of him. In that battle, Kamilan would need every hand it had, and every piece of iron, and every cunning mind.

"You know what some men say, lady?" he muttered. "They say it's a coward's way of fighting."

"And those who make war on us," Marwen replied darkly, "without cause or provocation, with forced levies and the wealth of empire—are they brave?"

"Never argue with a woman, captain," Borosar said, turning briefly to Caithland. "It's like having a swordfight with fog." He leaned back in his chair, stifling a belch.

"I have a lot of faith in young Shadrak," he went on. "I always have had. Thyrsian blood in a man is like wolf blood in a dog; it always shows. An old friend of mine once put it to me this way: The gods made all the fighting peoples, one by one, trying to get them right. They made the Sardas men first, and that was so bad everyone laughed. So they made the Dorathians and the Vards and the Almedes. Then they experimented with a great many others, and finally they made Telhiron. They were pleased with him, so they made the Kamils, and that was even better. Then they made the Thyrsians, and that was when they quit, because they had gone too far."

Marwen smiled and sipped her wine.

"He's wasted in Belengar," the warlord said. "I told him that myself. He should have at least a legion. If he proves himself in this, I will make him a warleader. We can't waste good men at a time like this, can we, captain?"

"Indeed not," said Caithland.

Dinner with Borosar, Kiri reflected, was fascinating.

15. The Matter of the Queen's Marriage

Angmar the Wise had never wanted to be the young queen's guardian. He had accepted the burden only out of loyalty to his dying king. He was aging; he had spent nearly thirty years of his life in the heart of Kamil politics; it was enough.

Don't give her to me, lord, he had pleaded. *In the name of Mohr, give her to a husband!*

But it had been too late for that. By that time the king admitted he was dying, death was only four days away, and he was rambling with fever, unwilling to deal with the kingdom which had so utterly disappointed him, or with the child who disappointed him even more.

Nothing could have made up for the fact that she was not a son. Still, if she had been pretty—if at the very least she had been sweet and warm and full of laughter, as a girl child should be—the king might nonetheless have loved her. But she had crooked teeth, and too much nose, and a thin, hard little mouth, and gangly limbs; there was nothing soft about her anywhere.

143

She was still very young when she grasped the fact that she would be queen—the fact that the king had no sons, and was not likely to have any. Her seriousness grew deeper. She watched everything happening around her with a quiet, fox-like alertness, as though she already understood that her life might depend on decoding what she saw.

She learned the formal things quickly and well: how to act and speak in court, how to carry herself, how to manage servants and keep accounts. But Angmar saw that many deeper, more essential things were not being learned at all, and that was Medwina's doing. The princess did not respect the gods, or the traditions of Kamilan—or indeed, even her own rank, except as a means of having her own way. She grew fiercely proud, in a manner which might have suited the bravest of warriors, but which was vulgar and offensive in a woman. She was never openly rebellious, and indeed it would have worried him less if she had been. Rebellion usually burned itself out. The quiet core wilfulness in this girl seemed only to grow, and to wrap around itself a shield of cold, unnatural strength.

He honestly did not like her, yet when the Dravians took her he was deeply grieved—not least because he knew how bitterly she would provoke the Dravian prince. And Held would not tolerate it. He would break her as men broke intractable horses, blow by blow, until they shivered in their harnesses, dull-eyed and ruined, but obedient.

That was what Angmar had expected. Yet the matter turned out differently, and he was not at all sure he knew why.

He sat across from the queen in a quiet chamber set off from the great hall. It was called the shield room, because Adelmar had kept there his ancestral treasures of war: old bronze weapons; ornate swords and scabbards; a bow which legend said once belonged to Alyth; and seven painted shields, all of them different, all of them wrapped in ancient stories.

This was the place where Angmar had usually met with the king, and he knew Marwen had brought him here—rather than to the queen's apartments—for precisely that reason. He was no longer her guardian. He might speak to her now only as a loyal advisor to a lord.

She was wearing a beautifully embroidered tunic, with a gold belt and a throat-piece of finely worked gold, studded with amber. She was still plain, but her astonishing poise and splendid hair gave her a certain uncanny grace. She was the kind of woman men would glance at, pass over, and then suddenly turn and look at once again, puzzled, wondering what it was that had caught their attention.

They spoke briefly and politely of his family, of the administration of the palace. He did not mention Caithland or the shield women; he had no wish to anger her before they began. It was she who opened the discussion.

"I think, Angmar, you had a particular reason for asking for this meeting?"

"Yes. I hoped to discuss your marriage. I know you prefer not to speak of it in Council—"

"I prefer not to speak of it at all." She let the silence lay between them for a moment, and went on: "But since you've come to speak of it, very well. You, and the other lords of Council, want me to take a husband. Is that not so?"

"Yes, lady. But it's not simply a matter of what we want. It's absolutely necessary. Kamilan needs an heir. And you must be protected." He leaned forward a little, speaking quietly and earnestly. "Had you married while your father lived, you would never have been carried off to Dravia. I blame myself bitterly that I did not insist on a marriage. Your father was ill, and he delayed because of it. I had no excuse. Indeed, because he was so ill, I should have insisted all the more."

"I was thirteen when my father died, Angmar. Would you have had me married even then?"

He made a vague, helpless gesture. "I yielded to Medwina because of that, lady. Because you were so young, I held my peace. And then your father died, and Council would agree on nothing, and you were carried off, and violated, and held captive in an enemy land. Wouldn't it have been better to be safe and honourably wed—even at thirteen?"

Her mouth twisted bitterly, but she did not speak.

"You are of age now, lady," he said gently, "and free to choose. That is a privilege—"

"No," she said coldly. "That is not a privilege; that is a right—a right which once belonged to every Kamil queen, and every Kamil goat girl. Don't ask me to be grateful for what is my own. And don't tell me I have no choice but marry, and then tell me I am free to choose. Surely Angmar the Wise can see the absurdity of that."

145

He had said to Theron: *The child who went to Dravia did not come back.* But in fact she had. She was as wilful and unreasonable as ever; misfortune had taught her nothing at all.

He made his voice carefully bland. "No one is entirely free, lady, least of all a sovereign. You have a degree of freedom which most queens in the world would envy. You also have the duties which you inherited. You may neglect them, but not without consequences."

"I'm not neglecting my duties," she snapped. "Who speaks of what in Council? We're on the brink of a war; we need more troops; we need bowyers and fletchers and smiths; we need copper and tin and iron; we need stores of grain; we need watchtowers and runners. I want to deal with these matters, and the lords of Council want to deal with my household affairs and my bed!"

"You're absolutely right, lady. In the matter of the Dravian threat, Council has been very . . . slack. On the other hand, they see another problem which is just as real, and every bit as dangerous. Until you have a consort and an heir, we will have no stability in Kamilan."

"Angmar, I'm not even eighteen. There's plenty of time for children."

"And if you're kidnapped again?"

"Held is dead."

"Forgive me, lady, but I wasn't speaking of the Dravians."

She went rigid, like an animal freezing into its shadow at the sight of a hawk.

"I'm sorry," he went on. "It's not my wish to frighten you. But I must speak plainly. Shall I tell you how one man put it to me? An unmarried queen, he said, is like a carcass drawing wolves."

"I see."

He had never thought of her as having an expressive face. That was a quality he associated with emotion, with softness in a woman's manner. And yet her face changed constantly, like a summer lake, full of uncertain currents and altered by every shift of cloud. That was one of the things which made men pause, and look at her again. The currents he saw now unsettled him. Dravia had not changed her nature, perhaps, but it had made her harder, more unpredictable. Prince Held had not broken her. Prince Held was dead.

"It was foully spoken, lady, but it is foully true." He paused. Deliberately, he reminded himself that she was only a girl. "I know what you would wish. First of all, to forget what you endured in Dravia. And then, in a year's time, or in three, or in five, to find a consort according to your heart. I would gladly see you have your wish. Only it isn't possible."

If you had been taught by anyone with sense, rather than by Medwina, you would know that, and I would not have to bludgeon you with truths which every twelve year old princess takes for granted.

His words had struck home, at least. She was pale, and no longer defiant—at least not outwardly. Inside . . . inside, the gods alone knew what she was thinking.

"I have been back less than a moonturn, Angmar," she said. "Even if I were to agree that you were right, it would take some time to find a husband. Or shall I pick one out of a bucket?"

He smiled faintly. "May I counsel you in this?"

"You will regardless."

"The purpose of this marriage is to establish your own security. With a strong consort you will be safe, and so will your children. The lords of Council represent, in one way or another, most of the powerful families in Kamilan, and they all have at least one unmarried kinsman of suitable age—for certainly no one would expect you to be a second wife. Landis of Maene, of course, is himself unmarried, and would be a most noble match for you.

"I have drawn up a list, lady, of the likeliest candidates. I know many of the men personally, and I've made sure that all of them are healthy and known to be of decent character—"

"Are we speaking of marriage, Angmar, or of buying horses?"

He sighed. "Lady, you had neither the time nor the inclination to do this for yourself. I did my best. The men I've listed are of excellent lineage, honourable, and young. I'm certain there is among them someone who will please you. I will not press you as to your choice; the decision is yours. I will act on your behalf, if you wish, with any of the lords, or with as many as you wish. There's no reason not to take the time to meet them all. And I will accept whatever choice you make. So will Council."

She took the list, but she seemed to do no more than glance at it, briefly, as though it were an irritation rather than a useful gift.

"And if I choose to accept none of them?" she asked calmly.

"You will put your life at risk, lady, as well as Kamilan. For in truth, if you were to do that, I couldn't vouch for the loyalty of the lords themselves. They aren't keen to serve a woman. They will do so if she's sensible, and creates a stable state, for then they will prosper more from loyalty than from rebellion. But if she's reckless, and isolates herself—if they look about and see that from day to day any wretch with a hundred men at his command might seize her and call himself their king—then they might well say: Enough of this; we'll choose our own king. Or one of them might kidnap her himself, on the grounds that if he doesn't, his rival will.

"I'm not your enemy, lady. I tell you this only because it's true. You must marry. You should do so before the spring."

He stood up, meaning to take a polite leave, and let her think over what he had said. She swept in front of him like a panther, more angry than he had ever seen her.

"Do you think it will be easy to usurp the house of Alyth?" she demanded bitterly.

"No, lady. It will not be easy. It may well tear Kamilan to pieces. Do you want that?"

"Do *I* want it? That is clever, sage! I should give up my rights, so they have no excuse for mutiny? Kamilan sounds more and more like Dravia. Don't annoy the prince, lady, lest he put you in a cage! Don't annoy the lords of the Council, lady, lest they start a civil war! Goddess of the world, Angmar, did I walk through the mountains of Dohann for this?"

Her rage was candent, painful to feel and to look upon. He could not meet her eyes, not because he felt himself in the wrong, for he did not, but because she seemed so alien to him, so unreachable, a being whose sense of life did not even touch his own, and never could. He did not blame her for her anger, no more than he would blame a forest creature howling in a trap. He could not spring the trap. He had not made the world. Her rage was empty, tragic, pointless. Female.

"You walked through the mountains of Dohann—or so I believe—to serve your people, and to be their queen. If you don't want to do that, then for your own sake you should have stayed with the Dravians, and been theirs."

"What kind of queen can I be when I'm commanded in everything I do? In Dravia, the queen can't set foot outside her house. In Kamilan, Council tries to tell her who she may take into her service, and whether she should marry, and when, and to whom; and they threaten civil war if she disobeys. That's no queen; that's a king's whore—a thing to warm his bed and breed his sons. If you didn't need that, you'd have no queens at all!"

"You're not commanded in everything you do, lady. And as for bearing children to carry on your blood, that comes with your rank. Warriors must fight, whether they want to or not. Healers must walk out in the middle of the night in snow and rain. No one escapes duty, lady, and only children try to."

"You're no longer my guardian, Angmar. Be careful what you say."

"I am being careful. And I will say one thing more. You're being offered an honourable marriage to a worthy consort. If you can see no difference between that and whoredom—"

"I can see no difference at all," she flung at him. "A bought woman is a bought woman. A soldier would offer me a copper coin; Council offers me a gold one. A large gold one, to wear around my head!"

He had had enough. "I will take my leave, lady. I trust you will consider what I've said."

And when you come to your senses, if you have any, we will discuss this again. . . .

16. Medwina

Life in Kamilan was the best life Kiri had ever known. She was the queen's minstrel; she played at the feasts, and spent much of her time learning Kamil legends and Kamil songs. She was the queen's confidante, and sat with her at night, just the two of them with a fire and a cup of wine, and talked about the world. She was also one of the queen's defenders, and when the first shield women came to the palace, and gathered in the parade ground outside the barracks to learn how to fight, Kiri was with them, honing the skills she had learned in Vanthala and on the caravan, learning new ones, and practicing with her crossbow until even Caithland grudgingly admitted that she was a far better shot than he was.

She missed the caravan sometimes, but she never missed it enough to want to go back—not even when she had played until she was exhausted, when her eyes burned from focusing on moving targets and all her bones ached from climbing and running and falling, when she fought her way through the tangles of Kamil history and genealogy—gods preserve us, who *were* all those people, and would she ever remember which was which?—not even then did she feel anything except fortunate to be here.

To the Kamils themselves she was a curiosity, as she had been to the Dravians, though not for the same reasons. The Kamils still remembered something of the world of the hill queens; they understood that a woman might want to be a minstrel, or a skilled archer—or that she might not be very interested in men. But what, they wondered, was a Dravian doing in the royal court of Kamilan?

Some accepted her wholeheartedly, as the soldiers had in Belengar, judging that she had earned her place. Others did not. There were keen sidelong glances, and sometimes whispers. Even those who did not actually mistrust her seemed to think that it was still simply . . . *inappropriate*. Dravs were always Dravs, after all.

But the shield women liked her and looked up to her. So when she came to Marwen's chamber one cloudy autumn morning, the young woman who barred her way did so with obvious reluctance.

"I'm sorry," she said. "The queen will see no one."

"Is she ill?"

"No. But she's told us to send away anyone who seeks her in the great hall, and to let no one into her room."

"Such an order would never include me. Let me pass."

The shield woman was visibly distressed. She was only half trained, and she knew that Kiri was stronger than she was, and tougher, and older. She knew also that Kiri was the queen's best friend, the one who had led her through the mountains. It was painful to stand rigid by the door and say: *No. No one may go in. No one at all.*

"Don't be ridiculous," Kiri said. "I have something important to tell her."

"No, minstrel. I am very sorry. I can't."

Kiri argued with her further. Surely, she said, the shield woman ought to understand what Marwen *meant*. There was such a thing as common sense. She, Kiri, went everywhere with the queen, and shared all her counsels; she would never be refused entry to her lady's chamber. Besides, the matter was important.

To each of her arguments, the answer was still no.

"She'll wring your neck for this, you little fool," Kiri snapped.

The shield woman swallowed and examined her shoes. "Better she wrings my neck for obeying her, than for disobeying."

"Good," Kiri said.

The woman stared at her in astonishment.

"I trained new guards for Mercanio sometimes," Kiri told her. "He said I could think up more stories than anyone he ever heard. I let you off easy."

"You had me scared silly."

"It gets easier. One day you'll shrug and tell Great Mohr himself to go jump off a ledge. Do you know what's wrong? Why the queen won't see anyone?"

"All I know is that Angmar was here. She was with him for over an hour in the shield room, and then she came here. She was angry, and she was crying, too. The gods alone know what he said to her. Why must they set upon her like hounds all the time? If only she were married; they would treat her better then."

If you believe that, Kiri thought grimly, *you are too innocent to be trusted with a sword!*

"What's your name?" Kiri asked.

"Mara. You look at me strangely. What's the matter?"

"Nothing. I knew another once who was named Mara. From Sardas. She's with the caravan in Larandau."

"What was it like on the caravan? It must have been exciting."

"Sometimes. I liked travelling around, but the rest of it was just work. I'd rather be a minstrel. Where are you from?"

"Getann. My parents were healers there."

Getann. The mountain of tin, where the slaves slashed out their days in an echoing, suffocating darkness of rock.

"Did they ever go to . . . to the mines?" Kiri asked.

"No," Mara said. "Those who died there, died." She shifted uneasily. "I don't much like slavery. They say the queen doesn't like it, either—though I guess there are some who are kind to their slaves."

"It's not possible to be kind to a slave," Kiri said. "It's a contradiction in terms. If the queen had her way, there would be no slaves anywhere in Kamilan."

"But who would do all the work? Who would mine Getann? It's a terrible place. Who would work there except a slave?"

152

"It wasn't always terrible. When there were no slaves, they used to keep the shafts clean, and even the clan chiefs went into the mines, as they went into the fields and the forests. There was no reason not to. The mines were part of their wealth."

"I can't picture that," Mara said. Then suddenly she began to giggle. "Can you imagine Lord Crayfe going down into a mine shaft?" she whispered shamelessly. "With that belly of his? They'd need a hundred men to dig him out!"

The sun was nearing noon when Marwen emerged from her room. She was calm, but the calmness was brittle; she looked drained and harassed. She said very little, except to summon Caithland and twenty-five of her guard. The shield women, she said, should come too. They were not yet well trained, but it was time Kamilan got used to seeing them.

"I'd like you to come too, Kiri, if you would," she said. "But I'm not sure what will happen. You may have to stay with the guards."

"I will come regardless," Kiri said. "But where are we going?"

"To the temple of Jana."

"But the temple is—" She saw the queen's face, and said no more.

They descended into the broad valley of the Magdal, through many leagues of splendid farmland, scattered with thatched houses, and from there into the forest. Here the road was narrow, with room for only two to ride abreast.

They came quite suddenly into a small clearing. In its centre was a long, low, sagging, thatch-roofed house, with a bit of garden and a tethered goat. They drew up, the guards forming a half-circle around them.

"What place is this?" Kiri asked, wondering why they would stop in so desolate a spot.

"The house of Medwina," the queen said, "high priestess of Kamilan, daughter of Alyth, conscience of the Kamil clans." There was a chilling bitterness in her voice.

"Medwina lives here?" Kiri whispered.

"Yes. Thus do the sons of Mohr honour the wisdom of their mothers."

Medwina emerged from the house, shielding her eyes against the sun. In the camp at Althen Field she had seemed a compelling and powerful woman; here, in clear daylight, she was old and almost haggard. She greeted the queen, and those among her companions whom she knew. Then she said simply:

"Let us go in." She paused, glancing at Kiri. "You have earned your place, minstrel. Please, come with us."

The building they went into was plain but comfortable. It might have seemed a farm house except that the walls were hung with strangely carved sticks, with horns and hooves and pelts and snakes and bundles of drying plants. In the centre of the room was a small stone altar, hollowed and blackened with fire.

The queen unclasped her cloak and laid it over a chair. To Kiri's astonishment, she wore beneath it a shirt of ring mail.

"Are we come to this, then?" Medwina said. It was not a question, and no one responded.

The priestess served them mead and cheese, and small seedcakes sharp with anise.

"Next time you come, Kiri," she said, "bring your lyre. I'm fond of music, and I hear so little of it."

"I'm sorry, lady," Kiri said. "I never thought of it, or I would have brought it today." She hesitated, and then, remembering that things usually turned out well for her when she was bold, she asked:

"Forgive me, lady Medwina, but why do you live here in the forest? Why don't you come to Kamilan? To my lady's palace?"

Medwina answered, looking at Marwen as she did so, almost as if to ask: *Did you put her up to this?*

"I'm a priestess, Kiri, not a courtier. I don't belong in palaces."

"But you lived there once."

"Aye. After my sister died, and her daughter had no one to guide her, or teach her anything except how to lower her eyes and bow to the will of men. She's grown now. She doesn't need me underfoot."

"I need you more than ever," Marwen said.

"I am in reach. I serve Jana, and I will have a temple. If this is the only temple I may have, then this is where I will live."

Kiri fell silent, fearing that she had opened a wound.

Medwina leaned back in her chair, resting her elbows and linking her hands.

"I saw you enter the forest," she said. "I saw fear in your heart. Why have you come, Marwen?"

"I've come for guidance," the queen said. "The lords of Council are determined that I marry, and very soon."

Kiri listened as the queen recounted her meeting with Angmar the Wise.

"He believes that if I don't marry soon," she concluded, "I risk both Kamilan and my life. He's certain there will be violence, perhaps even from within the Council. It seems an unmarried queen is like a carcass drawing wolves."

"Jackals, I would say rather," Medwina said. "Vultures. And let's not forget the worms." Her voice was soft, but Kiri winced at the hatred in it.

"I don't know what to do," Marwen said. "I don't like Angmar much, and he doesn't like me, but he is wise. He's the only one of them who isn't drunk with ambition."

"He's ambitious for Landis. Don't ever lose sight of that. Nevertheless he is right. You must marry."

Marwen's face fell. "I must?" she whispered.

"Yes. Or be destroyed. They will use violence to have their way. Have we ever doubted that?"

"Against their own queen?" Kiri asked bitterly.

"Against anyone. Rank is not important to men who crave power. They make a great deal of noise about it. They pretend it comes from the gods when they have it, or when their sons do, but they rarely honour it. Telhiron's own sons died by murder, and so have three Kamil kings.

"Even without this, sister child, I would have counselled you to marry. Kamilan should have an heir—perhaps two or three, in all this chaos."

"I don't need to marry for that. Alyth didn't."

"Alyth is dead!" Medwina said harshly, rising. "Dead so long they will soon begin to say she never lived at all, and the things she did never happened. Bear your children as Alyth did, and they will die in the hills, hungry as rabbits."

She limped to the table to fetch the mead. Kiri rose to help her, but she waved her back.

"No. Sit, little one. You are my guest."

She poured slowly, letting them think.

"Medwina," Marwen said at last, "for two years, night upon night, I shared my bed with a man I never wanted to be

155

with—never, not even once. It takes your soul away to do that. And when he began to care for me and wished to please me, instead of simply taking what he wanted—it wasn't better then; it was worse. I can't bear the thought of living like that again!"

Medwina gripped the back of Marwen's chair and turned away. She closed her eyes, as though she still could see everything she had seen when the Dravians came: the great bearlike hand reaching, closing, the girl prisoned like a rabbit in a snare, like Leya in the high-walled pit which Mohr had fashioned of the world.

She touched Marwen's hair with a slender, taloned hand. "Poor thing," she said. "I forget how young you are. You're wise beyond your years, and I forget."

She limped to her chair and sat.

"The world is what it is, Marwen," she said. "Angmar and I are alike in that: we see what is, and all our yearning for what is better doesn't blind us to the truth. It's Mohr's world. He has built it out of iron and bartered flesh, out of levies and slaves and concubines and whores, out of armies and cages and blood. It is his.

"So yes, child of my sister and my heart, you must marry one of them, because you have no choice. Even if you wished to turn your back on all of it, and live a private life, they wouldn't let you. They need your flesh; they have invested a kingdom in it. You may give it, on whatever terms you can devise, or they will take it. That is all. It is Mohr's world."

"You give cruel counsel, Medwina."

"Would a lie be kinder?"

"No." Marwen shook her head. "No. It would not."

"Aye. And cruel counsel is not hopeless counsel. They rule, but we're not powerless. I'm not telling you to surrender, merely to retreat. To bend, like a tree against the wind. Did you always defy Prince Held? Did you never stay silent, never smile, even? Never do what he demanded? No. I don't believe it. You would be dead. You must do the same now.

"It won't be like Dravia. You won't need to bed with him night after night, and once you have your children, you won't need to bed with him at all. Give them what they want. A proper queen. An heir. An empty smile. And bide your time, while he drinks and whores and imagines he is lord."

Kiri watched them, riveted to her chair. She understood completely Medwina's assertion that the queen had no choice, not even the choice of withdrawal from the field. And yet her mind rebelled. It made no sense. It was barbaric, pointless, mad. She understood it, and she would never understand it, no more than she would understand the armies which marched across the caravan roads: the armies and the slaves, the cities which turned to kingdoms, and then to empires, and then to dust. . . .

"Angmar wants me to marry Landis of Maene," the queen said.

Medwina went very still, like a marmot spotting a hawk.

"No," she said. "Heed Angmar in many things, but not in this."

"Why?"

"It's too dangerous."

"Medwina," Marwen said grimly, "if I must marry to protect my safety, and the safety of Kamilan, then I will do so—but why not do so, then, as effectively as I can? The house of Maene is the second house in Kamilan, and Landis is in Council, where Jana knows I need an ally."

"Landis wants to be king."

"They *all* want to be king! Goddess of the world, Medwina, that's the whole point of this wretched little game!"

"Yes," Medwina said. "They all want to, but not all of them have the means to do it. Landis does."

"Who would you have me choose, then?"

The priestess drummed her fingers thoughtfully against her chair. "Someone . . . someone *insecure*, I think," she said. "A man who has some power, but not enough to be dangerous. One who will support you now hoping to rule you later . . . only later will never come."

The queen said nothing. Medwina drummed her fingers a moment longer into the silence, and then stopped.

"You don't agree," the priestess observed.

"No. What's the point of defending myself with a wooden sword?"

"Because the iron ones will turn, and cut out your heart."

A heavy gloom hung over them as they departed. The bare trees and wind-scattered leaves seemed only to add to the sense of gathering cold and menace. It would snow soon. Marwen wrapped her cloak around herself, so that even her face was hidden in its shadows. She looked back once at the priestess standing stark and gray against the autumn light, and then she turned her horse and rode bent like a pilgrim into the darkening wood.

Kiri followed her in silence. The forest road had room for only one guard, and what, in any case, could she have said? Her experience had nothing to offer here. She was a minstrel, a wanderer of caravans, a woman without rank or power or importance to anyone, whose body was neither blessed nor cursed with kingdoms. She could not counsel flight. This time there was nowhere to run.

She fought back tears. Unbidden, the queen's words about Held of Dravia came to her mind: magnificent Held of Dravia, warrior prince without equal, dead and rotting in the woods of Dohann:

Do you know what was the greatest wrong he did me? He destroyed the future. He destroyed the peace we might have made, the honour in which we might have held each other. It is that, above all, for which I hate him.

Now she understood the enormity of Held's mistake—only it was more than one mistake, more than a single act. It was an entire damaged sense of life, a flaw running through the very essence of his being. The rest of him was sound; the rest of him was worth the entire Kamil Council. Together he and Marwen might have stood against the world. Instead, he was destroyed, and the kingdom he should have ruled and sheltered was Berend's now, and Berend would leave it in ruins.

Mohr, she reflected darkly, was not content to devour his daughters. His sons paid, too, for his savage glory. They paid differently. And, all things counted, they paid much less. But, gods of all, they paid.

17. A Visit from the Wolf

Kiri knew there were people in the world who did not care much what they ate. She knew because she had met some of them, but she did not understand how such creatures could exist. She felt sorry for them, as she felt sorry for people without ears or noses. Food was one of the great joys of life, and the food in the palace of Kamilan was wonderful.

When Marwen returned to her household, Malia the chief cook took one look at her, and said thereafter to anyone who would listen (and to some who would not) that the horrid Dravians had deliberately set out to starve the queen to death. It did no good to point out that Marwen had always been a rather lean and long-limbed girl, or that she had spent more than a moonturn as a fugitive in the wilds of Dohann. Malia would only sniff.

"She probably ate better in the woods than in Dravia, poor wee thing," she would say, and made it very clear that she, Malia, was going to repair the damage.

The cook was not an especially tall woman, but she weighed as much as two average men. Harad teased her sometimes, in his long-faced way, that he should pay her only half her wages because she had already eaten the other half. It was true that she ate too much, but everything cooked in her kitchens was irresistible. In Kamilan Kiri learned what it meant to eat like kings—or in this case, like queens. It was not the least of the things she liked about living here.

She sat happily with a great slab of bread in her hand, over which a servant had just ladled a scoop of creamy rabbit stew. After the stew there would be salted meats and seedcakes and cheese, and a hard sweet apple. And this was only breakfast, and not a feast day breakfast, either. The caravaners, she reflected, would kill her when she told them how she lived now: food like this every day, and a room with a fire, and twenty ells a year.

The gods alone knew if it would last. In a year or two the queen of Kamilan might well be dead, and her minstrel with her. Berend might be feasting in this hall, or Theron the high priest, or some other enemy whose name they had not even heard yet. But she would not tell the caravaners that. She would tell them about the baked doves and stewed quail, the ducks stuffed with plums, the venison turning slowly on its spits, the bowls of chestnuts and berries and stuffed eggs, the great slabs of salty cheese. And she would tell them about Malia, who had to have some of the palace doorways widened so she could get through them, and who spoke to her pots and pans as though they were people.

Engrossed in her thoughts and her food, Kiri was not aware of Shadrak's arrival in the great hall until he had almost reached their table. He was dressed for travelling, in soft high boots and a long fur cloak spattered with mud. Both garments were well worn. Most men of even a captain's rank would have passed them on to a servant, and bought something finer. Nonetheless he drew people's eyes, and held them. That was partly because of the fight at the Magdal bridge. But it was also because of the black Thyrsian look, the gaudy ornaments, the sense he carried with him no matter what he wore—the sense of predatory grace.

The shield woman Mara, sitting beside Kiri, leaned close and whispered: "The wolf of Dohann, am I right?"

"Yes."

"And the other?"

Trailing the captain was a soldier, gaunt and ragged and unpleasantly familiar. He walked slowly, like someone not yet recovered from a long illness. His right hand was missing; a dirty bandage wrapped the stump.

"I'm not sure," Kiri said. "But I think it's Tamon."

"The one who nearly shot you at Belengar?"

"Yes."

"I'm surprised the captain didn't hang him."

"It wasn't Tamon's fault, Mara. He couldn't possibly have known. The queen never blamed him, and neither did I. We were too happy to see a Kamil face. Even his."

"To some captains, that would have made no difference at all."

That was true. Simply to be wrong about something important was enough to get many a slave or servant or soldier killed.

Shadrak greeted the queen reverently. He was very happy, Kiri saw. He was riding within the hour for the north, he said, to begin gathering men for his new command.

"I didn't want to leave without thanking you, lady."

"There's no need to thank me, captain. Rather, I should thank you." She turned briefly to his companion. "It's good to see you well again, Tamon."

Tamon bowed—for the second time—almost to his knees.

However short their time was, the queen said, they must at least sit and share a trencher and a cup of wine; they would travel better for it. Shadrak glanced once at the laden table and accepted with thanks. For a moment nothing much was said. A place was cleared for them next to the queen, and servants hurried over with a fresh loaf of bread, cups for their wine, and the pot of rabbit stew which was steaming over the fire. When they had been served, Marwen asked:

"So Borosar has made a decision, then?"

Shadrak nodded, his mouth full of bread and rabbit.

"Clearly a favorable decision," Kiri said lightly—for in this, as in many other things, the captain wore his emotions dangerously unguarded.

It was more favorable than the queen had dared to hope. Borosar had given him a free hand, he said, to recruit as many as one thousand men, under his personal command.

"A thousand men, lady, trained as I want them trained: to read the woods and the weather and the wind; to learn an

161

enemy's mind from every small thing he does; to stalk and wait and care only about the glory of a final victory, not about the hope of glory in a moment. And to shoot, lady—on foot, or on horseback, or hanging upside down from a tree. Every one of them will be worth ten of anything Berend may send against us."

"I believe that," Marwen said.

The trencher was gone in a last hungry bite. He took a handful of seedcakes and attacked them with the same greedy pleasure.

"And once Borosar sees what's really possible," he went on, "he will give me more men."

Perhaps, Kiri thought. *Or he may take away the ones you have, quickly, while he still can. . . .*

Shadrak smiled at the queen. He was eager as a boy in the face of so many possibilities, but there was something guarded in his eyes, as though that other, darker possibility had occurred to him as readily as it had occurred to Kiri. To a man who had been a slave, nothing was certain, nothing was secure.

Except, she thought, the present moment: a board laden with good food, a fine morning to ride in, and the woman he loved sitting a hand's reach away, pleased with his loyalty and his skill. That was not enough, perhaps, but it was all he was prepared to count on.

Tamon, sitting beside Kiri, ate slowly, with his head down. He was ashamed of what he had almost done in Dohann. He would be ashamed until he died. At the feast in Belengar he had come and knelt at the queen's feet, and begged her forgiveness, and Kiri's too; and it had been given without hesitation. Still, though she did not blame him, Kiri did not think she would ever *like* him.

He was still ill, and he ate as though he had neither much appetite nor many teeth. She was surprised he was still with the army. Maimed fighters usually went home—some to live at last in comfort and content; others to rot.

"Are you well now, Tamon?" she asked him, and when he looked up like a startled animal, she added: "I'm very sorry about your arm."

"It be nothing," he said.

162

He had one hand now, he added, and the captain had three. "Cassian be his servant, maybe, but I be his shadow."

And he would do anything now for his captain. . . .

Shadrak had been fair to him—generous even, Kiri thought. But he had also been shrewd.

She watched Shadrak for a moment. Black, the Kamils called him, for his hair and because they had never seen real black people, the ones who came and traded sometimes in the southern ports of Sardas. He was not black, merely dark. But he seemed more alien than any ebony-faced trader she had ever seen, and infinitely more perilous.

He is half wolf. The thought just appeared in her mind, unbidden and unexpected. *Maybe what they say about the Thyrsians is true.*

And then she laughed at herself. The captain of Belengar rose—regretfully, she saw—to take his leave of the queen. He pledged his loyalty like any faithful soldier, and walked out into the very ordinary morning sun.

"If there were a man like that among my sixteen suitors," Marwen brooded, "the thought of marrying would not seem so dismal."

"Perhaps there is," Kiri said.

Marwen shrugged. They were sitting at a small table near the hearth while the servants cleaned away the meal, swept the floor with rushes, and alternately petted and cursed the palace cats, who were constantly underfoot, begging for leftovers.

The first thing the queen did when she returned to her own household was appoint Caithland as the new captain of the guard, with sweeping authority to reorganize their defenses and improve her personal security. The second thing she did was throw out the palace dogs.

She had never liked dogs much, and in Aralev she learned to hate them. Berend's dogs were as vicious as he was. One of them—before Kiri's time—had bitten her, and despite Berend's protests, the crown prince had killed it. It was one of those disturbing moments when she almost liked Held of Dravia.

On her second morning home she walked into the feast hall for breakfast and something growled at her. It only growled a little, and then it slunk away, but the damage was done. She looked around, saw a dozen or so other dogs curled up under the chairs and in front of the fire, saw water bowls and chewed-upon bones scattered among the floor rushes, saw Malia with a huge pot in her hands clumsily booting one of them out of her way. The queen called over the two guards who were manning the door.

"Get those creatures *out* of here," she said.

One of the men was much distressed. "Lady, those were your father's favourite hunters. I'll wager they cost him twenty or thirty ells apiece."

"You mean they're worth something?" she said. "I thought all they did was gobble food and bite people. Very well. In that case, get them out of here and sell them."

Kiri thought the man was going to cry.

In the end, she gave the dogs to Caithland, to keep in the barracks; the soldiers liked them, the soldiers could have them. And the palace cats, which had previously crept around the storerooms and the kitchens, hunting mice, happily moved into the great hall and grew fat.

The steward, Harad, padded to their table and placed three wax tablets at the queen's elbow. He had a long, hawk-nosed face and an air of absolute precision. He was the sort of man who would count the grains of wheat in a bucket, to see if one was missing.

"I have listed the provisions we will need for the festival, lady. Do you wish to go over it now?"

"Leave it with me. We can do it later."

"As you wish, lady."

He withdrew. Marwen glanced at the tablets, and shoved them aside.

"Even the Feast of Harash doesn't interest me today," she said.

"Lady." Kiri laid her lyre on the table. "I know what Angmar said—and Medwina, too. But is it really so? Do you have no choice but to marry?"

There was a long silence.

"I could gamble," the queen said at last. "My enemies are not united; with luck I could play them against each other and survive. If there were no war ahead of us, perhaps I would. But Kamilan is in the balance, too. A crisis of power in the midst of a war could undo us utterly."

"Would they really turn on you at such a time? It would be the worst kind of treason!"

Marwen shrugged. "Treason is whatever men choose to call it. They're not keen to serve a woman, as Angmar put it. He has a gift for understatement. Theron for one would probably rather see us ruled by the Dravians; at least the Dravians honour Mohr, and reject the Laws of Kind. And almost any of the other lords might persuade themselves that Kamilan needed a strong male hand—especially in war. They wouldn't call it treason; they'd call it rescue."

She paused. "I don't want to marry. But I also don't want to live all my days as bait, turning cold with every noise at the gate, every tramp of boots in the hall."

"There are many who would defend you faithfully—the captain of Belengar among them."

"And if we're fighting Dravians, shall I call him from the border to fight Kamils?"

Neither spoke for a time. One of the cats jumped up on the table and patted the strings of Kiri's lyre. It was a young cat, almost still a kitten, mottled and very playful. The queen picked it up and stroked it.

"They are such lovely things," she said. Then she looked again at Kiri, and went on:

"I think about it and think about it, and I come back to the same conclusion: that Angmar is right. But if I marry a weak man, I may see what power I do have chipped quietly away. And if I marry a strong man whom I dare not trust. . . ." Her mouth twisted. "It's lovely, isn't it, what men call choice?"

"What about your mother's kin? A man like Caithland? There must be others like him, who are loyal and have the power of Alyth's lineage."

"The power of Alyth's lineage, as you can see in my own case, is only half real. A kinsman would have the same strengths as I—and the same weaknesses. My mother's kin have few arms behind them, and less wealth. They have honour, and the love of the common folk, and names that are legends. Caithland can live as he wishes on the strength of that. And if an attempt were made to usurp me, my mother's kin would raise half of Kamilan in my defense.

"But I'm not sure they could win. Still less can they stop the lords of Council from backing me quietly into a corner— and keeping me there like a baited weasel until I die."

18. Feast of Harash

For generations, after their victory over Telhiron—a victory won by a goddess and a queen—the Kamils had celebrated every year, in a wild and splendid autumn festival called the Day of the Sacred Shield.

But it was always Mohr's way to take things which had belonged to the goddess, and change them into something which seemed to be his. The new priests could not forbid the victory festival; it was too popular, too deeply rooted in the passions and traditions of Kamilan. So they changed it. Once it had been held in honour of Jana, and in memory of Alyth who defeated Telhiron. Now it was held in honour of Harash, the son of Mohr, the male god of war and empire, the god whom legend called the sire of Telhiron.

It was a day given over to the glories of soldiering. There was an endless retelling of stories, and the bittersweet remembering of old wounds and old friends. By custom, no tavernkeeper charged a blooded warrior for his wine, and no woman took money from him for her favours.

The harvests were in, the trees bare, the air clean and bracing, the ground hard with frost. It was that time of the year which held a paradoxical sense of both adventure and completion. And on a plain called Althen Field, in the valley of the Magdal eight leagues from the heights of Kamilan, the city and the countryside gathered to drink and boast and admire a day-long, glittering feast of military pageantry and tournament. Most of the people stood in lines at the edges of the field, slipping away sometimes to warm themselves at the fires, and then elbowing and cursing to get their places back. Those who had horses shivered on top of them, willing to be cold and enjoy a better view. A raised stand had been built to seat guests of high rank; it was roofed and shielded from the wind. In spite of that, Kiri's hands and feet were numb, and the queen's face was pinched like a fox kit's inside its circle of fur.

Kiri sat on the royal bench, separated from the queen only by Caithland, master of the guard, and Crayfe, lord of the High Council. In the minstrel's mind an extraordinary sense of privilege collided with an equal sense of unreality. In private, she was Marwen's friend; that was one thing. But here she was a member of the queen's court, and that was different. It did not seem quite possible that the village girl from Vanthala, the ham-handed, square-jawed watchwoman from Mercanio's caravan, had found her way here. She had grown past the stage of expecting to be asked to leave. But she would probably never grow past the stage of feeling that she had somehow cheated her way in.

The day astonished her. Even in Dravia she had never seen such an eager, reckless celebration of arms, and it made her realize how much the Kamils looked upon themselves as a warrior people. The farthest-flung hilltop towns had sent out their captains, and from every valley came a lord with his retinue of men. Young boys raced and dodged amidst the crowds, chanting war cries and sparring with wooden swords. Three of the lords of Council would take their places on the field; only Angmar the sage and Theron the priest were honourably absent. Crayfe, who had never been in combat in his life, was most times a feared and powerful lord, but today he was a person of no importance at all: a fat, unmanly left-over in the world. And he knew it. He sat cloaked in malice at Caithland's side, his comments bitter and sharp as knives. He had brought with him a small leather bag of candied fruit, and he ate from it with a defiance so deliberate that Kiri could almost admire it.

It was impossible to look upon him as anything but a cruel man, cruel and corrupt. Nonetheless she wondered now if he had grown into such a vicious creature at least partly to shield himself against contempt. Kamil men were singularly proud of their horsemanship, their skill with arms, their fine bodies which they usually kept fit long after their hair was gray. And many of them, Kiri knew, looked upon a man like Crayfe as they would have looked upon a slug.

It did not excuse him. There were many kinds of honour to be had in life, even in Kamilan. But it explained, perhaps, why he had become so sharp-toothed and devious and full of hate.

The displays were impressive. There were cavalry charges and infantry manoevres. There were mock battles with blunted weapons which must have nonetheless left many painful wounds. Phalanxes formed, advanced, split, and formed again with astonishing precision. All of this would fill most of the morning. In the afternoon would come what everyone waited most to see: the tournaments. Here Kamilan's best fighters, without regard to birth or rank, competed in foot races, horse races, sword fights, pike fights, wrestling, javelin throwing, and archery.

The foot races and archery came first, Crayfe explained. Running, after all, was not what a warrior was supposed to be good at. And as for bows, well, they were like pikes: good weapons for the peasantry.

It was mid-morning when Shadrak appeared on the field. As warlord, Borosar no doubt had a hand in arranging the day's events; in any case the timing was perfect. Nearly everyone who was coming had arrived; excitement was at a peak; no one was sated yet, or so cold or hungry that they would drift away to the fires for hot drinks and food.

"What is this now?" Theron wondered.

Two huge oxen lumbered onto the field, dragging a structure Kiri had never seen before. It was a tower about twenty feet high. A braced pole extended outward from one side; at the end of the pole a straw-filled dummy dangled from a long rope.

"It's the mounted archery pageant," Caithland said, not to Crayfe but to the queen. "It's the first time we've had one. The captain of Belengar will have his chance to show us what he's been doing."

"Oh, yes, that is him, isn't it?" Crayfe said, as Shadrak rode by with a handful of his recruits. "Great Mohr, he looks like a savage. If all those animals he's wearing came back to life, it would clear the field in a hurry."

Among those blond and boyish riders Shadrak was a striking figure on a prancing horse, flamboyantly decked for war, his black hair shaggy in the wind. He led his young men to the far end of the field and spoke with them briefly. They swept in a single line towards the wooden tower, circled it once, and then broke into precision patterns, loops and spirals and reverse loops, all the time firing at the strawman which hung dizzy on its rope, swinging from the force of striking arrows. It was pretty to watch, and although it looked playfully easy, Kiri knew it was not. So did the crowd, which rewarded the archers with a surprisingly sustained burst of cheers.

"Are they praising that little bit of fancy riding," Crayfe wondered, "or the killing of Prince Held?"

"Both, I would expect," Angmar said.

Crayfe scowled. "I could understand that if he'd met the prince in a duel of honour. But as far as I have heard, Held was set upon by every Kamil who could get near him, and Shadrak hacked his head off while he was lying on his back, tangled up in a bunch of roots."

"Held refused to fight him," Marwen reminded them. "The captain challenged him, and he refused."

"He could hardly have accepted."

Marwen did not reply. Kiri thought for a time before she did so. She had been in Kamilan only a few months before; she had heard the endless, empty threats of war, the promises to march into Dravia with fire and sword, and put all of Aralev to the torch, and hang Prince Held from his own walls with his manhood stuffed in his mouth. But those who bragged so were Held's equals. It was an altogether different thing when a man who was not his equal brought him down. Denied honour himself, Shadrak was nonetheless required to offer it.

"Forgive me, Lord Crayfe," she said, "but I don't understand you. If a man scornfully refuses single combat, he can't afterwards expect its privileges in battle. Held's own arrogance was his death."

"It's not that simple, minstrel," Angmar said thoughtfully. "I don't blame the captain of Belengar. His duty was to protect the queen, and he did so. Nonetheless it was a tainted victory, and it was made worse by refusing Held the burial which any man of honour gives a noble enemy."

She stared at him, at Theron who was nodding faintly, and then at Crayfe. None of these men seemed to recognize what had really taken place. However grave Held's first act of violence against Marwen had been, his second was infinitely worse. The first time, armed with myths of conquest and with the belief that abduction was just another way of marrying, he might perhaps have made some small claim to decent if bullying intentions.

But to come back, after witnessing twenty-three months of Marwen's desolation and despair? After hearing her swear that she would rather die than give him to her people as a king? After she had thrown herself into brutal dangers to escape him? To come back yet again, as if nothing had happened, as if nothing had been said, as if she were a only a straying heifer—*(I've come to take you home!)*—to come back, and so bring death to seventeen of her men and nearly all of his own? No. Kiri shook her head. Any claim Prince Held ever had to the laws of honour or to the dignity of his rank he had left behind at the Dravian border.

"Was the prince a noble enemy?" Kiri asked. "Or a brigand who happened to wear a crown?"

There was an uncomfortable silence. Even Caithland would not look at her.

"Can you, as a Dravian, speak so against your lord?" Theron asked finally, harshly.

Crayfe smiled dryly, patronizingly. "Women," he remarked, "have never understood honour very well. I don't know why."

"Perhaps because it doesn't make very much sense," Kiri retorted. She saw the queen smile faintly.

"I think," Angmar said, "most people don't make the fine distinctions we might wish they did. Shadrak is very much a hero in the streets and the taverns, and I dare say they've had less worthy ones."

You sanctimonious, hypocritical old bastard!

Deliberately, Kiri turned her eyes back to the activities below, expecting to see the ungainly tower being dragged away again. Instead, a well-armoured soldier was climbing up to its roof.

"What on earth is he doing that for?" she asked Caithland.

"Just a guess, minstrel. But I'll wager he's going to make the strawman dance."

Shadrak rode alone to the end of the field, where a man missing one hand waited with a fresh quiver. He bent slightly from the saddle to take it, slipped the band around his shoulder, and took his bow in his hand. Every movement was at once both restless and calculated.

The long lines of clamourous watchers fell oddly quiet.

"We will see some shooting now, I think," Caithland murmured. "Watch!"

The straw man began to bounce wildly on its rope. Shadrak bent forward over the neck of his horse, gave a savage yell, and charged. She saw the bow draw and release and draw again, saw him pass the target and turn in his saddle, firing backwards, faster than she would have believed possible. The target danced like a crazy thing, speared with arrows. Shadrak reached the end of the field and galloped back. Suddenly, as though an arrow had speared him in full charge, he tumbled from his saddle. Marwen's breath caught in alarm. For one second Kiri looked away from the field and saw the queen's face stiffen with fear, and then melt into naked admiration. Crayfe's hand was frozen halfways to his slightly opened mouth, holding a forgotten piece of candied fruit.

She looked back, and saw a riderless horse thunder across the field—or riderless it seemed, but arrows were still finding their mark: the target spun from their impact. The horse swung around in a long arc and pounded back, this time on their side of the tower, and she saw the captain hanging as it seemed by a stirrup or a hair, no target at all to such enemies as might have been there, still firing his bow—now over the horse's back, now under its neck.

"Goddess of the world, he is good," Marwen breathed.

He slid back into his saddle and circled the target while they plucked the arrows out of it and held them up, one by one. The crowd counted them at the top of its lungs. Twenty-one.

Twenty-two. Twenty-three. This was not marksmanship, Kiri thought; this was magic.

"Twenty-four!"

Maybe it was mostly the cold, and the long morning; maybe they would have leapt on almost any excuse to shout like that.

"How many arrows in the quiver he had, do you think?" Kiri wondered.

"Forty-odd," the master of the guard said. "And he scored more than half of them, at a dead gallop on a moving target. Impressive, I would say. Very impressive."

"And he knows it," Crayfe observed.

Kiri had to admit that was true. Few men were given the opportunity for such a single-handed display of skill. Borosar no doubt had his reasons for showing off his captain, but Shadrak took full of advantage. His horse was restless from its wild running and he let it prance, drinking the glory like wine. From somewhere among the watchers—probably the mass of soldiers grouped near the far end—a chant had emerged, slow, rhythmic, rising with a ringing crash of shields:

"Shad-rak! Shad-rak! Shad-rak!"

It spread through the whole of Althen Field. Kiri's hackles rose on her neck.

"Holy Mohr," Crayfe said. "Do you believe this?"

"It's happened before," Angmar said calmly. "They carried Borosar all around the track on their shoulders once."

"That was Borosar."

"Precisely. Now they have one of their own."

"Their own? He's not even Kamil!"

"Will you tell him that to his face?" Angmar smiled.

Crayfe opened his mouth, thought a moment, and put a sweetmeat into it instead.

Below, Shadrak drew his long bright sword and raised it high.

"Kamilan!" he shouted. "The queen!"

And they chanted Marwen's name then, without a break in the strong, ringing beat. Kiri saw that Angmar was smiling, and it surprised her. Whatever his faults, she realized, whatever his capacity for sanctimonious hypocrisy or anything else, he revered the queen, and he was bound to her by compelling bonds of rank and honour. In his very arrogance was a kind of awesome loyalty. She would be careful to remember that.

173

She watched as the captain of Belengar rode to the edge of the field in front of the royal benches. He swept his gaudy helmet almost to the fetlocks of his horse as he bowed to his lady, and galloped out of the ring. No matter what might happen in the tournaments, Kiri thought, the rest of the day would be an afterthought.

It was.

The queen's hall was large, nearly a hundred feet long, and it was crowded as Kiri had never seen it. The feast had been lavish, with the choicest portions of everything going to the day's champions, who sat in the highest places of honour at the queen's table. Among them were Shadrak and the lord of Maene.

Kiri had been present when Harad and the queen tallied up the supplies which would be needed: two oxen, fifty hogs, one hundred chickens, four hundred loaves, forty barrels of ale and ten of wine—those were the staples. After that they discussed fruits and nuts and spices, honey and tallow, roots and small game and herbs.

Kiri had laughed. "Goddess of the world," she had said, "the Dravian army couldn't eat all of that at once."

"Watch," Marwen had retorted. "Just watch. They will eat every crumb."

She watched. Perhaps the queen's guests did not eat every crumb, but they did not fail by much. By then the room was clamourous, overheated from flaring tapers and too many people. She could feel sweat gather on her forehead, and see it on the faces of the men and women who listened to her sing. It was the feast of Harash, and the songs they wished to hear were songs of war and glory. She sang them willingly, for she loved such tales herself. She had spent weeks learning the legends of the hill queens, and the deeds of Kamil heroes. Last of all, to a room grown remarkably still, she sang the long proud ballad of Alyth's victory over Telhiron.

She had never sung so well, and it was well received. If the gathered lords and ladies noticed how pointedly she drew attention to the greatness of their ancient queens, so much the better.

She had not eaten with the others; her nerves had been too strained. But the servants made sure that choice morsels of everything had been saved for her. She took a tankard of wine and her trencher and settled gratefully into the first bit of empty space she could find. Only when she had eaten and drank the last of the wine did she realize that she was exhausted.

It was late, but no one appeared to be thinking of sleep. Some young men from Tamri had taken out their fifes and drums, and the hall was filling with wild music. The queen, as was her custom, had left her table to move among her guests; and several of the lords of Council had done the same. Lord Crayfe, still sullen and still nibbling, sat beside his wife, Lady Vanda.

Kiri always felt a little guilty when she disliked people without actually knowing them at all. But she could not help detesting this woman. Perhaps she would have detested any woman who could tolerate the seneschal. Unlike Berend's wives, who were powerless and very young, Vanda had been a widow of twenty-five when she married Crayfe—married him, apparently, of her own free will. She had helped to arrange his second marriage to the fourteen-year-old Dalia of Caerne—as a procuress, Kiri thought darkly, might have set about acquiring a particularly beautiful virgin for a favourite, well-paying customer. When Crayfe murdered the girl and her lowborn lover, Vanda's only public comment was that he ought to have gotten his bride-gifts back.

She was lovely, and as finely dressed as any Kamil woman of her rank would have been. Kiri looked at her, and then at Marwen, and marvelled at how much the eye saw what was in the mind. Of the two, it was the queen she found beautiful.

The room had grown dizzy with smoke and heat. The feast would go on yet for hours. Kiri slipped quietly away, stealing a small taper from the hall as she went.

As she walked she was still thinking about the queen and Lady Vanda, and about the whole troublesome question of beauty. Only yesterday morning Marwen had called her from the shield room, where she had gone to find a bit of privacy to practice her songs. The queen had ordered a new tunic for the Feast of Harash, but when it finally was finished, she said she did not like it. A half dozen other garments were tossed here and there about her room; she did not like them, either.

Sometimes, unexpectedly, the queen would remember that she was not beautiful. She would remember, perhaps, what the

Dravian princesses had thought of her, what Held had thought of her before her spirit and her defiance quietly seduced him:

Be thankful you have a crown on your head, lady. It would be a desperate man who would look at you otherwise.

Marwen held up her new tunic for Kiri to look at, and then tossed it over the back of a chair.

"Luned keeps telling me how beautifully dressed my mother was," she said. "That's her way of saying I am not."

Kiri sighed faintly, wondering what to answer. It was true the queen had no eye for elegance, the way the Dravian princesses did; nor did she have the personality to pursue the matter seriously. She was always doing something else. She liked sensual things: soft fabrics, perfumes, fine furs and leathers, things that glittered, whether they were valuable or not. But she would never be elegant, no more than she would ever have a curvaceous body or a stunning face. Her power to attract was starker, more elemental, and finally more compelling, as Held himself had discovered to his sorrow.

But when a young woman liked a man, she wanted to be beautiful, queen or goat girl, it did not make any difference at all.

Kiri picked up the tunic. It was finely made, of black and red silk. Warrior colours, she reflected, appropriate for the Feast of Harash, and also for the young wolf who would no doubt be sitting at her table tomorrow night, among the champions.

"Wear it, Marwen," she said. "It's pretty. And anyway, it isn't going to matter a fig what you put on. He will look at you all the same, and at very little else."

Kiri smiled to herself, thinking that Marwen looked very striking in her tunic. She walked without paying much attention. The passageway which led to the palace roofs was one she used often, even at night. The great hall was often crowded, and her own room, although she loved it, was small and a little close. She went to the ramparts a lot; they were windy and open—a good place to dream and to think.

She walked quietly, followed by huge, bounding shadows which always startled her when she caught a glimpse of them, even though she knew they were her own. She turned a corner, and at the far end of the passageway, just in front of the stairwell leading to the roof, she saw shadows which were not her own.

There was a small guardroom there, where Caithland's men kept a few supplies and came to warm themselves during their shifts on the roof. But one shadow clearly belonged to a woman, and Kiri stood still, uncertain what to do. She knew that two or three of the shield women had lovers in the guard, and no one objected to that at all. Servants had a right to their own lives.

But they were not supposed to visit while they were at work, nor in the guard rooms, nor anywhere else where the sharp lines of duty were likely to get blurred. Kiri did not want to cause trouble for anyone. At the same time, she reflected, security was too desperate a matter to allow for any carelessness at all. She doused her taper and moved closer.

She thought she heard the queen's voice.

She moved closer still, because she could not believe it. Marwen was in the great hall, surrounded by light and music and two or three hundred watching people.

But no, it *was* the queen's voice, speaking quietly—something about needing to be sure. Kiri halted in complete bewilderment, and caught the last of it.

". . . Borosar be trusted?"

The answering voice was Shadrak's. "He will support no action against you, lady. I'm sure of that."

"But would he oppose one? With arms if need be?"

A slight pause. "Probably." The captain's voice was troubled. "I'm not certain. But probably."

"And you, captain?"

"I would lead as many men in your defense as I could persuade to follow me, lady. Against anyone—even Borosar."

"I pray you will never need to. It's all quicksand around me, Shadrak. One day it seems they're all my enemies, and the next day we feast and laugh, and we're all friends."

"A man can walk a log across an abyss," the captain said, "and wonder after what it was he feared. But if a sweep of wind had come, or if the log had shifted. . . . I know your danger, lady, and I fear it."

"Then I will depend on you—not only to fight, if it comes to that, but to be watchful, and to advise me of anything you learn."

The queen's shadow hands met, parted, passed an object to her companion.

"Study the runes carefully," she said. "They are unusual. Any message, or warning, or command sent with this ring will be from me, or from someone who has my absolute trust. Heed it as though I stood before you."

He held the object a moment, and handed it back. "I will do so, lady."

Steps thumped on the stones above; Kiri heard the voices of the guards on the roof. She did not want to spy, and she had not meant to, but it was too late now to do anything except hide. She shrank into the shadows as the queen and her captain moved into the passageway.

"I will be missed, Shadrak," Marwen said regretfully. "Thank you for this meeting. I need your friendship very much, and I am grateful."

He bowed to go—a very small bow, as though he could not bear to take his eyes from her face.

"My sword is yours, lady, and my fealty, and my life."

She smiled. As he raised his head she reached to brush her hand across his bearded cheek.

It was not the sort of gesture Kiri would ever have called wanton. Yet in that moment, in that place, it was. There was nothing impulsive in it, or girlish. The queen's face was soft, but it was a woman's face, speculative and hungry. She caressed Shadrak's cheek as though she would willingly have caressed every part of his body, without restraint, there where they stood.

Kiri heard the captain's sharply indrawn breath. For a brief, exquisite moment he did not stir; then he reached quickly for the queen's hand, but she was already drawing it away.

"Lady. . . ."

"Farewell, Shadrak. May Jana keep you safe."

A door opened above, and a spill of light and voices tumbled down the stairwell.

"I will not fail you," he said then, simply. Armed and booted though he was, he was gone without a sound, like a wolf slipping into the night.

"Are you in love with him, lady?" Kiri asked.

It was the night after the Festival of Harash. They sat alone in the queen's chamber, on thick furs before the hearth. Often they would share a glass of wine before they slept; tonight they only talked. They had both drank more wine yesterday than enough.

"I think he's beautiful." The queen looked curiously at her minstrel. "Don't you?"

"For my own taste, no. But I can see what you admire."

"And what do you think I admire?"

"Grace of body. Daring. Passion. And you're also drawn to him because he's . . . different."

"What do you mean, different?"

Kiri smiled wryly. "When you asked me if he was beautiful, I should have said yes, and shut my mouth."

"But you didn't. What do you mean by different?"

Kiri groped for an answer somewhere between being honest and being careful.

"He is dark, and Thyrsian, and slaveborn, and I would suspect he was half wolf, too, except for his way with horses. And you're sick to death of princes and lords and priests, sick of men who want to cage you and buy you and sell you. What better way could there be to scorn them all?"

Marwen was thoughtful for a time, much like someone weighing a new and unexpected idea.

"You're shrewd, Kiri," she said finally. "But there's another side to it. Shadrak is not unworthy of being loved, even by a queen. They may think he is, but I do not. If I wanted to drag my honour down to spite them, it wouldn't be with him. He deserves better."

"You care for him a good deal, I think."

Marwen looked at her hands, turning the small bronze ring she always wore, the ring she had shown him as a token.

"Perhaps," she said. "I want him. I wanted him at Belengar, the night of the feast, and dear goddess, how he wanted me! Had I never been to Dravia. . . . But it was too soon. I didn't trust my own judgment; I dared not. I was terrified that I might find myself alone with him, and turn to stone.

"I don't know what to tell you, Kiri. What does it mean to ask me if I love a man? If I say yes I will lie, and if I say no I will lie as well. We can be very precise about killing; we have words enough for that. We can say a man was knifed or speared or garroted or drowned or poisoned. But I have only one word to name what I feel for you and Kamilan and Medwina and a good piece of roast venison and my kinsmen and my goddess and the palace cats. What is left for the wolf of Dohann? I will say that he's beautiful, and leave it so."

"I think," Kiri said, "you've answered me well enough."

"Don't jump to conclusions."

"One conclusion is certain enough: you will bed with him the first chance you get."

Marwen smiled faintly. "Do you disapprove?"

"No, of course not, lady. You know me better than that. Only . . . only it is still soon. Will you be all right?"

Marwen watched the fire. "I think so. I have other memories than Held. I know how good it can be." She paused, and added wryly: "You're surprised. Did you think I went to Dravia a virgin?"

"I don't think I thought about it at all. But if I had, I suppose I would have expected that. You were raised in a royal house, and you were very young."

"Not that young. I had danced through a festival or two. And the royal house of Kamilan is the house of the hill queens, and they were always free, and proud of it.

"There's a story we remember about Telhiron—a story you probably never heard, because they don't tell it in Dravia. After he had slashed his way through half of Kamilan, pillaging and raping, he arranged a parley with Alyth to demand her surrender. It led only to insults. He called her a whore, and he told her scornfully that his men had not yet found a virgin in all of Kamilan. And she said to him: 'I'm glad of that. I thank the goddess our women will have something better to remember than you.' "

"Ohhh. . . ." Kiri let out her breath with a slow smile. "I rather like that story."

"So do I. I told it to Prince Held one day."

"That was a mistake, I expect."

"Yes. It was a mistake. But it taught me something. Alyth defied Telhiron with a shield in her hand and an army at her back. Without those things she would have been nothing more than I was: a prize of war, a piece of booty in a tent.

"And I will tell you one thing more: I want Shadrak for himself, for his grace of body and his daring and his passion, as you put it; you describe him well. But he is also the wolf of Dohann. And that's part of what I see when I look at him and find him beautiful."

Their eyes met, and held, and fell.

"Lady," Kiri said at last, "don't you see the contradiction in that?"

"Yes," the queen said softly. "I see it very well. But I can't do anything about it.

"Kamilan was first built on the banks of the Magdal, did you know that? Who would choose to live on a stormswept mountain, when the valleys were sheltered and rich, and the fields could be close at hand? There was nothing up here once except a watchtower and a shrine."

"But I thought the Kamils were a warrior people since . . . since the first beginnings."

"In a way, perhaps. We loved our bright shields and our songs, and we could fight. Enemies who crossed the mountains rarely crossed back again. But we lived on hunting and farming and trade, not on plunder. There were no slaves; a Kamil in those days would have been ashamed to lead another human being around on a chain like a dog. And a cattle raid into Dravia every year or two was enough to keep the warriors' blood up.

"Then the invasions began. Small ones first; we just absorbed them. Then bigger ones. War became common. The valley towns were abandoned—all of them except Tamri— and the fortress towns were built, like this one, remote and high and cold. By the time Telhiron led his army across half the world, we had already changed. Had we not, he would have mowed us down like summer grass.

"I have no answer, Kiri. None at all. Medwina says the world is falling into darkness, and it may be so. But I still must choose. And I will follow Alyth. I will fight."

"And so will Shadrak."

"Aye. Better than anyone. He has a gift for it." She paused, and added ruefully: "If I were Alyth, I could invite him to the palace for a splendid feast, and we would lay together after, all night and for as many nights as we wished. And my friends would smile and say the queen had found herself a fine young wolf to run with. Oh, there would be a few black looks from highborn lords who thought themselves slighted, and black words as well: what kind of queen, they would say, beds down with a mere border captain, and a freedman to boot?

"But in the end they would shrug and accept it. They would say, well, it's her choice. She has no sense of things at all, but it's her choice . . . if I were Alyth, and this were Alyth's world.

"If I did it now, I would destroy us both."

19. Marrying

Autumn edged into winter. Snow fell in the passes of Dohann, and the herds of sheep and cattle came down from the hills. Woodcutters went into the forests by the hundreds, gathering fuel for the high city and dragging it in long caravans up the brutal mountain roads.

The suitors came.

One by one, decked out in their finery, laden with gifts, mounted on fine horses, surrounded by retainers and slaves, they came to pay court to the queen. The first of them came before the Feast of Harash, while the leaves were still yellow on the trees. The last came in snow.

They were, Angmar had said, men of suitable age and worthy character. Mostly that was true, though they numbered in their ranks a lad of fourteen and a widower of fifty-seven. One of them had put his wife to death for taking a lover. Another had not paid his tribute to the crown for seven years, though his men went out after every harvest and took a quarter of the crops and the calves and the wool. The standards by which men measured the worth of other men, the queen decided, were very generous . . . if the men had rank, of course. If they did not, no measure of worth was ever great enough.

She spent little time on them. She had other things to do. The city food stores were barely half enough for the winter; she spent a fortnight merely arranging to have them increased. She sent fresh delegations out after unpaid tribute. She visited the tin mines of Getann, and all the garrisons and forts which guarded the royal city. She spent whole days and half nights with Borosar's staff and sometimes with the warlord himself. All the border posts except Belengar had been ill-kept for years, he told her. The roads needed tending, if an army was to move freely and be properly supplied. And as for the supplies themselves, they had to be counted, replenished, transported, and safely stored.

What, she wondered, had Council been doing for the last four years? If men were so wise, so competent, so fit to rule, why was Kamilan in such disarray? Why was her marriage always the first thing on their minds, when it was the last thing on hers?

It seemed all they thought of, this business of marrying. They judged it far more important than food, or firewood, or broken wagon frames, or arrowheads, or hungry peasants. Angmar could barely hide his irritation when she kept his smiling suitors waiting—for hours sometimes, or even half a day. One young lord she received in her travelling clothes, with mud on her boots, and afterwards the sage had shaken his head and said,

"Lady, are you *trying* to offend every man who approaches you?"

"If it offends them to see that their queen must work, and that she does so without pretense, then I don't want them."

Angmar looked at the fire. When he spoke again it was with some difficulty.

"Lady, I will tell you honestly, I'm impressed with your seriousness and your ability. In truth, I didn't expect it of you. I admit that in all humility, and I regret my lack of faith very much. Will it seem incomprehensible now if I say that the more admirable and capable you are, the more urgent it becomes that you marry—the more urgent it becomes that you save yourself?"

Save myself? she mused silently. *Why, sage, is it my duty to save myself? Why is it not* their *duty not to destroy me?*

"I will marry, Angmar. But I will think before I do. You'll have to accept that."

It was snowing when Valdemar came. He was Lord Crayfe's cousin, a man well into his thirties, weathered and unbeautiful. He had been married some years before to a child bride, chosen by his father. According to the stories which were told about him, he had grown to love her passionately, and he had grieved for years when she died in childbirth.

He seemed a gentle man, well spoken, and wise in a fashion. The queen's youth appealed to him much more than did her rank, and she knew why. He wanted a woman who would adore him, who would wrap her life around his own and never want anyone else. In return he would love her very well.

She sent him back into the softly falling snow, and sent word to Angmar the Wise: *No more. I will see no one else.*

The temple was cold. There was only ash left on the altar stone, and only wind left in the world. It swept down the valley of the Magdal, gray and tasting of snow; it flung dead leaves against the windows, and clawed at the thatch roof. It filled her with a deep and quiet fear, with memories of long nights in Dravia when the only warmth in the room was a dying hearth and the sleeping body of the prince. She had crept to him sometimes like a cat, without waking him, taking his warmth, hating him more for the need of it.

Marriage by contract and marriage by capture were not all that much different, she reflected—not for the woman herself. It was no wonder Berend's wives had looked at her with their soft, uncomprehending eyes and asked themselves why she was so unhappy. Freedom—real freedom, as a daughter of Alyth understood it—freedom did not exist for them any more.

No more than it did for Angmar the Wise. When they spoke that first time, he had looked at her as though she were a forest creature, some kind of snarling animal which could be quieted perhaps, but never reasoned with. They had no common ground for argument. Of course women married according to considerations of rank, dynasty, and power. Male rank, male dynasty, male power.

Yes, men would offer them rewards. Men could easily do so; they controlled them all. *Do you want to eat well, woman?— do you want, perhaps, to eat at all? Do you want your children to make their way in the world? Do you want a wall and a sword between yourself and a world of ravishers and thieves? Marry me then, and build my fortune, and breed my sons.*

Save yourself!

What began as necessity in the face of conquest was quickly turned into virtue, into the order of the universe and the will of the gods. It was not discussed; it was how things *were*. Only a foolish child imagined that she might mate where she pleased, and bear her children when she was ready. Any choice at all was considered a privilege. A man was praised to Mohr's feast halls if he allowed his daughter to refuse a profitable match with an old lecher or a drunken fool. And she, mistress of Kamilan and daughter of the hill queens, should be grateful to tears to have a choice of sixteen highorn men of worthy character, still potent, and with all their teeth. What more could she possibly desire?

Marry one of them, Angmar said, or be destroyed. And he was outraged when she called it whoredom.

She placed the stones on the altar—sixteen small painted stones, all of them the same except for their colours. Smooth, cold, indecipherable. Lethal. Stones like these, flung from a simple sling, could kill.

She took one of them, and set it apart from the others, as in her mind, day upon day, she had begun to think of one of these men apart from the others, not with love, but with quiet calculation. If whoredom was what the world of men required of her, then that was what the world of men would get. But she did not want to make the decision utterly alone.

She bowed her head.

"Jana, I swore an oath in Aralev, and I will keep it, but to keep it I must rule here. Wise one, mother of the world, guide me now. For the sake of Kamilan, for the sake of all which has been lost to us, which can be yet regained, I beg you to help me. Tell me who to choose."

She knelt thus for a long time, aware of nothing but the wind, and the chill closing around her body like a shroud. She looked up at the sound of movement, and caught her breath. A wolf sat quietly on the other side of the altar—a large wolf, gray-black and powerful, watching her with ancient, cunning eyes. The same wolf. This time she felt no fear. She said nothing for a time, but waited. It seemed the wind would tear the temple into pieces, and scatter it across the world.

—*So, Wolf. Will you counsel me?*

—*You know your own heart.*

—*If what was in my heart mattered to anyone, I would not seek this counsel. Tell me who to marry.*

—*Marry who you must.*

—*That is no help at all.*

The wolf licked its paws. She challenged the animal then, bitterly:

—*Why did you come, if this is all you can offer me?*

It stood up, shaking itself a little, as if to leave.

"Wait!" she whispered aloud. "I'm sorry. You have your own purposes. But can you tell me nothing more?"

—*My purposes will be fulfilled. You are the one I seek, if you have the courage. Remember Belengar, daughter of Alyth. Remember Belengar, and wait for Tamri!*

It was gone. The single taper on the wall gulped and went out.

She sat back on her heels and stared into the darkness.

So that was how it was to be, then: she must choose for herself, without signs and without light. And she must take into her life a man she did not know, and could not trust, and would not love, as a child played pebble games behind its own back.

"What would you do in my place, Kiri?"

"You know perfectly well what I'd do, lady. Pack as many of my things as I could carry, sling my crossbow over my shoulder, and go to find Mercanio. But then, no one cares what I do—at least, they don't care enough to stop me." She pulled her fur cape tight around her neck. "I don't know if it was by accident or by choice, but I made sure of that quite early in my life."

"I envy you sometimes."

"Then we are even, lady."

"Really? I never saw you as someone with an appetite for power."

"Power, no. I wouldn't be queen for anything. I'm a teller of stories, Marwen, nothing else. If I had twenty lifetimes I would still be that. But. . . ."

She paused. She was singularly open about most things; it surprised the queen to see her look away, across the ramparts towards mountains they could no longer see for blowing snow.

"Sometimes," she said, "the singer would rather live the tale than tell it."

"But you did, Kiri," Marwen whispered.

"Yes . . . briefly. I may do so again . . . briefly. I touch life in passing, that is all." She shrugged. "You asked me what I envied."

"Would you like my sixteen suitors?" Marwen said. "You can have every one of them."

They laughed, and for a moment they watched the city pass below them: wagoners with slow-moving loads of wood, painfully creeping up the mountain roads; soldiers on horseback, bent against the bitter wind; children who ran as they ran in summer, and threw snowballs at each other; hurrying slaves, and women with their baskets, muffled like thieves, nothing showing of their faces but their eyes.

"You sent Valdemar away even quicker than the others," Kiri noted.

"Yes," Marwen said. "I liked him better than the others. In a way, I liked him better. He's a good man. How can I say this, Kiri?—he's a good man, but he understands nothing of the world. Crayfe would twist him this way and that like a piece of clay. As for me. . . ." She paused, and began again.

"He made me realize something, Kiri. I will never be a wife. I will marry, because Council demands it, but I will never be a wife. What Valdemar would ask of me I won't give to any man, not even one I loved. And he would never understand why I didn't. He would hold out his hands in bewilderment to all the world: *Look! I loved her so, and look what she has done to me. . . !*

"No, Kiri. Mohr has made marriage half marketplace and half camp of war. So be it. I'm going to marry for power, and I'm not going to pretend otherwise. And if one day my husband and I cross swords, at least we'll both know why."

Neither spoke for a time. The queen leaned her back against the rampart and let the snow tumble over her face. She felt herself dissolve into the storm, become one with it, powerful and cold as the wind, vulnerable as a snowflake.

Remember Belengar, and wait for Tamri . . . !

And what shall I remember about Belengar? The border, the cruel mountains, the feast, the dancing soldiers who made me a crown of gold leaves, the arrow that missed by a breath being fired into my heart?

Shadrak?

Shadrak who carries the wolf on his shield and in his blood, and hungers for me like a beggar in the snow . . . ?

She tasted the flakes against her teeth, felt the wind's fury wrap her body and turn itself to fire. She felt Jana's power all around her.

The goddess still lived in Dohann. She was not dead; she still blew the wind from her throat and spun the winter from her hair. She was cornered, perhaps, but only fiercer for that, and more cunning.

So, Mohr, hard god of cages and logic and war, you have not yet imprisoned all of us, nor persuaded us, nor killed us. And until you do, it will not be over. There is still one left of the sorceress queens. There is still blood in my veins, and strength in my will, and hate in my heart. Harry me as you choose, I will have my wolf, and I will have my kingdom. I will leave you the bones of those you send against me . . . aye, or I will leave my own, for the earth to fashion into some other creature, one who takes more willingly to cages than I!

She turned, resting her elbows on the tower wall, close beside Kiri's own.

"I will marry," she said softly. "One moonturn after the feast of midwinter I will take a consort. What happens after that is between the gods."

They went down from the ramparts, and the queen called for one of her couriers. She did not send him to Angmar. She sent him directly to the valley fortress of Maene, with an invitation to Lord Landis: the queen wished to dine with him, and to discuss the future of Kamilan.

"Shall we speak frankly, Lord Landis?" she asked.

"Indeed, lady. Nothing would please me more."

They had dined elegantly and well. They had wandered with the idleness of old friends to the shield room, where the fire burned high in the hearth, and a flagon of wine had been set out with two gold cups. They had toasted each other, sipped politely, and put the cups down. There was nothing left to do except speak frankly.

Marwen began. "Angmar has advised me that a marriage between you and myself would please you, and would be of great benefit to Kamilan."

"That is true, lady. I trust also that such a marriage would be pleasing to you?"

"I have asked for honesty, Landis, so I will give it. I would prefer not to marry at all. My heart isn't in it."

"Because of Dravia," he said. It was not quite a statement, not quite a question.

She was surprised. At the very least, the man was perceptive.

"What terms would you set for such a marriage, Lord Landis? What do you want?"

"I want nothing, lady, except to serve Kamilan, and honour you. And to see our son grow up to be a king."

"Nothing more?" She smiled, and saw that the smile made him faintly uneasy. "Then perhaps I should first tell you what I want. I made a sacred oath in Aralev. You're a man of honour; you know how binding such an oath must be."

"Indeed, lady. That is why I've never made one."

"I was a prisoner, and a prisoner will do many things in the hope of freedom. I swore that if I returned safely to Kamilan, I would restore the temple of Jana, and live according to her rites and laws. I mean to keep that oath. The man I choose for my consort must support me in this."

She saw him frown, and added hastily: "I command no one's beliefs, or choice of gods. That is Mohr's way, not Jana's. But I mean to restore the temple, and give the priestesses their rightful place of honour in the land. And then let the people choose whom they will worship.

"If I marry you, Landis, I'll expect your support in Council to make this possible. The goddess is well loved among the people; they will not object. But Theron and the priests of Mohr will be outraged. And so will those among the lords who have turned completely against the goddess."

She did not mention that Angmar was one of those. "They will try to stop me—and Theron, at least, is not above using violence. You're a man of high rank and great prestige. If you are seen to support me in this, many who might otherwise yield to Theron out of fear will stand their ground."

She picked up her wine cup and sipped it, so as to wait without seeming to do so. She could see that he was surprised, and that he was weighing it—weighing it less as a question of religion, she suspected, than as a question of strategy: What would be required of him, and what would it lead to? Would he make too many enemies? Did it matter how many enemies he made, if he had the queen? She had phrased the matter quite deliberately as a conflict with the high priest, for she knew that Landis detested Theron, and would be glad to see Theron's power undermined.

"Lady," he said, "I respect your oath, and I understand that you would wish to keep it. But surely you don't expect to restore the old religion from one day to the next?"

"That's how it was condemned," she said. "The Council met, my father expressed his judgment, the lords concurred. The palace garrison was called out, the priestesses were told to gather their belongings, and the temple doors were nailed shut.

"They can be opened the same way. That's what I am asking, Landis. Will you support me?"

"If it's that important to you, lady, yes." He spoke slowly, as though he were choosing his words with great care. "I'm not much concerned about the old religion one way or the other. Some men see harm in it; I do not. If you wish to keep your oath and re-open the temple, as your husband I would stand with you in doing so."

She watched him. A slender, poised, remote man. Intelligent, and not easily surprised. Perhaps also not easily moved. She could like him, she thought. There was something of Angmar's fine mind in him, and something of Caithland's cool resourcefulness. But he was an absolute stranger; neither in Council nor anywhere else had he shown her his inner self. If it matched his poise, his thoughtful and civilized demeanor, then she was choosing well. If it did not. . . .

If it did not, she thought, she would have an enemy who would make her regret Prince Held.

"I will marry you then," she said, "if you wish it. After the midwinter festival, according to the rites of Jana and the Laws of Kind."

She had wondered if anything could shake his calm. That did.

"The Laws of Kind? Lady, forgive me, you can't be serious! The Laws of Kind are . . . they are old and discredited!"

"Not among the people."

"We're not peasants!"

He read her face, and changed direction quickly. "Why did you say nothing of this to Angmar?"

"I'm not marrying Angmar."

"Lady, a wife married according to the Laws of Kind has no more rights or honour than a concubine. I would not so demean my queen."

"You're wrong, Landis. The traditional marriages are lawful. Even the priests of Mohr acknowledge them, for if a woman leaves her husband they accuse her of adultery—how could they do so, if they did not agree that she was married?"

"It's primitive and uncivilized. I can't see how you would consider it."

"But you said you didn't care about the old religion, one way or the other. How can you object to this? How can I tell ordinary Kamil people they can live by their beliefs, when I as queen refuse to do so?"

Landis was still, like a man who had bumped into something very sharp in the dark. He had lied when he said he did not care about the old religion, she thought. He strongly preferred the gods of men. But it was unlikely that he realized how closely religion was tied to power. It would take some time—years, perhaps—until he did. By then, please Jana, it would be too late.

"I can't claim to serve the goddess and not marry by her laws," she said. "I will not yield in this. I can't."

Not unless I have to. Not unless sixteen men rivalling for a chance at kingship can come together, and agree not make that bargain with me, and trust each other to keep the agreement? Goddess preserve us, how much chance is there of that? How much chance is there that even you will leave this room without the bargain made, and so risk that I might make it with another?

"Lady, you said we should speak freely."

"I did."

"By the Laws of Kind, after we have an heir, or if two years pass without one, you will be free to discard me, and marry anyone else who suits you better! What sort of marriage is that?"

Landis was not normally so blunt. Perhaps he did not see the long term implications of goddess rule, but a traditional marriage had clear short term implications for an ambitious man. The fact that he would have the same freedom to leave her was irrelevant; she was the queen. She chose her words very carefully.

"You wrong me, Landis—for why should I discard you? You are of the noblest lineage, and young, and honourable. That will be just as true two years from now, or ten years, as it is today. We're making a political alliance; we can't pretend otherwise. If we come to love each other, the Laws of Kind are not going to stand in our way. If we don't, you will be no more bound than I am, and no more free. You will still be prince consort, with all the rights and honours of your rank. Do you think that I would give you less?"

He flushed faintly. "No, lady. That wasn't what I meant."

Perhaps not, she countered silently. *But when men marry by the laws of Mohr, should the bride say to her husband: How do I know that you will not abuse me, and bring home concubines, and marry as many new wives as you wish, and leave me as nothing but a servant in your house, with no right to leave, and no rights even to my children? How do I know that you will not come and go as you please, and scorn my affections—aye, and murder me, too, if I turn in my loneliness to someone else?—for all of that is possible.*

The Laws of Kind said that a man and a woman were free and equal. One could not command the other. They could not ask of each other what they themselves would not give, and they could not be compelled to stay together. Mohr, great god of slaves and conquerors, might well ask: What kind of marriage is that?

"I have no wish to wrong you, Landis. I asked for this meeting, and spoke as frankly as I did, so that we might understand each other from the start. I'm not asking you to love me. I will not question where you take your pleasure, or where you give your heart. Your bond will be only to the queen of Kamilan, to support and to defend her; I'll keep no consort who is disloyal. And my bond will be only to the first lord of

Kamilan, to a prince and an ally. That's all I ask of you, Landis, and that's all I can promise. Do you accept?"

"A handfast marriage, lady? No more than that, to shield a kingdom?"

"The hill queens married so, and the kingdom was better shielded than it is now."

He hesitated. He had probably dreamed of this marriage since she was twelve or so. He had remained single in the driven hope of it, and yet he hesitated. Every bride had to make a naked leap of trust, but for her husband to do the same—oh goddess, that was different!

"Yes," he said. He raised his wine cup. His eyes were like blue slate, unreadable except for a small gleam of triumph. "You're a strange, hard creature, queen of Kamilan. But yes, I will marry you. Yes!"

In an unexpected gesture of abandon, he drained the wine without stopping, and laughed.

"May I kiss you?" he asked.

She smiled, put the cup down, and slipped her arms around his neck. He kissed her hungrily, but it seemed to her that he was kissing only the queen, the sceptre, the bright sheen of power. She felt his phallus harden against her.

"Let's go to the hall," she said softly, "and tell them all."

Ring the bells and sound the trumpets; shout it into all the winds of Kamilan, lest I lie awake tonight and weep, and change my mind!

20. In the Temple of Jana

Shadrak awoke in icy darkness. For a moment he did not know where he was. He heard the wind tugging at the roof, heard the harsh sounds of men dragging themselves out of sleep, cursing, making fires, banging doors and stumbling into furniture.

Althen Garrison....

He was back, then, in his own bunk. The room was bitter cold. The fire had gone out. Perhaps he had forgotten to replenish it; he had been so tired. He closed his eyes. The thong was still about his neck, and the ring was still on it. He could feel the faint ridges of its runes against his fingertips. It had not been a dream, then. He let himself remember.

Remember all of it, moment by moment, from the beginning....

It was sometime after noon, on the eve of the Festival of Sunturning, when the messenger came to Althen Garrison: a darkly cloaked figure so muffled he could not recognize it even as male or female. The voice, too, was indeterminate.

"You are Shadrak of Belengar?"

"Yes."

"You have been summoned by the high priestess of Jana, the lady Medwina." A gloved hand held up a ring. "Do you recognize this token?"

Any message, or warning, or command sent with this ring will be from me, or from someone who has my absolute trust. Heed it as though I stood before you!

"Aye," he said. "I recognize it well."

"Then come with me. Tell no one, but come at once, and come alone."

He stared at the messenger, trying to perceive a face, but there were only eyes reddened with cold. Snow still clung in little ridges on the stranger's cloak.

A thousand terrors flashed through Shadrak's mind. The queen's position, although it was holding, was extremely vulnerable. There had been no plots—not yet, but there was talk enough, and an awareness everywhere that men were watching and biding their time, waiting to see how events unfolded. The announcement of her coming marriage to Landis of Maene had eased his fear a little, painful though it was to think of her marrying anyone. Landis was powerful, and for the time being at least he would protect her. On the other hand, Shadrak reflected, the very fact that she had made her choice might well have moved some other lord to mutiny.

"Wait!" he said, and went to fetch his cloak and mittens.

Cassian sat by a window in the barracks hall, a scatter of mended and unmended bows laying at his feet. He looked up in surprise when Shadrak strode in and began to pull on his winter clothing.

"I thought you wanted us to finish—" he began.

"Finish," Shadrak said shortly. "And then go. Don't wait for me."

He tramped out again; Tamon and Cassian both dropped their work and followed him.

"Surely you not be goin' off, captain?" Tamon demanded. "Not by yourself like this? It be snowin' and cold." He glared at the messenger. "And who be that?"

Tamon was always respectful. When he sounded otherwise, he was frightened. For a second Shadrak felt that fear in his own throat. It was reckless to ride off alone with a messenger he did not know, a messenger who did not even show his face.

But the fear passed again. If he could not trust the queen's token, then he could trust nothing in the world.

"Leave it be, Tamon," he said. "I know what I'm doing. Go to the Festival, both of you." He smiled faintly, wryly. "Bed a pretty girl for me, and I will drain a cup for you. Is that a fair exchange?"

Cassian called after him, his voice taut with concern and disappointment. They had looked forward to enjoying the Festival together. Shadrak did not answer or look back.

They rode for more than an hour. It was snowing lightly. The wind was not strong, but it seemed to cut through his clothing like a knife. All around them the landscape huddled under a grey, descending sky. Bunched cattle stood with their heads down, their backs to the wind. Peasant huts sent up wisps of white smoke, scattering desolately in the wind. Shadrak and his companion passed a few travellers at first. Then the guide turned off the main road from Althen and led him into the forest; after that they passed no one at all. By then his hands and his feet were numb with cold, and his concern deepened. Surely Medwina would not send for him on such a bitter day unless there was grave need.

They came at last to a long low building, rising gray and shapeless in the gray light. Except for the smoke which drifted from its chimneys, it seemed utterly desolate and deserted. Icicles hung from the roof, and snow lay heavy against its sides. The messenger led him to a small doorway near one end of the building, and pulled it open without knocking.

The first rush of air within was warm and damp. It was obviously a kind of anteroom, barely furnished, and lit with a flickering taper. Only one person was there, an elderly servant who rose at once to greet him, bowing slightly.

"Welcome, Shadrak of Belengar."

He looked around. In the center of the room was a large bath, and cauldrons of water hung over a brazier, steaming in the chill. Nearby, laid out neatly on a bench, were articles of clothing which even in this poor light he could see were very fine.

These were no more than common courtesies offered by the Kamils to their guests, especially to those who had travelled far, or in harsh conditions. But at this moment they were utterly unexpected. He turned sharply to the messenger.

"I thought the high priestess wished to see me at once!"

"She will certainly wait until you have had a chance to refresh yourself, and get the winter out of your bones."

"But. . . ." He faltered. "There is no danger, then?"

"Danger?"

"To the queen. I thought there was a crisis of some kind."

"Not at all. I'm sorry you were alarmed. I would have told you if I had known. You have been summoned to meet the high priestess, and to honour the goddess on this most sacred of all her feast days."

"Oh." Absently, Shadrak took the cup the servant handed to him. The drink was hot and spicy and there was wine in it. "I wish I had known," he said. "I brought no offerings of any kind."

"Surely you have some coins in your pouch," the messenger said. "They will suffice. I will leave you now; Seldon will take care of you. Don't worry about your horse. It will be fed and sheltered." He bowed faintly and turned to go. The door opened with a rush of bitter air, and closed again.

Shadrak drained the cup quickly, craving the warmth of it. He was swept by relief. There was no crisis. The queen was not in danger.

Then, when he had a moment to think about it, he was swept also by annoyance. If there was no crisis, why did Medwina need to see him today? It was Sunturning, and tonight the whole of Kamilan would revel. The tavern roofs would shudder with the sound of drums and dancing feet. Laughing women with masks on their faces would hang their arms around his neck, and press their bodies close, and maybe when the dance was ended one of them would lay with him, and laugh, and dance away again, nameless and still laughing. At Festival all women were the goddess—infinitely generous and infinitely elusive.

He sighed. He was starved for pleasure. He had spent too many Festivals in tents and trenches and desolate border posts. Now, living four leagues from the royal city, he did not want to spend this one in a broken-down temple in the woods.

Was it asking too much of the wise and worthy to ask them to remember how much small things mattered, when small things were all a man had?

"Well." He put the empty cup down. It was still early. Perhaps Medwina would not keep him long. He nodded at the servant to pour the bath for him, stripped quickly, and jumped in.

He stepped through the door into the temple sanctuary thinking of nothing except that with luck he might still enjoy the Festival. The thought was gone before the door closed behind him; from that moment his life would never be the same.

He had seen Medwina only once before, at night and from some distance, in the camp where she came to welcome the queen. He remembered very little, and he might well have disbelieved that this tangle-haired, twisted crone was the high priestess of Kamilan, except that, dreadful as she seemed, he sensed in her an ancient and compelling power.

She wore a loose robe which hung to her ankles. It was thin and open to the waist, where it was belted with an embroidered sash. He could see the gaunt outlines of her limbs, and the hanging flesh of her breasts. She was aging and drawn, but there was no mistaking the sensuality of her dress—or of his own. She had laid out for him a beautifully embroidered tunic which fell to mid-thigh, sleeveless, with a fine gold belt, and soft shoes for his feet—garments which would serve equally for a temple or a bedchamber.

Or a sacrificial altar. . . .

The room was bare and cold; the altar stone stank of old ashes; the tapers smoked and guttered.

"Enter or depart, Shadrak," she said coldly. "But close the door."

He could not move. He was overwhelmed with humiliation and despair. This woman who was the face of the goddess on earth was nothing but a spent harridan, coarse and sordid, staring at him greedily across an empty, ruined shrine. He could feel time in her like a mountain—time and blood, and the awfulness of death, and the darkness of cunning.

The followers of Mohr were right, he thought numbly. There was nothing left of Jana, just old twisted dreams of power, old lusts, old treacheries. Who would worship in such a temple as this? What deity would accept such worship? And what, in the name of all the gods that might be, what was he doing here, dressed like a lover for this carnivorous hag?

Enter or depart. . . !

Depart to what?

Althen Garrison. Dohann. War and pain and death, and nothing at all between him and the closing sky.

Jana had always been there . . . she of the clouds and the soft rains, of the signs in the wind and the grass and the broken leaf. She of the floods which drowned the hosts of Telhiron, and the roots which closed around the bones of Prince Held. He did not know what she was, perhaps a failing goddess, imaged in this failing sorceress. But she had shielded him, guided him, kept him whole. With her, he was still a warrior of Kamilan. Without her, he was a grain of salt in a stream, dissolving and scattering into the void.

He pulled the door shut behind him, walked across the room, and knelt before the priestess, placing his few coins on the burnt stone at her feet.

"Why have you come to the house of Jana, Shadrak of Belengar?"

"To honour the goddess, and to seek her protection."

"You must swear an oath then, that all which passes here, and all which is spoken, and even the fact that you have been here at all, will never be revealed by you to anyone. A sacred oath, Shadrak, which if forsworn will bring you to ruin. But you must take it, or withdraw."

He hesitated. Such an oath, sworn beforehand, was profoundly dangerous; and though he gave the priestess homage, he could not forget the dark fear she had stirred in him.

Yet she had sent for him with Marwen's ring. She had Marwen's absolute trust.

"I will swear." For a moment he could picture Cassian standing before him, shaking his head: *You are mad, my friend*, Cassian would say; *you are completely mad.*

He bowed deeply and repeated the oath. Her hand closed gently on his shoulder, motioning him to his feet.

Perhaps it was a sorcery of the light, or of her will, or perhaps he had only changed inside himself. But she no longer seemed terrible. She seemed, in fact, a magnificent woman. The sharp lines of her face must have been exquisite once, and there was majesty in her, and the wise blood of the hill queens. And although she looked at him with the frank appreciation of a woman who had known men and liked them more than well enough, that regard was only one of many things in her face. Mostly there was sadness.

"The goddess is not always beautiful, Shadrak," she said softly. "Those who turned their faces away from her, to worship her sons—they could not bear that. They could not forgive her for reminding them that they would die. As I will. And you. And everything which lives upon the world. Kamilan itself will one day be dissolved and gone, and the earth and the stars, too, and the young gods who imagine they are eternal. And there will again be only her, who gave birth to all, and to whom all will return to be born again, utterly different, for only so is infinity possible.

"I don't ask you to believe this, for it is so, and it will continue to be so whether you believe it or not. For your own sake only do I counsel you. Never trade life for immortality. That's a fool's bargain; it will leave you with neither. It is the bargain which will undo us all."

There followed a silence, whether long or short he did not know; but he knew that coming here was worth more to him now than any Festival which might have burned the winter from the streets of Kamilan.

"I'm sorry I doubted you, priestess."

She smiled. "And I'm sorry I tested you so harshly."

"Tested me? Then what you showed to me was. . . ?"

"Absolutely real. What would it serve to test a man with lies? I am old, Shadrak, and nearly used up. And yet I have great power, for I am cunning, and devious, and sometimes malevolent—yes, and sometimes lustful, too, and I don't care who knows it. I'm not soft, as men imagine women should be; I can be an enemy to fear. What you saw was real. It was a face of the goddess, and of woman, and also of man, though many men refuse to admit it. They won't look on dark and light and see themselves. They must have witches and whores to carry their darkness for them.

"I saw how it wounded you to see me thus. But I needed to know how strong was your faith in Jana, and your courage. I don't mean your courage as a warrior, for that is known to everyone. But there are other kinds of courage. I'm not disappointed in you, Shadrak."

He bowed faintly. "I am honoured, priestess."

She walked to a table, moving slowly to minimize her crippling, and brought back two small cups of wine.

He thanked her, and drank. The wine was spiced and potent, and sent a shock of fire into his blood. He looked curiously at the cup, and then at her.

"The nights of Sunturning are long," she said dryly. Then, with no warning at all, the smile faded from her lips and from her eyes.

"Do you love the queen, wolf of Belengar?" she asked.

He froze, the cup poised at his lips, knowing not what the question meant, or how he might answer it, except that he knew he dared not lie.

"I love and honour my queen with all my heart," he said carefully, "and I serve her loyally."

"That's not what I asked you."

He met her eyes. There was no warmth in them now, nor was there enmity. There was only power.

"What do you want of me, priestess?" he asked bitterly.

"The truth."

"The truth is that I'm a freedman, born of a Thyrsian slave, without wealth or clan or power, and I love the queen too well to imagine that I have any right to love her."

"But you do."

The words pinned him like a sword-point.

He put the cup down.

"Yes," he said harshly. "Make of it what you will. I love her more than my life."

"Then go to her. She is waiting for you."

"What?" He stared at her, unable to comprehend, unable for a moment to respond at all to what seemed like merely another sorcerous twist of words. She made a small gesture with her hand towards a door, different from the one he had entered, and he caught his breath in disbelief and hope.

"She is here?"

"It was she who sent for you. I merely meddled, as I always do."

He was swept with confusion and desire. She was here. She had sent for him. It was the night of Sunturning and she had sent for him to come to her, in a sacred place, alone. . . .

"I will give you one counsel more," Medwina said softly, "for I think you're wise enough to follow it, but too young, perhaps, to have thought of it yourself. She endured a bitter captivity in Dravia, with a man who looked upon her only as a prize of war. Treat her gently.

"You will be safe here. Few are abroad, and if they pass this place they will not see it, and if they see it they will not remember. The year dies, the year lives, but this night will not return.

"Go."

He stepped through the door and stood utterly still. The room was curtained against the wind, and lit only with a single taper. It had been prepared as carefully as a bridal chamber, though he did not notice that until later. A magnificent fire burned in the hearth, spreading the room with warmth and shifting light. It had been scattered with sandalwood and linden flowers, and the air was filled with sensuous fragrance. There was a small table laid out with a flagon and two silver cups, and a tray piled with delicacies of food. On the floor in front of the fire was a bed of soft rushes, spread with fine linen and covered with furs.

He saw none of that, at first. He saw only the queen, standing a few feet away. She was wearing a pale blue chinon, fastened at one shoulder with a gold clasp. Her hair glinted in the firelight.

"Lady. . . ." The word was barely a whisper. He could not move, or speak more than that one word, all the other words dying in his throat. In his most reckless dreams he had not imagined this. For one second he remembered Belengar. He remembered the gaunt fugitive with bleeding feet, laughing at his feast table as one who had almost forgotten how to laugh, drunk with freedom, so lovely then in her youth and pride and courage, lovely as a deer now in the changing light, supple, shimmering with promise, moving towards him.

"Shadrak." She touched his bare shoulder with her fingers, the caress delicate yet hungering. She smiled. It was a small, uncertain smile, but he would have died for it, and for the soft question in her eyes. Then she lowered them, bending to press her face against his shoulder.

He could scarcely breathe. Her hair wisped over his face, tangled itself in his hands as he reached for her. His voice was harsh with emotion.

"Lady, is this possible? Are you real, or are you made of dreams and potions?"

Her arms prisoned him. "Say my name, Shadrak," she begged. "I want to hear you say my name."

"Marwen."

How many times did he say it through that long night?— Marwen, Marwen, Marwen; a reckless litany of desire, mouthed against her face, her fingertips, her eager, graceful body.

"Marwen, my love, my life, my queen. . . !"

His hands hungered over her body. The chinon was thin silk, and she wore nothing beneath it. Her breasts flowered at a touch; her mouth reached for his. For a time he did not measure they stood so, coiled together, caressing each other with more and more abandon. Then he drew back and undid the clasp of her chinon; it fell with a soft rustle to her feet.

She was clean-limbed and slender as a reed. "You're lovely," he said hungrily, and saw that she was pleased. Proud queen though she was, she was still young, hardly more than a girl, and she very much wanted her lover to find her beautiful.

To him she was more beautiful than words, but he found what words he could. He said them over and over as he took her body with his hands and his mouth, said the words and said her name, endlessly, Marwen, Marwen, Marwen. At last she drew back in turn, unbelted his tunic and helped him lift it over his head.

He would have bent then and swept her up and carried her to the fur-covered bed, as he might have carried a hot-blooded country girl to a grove or a pile of hay. He caught himself just in time.

She endured a bitter captivity in Dravia, with a man who looked upon her only as a prize of war. . . .

"Come," he said softly.

Even so, as they knelt together, her eyes changed; something dark came into them. Not fear; she was not afraid of him. And yet there was something, he was not sure what; perhaps just . . . *remembering.*

He hated Prince Held then as he had never before hated him, even at the Magdal bridge. He knew it was said that he had not slain his enemy honourably. He did not care. He would have killed the prince any way he could, with an arrow in his back if need be, and cut off his head a hundred times over, simply because of this alone: this dark, savaged look in Marwen's eyes.

What he did then, he did by instinct, without conscious thought. He sank onto his back and let her come to him. It was a small thing, perhaps, an animal offering of vulnerability instead of power, but it was enough. She slid one arm across his body and pressed her face into shaggy chest. For a moment she did nothing more than that, and he did not ask for more, only stroked her hair and her shoulders, *Marwen, Marwen, Marwen* . . . goddess of the world, but he loved her, he would die of loving her like this.

Her body came soft and serpentine to his. Her mouth ravished him, turning his nipples into burning copper beads. She knelt to take him into her loins, and then sank full against him, slowly, her hands sliding in a long caress up his belly, over his chest and his face, at last winding and tangling greedily in his hair. Her eyes were burning shale.

"Black as a raven," she murmured. "Beautiful black-haired Thyrsian border wolf. Kiri was right."

He was bewildered, undone with desire. "What in the name of any gods at all are you talking about?"

She laughed. It was the first time since Belengar that he had heard her laugh so. The sound of it melted what was left of his heart.

"You, my love," she said. And kissed him, and began to rock in his arms.

They did not sleep until day, and then only a little. They laughed, and drank wine, and fed each other pieces of cheese and chicken and sweets filled with cream. They stoked the fire, and talked of the past (*I don't want to speak of the future,* Marwen said, *not now.*) Mostly they talked of his past, for they did not want to speak of Dravia, either. And again and again they came together, hungering, wanting more than simple coupling, wanting everything, wanting insatiably to look and touch and taste, to possess each other completely, every way they could. The storm swept around the temple, burying it in soft white darkness, locking them in pleasure. And yet he could not get enough of her mouth on his body, or the glint of firelight on the naked sweep of her thighs, or the sound of her name in his throat. He could not bear to think that, after tonight, he might never be with her again.

Finally, though he had agreed that he would not, he talked about the future. He thought of many ways to frame the question, but it came out at last without much thought, like an unexpected and unbidden gulp of pain.

"Do you love the lord of Maene?"

"I may come to," she said. She met his gaze openly, hiding nothing, not even the uneasiness in her always changing eyes. "But I don't think so. It's a political marriage, Shadrak. I don't think it will ever be more than that . . . or less. I will do what I must to survive."

"And then?"

"And then I will come back to you, my wolf." There was a ghost of a pause. "If you wish."

"Yes," he said simply, eagerly, reaching for her. She smiled with open delight, and he realized that she had not been sure of him.

He found that almost impossible to believe.

They slept at last, and woke somewhere in the middle of a timeless gray day. The sun had turned, but there was no sign of it; there was barely light against the storm. They made love again, tired but unwilling to let go, unwilling to face the moment when they would ride, each of them alone, into the snow.

She took from her finger the bronze ring she had shown him as a token.

"I bought it from a gypsy trader when I was ten," she said. "He had black hair, and he was very beautiful. My father would let me have only a few coins to spend, so I chose this ring. After I'd paid for it, the gypsy gave me a warning. It was a love ring, he said, and I must not give it lightly, for it had a fate upon it."

"Did he tell you what it was?"

"He said no matter who I gave it to, it would one day be given back. And then I wished I'd never bought it. But he only smiled, and said such things were never simple. 'Choose wisely,' he told me then, in a soft dark voice, as though he himself saw something he wished he had not seen. 'Choose wisely.' "

She looped the ring into a leather thong and slipped it around his neck. She did not smile.

"It's yours, Shadrak. Since you're fated to give it back to me one day, I hope it will be in friendship, and not in anger."

"I will never give it back," he said. "Not unless you command it."

"He didn't speak of commands."

"I don't know what he spoke of, Marwen. But I love you. Much will change in the world before that changes."

"So be it, then." She stroked his face. Her eyes were tender again, her caresses soft as rain. "You are beautiful, wolf. Beautiful and valiant, and I wish I could have you by my side."

"You need only to ask."

"And see you killed? No. That's too high a price for love."

"They won't find me easy to kill."

"No. But they would do it nonetheless. I won't even think about it." Her finger traced the scar down his face. "You will eat with us before you go? It's a long way back, and cold."

They ate. They said good-bye many times. Last of all she brought him a parting gift, held out white and shimmering in the hollow of her arms. It was a cloak of white fox-skin, long and hooded, sweeping and proud such as a king might wear.

"It's not armour," she said. "It can't turn back a sword thrust. But all the skill I have is in it. It will shield you from many things besides the wind."

He thanked her, and held her as she wound her arms around his neck and clung to him. Proud and brave though she was, she could not hide from him the fact that she was bitterly afraid.

Book Three.
The Goddess Returns

We shall burn incense to the queen of heaven, and shall pour her libations as we used to do. For then we had plenty of food, and we all were well and saw no evil. But since we ceased burning incense to the queen of heaven and to pour her libations, we have wanted everything and have been consumed by sword and famine.

Book of Jeremiah

Many evils did the Kamil queen visit upon her people, bringing sorcery and wickedness back into the land. . . .

Chronicles of Larandau

And I will judge thee, as women that break wedlock, and shed blood are judged.

Book of Ezekiel

21. Gods, Men, and Power

Five days after Sunturning, on the day which was counted as the first of the Kamil new year, more than a thousand men and women from both the city and the countryside gathered outside the abandoned temple of Jana. They hacked down the fence, and with great iron bars pried away the timbers which had closed off its gates. Then, with what Kiri judged a fine bit of irony, they cut the wood into hearth-sized pieces and piled it in the temple storerooms for fuel.

They cleared out the snow, and swept the courtyards of leaves and debris. They restored the outbuildings and the lodgings of the high priestess. And in the sanctuary itself, they cleaned away the rat's nests and cobwebs, scrubbed down the walls and the floors, and polished the altar stone until it glistened.

Then, in endless processions, they brought gifts: grain and jars of oil, tapestries and linens and pottery and tools, more wood for heating and for the sacred fires, chickens and calves and great rounds of cheese, and everything else the keepers of the temple would need.

This outburst of reverence for Jana seemed to Kiri to have in it an overwhelming sense of relief, as though the Kamils were not merely thankful to have the goddess back, but even more thankful to be allowed to say so—to be able stand in clear daylight, before their neighbours and the world, and acknowledge publicly what they had always privately believed: their mother was not dead.

Of course there was opposition. Mohr's rule was powerful, if not absolute, and it was mostly the richest and mightiest of the Kamils who served him. Bands of young men gathered almost daily to fling insults at the workers; sometimes they flung stones. Twice it came to swordplay, but Caithland's men were there, flying the queen's standard. There also were three hundred men of the warband of Maene. At Landis's insistence, their leader Ranir commanded them in person.

Even the angriest of Theron's supporters were not about to challenge so formidable an armed force. And although Theron demanded it of nearly every Kamil lord in turn, none of them was prepared to send a warband of his own to contest the matter.

That surprised Kiri until she thought about it a little; then it seemed quite predictable. Mohr was the god of the great lords. His laws provided them with the moral and social foundations of their power. But they were often at odds with his priests, usually over their private morals or their treatment of the people. In Dravia, during her girlhood, King Algard had put over a dozen priests to death.

"Theron is a bitter, quarrelsome man," the queen said. "His personality alone has earned him enemies. And he says many things the lords don't like. He says they take too much tribute from the people, and waste it on luxury and pleasure. And he says they don't give enough to the temple. He wants to establish a tithe based on wealth and rank, to force them to give more."

"The problem goes deeper, I think," Kiri said.

"Oh, much deeper. These men want a god who orders everything in the universe except themselves. Mohr is a god of mastery; that's why they like him. Those who serve him are to have dominion over the world, and everyone else must obey them—wives, children, slaves and servants, other nations, beasts, the earth itself. Everything is theirs.

"But how can you give men all that power, and go to them afterwards and say: Be good? Don't pillage, don't rape, don't murder, don't exploit the weak and the poor! Can you imagine, Kiri, how many of them will listen?"

Few enough, Kiri thought. The priests of Mohr were doomed to failure from the start. They fought two wars at once—one war against the resilient, ever-encroaching presence of the goddess who would not die, who kept whispering to the world: *Mohr is not master, there are other truths and other ways.* And they fought another war against the power Mohr himself had unleashed upon the world, against the men of power whose cruelty and corruption everywhere surrounded them. The priests condemned that corruption, and in the next breath they reaffirmed the power which made it possible. They pleaded for humanity, but whenever they had to choose between humanity and Mohr's dominion, Mohr came first. And the crimes they railed against went on.

They never saw the contradiction. They could not allow themselves to see it, for to see it was to give up being chosen, to give up being the masters of the earth.

A week before the queen's wedding, Harad the steward went to his mistress, with a certain degree of embarassment, and asked if he might buy from her stores a cask of good Sardas wine to pay a bet he had made—and lost—with Luned.

That night there was a party in the palace kitchens. Kiri sang for them as willingly as she sang in the feast hall, but there were fewer songs of ancestors and war, and more of common things. Here vagabonds travelled the roads, lovers outwitted jealous mates and bullying parents, and Owen the farmer lamented his lost fowl:

> *Where are my chickens, old fox, old fox?*
> *Bring back my chickens, I swear,*
> *Or I'll pull out your teeth, and your fine bushy tail*
> *I'll give to my goodwife to wear. . . .*

As the night deepened, gossip flowed like Luned's wine, more and more freely. All of Kamilan was talking, amazed by the queen's decision to marry according to the old laws, and to open the great temple of Jana. Fact and rumour were no longer separable, except with great effort. For a while there had been talk of mutiny in the east. Since the days of the first kings, the lords of Tamri had rebelled or threatened to rebel nearly every generation over one thing or another. This, the gossip said, would trigger a new upheaval.

But Landis rode boldly to Tamri to present his case, and just three days ago Favian himself arrived with bridal gifts worth more than a thousand ells, and an escort so large it seemed like a small army, and announced that if the lord of Maene saw no reason to keep the temple closed, neither did he. At that point, they said, Theron the high priest took to his bed and was close to dying of fever and rage.

Kiri, content to lay her lyre aside, got herself a mug of wine and sat back to listen.

—*But Favian was always one of Theron's men. He danced to whatever the old crow sang.*

—*That's the whole point. Landis calls the dances now. And he's not even prince consort yet.*

—*Judging by the embassies he's been sending to every corner of the land, he thinks he's already king.*

—*He's winning allies for the queen. What's wrong with that?*

—*He's winning allies for himself. The trouble with you, Luned, is that you can't see beyond a handsome face.*

—*Ah, leave off, steward. You're just mad at her because she won the bet.*

—*It will be such a wedding! Have you seen her gown? Not even Queen Arden's was as fine. And Landis has offered five hundred of his finest horses for a bride-gift.*

—*I wager she won't keep them for a week. She'll give them to Borosar for the army.*

—*I think we've had enough of wagering. But I expect you're right. She is a queen born of Alyth's blood, that is certain.*

—*Do you know what Lord Crayfe's wife said? Lady Vanda? At the Feast of Harash, when the queen gave the champions their laurels, and led the dance with them, Lady Vanda said— there's no need to smile like that, Malia, I heard her myself— she said she wondered if the queen meant to be like Alyth in everything.*

—*So?*

—*Don't you know? They say Alyth slept with all her captains. Some say she slept with every brave man she met.*

—And *every beautiful one.*

—Why should Lady Vanda care? Her husband wouldn't be in any danger—not on either count.

A ripple of laughter went around the room. Kiri grinned into her wine cup. There was a very special pleasure common people took in sitting around now and then, picking apart their betters. Especially when their betters really had it coming.

She looked up, and saw that Harad alone was not smiling. He sat quietly, staring at nothing in particular, with a face which belonged at a funeral. The steward was a terribly serious man, a little bit pompous, but he was not so petty that he would pout all night because he had lost a bet. He had grave doubts about what lay ahead—for the queen and for Kamilan. Nearly everyone did, though what some feared, others rejoiced at; and what they rejoiced at, others feared.

Probably the only two people in the land who were truly content tonight, she reflected, were Luned and the lord of Maene.

For the first time in sixteen years, the high priestess Medwina rode in state into Kamilan, in a royal chariot, with an honour guard of Caithland's men in all their finery, and twelve of the queen's shield women, and two hundred warriors from Althen Garrison. Command of the escort had first been offered to Lord Crayfe, as seneschal of the royal city; then to the commander of the garrison. Both of them politely declined. If the queen was reckless enough to bring the sorceress back, and the Lord of Maene was mad enough to let her, so be it; they would not say more. But neither would they ride in her honour guard. So the escort was captained by Shadrak of Belengar. Thus, unwittingly, the lords placed him again in the full gaze of the Kamil people, in yet another role they would not easily forget.

For the people were following Medwina that morning. A procession of worshippers stretched halfway down the mountain road, bearing evergreens and torches. They came before the sun cleared the eastern peaks; from the fortress wall they seemed like living fires. Their chanting rose and fell as the wind bore it, now towards the high city, now away:

> *Mother of light, mother of darkness,*
> *Bearer of the gods;*
> *Bearer of the world and all that lives,*

Virgin, mother, and crone:
We welcome you, we honour you,
*   we ask for your forgiveness;*
We give you back the city of the queens. . . .

For a long time Kiri and Marwen watched them in silence. Only parts of the long road were visible from the ramparts. But on every bit of road which they could see, the procession wound endlessly, as though all of Kamilan had come to join it. Dawn light was breaking in the east, muting the torches, making them strange and fey.

"Even I did not expect so many," Marwen whispered. "They have never loved Mohr. They fear him, perhaps, but they have never loved him."

Steps crunched the snow behind them. Angmar the Wise, wrapped in furs as they were, moved slowly towards them. Even in this gray light Kiri could see that he was ashen, almost ill with defeat. He had his most desired wish—that the queen should marry Landis of Maene. But he had it at a cost which turned his triumph to bitter gall in his mouth. For weeks he had argued, pleaded, even threatened. He was a man of many skills, and he had used them all to prevent this. But against the queen's resolve and the lord of Maene's ambition, all his skill had gone for nothing.

"Do you know what you've done, lady?" he asked at last. There was no anger in his voice; he was beyond it now.

"Yes," Marwen said.

He hunched his shoulders. "No," he said. "You don't know. You cannot. You are not that corrupt."

It was an astonishingly harsh thing for him to say. Kiri expected the queen to reply in the same fashion, but she did not. For a time she watched the road below, where dancers, indifferent to winter, followed Medwina's chariot, clashing their cymbals as they snaked and spun.

"This is not about virtue or corruption, Angmar," the queen said. "This is only about power. Wise as you are, you've never been able to see the difference. You are like Mohr: what he rules is good, what he cannot rule is evil. That's why he tried to kill the goddess, and burn her flesh, and keep it in golden urns inside his house.

"He failed, Angmar. She is alive. She is free. *She is back!*"

216

Marwen spun around to face him. Never had she seemed more truly Medwina's kinswoman, or Alyth's heir, as though the power of the goddess approaching her gates was already in her hands and in her eyes.

"She is back!" she cried again. "And while I live, she will never leave these walls!"

Their eyes met like swords. It was the sage who finally looked away.

"I pray that spirits do not walk," he said bitterly. "I pray the dead king sleeps, and doesn't see." He turned and left the wall.

"Aye, wise one," she muttered after him, "and what of the dead queens?"

She kneaded bits of snow into balls, and tossed them away. "Well, Kiri, it is time. I must go and dress for my wedding."

She had not slept; her eyes were deep and shadowed. "In Dravia I swore I would choose my own husband," she brooded. "And so I do, and I do not. On these very walls I swore I would have Shadrak. And so I do . . . and I do not. Is everything fated so, Kiri? That after we've done everything we can, we find we have done so little?"

"Do you fear this marriage, lady?"

"Yes."

"Landis seems. . . ." Kiri hunted for a word. "Honourable."

"Oh, no doubt he is, in his fashion. So was my father. So was Held. So is Angmar the Wise. Fine men, all of them, men the world will remember with admiration. And all of them, for their own honourable reasons, wanted me caged."

Everything was white. The night before, Jana had shaken out her hair, and fresh snow clung to every roof, every path, every branch of the trees. The sun did not come out at all, but it often did not at this time of the year, so no one saw that as an omen. Rather, the clean beauty of the morning seemed to herald hope and fresh beginnings.

That day even Marwen's sternest critics agreed that she was striking. Those who loved her swore that she was beautiful.

She was no longer gaunt as she had been in Aralev. Her fine gown of white and gold draped a body with distinct if delicate curves. There was colour in her face, and her hair in its splendid bindings shone like spun gold. Malia, bustling madly with preparations for the feast, nonetheless found time to comment on the miracles which could be wrought with food.

The miracles which could be wrought with freedom were not mentioned.

The great hall was hung with boughs of evergreen, and the air was filled with sandalwood and incense and music. The bridal couple exchanged their gifts. Landis had brought for the queen the splendid horses he had promised, and many pieces of jewellery. To him she gave two of the small estates which had come to her father over the years, a magnificent set of weaponry and armour, and several beautifully crafted garments—boots, an embroidered tunic, a gold belt, and two silk shirts.

"As if he weren't elegant enough already," Malia sniffed. But she smiled, caught Harad's eye, and winked.

Angmar, solemn as a king himself, approached the table with two servants, who carried between them a locked iron casket. They heaved it onto the table before the queen.

"Lady," he said, "this was put aside for you soon after you were born, by your mother Queen Arden, your father King Adelmar, and the lady Medwina. I have kept it for you—sometimes against the advice of others, and sometimes against my own better judgment, for our need was often very great. Now I'm glad beyond telling that I did so."

He took a key from the chain on his belt, unlocked the casket, opened it, and handed the key to the queen. Silence fell on the room in waves, and then a soft ohhh! of wonder. The casket was filled to bursting with jewellery and gold ells.

"Your dowry, Lady Marwen. May it enrich the royal house of Kamilan forever."

"Thank you, Angmar." There was a hint of tears in the queen's eyes. "In this, as in all things, you have been the most loyal of men."

Harad's eyes were fixed on the lord of Maene. "He's pleased enough with that," the steward whispered unpleasantly. "That is worth a good deal more than five hundred horses."

"Maybe so," Malia whispered back. "But it's hers; it isn't his."

Harad smiled.

The priestess Medwina brought the queen and her consort a single cup of wine, from which they both drank, and a single piece of bread, which they broke in half and ate. Lastly they were given two weapons—among the poor these might be only staves; here in the royal palace they were two gleaming swords with jewelled handles. These they held high, with their sword-arms linked, affirming that they would defend each other against all dangers.

So, according to the rites of Jana and the Laws of Kind, Marwen of Kamilan married the lord of Maene, and all which came after was from that moment laid in place. For the rest of her life Kiri wondered how it might have been different, what better or worse fate might have come upon them if the queen had married Valdemar, or Borosar's son, or any of the others, or if she had dared not to marry at all.

Late into the night, when most of the guests had gone home or fallen asleep in the hall, Kiri sat with Medwina. In spite of many braziers, the hall was chilly unless one stayed close to the fire. Across the room Shadrak, prisoned there by his duty to the high priestess, wrapped himself in his fox cloak and slept . . . or pretended to sleep; it was easier than hiding his pain.

Medwina did not trouble to hide hers.

"Well, we have said it all, Kiri," the priestess said, "and nothing we say makes any difference. Do you know, when Angmar looked at me so many times across the feast table, with so much bitterness in his eyes, I grieved for him? He has been given his heart's desire on the point of a spear, and so have I. I know exactly how he feels." She drank deeply, and stared into her glass. "So much was lost," she brooded, "lost for no reason. If only he had remained my friend. . . ."

She looked up, and saw Kiri's bewilderment. "Marwen never told you? I saved his life many years ago. He came back from the battlefield shattered with wounds, and no one thought he would recover. His mother sent for me in secret— his father would have let him die rather than give him into the care of a witch. I healed him, and we became lovers."

"You and Angmar?" Kiri whispered.

"Yes. Why is that surprising? We had many things in common. I taught him much of what he knows."

"Then he is Angmar the Wise only because of you."

"No. Not only because of me. He had gifts of his own; that was what drew me to him. He learned from me, and I learned from him. I will not say who had the better of the exchange.

Not yet. But almost from the first he was divided inside himself because of it. He wanted my wisdom, and he wanted me; before a year had passed he cast both away, and taught himself quite resolutely to hate me."

"But why?" Kiri demanded.

"He feared my power. He feared the goddess and the earth; he feared us then as he does now. And yet he knows he can't defeat us. Why do you think I was allowed to raise Marwen after her mother died? He couldn't prevent it. He knew of no way, neither in his mind nor in his heart, to do so. I will give him this, Kiri: he is honest. He wants the world of reason and absolute order Mohr promised him, but he knows in his blood that it can't be, that it's only a fiction of men's minds. I, on the other hand, am real . . . but I am lascivious, and irrational, and dangerous."

Medwina sighed. "So now we're come to this. . . . Do you know what he said to me, when he told me he wouldn't see me again? He said I stood between him and his duty to Kamilan.

"I keep no lover against his will, Kiri. But I laid a bond on him, a bond he will never escape. I told him this: I don't stand between you and Kamilan, but if it ever comes to pass one day that another does, you will make this choice again. You will choose Kamilan, though you tear your own heart out doing it."

Neither spoke for a time. They were exhausted, and half drunk, and cold, and yet to rise from their table was to acknowledge that the day was finished and the dice cast, that Landis of Maene was the queen's husband and consort, part of her world and her life, and if she had misjudged in choosing him, the harm might well be too bitter to contemplate.

"Any other man, Kiri," the priestess murmured. "I would have seen any other man by her side, rather than that one."

22. The Lords of Maene

The world did not end when the goddess returned to Kamilan. Indeed, on the surface nothing changed very much at all. Nonetheless, for almost two moonturns Angmar the Wise lived in seclusion in his great stone house. He did not do so out of pique or wounded pride, but out of genuine exhaustion, and the wish to be alone to read and think. Generously worded invitations came several times from the palace, asking him to join their feasts; often the messengers brought small gifts. Angmar pleaded illness and stayed home.

Finally one evening, with no warning at all, a servant appeared at the door of his study, and announced that the prince consort had arrived, and wished to see him. Angmar sighed, and invited him in.

Success agreed with Landis, as it did with most men. He looked splendid, and he settled into Angmar's chair with an easy self-assurance which was the closest thing to sheer pride Angmar had ever seen in him.

"I'm glad to see you're better, cousin," Landis said. "The queen and I have been concerned about you."

"I am weary, Landis." He smiled. "You look well. I'm glad you came."

"I would have come sooner. I thought perhaps you didn't want to see me."

"I'm not angry at you."

"You were for a while."

Even that, Angmar thought, was only half true. He had been angry at everything: at the queen, at Medwina, at fate, maybe even at Mohr, for failing him, for not being god enough to keep what was his.

"So fill me in, Landis. What's been happening?"

"Really, Angmar, your servants and your friends tell you everything that happens, without needing to be asked."

"Yes, they do. And every one of them puts his own slant to it. I want your view. What's Theron doing about all of this?"

Landis shrugged. "Making a great deal of noise, and not much else. He rails against Medwina, and she rails against him, and it keeps both of them busy. To tell you the truth, when I agreed to the queen's terms, and let her open the temple, I had my doubts about it. I thought the last thing we needed in this country was something else to quarrel over. But now I think it might prove useful, having those two old ravens at each other's throats."

"And what about the people?" Angmar asked softly.

Landis shrugged. "Did serving Mohr ever make them wiser or less quarrelsome?"

"In time it would. That's how men grow, slowly and with time, as they are given better things. Now we've given them something worse."

"Have we really? What does it matter where they bring their little offerings? You said it yourself: who cares what peasant women mumble in the dark? The queen is pleased with me for helping her, and even Favian isn't as angry as I thought he might be. You worry a great deal over nothing, my friend."

"What peasant women mumble in the dark, and what the rulers of the land allow in the light of day—those are two very different things. We are welcoming unreason and corruption into the centre of our lives."

"Now you sound like Theron."

"Theron isn't always wrong, Landis."

"That may be. But nothing is forever."

"The queen will never let you take your agreement back," Angmar said grimly. "Never. You yourself argued that you had no choice except to make it. Having made it, you will have even less choice, except to keep it."

Landis was looking at him oddly—almost wearily, it seemed. *Does he see me as another of those croaking ravens?* Angmar wondered.

"Things change, Angmar," Landis said quietly. "The queen is young, and finds it pleasant to be mistress. That will wear thin. After she discovers how burdensome it is, and how much beyond her strength, she will be glad to see me take on more of it, and still more. Oh, I know she's too proud to admit it, don't look at me so. It will never be acknowledged; it will simply happen. And who can say then what agreements will be made—or taken back?

"I don't understand you sometimes. You say over and over she's not a king, and yet sometimes I'd swear you think she is."

Angmar laughed a little. It was so like Landis, cutting to the heart of the issue with a single stroke.

"Thirty years of habit, my good friend. She's Adelmar's heir; I can't help it. You're right; she's just a girl. But she's as wilful a girl as the gods ever made."

Landis smiled faintly, like a man who had been told the world was flat. What further comment could possibly be called for? Still, he looked content.

"Things are going well, I trust?" Angmar said. "You're happy together?"

"Happy?" Landis shrugged. "When did that become necessary?"

"I merely asked. It's not necessary, but it makes life . . . sweeter."

"She's hardly the sort of wife to make a man besotted, Angmar. Nor would I wish her to be. She's cold, and after Dravia who would be surprised at that? When we have a few children she'll be content to be left alone. And I would just as soon keep my passions out of the council room."

Right again, of course. Landis was always right. It was tiresome at times.

"Have you ever been besotted, ever in your life?" Angmar asked. He had intended the question as playful. Somehow it came out sounding like a challenge.

"I suppose so," Landis said dryly. "I've had various plagues and fevers. Fortunately, I recovered from them all."

Aye, Angmar mused silently. *I recovered, too, and I'm glad I did; she would have destroyed me utterly. Why then do I still feel so much regret?*

"You've been brooding here too long," Landis said. "You must come and play chess with me again."

"Teach the queen to play."

"She already knows."

"Odd. I never taught her."

"She says she learned in Dravia."

"Is she good at it?"

"She wins sometimes. I don't much like playing with her. She takes it too seriously. She takes everything too seriously, Mohr knows."

"Would you rather she were frivolous?"

"No. I would rather she were . . . how can I say it? . . . *womanly*, perhaps? She thinks of nothing but the war. She spends half her days with messengers, sending here for tribute, there for grain, some other place to strike a deal for a shipment of iron. And that old fool Borosar sits there like a schoolboy: yes, lady; no, lady; what do you think about this, lady? He doesn't even notice any more that she's a *child. . . !*"

He paused, and laughed ruefully, leaning back in his chair. "I don't mean to sound disrespectful, cousin. You must understand that. And I don't wish that she was frivolous. But she has a husband now. I wish she could see how it looks. I'm not used to being a . . . a *bystander*. Especially in those things which are especially a man's concern, and not a woman's."

"Well." Angmar rang the small bell beside his chair. "I would like something hot to drink, I think. Will you join me? Cider perhaps? Or some lemon barley water?"

"Cider would be fine; thank you."

The servant came, listened politely, departed. When the door had closed, Angmar said,

"Surely you expected some of that, marrying a queen? And you said she will tire of the burden, and willingly give some of it to you?"

"Yes."

"Then be patient. You waited many years to marry her. You can wait a few more years till she grows up. Don't make her your enemy. She's not a woman who easily forgives."

"And what of her mistakes? We're on the brink of war, and she thinks she knows how to conduct it. She doesn't."

"She hasn't made any serious mistakes yet. When she does, we shall have to deal with it. All of us. In a sense we're still regents, and we will be until we have a king."

Angmar sighed, staring at his hands. After a moment he went on grimly:

"I swear to you, Landis, if I'm still alive when we have a king, I will use all the influence I possess to somehow make it law, forever, that only a male can inherit the crown. If there are no sons, then we'll choose a grandson or a nephew or a cousin, and if there are none of those, then by the gods we'll start over with another house. But no more of this. A whole nation must not be held hostage to a woman's loins. Do you realize, Landis, if she had borne a son to Prince Held, the lawful right to rule us would have passed to the Dravians? I can't tell you how many offerings I've made in gratitude, that Mohr saw fit to keep her barren."

There was a soft tap at the door. The servant entered, carrying a tray with two steaming mugs and a plate of honey cakes.

"Now," Angmar said moodily, "I pray he'll do the opposite."

"Be content, then. She is with child."

Angmar looked up sharply, eagerly. "You're serious? Already?"

"What do you mean, already? Don't you have any confidence in me?" Landis laughed softly. "I came especially to tell you."

He took his cup and raised it. "Now! Let's drink to the king of Kamilan!"

23. The Field of Fire

Kiri had forgotten how harsh the mountain winters were. On the caravan she had spent them alternately in Sardas, where there was no winter at all, or in the south of Larandau, where the leaves turned gold and an occasional snowflake fell, but where flowers bloomed again two months after Sunturning.

Dravian winters were bitter, and Kamil winters only slightly less so. But the Kamils had more taste for pleasure than their neighbours, and there was plenty of feasting and story-telling, and all sorts of games. Kiri liked card games, but after a dozen or so tries she gave up on chess. She had no head for it. She was content to play her lyre, and watch the queen play with Landis.

Kiri's opinions regarding the lord of Maene were still completely fluid. To her first discreet questions Marwen had made equally discreet replies. He was nice, she said; he treated her well. That was all, and it seemed singularly little from the woman who had lain dreamily on her rug, toasting her feet by the fire, telling Kiri how beautiful Shadrak was, how generous a lover, and how they had not slept the whole night of Sun-turning.

Certainly Landis was always respectful, and often thoughtful in small ways which Kiri frankly admired. He was a singularly *polished* man; a man to whom bad manners and bad taste were inexcusable. He was also very obviously intelligent, and deeply concerned with affairs of state. At times Kiri could see perfectly well why Luned adored him, why Luned thought her mistress the luckiest woman on earth.

He really is quite splendid, she would think. *I can't imagine why Medwina fears him so. Perhaps her own quarrel with Angmar has somehow blinded her judgment?*

But she could never quite bring herself to believe that Medwina was wrong; nor could she determine why not. Sometimes she wondered if it were precisely because Landis was so correct: never a wrong word, never a hair out of place, or a gesture, or a drop of sweat. A man had to *work* at being so controlled—in particular he had to work at making it seem natural—and the question Kiri asked herself was why a man would. His rank did not require it; neither did his family nor his peers. There was something inside himself which required it. And she could not even begin to guess what that might be.

As the winter went on, he spent less and less time in the palace. Within three months of the wedding, the queen confirmed that she was pregnant. After that he was often absent from her table, and more often absent from her bed.

"I thank the goddess," Marwen said, "that I didn't marry him for love. As it is. . . ." She shrugged, and then wrapped her arms around her knees. "As it is, it's just as well."

"He has no. . . ." Kiri hunted for a discreet word. "No . . . interest in you at all?"

"He was eager enough to make an heir. And he's not without desire; I don't mean to suggest that. But his desire is cold, Kiri, and don't ask me how that's possible, because I don't know. It's as though he hungers only with his mind. His body is a tool; it does what he expects of it. He must beget a king, so he must lay with me. He enjoys it, in a fashion, and yet there's a part of him, I think, that wishes it weren't necessary—that wishes none of it were necessary, neither birth nor death nor food nor passion of any kind. I think he wishes men could just *be*, without having to deal with their bodies at all."

So many of Mohr's men wanted that, Kiri reflected: to somehow escape the world; to escape the cycles of life and the unpredictabilities of flesh into some kind of abstract, totally structured world of mind and spirit. She sighed. She rather liked Landis. It depressed her to think that his best qualities might have nothing to do with courtesy or affection, only with the wish to be always in control.

Still, there was one question she had to ask, so that all possibilities might be considered. It was part of what Marwen expected of her.

"Do you think perhaps because of Dravia, and because he knows you don't want him very much, he's spending his time elsewhere out of kindness?"

"It's possible," the queen said. "He's not an easy man to know. And he wants it that way."

She shrugged faintly, reaching for an orange. "I think it more likely that all he wanted was an heir. Now that he will have one, he has more important things to spend his time on than his wife."

She caught Kiri's eyes on her and smiled. "You've been wanting to ask me for weeks, haven't you? If the child was his?"

"It's not my place to ask that, lady," Kiri said. "But yes, I have wondered."

"I'm not a fool, Kiri. If the child were Shadrak's, and if it resembled him even a little, Landis would know at once that it wasn't his. So would everyone else. And it wouldn't take them long to guess whose child it was. Can you imagine their anger?" She shook her head. "Trying to *marry* Shadrak would have been less reckless than that."

She paused, and added quietly. "And quite apart from anything else, I made a bargain with Landis, and I will keep it. The heir is his. There's nothing to fear. I bled four days after Sunturning, as I knew I would."

Kiri hugged her knees. "I guess if I'd thought about it even for a minute, I would have realized that," she said.

"In the days of the hill queens," Marwen went on, "such things were known to all women. There are times of the moon when the goddess will send a child, and times when she won't. There are plants which keep you from breeding, too. And there are many ways to end it. All of that was known to everyone. Now it's mostly just the priestesses who know. The men of Mohr call it sorcery, but it isn't. It's simply wisdom—a wisdom they don't want their daughters to have—or their wives. And so the knowledge is being lost."

It was commonly said that women blossomed with pregnancy. Kiri knew that some did not; her own sisters declined into haggard exhaustion. That was not the smallest of the reasons she swore she would never marry. But Marwen looked more splendid every day; and also more distinctly and compellingly female. She did not seem to be any less a sovereign, merely less a girl. If anything, the sense she conveyed of the power in her person and in her rank was growing.

She would give Kamilan its future. And Kiri knew there was no doubt in the queen's mind that the heir and the future were hers to give, and no one else's. She was not, like the wives of kings, an exchangeable vessel; she was the source. And it was that fact, as well as the fact of her own personal sovereignty, which so troubled the lords of Council and the priests of Mohr. Like Jana's temple it was a reminder that things had once been different.

In the days of the hill queens, and as long before that as anyone could remember, women had shared the power which warriors now claimed only for themselves. In the days of the hill queens, children belonged to their mothers' families, and land belonged to the clan. A man's bonds were to the young his female kin might bear, and not to the young he might father—for how could he know whom he had fathered, when he went where he chose to find pleasure, and when women were as free as he was? His pride was in his skill and his courage and his loyalty to the clan. He had no slaves in his fields, and he had no need for any in his bed.

All of that changed with Telhiron, with the men who came in ships, with the great god Mohr. For them, bread and land and joy in life were not enough. They wanted gold and slaves and kingdoms, too, and always more of them. Their own freedom they laid aside as a trifle; freedom for women was to them absurd. Women had other uses: they were for breeding and raising heirs—not the heirs of the clan but the man's very own. Women were the vessels he needed to pass on land and power to his sons. They were the peace offerings between kings, the ambassadors of alliances, the hostages of ambition, the cement in the walls of empire. They were shields against the darkness in a man's own mind, and against the terror of his own sins. They were the warm presence in the night, the smile of forgiveness, the unquestioning approval, the reassuring obedience. They were the owned flesh upon which all other ownership of flesh was fashioned, the first conquest by which all other conquests had been made possible. Once a man owned his wife, he need not stop until he owned the world.

And for that women had to somehow be controlled—controlled by force or by persuasion or by hunger or by the fear of god. And most effectively they were controlled by ignorance and lies. The wisdom of the past was silenced, the priestesses exiled, the witches destroyed, the creating goddess transformed into a destructive monster, and the free woman into a joke or a whore.

When Kiri left Vanthala, every person who was close to her had been appalled. "But when you come back," they said, "no one will want to marry you!"

"And then the rivers will dry up," Kiri had told them scornfully, "and the stars will fall out of the sky, and the sheep will fly south and leave their wool in Kamilan. Gods of the world, what does it matter if someone marries me or not?"

They had looked at her. They had not said anything. They had just *looked*. Their whole sense of proper living was offended. Women had to marry; that was given, and not open to debate. Or else, in spite of everything, they might still escape control.

The thing which surprised her most in the world was that it was not half as hard to live there as she had been led to believe. And the second thing was the discovery that there were other women like herself, quite a few of them, warriors and traders and ship captains and farmers and carpenters and smiths, strong-minded women who decided to make their own way and often prospered doing it. They were there and they always had been there, and probably they always would be. Nonetheless the world went on pretending they did not exist, and erasing them from memory the moment they were dead.

Unless of course they had been evil, or could be made to seem so. Then they would be remembered until the end of time.

I will be forgotten, she thought suddenly, darkly; *and Marwen will be condemned. And the world will nod and say: See? It's like the priests say; it's the nature of things.*

After what seemed like forever, the winter began to end. The sun came out day after day. Bare crags began to show on the sides of the mountains, and water began to murmur under the snow. The ice broke in the rivers. People still wore their furs, but they wore them unbuttoned, with the hoods thrown back; and the winds coming down from Dohann began to feel like gypsy winds, full of restlessness and promise. There was still snow in the woods when Shadrak took his men north. Summer would open the passes, and the war with Dravia would begin again.

They were hardly the cream of Kamilan's warriors, and their quiet march out of Althen attracted little attention. They had known little about horses when he recruited them, and less about swords. However, being mostly peasant lads and foresters, they knew bows. They could stalk and hunt, and they could shoot well with the short bows they used for game. The captain had drilled them hard all winter, day after day, and he was not displeased with the quality of his men. The quality of their weapons was another matter. The queen had set scores of Kamil bowyers to work making Thyrsian style bows. Unfortunately the making was slow, and could not be hurried. The woods had to cure, the resins had to dry. Adaptations had to be made to suit the Kamil climate, which was different from the eastern lands where the bows were first made.

Only a handful of Shadrak's men had the weapons he wanted them to have. Hunting bows were lethal only at short distances, and were useless against even light armour.

"I'm not sure what that ragtag troop will be good for, in the end," Borosar told the queen. "But they are keen to fight. Whatever else, Shadrak can inspire men."

"Does that surprise you?" she asked.

He shrugged. "When I gave him Belengar I had my doubts. Oh, not about his competence; that was obvious. But I wondered how the men would feel, captained by a freedman, if they would . . . hold back, perhaps. I always thought men had to be born to leadership."

"Perhaps they do," the queen said. "But not in the way you mean."

He thought about that a moment. "Then the gods help those who have such skills in their blood," he said, "and are born to obedience."

Borosar, of course, was thinking about men. Kiri did not ask him to stretch his observations further.

Everything sang with life: it sang in water and wind and blood. The air was flesh-warm and sweet with resin. Except for the wild clamour of shawms and drums, one could have heard everywhere the sound of a thousand rivulets and streams laughing into each other's arms. In the valley below the royal city, in the place which was called the Field of Fire, the rites of the Planting Festival were about to end.

For sixteen years the Kamils had honoured this feast day without a temple. For more years than anyone could name they had done so without a reigning queen to make the first gifts, to lead them into the fields and bless the earth, to light the three sacred fires of the goddess, and now, at last to begin the dance. The day had been laden with reverence; the night would burn with ecstasy, and that too was reverence. For as men and women whirled away from the sacred fires to lay together, they united themselves with all living things, with trees and animals and water, and their passions replenished the earth. Boundaries dissolved. People forgot their age, their rank, their names; many wore masks and dressed as forest creatures. And what passed in the dance was sacred. All might choose, but no one might command or forbid, and no one ever asked another's name.

The fires were splendid, leaping so high sometimes that the light bounded off the crags above. The drum beat made Kiri's blood race; it rose and fell; it was constant and yet somehow uneven, like a fevered pulse; the mountains caught it and tossed it back. The whole valley seemed filled with fire and music, and at the same time surrounded by darkness and silence, and by all the things which were there before the people came. And it was that, more than anything Marwen had said to her, which made Kiri understand the meaning of this festival. It was not simply to bless the crops and the lambs. It was not simply a ritual of fertility, a plea for the earth's bounty. It was also a ritual of making peace with the earth, for it recognized that the earth was dangerous as well bountiful.

As the goddess was. . . .

Landis was returning, graceful as an arrow in the changing light, pale-haired and slender, his cape flung open and trailing in the wind. The queen turned to greet him, an eagerness on her face which Kiri had never seen before. He was not the black wolf she might have wished to spend this night with, but he was young, and fine enough to look upon. He was the consort she had chosen, and he belonged beside her now.

"Landis." She moved towards him, reaching for his hand. "You are here. Everyone is waiting."

"It took some time to locate our escort, lady. It seems they thought they could stay here all night."

She took his arm. "Well, half the night at least. Come, let's begin the dance."

He did not move. "The men are ready, lady. We are prepared to leave."

"Leave?" There was pure bewilderment in her voice. The world was bursting into leaf, into flower, into flesh. The sky was afire, the wind tasted of honey. *Leave?*

"This is no place for you, lady," Landis said.

She smiled with sudden understanding. "I'm not three months gone, Landis. Dancing won't harm the child."

Nor will a soft bed after in the grass. The queen's eyes were soft. She meant to do more than lead the ritual with him, Kiri saw. She meant to draw him into the fire and the music and the passions of the earth. At festival, they said, all women were the goddess.

"Come, Landis. The dance, and then the dark."

He looked across at the waiting people, their faces horned and fanged and leaved, their bodies wrapped in furs or rags or nothing at all. In the firelight they were both savage and vulnerable. And this man, Kiri knew, meant never to be either.

"Surely you don't mean us to take part in this," he said.

"Of course," the queen said. "Why shouldn't we?" The arm which had held his own released it, and slipped around his waist.

He stood rigid, and Kiri backed out of the light, unable to take her eyes from his face. There was more in his dismay than a fastidious man's distaste for excess, more than an ambitious lord's strict sense of personal dignity. Those things could be bridged. Festivals existed in part for that very bridging, for lowering barriers and forgetting self, for remembering that all life was finally alike. But she saw that there was more, that most of all, Landis was afraid. He dared not give himself over to laughter and abandon, to the fire and the music and women's flesh, to being young and animal and free, and waking in the morning dirty and wet with dew and less correct, less ambitious—for what did it all matter, in the end?—life was flesh and flesh lived for a small time and died, the dance and then the dark. . . .

"I'm expected to lead them," the queen said. "It will look ill if you don't join me."

Thousands of people waited around the fires, the same thousands who all day long had cheered and thrown garlands at the queen and her consort. Landis stood motionless, trapped between his own revulsion and what must have been a powerful political imperative. *It will look ill if you don't join me.*

"Very well, lady," he said, and let her lead him towards the fires.

Kiri did not follow them. Like the queen she had brought a mask, and wore peasant garb under her own clothing. She would join the dance alone, not as Kiri the minstrel but as one of the people. She did not know what would happen. Such revels were still held in Dravia, in isolated places, but she had never been to one. It would be good to dance to the edges of being, she thought, good to be reckless for a small time, good to forget that she was too often alone. She did not want to change her life; she knew already that no lives were perfect, that every other person who walked upon the earth carried wounds. That was why they made festivals, why they needed them so much.

In her early youth she had wanted to marry, in a fashion; she had wanted to find a man to love. But she had looked at the world, at the hills of Vanthala, and the roads which wound to High Kamilan, to glory and adventure. She looked at her mother's life, and the lives of her sisters. She looked at the men whom other women married, and saw what they expected, and she saw that above all they expected to be lord. Even the best and most generous of men took as given that a woman's life would be shaped around his own. Her work, her thoughts, her destiny became his. Men married and the story they lived in went on. Women married, and the story they lived in was over.

Even as a child it had appalled her: that sameness, that terrible finality. *This house, this garden, this tiny fenced place from which she must wait forever for the world to come if it chooses—that's all there is, and all there ever will be!*

She would never marry. Freedom was too precious. She might give it up, perhaps, for something very good—men and women bonded sometimes in ways that were beautiful; and maybe if she spent a lifetime looking she could find that. Maybe, and maybe not. In any case she had only one lifetime, and there were so many other things to do. . . .

She would never marry, or even take a lover except in passing. But tonight, on the Field of Fire, without a past or a future or a name, with only her flesh and the drums and the wind, she would dance, and she would not ask where the wind or the drums or her flesh might lead her.

To his own surprise, Landis found his head strangely clear in the morning, clear as the dawn light which crept over the trampled Field of Fire. The valley was wet with dew now, and rank with dying fires. It was like a battlefield, he thought, staring at it from the palace ramparts, a battlefield without honour or victory, only death.

He remembered Caithland's face with a stab of humiliation. The captain of the guard had dutifully waited for them—the queen's loyal hound, sitting all night with his circled pack, his head on his paws, looking up with such satisfaction at the sight of the prince consort, the proud lord of Maene, reeling with weariness and wrapped in a filthy goatskin, no different from a peasant, no different from a dog run ragged by a bitch in heat.

And how the damned eunuch had smiled!

All day, Landis had picked his way through the tangles of ritual without difficulty. None of it mattered, except as a means to an end. It would reaffirm his place at the queen's side and legitimize him as prince consort in the eyes of the common folk. It would make him, even more than before, a public figure; a man whom people watched and admired and looked to for leadership. They shouted his name along with the queen's, and dancing priestesses hung garlands of flowers around his neck. There had been no reason to resist any of it— no reason at all except Angmar's silly fears of witches: *You're giving them credibility, Landis,* he had said. *Think about what you are doing!*

He had thought about it, and he had gone ahead. He had not hesitated at all until the Field of Fire, and there his hesitation had been purely a matter of dignity: *Surely, lady, you don't expect us to take part in this?*

He had walked into it with his head up, seeing embarassment, perhaps, but no danger. And she had conquered him as a warrior might conquer a child, without effort, even with laughter. She had spun him into the circle of fire, into the wild hammerbeat of drums, and a moment came when he was no longer himself, when he was no longer anything at all, except whatever slavering thing she might allow him to be. He could not identify the moment even in clear light. The maelstrom was vivid enough in his memory, but not the fall; it had simply happened.

She had been more in that moment than a woman, more even than a queen. She had been a goddess and a sorceress. She had been power and blood and fire, flesh consuming flesh, devouring boundaries, undoing stars and seas and earth in a blind dream of oneness. The drums pounded in his brain and in his loins. He was aware of nothing in the world except her body, and his own; her wild hair, her laughter as she spun him into darkness, her arms pulling him down.

He was a man of normal passions; he had tasted lust before. It was good, healthy, and ultimately simple, like food. A man ate; he ate well if he could and poorly if he had to, and then he forgot about it until he ate again.

The Field of Fire had been different. Different not simply in the intensity of his desire, but in its nature. For the first time in his life he had not been in command of it. She had forged it, honed it, maddened it; she had reduced him to soft clay, shaped by her every touch. She had melted him down like a gold ingot and she meant to wear him so, like a falcon's chain around her wrist.

Angmar had it all wrong. Angmar feared phantoms, goddesses riding the thunder, sorceresses in the black night. The queen, like every other ambitious woman born, knew perfectly well what it was that men were supposed to worship. She might name it Jana, and build a temple for it, and anoint her priestesses, but at the Field of Fire it had all been very earthy, and very clear. Marwen had used her body to bring Landis of Maene to heel; and had Landis been any other man except himself, she would probably have succeeded.

He saw that as a simple fact, a given. Nonetheless he was surprised at the impact she had on him when she came very late into the hall for breakfast. She wore a simple tunic and slippers and her hair hung unbound. She looked tired but utterly sensual, a hind from the forest, a wild creature from the Field of Fire, with the scent of smoke still in her hair. . . .

His stomach knotted; his loins flooded with heat. Gods of the world, but he wanted her! He did not love her. He did not imagine—not yet, great Mohr protect him!—he did not imagine for a moment that he loved her, or that he ever would. But he wanted her.

He watched her cross the room. He made himself acknowledge, very deliberately, that she was not beautiful. Her nose was too large, her teeth were uneven, her arms were too long, her knees beneath that tunic looked like knobs on a tree. But she was graceful; her skin was like flowers, and her mouth sweet as honey. Her hands were smooth and cunning; they could read a man's body like a sculptor could read wood, knowing exactly what, and where, and how; her loins could draw him deep and close on him—stroke him, almost—until he cried out from the pure, drowning pleasure of it.

She moved towards him. He felt his own desire like a wound, but its very intensity was a strange exoneration. This woman had an extraordinary, fascinating power. She compelled in everything she did, everyone she touched.

What becomes of people who get close to you, lady? he asked silently. *Your Dravian minstrel betrayed her country and her liege, and thinks nothing of it. Prince Held followed you to a bitter death. Even that half-caste barbarian from Belengar offered to throw himself on Held's sword for your sake, though he would not have survived long enough to curse you for it if they had actually met in single combat. You use your power like a maelstrom; you pull men down in it until they cannot breathe, until they offer you anything you want,*

*flesh or gold or power, and you take it all, and give back a
smile for payment.*

*And now you hope to have the same from me. My house is
as old as yours, and as powerful. Luck made the first Adelmar
king, luck and Landor of Maene, whose armies brought the
Kamil rebels to their knees and kept them there. Adelmar
would never have been king without him, and more than one
of Adelmar's sons and grandsons would have been hung
upside down from their palace walls but for the lords of
Maene. Your own father was nothing without Angmar—just an
impotent fool more worried about witches than about the real
enemies in his realm.*

*What is any of that to you? You ask my counsel when it
suits you, and follow it when you fancy. You think you are
seneschal and warlord and king all in one. And you think you
can pull me down as you have pulled down others, gods know
what you offered them with your cold smiles but I know what
you offered me, I have bedded whores before, only the others all
took their coin and went away, they did not imagine they could
use their hot thighs to weld a collar around my neck. . . !*

"Landis." She took his hands, brushed her lips across his own.

He smiled. "Good morning, lady."

"Have you eaten?" she said. "I'm starving."

He wanted to pull her into his arms, press her against his
body, lead her laughing back to her bedchamber.

*All these days and weeks I tried to be kind to you. I thought
you were wounded. I took account of your youth, and Prince
Held's reputation as a lustful man. Why did I bother? You
probably enjoyed him. Aye, and laughed at him, too, and
played him like a wooden whistle, and led him like a besotted
fool to his death!*

"I've eaten already," he said.

He waited a week. He did not want it to be obvious. He did
not want to create an open break, or even an apparent wound.
He told her there were matters on his estates which had been
festering for some time, and which needed attention. He had
put them aside, he said, but he could not do so indefinitely, and
with war on the horizon he should see to them now.

She did not challenge him. She did not try to seduce him
again. By the time he left, she had already noted his withdrawal,

already recognized that what had happened at the Field of Fire belonged to that time and to that place, and would never happen again.

He rode with pomp and ceremony from the gates of the royal city, preceded by fanfare, followed by glittering retainers and men-at-arms. He felt proud. He felt himself at last, the true lord of Maene, the father of the kings of Kamilan. Just once he looked back, and saw—or imagined that he saw—a woman on the ramparts, silent and motionless, her tawny hair blowing free in the wind, a woman who could have been his, had he only accepted her terms. He turned his gaze resolutely ahead, acknowledging that he wanted her still, that it hurt to leave her. But it was a blunt, physical hurt, a pain which had nothing to do with his real self. Like a blow from a club it had smashed into him from the outside. Like any blow which was less than lethal he had survived it—aye, and he was wiser for it. He would never get close enough to be wounded again.

24. Mercanio

Three days after midsummer, travellers brought to Kamilan the first word of Mercanio's caravan. It had passed Belengar a week earlier, battered and half in ruins, and was now limping down the Magdal valley, covering only a few leagues a day. When the traders at last made camp at the base of the mountain, Kiri took a handful of palace guards and three shield women and rode down to greet them.

She had been warned, and yet she did not expect to see so desperate a sight. More than half of Mercanio's wagons were gone. Those which were left were scarred by axes and arrows; some had obviously been set afire. For a time she sat silent on her horse, staring in disbelief and sorrow as they set up their ragged, overcrowded camp. She spotted three hostlers leading a line of spent horses towards the river.

"Tharn!" she cried, and spurred her mount. The men turned, shielding their eyes against the evening sun. She pulled to a sharp stop, the horse hooves spattering earth, and jumped off.

"Tharn! Parel! Gareth!" She exchanged quick greetings, hugged them all, even Parel, and then asked:

"Gods of the world, Tharn, what happened to you?"

"Three times we are attacked, Kiri. Each time more we lose. We had need of your bow, but glad I am you weren't there. Many are dead."

"Mercanio?"

"He took a spear wound in his side," Gareth said. "But he will live. He's as tough as an old boar. Is it true you ran away with the Kamil queen?"

"Of course is true," Tharn said. "She is here, can you not see that?"

Kiri did not want to talk about herself just yet. "Who attacked you?" she asked.

"Dravians," Tharn replied, prefacing the name with the worst obscenity she had ever heard him use.

"Bandits," Parel corrected him. "We were attacked by bandits."

"*Dravian* bandits," Tharn said, repeating the obscenity, and ignoring Parel's scowl very pointedly. "And the soldiers do nothing. Hundreds we pass on the road, we have blood all over us, and they laugh. 'Go tell the witch of Kamilan about bandits,' they say; 'we have more important things to worry about.' Is king there now a madman, Kiri. A lunatic. I do not go back."

They talked quickly, recounting what had passed, naming the dead. Lafe was gone, and Mercanio's steward, and eight others.

"And Mara?" Kiri asked. "Is she with you?"

"She is dead, too," Tharn said. "In Larandau. She caught a fever, and would not eat or speak. Her jaws they had to force open to give her medicine, and she spat it out. She wanted to die, and for one I do not blame her."

He paused, looked away for a moment, and spoke again. "Will you stay and sup with us, Kiri?"

"Actually," she said, "I've come to invite you to the palace—Mercanio, and any others who wish to come, and can be spared. You'll be the queen's guests for supper."

She had so looked forward to this meeting, to seeing them all again, and celebrating, showing them how good her life was. Maybe even boasting a little. Now. . . .

"Please come, Tharn."

"I am senior hostler," Parel said. "I will decide who can go."

"And I am Kiri's friend," Tharn said coldly. "I go, and I do not ask you. That is mutiny, yes? Good. Tell Mercanio so. I caravan no more."

Mercanio greeted her with pure delight, brushing aside her concern and insisting that his wound was little more than a scratch.

"You won't believe what tales they tell about you!" he said. "We were in Vianon when we heard. You know the Larandavs, Kiri, so cynical they are: they believe nothing, and also everything. So all we heard was rumours. The Kamil queen was fled, and her minstrel with her, and then the prince was killed—aye, it was a story for the fires. Some said you had been a Kamil agent all along. A good laugh we had over that. The whole story we did not hear until we got to Belengar, and some were disappointed; the rumours were so much better. It was even said that you and the queen changed yourselves into ravens and flew out the window and over the mountains of Dohann!" He raised his arms a bit and flapped his hands, laughing.

"Gods," Kiri said, "I wish it had been that easy."

The arms fell again with a wince of pain.

"Mercanio! That was no scratch you took. I know better. I talked to the men, you know."

"It's not so bad, Kiri; it will heal. Other things will heal less quickly. Oh, don't look so troubled, I'm not ruined. After twenty years I know tricks no bandit even thinks of. But I'm poorer than I was, and sadder." He straightened a little. "You look well. Do you miss the road?"

"Yes," she said honestly.

"It gets in the blood. So the queen has asked me to supper? Well, I will come, but I have nothing to tell her that I haven't already told her warlord and the wolf of Dohann."

"You met with Shadrak?"

"Aye," he said. "And three hundred of his bowmen. Gods, they are the deadliest looking men I've ever seen. I thought he would swallow us alive for tribute, but he took one look at the mess and invited me to sup with him instead. And he wouldn't let me go until he had wrung out of me every detail of everything I'd seen and heard in Dravia—not once, Kiri, but two or three times, to make sure we both got it right. So you see," he added, smiling, "I know what to expect."

Kiri laughed. "I have no doubt the queen will question you. But you would have been our guests in any case."

"Kiri, truthfully, what is she like? You wouldn't believe what people say. No, you have caravaned; perhaps you would. Is she a witch?"

"What is a witch, Mercanio?"

"Ahhh." He smiled faintly.

"We *walked* through the mountains of Dohann," Kiri said. "We didn't fly. Which is more astonishing, when you think about it?"

"I wish you'd never left us," he said. "Times there were when I nearly strangled you, but it was always so interesting having you around."

"King Berend is not mad," Mercanio said. "At least he is no madder than twenty other kings in other countries. Crueler than most, but not mad."

The caravaners had eaten like starving fugitives. Wounded and still ill, Mercanio ate modestly; the others gorged, downing trencher after loaded trencher and cup after cup of sweet, watered wine. The trader, seated at the queen's elbow, leaned back in his chair.

"I will tell you a story, lady," he went on. "It says much about the king. There was an old man, a farmer, who had lost all his sons in King Algard's wars. Only one of them had lived long enough to have children; he had three boys before he, too, was killed. The lads were raised by their grandfather. They were of fighting age now, and in the spring, as soon as the crops were planted, Berend's men came and took them for the army. So the old man went to Aralev and begged an audience with the king. 'Please,' he said, 'don't take them all. Take two, if you must, but leave me one.' King Berend said that he would give it thought. The next day he sent for the old man. 'I have thought,' he said, 'and I have judged. Because of your request I shall allow all three of your grandsons to remain in Dravia.' He pulled aside a curtain, and there were the three boys, stripped like prisoners, with their hands bound behind them. The king gave a command, and a soldier stepped forward and cut their throats—all three where they stood, with the old man watching. And then he had the bodies thrown into the great square, and he stood on the wall and shouted: 'Know then, all of you, your duty to your king!' "

"And the Dravians will follow such a lord?" Marwen asked.

"Yes. Because of Held. May I speak frankly?"

"There is no other purpose in my asking questions. Speak as frankly as you can."

"They want revenge, lady. They don't love Berend. He's a monster; even the loyal ones can see that. And so they mourn their dead prince all the more. And they blame you all the more, because he died in Kamilan."

"But as you say, Mercanio: he died in Kamilan! We didn't go to Dravia to kill him. He came to us. He came in arms to take me prisoner!"

"I know that, lady. But people are not rational about such things. They are bitter at his death, bitter because he was proud and handsome, bitter because he was replaced by Berend who is foul and cruel, bitterest of all because he was brought down by a slaveborn alien without rank or lineage, in unfair combat—whether it's true or not, lady, it is what they believe—and that he was left for carrion, without honours or a grave. That they will avenge, Berend or no Berend."

There was a brief but heavy silence.

"He doesn't lack for men, then," Caithland said. "So he will invade before the summer is out."

"We saw soldiers everywhere," Mercanio said, "but not massed armies. He is still gathering men and supplies; there is no question of that. And the two legions the emperor of Larandau has promised him are not likely to arrive soon. Dravia is simply not a high priority in Vianon. There are men there, I think, who don't even know where it is. And some who never heard of Kamilan, and who don't believe there are any queens left in the world—queens in their own right, I mean. I hope you're not offended, lady, but one such fellow laughed at me, and asked what sort of men the Kamils were then, that they would take orders from a woman: did they wear swaddling clothes as well, and suck their thumbs? Barely does Larandau know these mountain lands exist, and it is better so.

"But as for Berend, and what he will do, there is no way to be sure. Such a man I don't pretend to read. He may attack with the forces that he has, or he may wait until he believes he has an army nothing in the world can defeat. There is hate in him, and he may wait—if you understand me, lady, he may wait precisely because he hates so much."

"Why should he hate us so?" Kiri asked. "If the Kamils had not killed Prince Held, sooner or later he would have done so himself. They couldn't walk into the same room without quarrelling. And Berend said more than once that his brother was soft, and wasn't fit to be a king."

"Of course," Mercanio said dryly.

Yes, she thought. Of course. All the hatred Berend carried for his brother was transferred, without a catch of breath, upon those who killed him. He could weep now; he could rage to the heavens over the sacred blood of kinship—and so erase, even from his own memory, his own guilt.

"He has promised his people more tribute than Kamilan could ever pay," Mercanio went on. "And in return for the Larandav legions he has promised the emperor five thousand Kamil slaves. This city he swears he will leave in ashes, and the queen, too—for he says you are a witch, lady. And Shadrak of Belengar will do well not to fall living into his hands.

"All of this I spoke to your captain, just as I am speaking with you. And he told me that he had made his own oath, and that I should tell it to King Berend when I returned. An oath not to the usurper Mohr, he said, but to the great mother Jana, first and last of all the gods. 'I have sworn,' he said, 'that no one will rob my lady of her lands, or her freedom, or her life. I don't care who or how many they may be, I will kill them all; I will give them to the rivers and the fires and the frozen rock, until they come no more.' "

Mercanio paused faintly, and went on. "I must tell you, lady, when he spoke so my blood ran cold—for it seemed to me not simply that he meant his words, but that he could carry them out. It seemed absolutely certain . . . there, among a mere few hundred men, in a tent which did not even shut out the rain . . . so compelling is he, lady. So. . . ." Mercanio hesitated, as though the word was not quite right, but he could find no other.

"So . . . *dark*."

Kiri sat silent. This was Mercanio of Sardas, the most worldly of traders, who had seen every land there was, and every kind of people, and who looked upon everything he saw with a shrewd, unemotional merchant's eye. This was Mercanio who made few mistakes in judgment, and who always noticed when other men did.

Then, as if Mercanio himself suddenly realized that he was waxing poetic for the second occasion in his life, he smiled and said dryly:

"It may be that someone will take that oath to King Berend, but I will not."

When everyone had eaten every morsel they could, and Kiri had entertained them with many songs, the queen left most of her guests to linger over their wine and a game of counters, and took Mercanio and Kiri into the shield room. One of Caithland's men followed them, and, when Mercanio was seated, placed a bow on the table beside him.

"What can you tell me of this weapon?" the queen asked.

He picked it up and examined it briefly.

"It is a composite bow, lady, made of wood, horn, and sinew. It is used widely among the Thyrsians and the people of the steppes. Few have I seen in the mountain countries, though some of your border troops in Dohann had them. It surprised me."

"Why? Is it not a good weapon?"

"It's a very fine weapon, lady. It's the fastest of all bows, and only a crossbow can compete with it for accuracy. Also it can be used on horseback, which is a great advantage. But hard they are to make, and require much skill to use."

"That they are hard to make we've already discovered. Are they also hard to buy?"

The trader's one shrewd eye rested on the queen for a moment, and then turned to Kiri.

"What did you tell the queen about me?" he asked.

"That you've been a caravaner for twenty years," she said calmly, "and that there is none better. That you are honest, competent, and capable of infinite discretion."

"I see," he said dryly. "You learned things on the caravan I never taught you." He looked then towards the queen. "The bows can be purchased, lady, I would think, though I don't know how many, nor for what price."

"I want a thousand of them," Marwen said. "And as many bowyers as can be found who know how to make them and will come to Kamilan; I will pay them thirty ells a year. As for the cost of the bows, you must have an idea?"

He shrugged. "Perhaps ten ells apiece."

The queen looked at Kiri.

"Perhaps nine," Mercanio amended, "if a man bargained well."

You will get them for five or six at most, you old thief, Kiri thought grimly, *and you know very well I'll tell her so!*

"I'm sure you bargain well," the queen said. "I will pay you nine ells for every bow, and one ell for every two hundred arrows, and twenty more for every bowyer you bring me. That is, of course, if the weapons are warworthy and the craftsmen skilled. If they're not, I will pay nothing. I will pay you a bonus of two hundred ells if you return with at least half of my request before the winter. And I can advance you a thousand to repair your caravan. Do you accept?"

He clearly did not know what to say. He had spoken to Kiri of leaving the road. But this enterprise, if successful, would recover much of what he had lost in Dravia.

"May I . . . consider?" he asked.

"Of course. But I wish to show you one thing more." She motioned to the guard; he bent and she whispered to him briefly. He disappeared momentarily, and came back with two others, carrying a large iron coffer. Kiri recognized it at once as the queen's dowry chest.

"Kamilan is not a wealthy country, Mercanio," she said. "I know you're aware of that. But I have the means to pay you." She opened the coffer and smiled. "In gold."

"Your queen," Mercanio said, "is a hard woman."

"Would you have noticed," Kiri asked, "if she were a king?"

He chuckled. "Kiri, you never change." The laugh died away, and his face grew thoughtful. "Never they fight in the mountains with bows. Oh, perhaps a little; bows are always good in a siege. But in the field?—it was unthinkable. This will change everything."

"Yes," Kiri said.

"I meant to retire," he said. "What will I tell my wife?"

"Tell her what you told her the last four years. Just one more caravan."

"You're as hard as your mistress. In Dohann I think you ate rocks."

"No. Just raw partridges."

"Raw? You ate them *raw*? Mohr save us, what did they taste like?"

"Awful," she said. "You will accept her offer, won't you?"

For a time they watched each other across the campfire. It was very late; the moon was almost gone behind the western peaks. Most of the caravan slept, curled in blankets beside their wagons. Nearby, someone was playing an ill-tuned wooden flute.

"He doesn't play half as good as you," Mercanio said. He smiled. "I am a fool, the gods know, but I never could resist a chance to be a rich man. Yes, I will accept. But tell me this, Kiri—when the Dravians have the same weapons, what will your queen do then?"

25. The Wolf Unleashed

On a warm night in the moonturn of high summer, some twelve hundred Dravian warriors appeared in the high reaches of Dohann, to the east of Belengar. They marched unopposed for more than forty leagues. They were singing, it was said, and making jokes about the Kamils hiding in their beds. On the third day they were ambushed in a narrow valley: ambushed by men who would not stand and fight, who would not even show their faces, but who rained arrows at them from the trees, and fled.

Only a few Dravians were killed. More than a hundred were wounded, but the arrows did very little damage, except to draw a little blood. Some of them fell again from their own weight before the warriors could contemptuously toss them away.

If this—so the Dravian captain was reputed to have said—*if this is what the Kamils have to fight with, then we shall be feasting in the witch's hall before the leaves turn gold.*

By morning all but three of their wounded men were dead. The next nightfall they were attacked again. By the end of a fortnight the last survivors, perhaps two hundred men, scattered and on foot, stumbled back into Dravia. They had never fought a battle, and they had killed fewer than forty of their enemies.

A shock of triumph swept through Kamilan. Bonfires roared in the streets, and country folk came in long processions with gifts for the temples: for Harash the god of war, for Mohr the great father—but especially for Jana. It was Jana most of all whom they praised with hymns and offerings and dances.

Angmar watched them sadly and shook his head. They could not see beyond the moment, beyond their own simple aspirations. So it was all perfectly clear to them: Jana had returned to Kamilan, and the Kamils prospered. The crops grew lush, the trees were laden with fruit, the lambs and calves were fat. And in the borderlands a Dravian warband had been defeated and destroyed—defeated, they did not fail to notice, by the man who had fought for the queen at the Magdal bridge, and who had marched in defense of Jana's priestess. It was all very clear to them.

But for Angmar, as for his peers, the shock of triumph had in it a shock of horror. What had passed in Dohann was not the Kamil way; it was not the way of men at all. Young Lord Favian, who was a bold and skilful fighting man, paced and threw his arms about and swore that no Kamil warrior could ever hold his head up after this. He cursed Borosar for holding the army back and letting Shadrak range the borders.

"We should have been there!" he said. "By Great Harash, then there would have been a fight!"

The only fight Favian got to enjoy that summer took place in the royal city itself. By the main market square, not far from Mohr's temple, a huge brawl erupted between his men and a mass of revellers who were yelling *Glory to the wolf!* at the top of their drunken lungs.

But when the seneschal's troops restored order again, and the broken heads were carried away, it became obvious that the lines of battle had not been very clearly drawn. It was not simply the riffraff, crashing their tin cups in the taverns, who admired Shadrak's victory. Nearly everyone did.

Something was afoot in Kamilan, Angmar thought: a mood which was not easy to name, which one could sense more in its effects than in its essence. It was visible in Theron's rapidly waning power—and indeed, in Angmar's own. It was visible in the willingness of even well-taught and highborn men to forget their generations of slowly acquired wisdom, and to be fascinated anew by the promises of a sorceress.

And now a slaveborn Thyrsian savage made war with ill-trained rabble and poisoned arrows, and the warlord of Kamilan did not appear to object, and the queen sent a royal courier with fulsome praise and gifts, to commend them both.

"Well," said Crayfe, "what else would you expect from a woman?"

Angmar did not enjoy travelling. Wagons and chariots were dreadful things to ride in for any length of time, and even in his youth he had never been a great horseman. He ached in every bone by the time he reached Borosar's camp at Getann. For the first time in years he felt and looked his age.

They were not old friends, but the warlord embraced him as though they were—though he could not resist a jibe at Angmar's wooden walk.

"You look," he said, "like you haven't sat your backside on a horse for twenty years."

"Well, I haven't," Angmar said shortly. "I detest horses."

"What a thing for a Kamil to say."

The warlord cleared a room for him in the small garrison, with a bath and fresh clothing, and ordered wine and food. They sat outside then, with a bit of awning for shade. It was a magnificent day; the summer wind was sweet with mountain flowers.

I spend too much time in the city, Angmar thought regretfully. *It is so lovely here.*

The camp was surprisingly empty of men. Although Borosar was not fighting, he was by no means idle. His men were escorting tin shipments from the mines, repairing roads, recruiting, collecting stores, breaking and training horses—and practicing, the warlord said, till they stumbled to their tents from exhaustion.

Borosar rarely bothered with pleasantries. The food was served and the wine poured. He leaned forward a little in his chair, and said:

"Well, sage, you didn't ride two hundred leagues to play a game of counters with me."

"No. I didn't."

Borosar waited, and when Angmar did not go on, he smiled a faint, cold smile, and said:

"So you've come to tell me the Council is unhappy. Theron is outraged. Favian is hanging his head in shame. And Crayfe is stuffing his fat face and saying: 'Oh, my, has old Borosar put his foot into it now!' Am I wrong?"

"No. You're not wrong." The warlord was not a deep man, Angmar reflected, but neither was he a fool.

"And what does the prince consort say?" Borosar asked.

Angmar frowned slightly. "He says that since the captain of Belengar is a slaveborn foreigner, and his men only common folk, though he himself disapproves of their methods, he doesn't think their actions necessarily reflect on us, or on our honour."

"Trust Landis to be so practical."

"Borosar." It was not easy to begin. Where did one start, and what words said the thing properly? Honour was such a simple thing when it was intact, such a complicated thing when it came undone. And it began to come undone long ago, when the king had no sons. Honour could not exist in a vacuum; it was part of a clearly defined order, a social fabric which was already unravelling, which had been unravelling for years. Prince Held savaged it further when he took the queen. Since then they had been slipping from one small dishonour to another, and each had seemed unavoidable. And now this. . . .

Crayfe had said: what else can you expect from a woman? He had spoken out of spite and malice, but underpinning his question was a truth.

Angmar decided to begin as politely as he could. "Why are you holding the army back, Borosar?"

"Because," the warlord said simply, "when Berend begins this war in earnest, I'm going to need it. I'm going to need every warrior, every weapon, every outraged peasant with a club, *and* the wolf of Dohann."

"You approve of what he's doing, then? You agree that we should defend ourselves by hunting men down without giving battle, and killing them with poisoned arrows?"

"I don't approve. I simply ask you—and the rest of Council—what the captain asked me. What choices do we have? You used to be the most sensible of men, Angmar, the one who always accepted reality. I must say I am surprised at you."

"And you used to be the most honourable of men. I am surprised at you."

Borosar flushed slightly. "We have five thousand blooded warriors," he said grimly; "the best in all the world, but only five thousand. We can recruit and arm another ten thousand commoners—but what kind of soldiers will peasants and foresters turn into, with a mere few months to train them? Shadrak is succeeding with his men because he taught them to be hunters more than to be warriors, and hunting was something they already understood.

"Five thousand good men, Angmar. Berend can send that many as a scouting party. How many times can we fight them, man to man, and still have any fighters left?"

"So we abandon our honour, and act like dogs in a pit, like barbarians who have neither religion nor shame?"

"You put the matter very harshly."

"So do others."

"Aye, no doubt. And some are dancing in the streets."

"Any fool will dance in the streets if you tell him an enemy has been defeated," Angmar said wearily. "Surely it's for men like us to think a little farther than that." He paused, choosing his words. The warlord did not like to be criticized, least of all by one who was not himself a soldier.

"If we are not men, Borosar, then we are nothing. If we fight with all the skill and courage we have, surely we may yet prevail. Even I will take my sword from the wall, and mount a horse again, if it is needed. And so will every man in Kamilan. We don't need this barbarism. We will never win the gods' favour in this way, and without their favour, what hope do we have in any war?"

For a time Borosar did not answer, and the sage knew his words had struck deep.

"I agree with you, Angmar," he said finally, heavily. "In one part of my mind I agree with you. In the other. . . ." He took a long drink of wine. "I talked to Shadrak, you know, when I learned of this. I sent runners all over Dohann to find him, and I wasn't gentle with him, for I knew I'd have to answer for all of it. I called him a miserable savage, among other things. And when I asked him what he had to say in his defense he said: 'Nothing.' He was sick to death of talk about honour, he said.

" 'Honour is all very well for you,' he said, 'and for all the other lords. If you're killed in battle you're a hero, and they sing about you in the feast halls. If you're captured, your kinsmen will ransom you. If you're defeated, after the dust clears and the anger cools, likely as not you'll still be lords, even if you serve another liege.

" 'The rest of us,' he said, 'will go to tin mines and to galleys. The common people will be taken in caravans of slaves, and scattered across the world; the old will die of hunger because the crops are gone for tribute. The queen will be a fugitive, or torn to pieces in their camps, or kept in a cage for Berend's pleasure.

" 'There is no honourable defeat for us,' he said. 'Only for men like you. You may not get it, either, but you can hope. After all, you're the ones who make the rules—on both sides of the border.' "

The warlord shook his head. "Five years ago, Angmar, I would have struck down a man who spoke to me so. Instead, I kept thinking about myself when I was his age, how many times I'd ridden into battle like a wild man, looking back again and again to make sure that everyone was watching, that everyone had noticed. Glory, Great Harash, how I wanted glory! I never thought much about slaves or tribute."

Borosar drained his cup and filled it again. "This will be my last war, I think. I doubt I'll live to see another. And I find that I don't care much about anything except Kamilan. Not glory, nor rank, nor what is fitting to a man like myself or to any other man. I don't care a fig if they never hang another champion's wreath around my neck. I care about these mountains, and these fields. I want to keep them. No, wait, Angmar, hear me out! I want to go to my death knowing that whatever else I have done or failed to do, I have kept Kamilan whole.

"You speak of the gods' favour. Well, if they are set against us, no doubt we shall soon know. But maybe none of this is as simple as it looks to a wise man. I sat there with Shadrak and I thought: This man has no social rank, no lands, no lineage, no name even, except some foreign snarl that sticks in the throat.

He doesn't understand honour. He can't even see the purpose of it. What is honour to a hawk, or to a hare? But he will keep these mountains. He will harry the borderlands like a wolf, and even a large army will be bleeding by the time it gets to us. And I'm glad.

"I know what you're thinking, Angmar. We are an honourable people. But by great Harash, it's *our* land—why shouldn't we defend it?"

He paused, and added pointedly. "The queen has already commended both of us—Shadrak for the victory, and myself for having the good sense to promote him, in spite of his low birth."

"The queen is a woman, and thinks with her feelings. She hates the Dravians beyond all reason; and she's frightened of losing her power. I don't blame her for any of that, but it hasn't sharpened her judgment."

"Well, and what is blunting my judgment, do you think?"

Angmar ignored that. "We've been fighting Dravia for seventy years, without the likes of Shadrak of Belengar, and we're still here." He paused, aware that nothing he said was going to make any difference, wondering if there was any point in going on. Nonetheless he did so.

"The lords of Council, with the exception of Lord Landis, have asked that you reconsider, and withdraw the command you've given to Shadrak, and absorb his men into your other forces or dismiss them."

They had been, Angmar recalled, a good deal more blunt. They had said: *Tell Borosar to strip that gutterbred savage of his rank and send his rabble home!*

"And how would I justify this to the queen? Did they tell you that? Or is that my problem? How do I justify it to my own men? You would be surprised how many of them see Shadrak as a hero."

"As you phrased it yourself, Borosar, the man has no social rank, no lands, no lineage, no name. The command you gave him, under those circumstances, was an extraordinary trust. He has dishonoured that trust, dishonoured Kamilan, and dishonoured the queen, whether she acknowledges it or not. That is how you justify it."

The warlord was silent for a moment. Then he shook his head.

"You haven't been listening to me, Angmar. Neither rank nor honour are the issues here. Kamilan is. How it will all be judged in the end I leave to the gods and the songmakers. But Kamilan I will defend as I see fit. I will not leash the wolf, and you may tell Council so—and you may tell them I made that decision in Dohann, before the queen's messenger reached me. I know a warrior when I see one."

"You admire the man," Angmar said, and wondered why that had not occurred to him before.

"I admire *skill*," Borosar said. "And by the gods, he has it. Skill and audacity, like you see once in a lifetime."

This man, Angmar thought, was hopeless.

"We speak at cross-purposes, warlord. I will leave you in peace. But I have one counsel more, whether you want it nor not. Don't give your captain too much lead, or you may have more to answer for than any of us will swallow—even the queen."

Riding to Getann, Angmar had paid careful attention to the landscape, drinking in the lushness of the pastures and fields, the brooding darkness of the forests, the splendour of the gathering mountains. Riding back he noticed little. He was lost in his own thoughts, ignoring even the discomfort of his body.

He felt as he had often felt at the side of King Adelmar: that all of men's wisdom, all their finest intentions, all their most carefully made decisions were little more than groping motions in the darkness, trivial gestures against the chaos closing everywhere around them.

Hard things were being said in Council, sometimes in pretended jest. Usually it was Crayfe who would say them, Crayfe who was willing to be the headsman, so to speak, the verbal executioner of other men's grimmest thoughts. It was a role they had come to expect from him, and which he took great satisfaction in fulfilling.

Borosar, Crayfe pointed out one night, had never been the sort of man to cater to a woman. Quite the opposite. And now their hard-nosed, hard-mouthed, hard-drinking warlord jumped to the queen's every whistle, just like a puppy dog. Curious, Crayfe said, was it not?

Theron did not think it was curious. Theron considered it perfectly obvious that the warlord was bewitched.

Angmar did not believe that—at least he did not believe it with any part of his mind which was the mind of the politician and the sage. Still less did he believe that Borosar was moved by infatuation; in this Crayfe's judgment was correct. The warlord had never been a man to cater to a woman, and he was not such a man now. What he was—what he had always been—was ferociously ambitious.

Any man who made combat his life, Angmar believed, was a man with a deep passion for winning. Glory and skill—the things which he claimed were at the heart of it—were in fact secondary. Skill was merely what you needed to win, and glory was the proof that you had done it.

Borosar, aging and cornered, wanted to win. And although the man was not deep, he had good instincts. He might well believe—not without cause—that if he won this war for Marwen he could name his own reward.

Even. . . . Angmar's mind faltered a little, and then took the thought head on. *Even the queen herself.*

The warlord had not pressed very hard for a marriage between the queen and his son. He simply could not do so; the lad was an idiot, and even Borosar knew it. But if he smashed the Dravians, and saved Kamilan, and perhaps even had something left of his army when he finished. . . ? His own marriage would not stand in his way. He would give his wife whatever honour money she demanded and send her back to her clan. The gods knew he would not regret her, and she would not regret him.

Angmar did not believe for a moment that the old warrior had suddenly been seized with love for Kamilan's mountains and fields. Neither was he being a hypocrite. The warlord, more than any man Angmar had ever known, was an emotional chameleon; a man who could, with astonishing ease, take on attitudes and beliefs as he needed them; a man who could become, without any sense of dishonesty, whatever he needed to become in order to be at peace with whatever decision he had just made. His passion for Kamilan was the effect, not the cause, of his decision to hold it at any cost.

Angmar sighed, feeling utterly overwhelmed. Nothing was happening as he had hoped it might. His cousin's marriage to the queen, which he had dared to believe would make Landis singularly powerful, had instead made Landis vulnerable.

257

From the day he had accepted her offer of marriage, Landis had become not her lord and leader, but her follower. Calmly he let the goddess return, and let Kamil life be corrupted anew with sorcery and decadent excess. He allowed Theron to be isolated, and the Council split like a melon. And now he shrugged his shoulders at the savagery in Dohann. *The man is lowborn; it does not reflect on us.* Dishonour crept like wetness through a sponge, and soiled them all.

The horse Angmar was riding nickered suddenly, and he looked up. They passed a small group of peasants, with an old half-blind horse pulling a wagonload of wood.

"The gods preserve you, lord," one of them shouted pleasantly. "It be a fine day on the road, be it not?"

He returned their greeting and rode on, sadder than before.

Great Mohr, what is to become of us? Give the queen wisdom, great father, and give us time. Stay your hand, and keep us together until we can raise up a king. . . !

26. The Winter Before the Great War

The Dravians sent no more armies to Kamilan that summer. Rumours flew readily enough, and twice Borosar marched north to meet a threatened invasion which failed to materialize. As the summer passed, it became clear that Berend simply was not ready. He had tested Kamil defenses with that one ill-fated raid, but he would not fight in earnest until he had an army strong enough to win. He wanted more men and more stores. He wanted the promised Larandav legions. And he wanted every Dravian fighter armoured from head to foot. As far as anyone could remember, a helmet and a good mail shirt or leather cuirass had been standard protection in the armies of the mountains. Now, after the slaughter in Dohann, he wanted gauntlets, greaves, cheek-pieces, heavy boots, everything. He would roll into Kamilan an unstoppable machine of war, and crush everything in his path.

The harvest was magnificent that year, and the weather held, so that every coil of hay was stored dry, and every patch of grain ripened and garnered without loss. The forests were plundered for nuts. The cellars were piled with mountains of cheese. Fat pigs rooted and grunted in their pens. The Kamils could scarcely remember such a year of bounty. And it was all theirs. None of it had been burned or trampled or dragged away for tribute by the Dravians. Jana had kept it safe for them, and they honoured her for it with songs and processions and wagonloads of gifts.

Theron, high priest of Mohr, thundered and pleaded from the steps of his temple:

"People of Kamilan, look how you've wronged Great Mohr, and look how he's forgiven you! He has stayed his hand! He has given you time to see your own folly, and make right your betrayal. All these gifts are Mohr's! The crops are Mohr's! The cattle, the lambs, the fruits of the forest, the grain, the wind, the sun, *the earth itself is Mohr's!* Don't believe the sorceress. Jana is no god. Jana is a demon who can only bring ruin, not blessings. I beg you, before it's too late, drive out the evil that is among you! *Save Kamilan while you can!*"

Kiri listened to him with fascination. He was perhaps a little mad, but only a little. He shouted when other men whispered, but he was not alone in his thoughts. Kamilan was deeply divided. It was a nation which had been conquered, but unlike Dravia, its conquest had never been complete. In nearly every part of Kamil life, from its bedchambers to its battlefields, from the royal house to the mine pits of Getann, a new order had been everywhere imposed upon an old one. The new had dominated for a long time. The elites of Kamilan were mostly sons of the conquerors; they were the followers of Mohr. But even they had needed their alliance with the daughters of the hill queens, and so even the Kamil aristocracy was split. The new dominated, but the old stubbornly remained. Now, with a true queen in the palace and Jana back in her temple, the old was lifting its head and scenting power.

And the men of Mohr were afraid!

It was that which Kiri found so fascinating. They had most of the land and the wealth. They had the swords. They had the power of command and the confidence which came with it, the sense of their own worth and rightness. And yet they were afraid. The fact that Jana's people had numbers on their side, and some real if limited power, and the sovereign—none of that, in Kiri's view, accounted for the extent of Theron's fear, and the fear among all who followed Mohr. What they feared most was inside themselves.

"You must never weaken, people of Kamilan!" Theron cried. "Do not yield to witchcraft and harlotry! Do not believe in the false promises of false prophets! Mohr's people must be a stern and steadfast people!"

"And they must never," Medwina said scornfully, "think about living. They must never lust or revel or run wild like children. They must never imagine that it might be nicer to lie in the sun with a lover rather than lie in a ditch with a spear. One day I'll put a hot coal down that old raven's throat, and he will croak no more."

"He croaks so much because he's afraid of you," Kiri said.

"Yes."

"But why?"

"I am stronger than he is."

"Yet you believe that he—that they—will win. You've said so many times."

Medwina linked her hands, kneaded them thoughtfully. "Both things are true," she said. "It's not easy to explain. The men of Mohr—the men of violence and conquest and power—are ranging over the earth. The peoples they are conquering have two choices: they can try to fight, or they can go down. Most have gone down, whether they tried to fight or not. And if they want to fight, they'll have to be very good at it. After a time, it will be hard to tell them from their enemies. Either way, it becomes Mohr's world.

"Yet Mohr will live in Jana's shadow till the end, till he is brought down himself. He will cage her, but she will escape. He will cut out her tongue, but she will learn to speak anew. He will imagine that he has killed her, and she will spring up in every spot where he's not watching. His own sons will stumble into her arms, and see that she is beautiful, and go back to their father and say to him: *What have your done?* He will have no peace. He will break the world to splinters to control her, but he will fail, and he will have no peace.

"So, yes, Mohr will win, but we are stronger. And out of that will be fashioned the darkest story of all. For if Mohr could conquer utterly, his followers would soon erase themselves—

and him—from the history of the world. It is we who will keep them alive—we who dance and love and dream and make things for pleasure. We who do not care for conquest will make sure there is always another world to conquer. We will keep rebuilding the world so he can trample it again. It is that, Kiri, it is that above all which makes me . . . despair."

Neither spoke for a long time. It was all true, Kiri thought. Already Marwen was fighting Mohr's men with Mohr's weapons. And however complete her triumph might be, how long would any of it last beyond her own lifetime? Kamilan, only half-conquered, was already an aberration, an island. In Larandau men laughed at the thought of a queen ruling in her own right. In Thyrsis, although they still worshipped the goddess, they buried every chieftain with the strangled bodies of his wives and concubines beside him. In Sardas no respectable woman left her house alone, and many women of rank never left their houses at all.

How long was one battered mountain kingdom going to be different?

It is as Medwina says. Men of violence determine the order of the world. Those who are attacked can only choose to surrender or resist; they cannot choose to be left alone. If they are destroyed, violence has won. If they want to survive they must become fighters, and violence has won again.

Consider ourselves. We honour Shadrak above all men; we empty our granaries and melt down our gold for him. Kamilan has given him its heart, and the queen has given him her bed. And it is true that he is a man of integrity and courage, but there are others among us who are equally good, and they are not equally rewarded. It is the wolf we bring our offerings to, and it is the wolf whom Marwen loves. Without the violence that he wields, we are levies in the armies of Dravia, slaves in its tin mines, whores in its brothels; we are erased from time, the only trace of our existence a smear of blood on a sword without a name.

Whatever the outcome of this war, violence has won.

Marwen's child was born late in the fall, a fair-haired, blue-eyed boy child. He was carried in great splendour to the temple of Jana, and presented to the goddess, and the name of Alyth's brother Aran, who had been a warrior and a bard, was given to him. The queen thought he was beautiful, but Kiri could not see why. She liked children when they were old enough to talk to, when she could think of them as people like herself, only a bit younger. Babies were strange creatures, noisy, demanding, and unpredictable, and they all looked the same. The fact that she had once been a baby herself in no way changed her opinion on the subject.

But the queen doted on the little wretch, and in spite of herself Kiri noticed how bright and alert he was, how quickly he responded to things, how quickly he learned. He was intrigued by her lyre, and in no time at all developed a liking for the sound of it. She sang him to sleep, and learned silly baby songs to make him giggle, and after a few weeks she decided that, although she would never be one of those women who cooed at every baby they met on the street, she could find a *particular* baby quite charming.

Luned, of course, thought he was wonderful, too—proof of how perfect the match was. Luned bragged about him even more than his father did. The best blood in the world was in that little prince, she said: the house of Alyth, the house of Adelmar, the house of Maene. He would be a king to reckon with. And then she would wink, and hint as broadly as a tavern wench that the queen and her splendid consort would soon make another.

But Landis did not return to the queen's bed, and as the skies lowered and hung black over the peaks of Dohann, he gathered up his men and returned once again to his own estates. There, for the first time publicly since his marriage, he chose a concubine, taking her not only into his bed but into his feast hall. Realists in the court interpreted his action as a frank admission that his bond with Marwen had been purely political, and having produced an heir, had served its purpose. In a year or two, when the war was over, they would perhaps choose to have another child; certainly it would be wiser if they did. Except for that, they had neither any need nor any wish to share their lives.

So be it, Kiri thought. There was something cold and bleak about it all, perhaps, but dynastic obsessions left honest men and women little other choice. She felt a genuine respect for Landis of Maene. Whatever else, she thought, he was not a hypocrite. So she was surprised when, a fortnight or so later, as she and Marwen sat alone in the shield room, the queen said, without any warning at all when Landis's name happened to be mentioned:

"I don't trust him, Kiri. I did at first—as much as I could trust any of them. But not any more."

"But, lady, I would have thought. . . ." Kiri paused. "It seemed to me that he did much to earn your trust."

"He did. But something happened between us which puts everything in a different light."

She did not immediately go on, and Kiri asked softly: "Was it the Festival—the Field of Fire?"

"Yes. We were like lovers that night, Kiri. And I admit I seduced him—quite deliberately. It would be better between us, I thought, if we shared some pleasure, if we could enjoy each other's company a little. He was always so self-contained, so unyielding. And the fire was in my blood, too, and the drums—who could help it? So I pleasured with him as I've rarely pleasured with anyone. You would think me most unqueenly if I told you everything we did.

"He hasn't touched me since."

That, Kiri thought, made no sense at all. "Surely Landis is not ashamed of bedding with his own wife!"

"Not ashamed, Kiri. Afraid. Afraid of loving me. Afraid even of desiring me too much."

"Perhaps he's afraid that you won't love him in return. That he'll only be hurt."

"Perhaps. But he's proud, Kiri—proud enough to think himself worthy of a queen's love. And all his life he's gone after what he wants with single-minded determination. He waited years to marry me. He accepted all my terms. Should I believe he would abandon me, out of fear of loss, precisely at the moment when it must have looked to him that he might win me?"

The queen shook her head, in answer to her own question.

"Medwina was right," she went on. "He wants power. That's the reason he married me, and it's the only reason. He wants power so much that even the thought of being happy with me must be kicked aside like a rock from his path."

"Would it have been possible?" Kiri whispered. "Being happy with you?"

Marwen shrugged. "Only Jana knows that. I don't love him. But he could have had pleasure from me, and friendship, and political advantage, and freedom to love anyone he wanted—is that enough to make a man happy? I don't know. I suspect happiness never was the question."

"Still, you can't blame him for withdrawing—"

"I don't blame him for withdrawing. The Laws of Kind give him every right to do so. I'm troubled by the reason for it, that is all."

Kiri was silent for a time. She loved Marwen dearly, but she knew nonetheless that the queen was proud—too proud, perhaps. Was she piqued because the equally proud lord of Maene had walked away from her bed—piqued when she should have been thankful for both their sakes?

"Whatever the reason, lady," she said, "isn't it better this way?"

Wind hammered against the palace walls, making the tapestries shift and sway, and the tapers gutter and leap. There was snow in the air; it was already failing in Dohann. The queen pulled her shawl close about her shoulders.

"If nothing were involved but our own lives, yes, it would be better this way. Then again, if nothing were involved but our own lives, I would never have married him. It's all a question of power. And I have lost this exchange. I'm certain of that. I can't prove it, and maybe fear is making me misjudge the man—fear and Medwina's warnings, which I never forgot for a moment, even when I ignored them."

She paused, and looked at Kiri with an unexpected, enchanting smile.

"Don't be so downcast, my friend; it's not the end of the world. I was foolish to imagine that it might have been different. The lords of Council are lords of Mohr—all of them, even Borosar. They will never build me more than a paper house, with the key in their pockets."

She glanced at the window. It was still full day, but the sky was so dark it seemed like evening.

"Shadrak will be here in a few days," she said.

"You've had word?" Kiri asked.

"No." The queen smiled faintly. "I'm not Medwina. But I *am* her kinswoman. There are things I simply . . . know."

Something cold went deep into Kiri's bones. "And is the heart of Landis of Maene one of those things?" she whispered.

There was a brief silence. When the queen spoke again, Kiri grew colder still.

"I think it always has been," Marwen said.

Two days passed. On the morning of the third a messenger arrived from Borosar the warlord. The danger of invasion was over until the spring. Oswin of Tamri and the other warleaders had dispersed with their men to their own estates. The rest of his forces would winter at the garrisons of Getann and Althen. The warlord himself, along with Shadrak of Belengar and some two thousand men, would reach Kamilan in two days.

Kiri never forgot that procession. She had seen others far more splendid; the queen's arrival, after her flight from Dravia, would always be the best of them. But she never forgot Borosar's last march into Kamilan. He came hours before the first snow, with the clouds hanging so low one could almost have reached up and touched them. There was a breathless quiet in the mountains, and the world was shifting with fog. Sometime after noon came the sound of feet bounding up the steps, a rush of voices at the door, and then one of Caithland's young guards running across the hall:

"They're coming, lady! They're coming!"

Kiri ran with the others to the palace roof. Everyone was staring and pointing and shouting, and then everyone fell still, realizing that there was nothing to see. The twisting road down the mountainside was empty, and the valley was mist-wrapped and desolate. The boy had made a mistake.

Then she heard it, and in a thousand years she would never forget the sound. It was a Kamil warsong, indistinct with distance, a muted cry of fifes echoing among the crags. It was impossible to tell where it was coming from. It leapt from earth to sky and back again, from mountain to mountain, fading sometimes until only the slow beat of a drum remained, rising again closer and wilder but still lost in mist, as though the warriors who followed it were marching just beyond the edges of the world.

Her hair rose on her neck, and her breath caught in her throat. It was unbearably beautiful, and no amount of rational thought could undo that beauty. She hated war, and she hated the men who had turned conquest and dominion into a virtue and a way of life.

And yet . . . and yet . . . and yet . . .

Vague shapes appeared in the valley, resolving slowly into horsemen, still gray with distance and fog. Their standards were muted splashes of colour, all the more splendid for the lowering skies around them. The fifes cried like wind, reckless with pride. Someone on the roof shouted, and a wild cheer swept across the queen's ramparts, so that people in the streets below looked up. A guard cupped his hands beside his mouth and shouted down to them, at the top of his lungs:

"Borosar!"

In minutes, the entire city was in the streets.

Kiri understood their excitement. She had run like a hare through the fields of Vanthala more times than she could remember, abandoning whatever she was supposed to be doing, merely to catch a glimpse of a raiding party coming in, or a band of soldiers from Aralev passing by on their way to the border. It was always splendid to look at them, and it always would be.

She did not know why. None of the answers anyone gave her ever satisfied her. Sometimes she looked at herself with scorn, called herself a liar and a fool—the worst kind of liar, the kind that lied to herself. *We are a race of predators,* she would say, *and we always have been, and you, Kiri the minstrel, are no different from the rest. You do not kill, you merely make songs about it—does that make you better? Or does it perhaps make you worse?*

But that was not the answer, either. Humans *were* a race of predators, perhaps, but they were also a race of planters, of poets, of gossips and healers and friends. So what then was this love of glory, this passion for drum beats and horses and ships, this thing which had sent her hungering out of the hills of Vanthala and knotted her throat here on this foggy rampart? Was it nothing more than savagery? Or was there something else at the core of it—in her and in all of them—something other than conquest and dominion, something which once had been whole and sound, something the makers of empire had taken, and twisted, and turned to their own use?

So began the winter before the Great War. It seemed to Kiri that the queen grew more daring as it passed, as though both the victories behind her and the menace which lay ahead were spurs to action, to seize what she could while it was still in reach. The lords who for years had not paid their tribute found armed men at their gates, the queen's banner flying high from their standards, the queen's command harsh on their lips: *Pay, or be charged with rebellion!*

One of them, a kinsman of the house of Maene, came to her then himself, storming with wrath:

"What's the meaning of this, lady? I sent a messenger at summer's end, when the harvests were taken. He told you I couldn't pay this year, and the prince consort assured me that I might wait, because my debts are so pressing. Do you now break your word?"

"I'm not breaking my word," she said grimly. "I never gave it. I don't know what the prince consort promised you; it was not his place to promise anything without consulting me. The harvests were good, and you've taken your share. You have no reason not to pay."

"I have more than five thousand ells in debts, lady. We have expanded our holdings, and cleared new land, and built a fortress at Haring. All of that takes money, lady."

"And all of that enriches you. Your wife wears more gold around her wrists than I can find in the Kamil treasury. Pay some of your debts with that!"

He was overwhelmed with rage. "By the gods, would you begrudge a woman her husband's gifts? What will you demand next? The roof above her head? This is outrageous!"

"Had you paid your tribute year by year, as the law demands, you would never have bought so many gifts. I have a war to fight. Pay, or be held in rebellion."

"I will speak about this to the lord of Maene!"

"So will I," she said.

Moves like these were provocative, but they were also widely popular. The common folk saw no reason why a lord should not pay his tribute to the sovereign, when they paid theirs to the lord every year, good crop or bad, and no one caring a fig if they were hungry. Even Angmar approved. It was time there was order in the land again, he said. He could not imagine what Landis had been thinking of, telling the man he would not have to pay.

Time was short. The queen moved against every weakness she saw, honed every weapon, made every possible friend. She threatened, when she judged it necessary, but mostly she reasoned, and sometimes she smiled. Borosar had smiles enough to feast on for the rest of his life; smiles enough to set all of Kamilan wondering and gossiping.

So, too, she kept her slaveborn captain by her side, and despite the ongoing crisis in which she lived, she met with him boldly and often. She was not unaware of the danger, but she was strangely cool about it. It was as though she looked at the world from a different place, and saw the danger differently—as something false, something wrong in the very fabric of the world—a thing to be heeded, perhaps, but never treated with respect. Her right to love could not be sacrificed in the name of sovereignty. It was part of sovereignty, and she would claim it as fiercely as she claimed her crown.

In the time of King Algard's wars, in those terrible years which Marwen had spoken of in Dravia, Medwina had ordered a tunnel dug from the palace, in case the city was overrun or the king betrayed. It led from what were then the princess's chambers into the cellars, under the fortress wall to the house of a tradesman, a kinsman of Medwina's who made leather goods and toys. As it happened, the tunnel never needed to be used, and only a handful of people in the queen's household ever learned of its existence. The tradesman had since died and the house belonged to his daughter, a priestess of the temple of Jana.

In that house a room was set aside for the queen's use, finely furnished and warm with tapestries and fire. Sometimes her meetings there with Shadrak were private and brief, but often they ate together with one or two guests. Medwina joined them occasionally, and so did Caithland, who was becoming more and more deeply involved in devising strategies for the queen's safety.

Tonight only Kiri was present, playing her lyre as they ate and laughed together and toasted each other with cool, fragrant wine. Watching them, Kiri sometimes remembered Dravia, remembered the queen and Prince Held. She understood more than ever how bleak that life had been—how bleak and unsatisfying for both of them. If Held could come from his spirit world and see, she wondered, would he weep for what he had thrown away? Or would he look upon their happiness and hate them both?

Shadrak's hand was in the queen's hair, his face bent to her neck. She murmured something, and he laughed, and drew her back against his body. Kiri rose, tucked the lyre under one arm, and prepared to leave.

"No," the queen said softly, turning her head a little. "Don't go, Kiri. Stay and play for us, if you would. It's so beautiful."

"Oh." She was not embarrassed, but she was genuinely surprised. "If you wish, lady."

She sat down again and began to play, choosing a love song she knew the queen particularly liked, paying self-conscious attention to her instrument, aware nonetheless when they rose, when Marwen's gold belt tumbled with a soft clatter to the floor, when the captain tugged off his boots, when the softness of their voices became uneven and harsh. How many songs that took she could not afterwards remember, but finally, forgetting herself, she looked up and saw them tangled together on the bed, animal and lovely, the man's dark body rising and falling, the woman's thighs enclosing him, her hands greedy against his back and her body coiling eagerly to his. Kiri's breath caught. She watched, forgetting to play, forgetting everything except the splendour of it and the knowledge which swept her, as though a window had opened not merely on her world but on all worlds past and to come: the knowledge that the anarchy of passion was an enduring enemy—the best and most enduring enemy—of Mohr.

Here was neither queen nor slaveborn soldier, neither caste nor rank nor dower, no family, no sacred blood, no *patria*. Mohr's power needed all of those things. Dynasties could not be founded without them, empires could not be built, slaves could not be kept as slaves, whole nations could not be bought and sold with the trading of a princess. And ordinary men could never be persuaded to throw away their lives for someone else's glory.

So the sons of Mohr called bound flesh virtuous. And this now, this sweet uncalculated pleasure on the queen's soft bed, was defilement.

For this women died, and men too, as Mara and Clodis had died, and the princess of the Almedes, and the bride of Crayfe the seneschal, and Jana alone knew how many others. She gathered their broken bones from death pyres and gallows, from rivers and ravines, from lovebeds bloodied with swords, from family council rooms where fathers and brothers did their duty, stone by stone, in the name of the race and the gods.

Rage clenched Kiri's hands against her lyre, and scalded her eyes with tears. One day, she thought, one day she would look on all this death and it would be one death too many, and she would take her rage and notch it against a bowstring and some of these dutiful and rational and blood-loving men would die—aye, and she would not stop there, not if it were possible for a woman to lodge an arrow in the arrogant heart of a god! Tears spattered onto her hands. She wiped them away and began to play again, softly, the words of a song taking sudden shape in her mind:

> *In Amaran the fruits grew kissed with sun,*
> *The flowers with rain;*
> *Ah, weep for Amaran, for to its wideflung hills*
> *The great god came. . . .*

The song almost leapt to her lips. Her hands fumbled with the strings, finding the music slower. The words, dear goddess, the words were there whole, had been there for years, waiting to be sung. Verse after verse, the story long and bitter, ending without an ending, ending only with knowledge:

> *Leya, do not go back to Amaran;*
> *The earth is gone there, and the fair things die.*
> *For he has made of all of Amaran*
> *A prison and a lie.*

The tapers had burned low; the queen and her lover were asleep. Kiri put aside the lyre, stoked the fire, and went back to the palace, pausing once at the door to look back at them.

You will not die, Marwen of Kamilan, she promised silently. *And if you do, then by the sacred goddess, by all that lives, by that one last cry of Leya which Jana gave life to forever, I will avenge you!*

It is enough!

27. The Quarrel

After his years in Dohann, Shadrak still found the royal city crowded and full of clamour, and the queen's hall a luxurious and perilous place. The winter was almost gone, and as it passed he grew not less but more wary of the men who surrounded him.

This night as always he had eaten well. But he drank his wine sparingly, engaged himself in a long, boring conversation with the man beside him, and otherwise left few shadows in the room, and few tracks. Once, he slipped out of the hall to relieve himself; Tamon as always following like a shadow. When they turned to go back, Tamon said softly:

"There be rats in this place, captain. More rats than enough."

"I know that," Shadrak said.

"The seneschal be watching you. All the time." Tamon spat. "The fattest rat I ever sees, that one, and the meanest. Why he hates you, captain?"

"He hates Borosar; they've been enemies for years. I'm in Borosar's camp, as he sees it. So I'm an enemy, too."

Tamon thought a moment, and shook his head. Politics was not very real to him.

"There be more," he said.

"Perhaps," Shadrak said grimly. Probably there was more, but he had no way to know. The queen's court was a chess board, a place where he felt no security—less for reasons of rank than because he could not sort through the layers of jealousies and old feuds; the constant trade-offs of power; the pretended alliances which he knew could dissolve in a breath.

And there was, he knew, no security for Marwen, either. She played the board well—too well, some said—and she was still very much the queen. But the ground kept shifting. Landis had gotten her with child, and then left her. He came to see the prince born and named and presented to the world, and then left again. They were clashing now, quietly, over small things: a kinsman's unpaid tribute, Angmar's wish to have the child blessed in the temple of Mohr, a hundred horses the prince consort had promised to Borosar and then given instead to his warleader, Ranir. That Landis took a concubine openly into his feast hall probably had less to do with desire than with defiance. Marwen was a woman, and he a man. He had made all the concesssions to her that he was going to make.

He was, of course, still formally loyal—they all were. How much their formal loyalty would be worth in a crisis Shadrak did not know. But the queen, having lost any hope of a having a powerful ally in Landis, was determined to keep the one ally she had left. Borosar the warlord moved triumphantly into the place Landis had abandoned: at the queen's table, and in her counsels. And perhaps also—so it was whispered now, more and more openly—perhaps also in her bed.

A burst of raucous laughter came from the hall, and a moment later a young man stumbled out to use the privy. It was one of Crayfe's men, very drunk and singing to himself. He saw the others, and fell silent. Then he grinned.

"What a surprise," he said. "Borosar's pet wolf. I would have thought your sort would go out and find a tree."

Anyone who used violence in the queen's hall was in instant disgrace. Shadrak considered that before he responded.

"You look a lot like a tree to me," he said.

It took a moment for the implication of his words to register. The man's grin turned slowly ugly, and faded altogether. He was reeling drunk, but not quite drunk enough to fight. He would be barred from the court, but more than that, he would lose the fight, and lose it badly. He muttered a huge obscenity, relieved himself long and noisily, and went back into the hall.

"You be challenging him, captain?" Tamon asked hopefully.

Shadrak shrugged, and shook his head. "No," he said. "It wasn't public."

"It never be public. They never dares."

That was true. No one would force his hand. But it was only partly because they did not dare, because they feared his skill. It was also because, finally, he was too far beneath them. And nothing would change that, neither Borosar's confidence in him, nor the queen's favour, nor the cheers of Kamils waving their scarves and bonnets in the streets. To the hard core of the Kamil aristocracy he was not even a wolf, but a dog; and the higher his fortunes seemed to rise, the more bitterly they would bait him and try to bring him down.

You're in a maelstrom, Cassian kept saying to him; *you will drown in it if you don't get out. . . !*

But there was nowhere to go, even if he wished to get out—nowhere except back to the border, to a life whose bleakness and savagery he had once scarcely noticed. Once, it had been enough to be free, to be armed, to have a good horse and a good bow and the wind in his face, to know that women would smile at him and men follow where he led. That had been splendid. That had been more than he had ever dared to dream of in the slave quarters of Tamri.

Then the queen wrapped her long, pale arms around his neck and life was never the same again, and never could be. To return to a place like Belengar now would be exile, not liberty.

—*If I drown, Cass*, he had said, *then I drown. Let me be.*

—*You're a fool, my friend. There's no outcome possible except that you will come to grief. You will be discovered. You will be betrayed. You will be murdered. She herself will discard you in the end. Even if she doesn't want to, she'll have no choice. One of those things will happen, Shadrak, or all of them. You're mad to pursue this.*

—*You're forgetting something.*

—*What am I forgetting?*

—*I'm in love with her.*

274

That had been worse than no answer at all. Cassian threw up his arms and stalked out of the room, slamming the door behind him. Had the woman in question been anyone but the queen, he would probably have said what he was thinking: that a woman was a woman, they were all the same in the dark, and a man who would throw his life away to have one rather than another was worse than a fool; he was a lunatic.

It did no good to explain. Had their situations been reversed, Shadrak supposed he would have said the same things. *Give it up; it's not worth it. It's going to ruin you.* He could not explain that the choice was not between certain ruin and probable survival; it was between probable ruin and certain despair.

All down the long road from Dohann he had thought of nothing but her, remembering her body in his arms, her soft mouth, her promise: *I will come back to you, my wolf.* . . . In the palace courtyard she had greeted Borosar and the other lords, according to their rank; then she had turned to him with poised courtesy, thanked him for his loyal service, and moved on. The hall was full that night, his place far from hers. Most of the time he could not see her, and that was just as well, for he would have looked at nothing else. Goddess of the world, why did she not give him some small reassurance, a look, a word, *something?*

It was the minstrel Kiri who sought him out, quietly, pretending to want stories about Dohann, and being a bit flirtatious as well. The revelry was loud by then, and many of the guests were drunk; a few were leaving for their own houses.

"Take your leave," she said softly, after a bit of talk. "I will wait for you at the door."

She led him into a small hallway, through a narrow door and down a set of stone steps to a room full of sacks and barrels. It smelled like an old granary, musty and full of mice. Kiri stuck her taper onto the wall and turned to him.

"If you'll wait here, captain, the queen would like to see you." She paused, and added softly: "It can only be for a few minutes, but she wanted at least to greet you. I'm sorry it's such a gloomy place. There are servants underfoot all over tonight, and we've had to put some guests even in the storerooms."

"The place doesn't matter," he said. "Has she been well?"

"Yes." She smiled. "I was serious about the stories, by the way. I do want them. My fee for carrying messages. Agreed?"

"Agreed."

She was, he reflected, a most unusual woman. He wondered how much she knew, and decided that she must know everything. She certainly acted as though she did.

There was something vaguely intimidating about her. It was not power; Marwen was a far more powerful woman. Nor was it any malice or ill will, or any falsehood. He did not distrust her. But he felt when he first met her at Belengar that she was odd, not so much dangerous as invulnerable, a woman whom no man would ever reach, and whom women would reach in ways men did not understand.

It was some time before Marwen came to him. She stepped through the door and closed it softly behind her, and he understood why she had been so poised towards him, so correct; she had not dared to be otherwise. She had not trusted herself to keep from her eyes the passion that was in them now.

"Shadrak."

He reached to touch her face and she came to him with a harsh whimper of hunger, her hands in his beard and in his hair, her mouth gulping eager, desperate things between kisses, *I missed you, oh love, I missed you so. . . !* He pulled her hard against his body. The touch of her was like a torch to autumn grass, dissolving him in a sheet of flame. He was never quite sure what happened after that. Reality intruded vaguely once or twice, the realization that he did not know precisely where they were, if it was safe; a few soft curses over the impossible clumsiness of clothing; the rest was a blur. They mated where they stood, saying little except raw animal words of need, indifferent to the lack of comfort, the smell of cellars; indifferent to dignity; he had not meant to do this, she was the queen, not some wild village girl.

"Lady. . . ."

Sanity returned—some kind of sanity. He heard the torch gutter and snap, felt the cold of the room on his naked thighs, felt her breath burning against his neck, unsteady and harsh.

"Marwen, I'm sorry. I shouldn't have . . . not here. . . ."

She looked up. Small tendrils of hair matted damply on her face. She had not meant to do it, either; in the languor of her eyes were both pleasure and bewilderment.

She did not withdraw from his embrace, not even the small bit that would have made it easier to breathe.

"My beautiful wolf," she said. "I love you. I love you more than anything in the world."

What could Cassian say that mattered, what could anyone say? What more could the world offer—any world, least of all the world of a slaveborn border captain? What shabby security might he find elsewhere? What small and insignificant death might he pursue that would be better than loving her, aye, and dying for her if it came to that? Of course it was dangerous; what of it? In the slave quarters of Tamri he had learned two enduring lessons—lessons which his life as a soldier merely confirmed anew: joy was fleeting, and everything was dangerous.

So he met with her, all winter, as often as three or four times in a moonturn, and for a while he cared about nothing except the wild happiness of it. She was as eager and wanton as any village girl in his bed; as thoughtful as any quiet, grey-eyed king after, sitting with her arms around her knees, talking of politics and war. The world was his; at first even the contempt of the lords could not touch him. But the winter passed. His enemies' hatred deepened as they found they could not dislodge him. The lords of Tamri came to Kamilan for Sun-turning, manoevring for advantage every way they could. The ground around him kept shifting, shifting, shifting. And the whispers about the queen and the warlord grew franker, blunter, uglier. The warlord, they said, had set up his winter quarters in the queen's bed, and mapped his campaigns on her pillow, and kept his lance well polished between her thighs.

Some said it with outrage, as though no worse thing could be said of any woman, especially a queen. Some said it with amusement: how else had women ever gotten what they wanted? The world was always this way, and the parade of men through the bedrooms of the world was a long parade of fools.

Cassian wisely held his tongue, but Shadrak could read his eyes; they had been friends too long.

You're being used, my friend, Cassian's look said. *You're a diversion for her, that's all. Did you imagine, slaveborn and powerless as you are, that you could ever have been more?*

He asked her about the warlord, finally. He had to. The question tormented him, gnawing at his sleep, spoiling the soft edges of his pleasure in her. He was jealous of any man who might so much as touch her, yet it was not jealousy, finally, which proved to be most unbearable; it was fear: the fear that he would lose her; the fear that she had never been his at all. He wondered, and shoved the talk aside. He wondered again, and believed. And at last, unable to be silent any longer, he spoke.

They were sitting as they often did, sated and easy by the fire. She was talking about Borosar's suggestion that the Dravian army was likely to be over-armoured, over-supplied, and over-confident; it was Borosar said this and Borosar said that. He lifted his wine cup to drown the question, and then put it back untasted.

"You seem to know everything he says or thinks," he said. He had waited too long to say anything at all; now the words came out blunt and bitter.

There was a moment of silence. She rubbed at a scratch on her finger, refusing to look at him. It was the first time there had been even a breath of coldness between them. He was astonished at how desolate it made him feel.

"Everything in Kamilan may one day depend on what Borosar thinks," she answered simply.

That was true, and a part of him wanted to leave it so; to say nothing more. Nonetheless he plunged on:

"They say you bed with him. Is it true?"

There was another small void of silence. But when she looked up and met his eyes, her own were grey and cool and steady.

"Does it matter?"

"Matter?" he said harshly. "You can tell me that you love me, and then ask me that?"

"I told you when I married Landis that I would do whatever I had to, to survive. You accepted that. What's the difference—?"

"At least that was an honourable marriage—"

"*Honourable?* Don't talk to me about honour! After what passed in Dohann a few moonturns ago, you're the last man alive to throw that word in anyone's face!"

"You commended me for my action at the time," he said bitterly. "You change with as little conscience as the wind!"

"*I* commended you, wolf—the lords of Council did not. All they talked about for weeks was honour, and how you didn't have any! Now you do the same to me! I didn't choose to marry Landis; I was compelled to. Marry or risk a civil war; that was my choice—what's honourable about that? When Prince Held carried me off and raped me, he didn't lose his honour, I lost mine—and had it given back to me when he called me wife, even though I never called him husband, even though the price of my precious honour was the whole of Kamilan! Oh, honour is splendid, Shadrak! Like a fine gold chain for a slave! I thought better of you than this!"

"And I of you, lady."

"Shadrak. . . ." She rose, walking aimlessly, making small empty gestures with her hands. She turned to him again, the anger gone.

"What have I not given you?" she said gently. "You have my heart, my hopes, my bed. You have all the protection my rank can give you. Do you think I use my influence with Borosar only for myself?"

"I never asked you to whore for me."

"Oh, you're a fool!" She paused, and went on desperately: "I see a side of him the world doesn't see, Shadrak. He's weary and afraid. Hardly anyone would believe that, but it's true. There's no telling what decisions Council might persuade him to make, if I didn't persuade him to make others."

She reached, linking her arms around his neck. "He says he'll make you warleader, equal to Ranir and Oswin. He even thinks it was his own idea." She smiled faintly, briefly. "I don't know whether he'll do it, in the end; I trust him, and I don't trust him—"

"Aye, lady. And do you say to him, too: *Shadrak will do thus and thus, at least I think he will, but I don't entirely trust him!*—"

"Why are you saying this?" she whispered.

"Why shouldn't I say it?" he said bitterly. He siezed her wrists, pulling them away from his neck and forcing them back. "You're using all of us. Landis. Borosar. Anyone else, no doubt, who might cross your path to power. Why should I believe I'm different from the others? That you care for me at all?—oh, perhaps a little; the queen can have a favourite dog, a favourite slave—both of them stupid enough to believe they're something more. I was blind with love for you. I would have died for you willingly. But I'm just another counter on the board, am I not?"

She stared at him. "That's not true," she said.

"Why should I believe you? You're false to everyone else."

"False by whose terms? The terms of men who fashion every law to their own advantage? Do you think they won't lie to me when it suits them? Do you think the honour they thrust in my face—and in yours—will keep them loyal one minute longer than they choose?"

She twisted her wrist to free it, found that she could not, and let it fall limp in his grip. "I love you," she said fiercely. "I thought you understood. I will never betray you! What can I say to make you believe that? Tell me! What can I say?"

He was torn by the wish to close his arms around her, and bury his face in the soft curve of her throat, and tell her there was nothing more that needed to be said. Had she been slaveborn, like himself, he would have done so. She was young and surrounded by enemies, and fear could inspire almost any kind of desperate act.

But she was not like himself. She was a queen, a powerful and clever woman who could seem anything she wished to anyone she chose. Why indeed should he think himself different from the others—himself least of all, a slaveborn soldier without land or wealth or power? Why should he imagine himself more than a pawn: at best a talented minion for Borosar's army, at worst a mere amusement, all the more amusing for being lowborn and forbidden? She would not be the first highborn lady to treat a man thus and think nothing of it.

"If there's anything you can say to make me believe you, lady, you shall have to find it. I don't know what it might be."

"I could have lied to you," she said bitterly. "I could have sworn that I had never lain with Borosar, that I never would, that it was all malice and gossip. You would have believed me. Instead I tell you the truth, and you call me a liar. May Jana preserve us from the wisdom of men!"

"And from the faithlessness of women!"

"I have not been faithless."

"No? What do you call it, when you go from another's bed to mine and back again?"

"You don't own me!" she cried savagely. "And don't look at me like that! It has nothing to do with your rank or your birth. I wouldn't care a fig if you were the emperor of Larandau; you still wouldn't own me! Goddess, I thought you knew me well enough to know that!"

"I don't think I ever knew you at all."

He dressed quickly, quietly, looking up once to break the silence with a question even he did not want to confront:

"He is my captain, lady. Suppose he learns the truth—then what happens? Did you think about that at all?"

She looked at him, and looked away. She had thought about it; that was quite obvious. Realizing it only made him angrier.

"Suppose your plan at Medra hadn't worked, Shadrak? Your hundred men and your drums and your cave? What then?"

"We would have been no worse off than before."

"And will we now?"

"At least he wasn't your enemy before. Nor was he mine."

He pulled on his boots and his cloak. Her cloak, he reminded himself. He could not leave without it; it was dead of winter. He would send it back to her tomorrow, and the ring, too.

She stood by silently, watching him with bitter accusation, as though she were the one betrayed. Once she moved towards him, began to speak:

"Shadrak, don't! *Please. . . !*"

She met his eyes, and her own went dark. "All right, go then," she said. "Go and rot in Dohann. I wish I had left you there!"

Nothing could have wounded him more than that.

"Never fear, lady; I can find my way back." For a moment he hesitated; she was the queen, after all. And then he did not care. Everything was finished. The world and all its queens could do to him what it wished. He drew a handful of copper coins from his pouch and laid them on the table beside the door. A generous handful. As many as any well-pleased soldier would offer to a splendid whore.

The instant he had done it he was sorry. Her mouth trembled, and tears welled in her eyes. She looked at him unbelieving, like an animal who had been smashed with a club for no reason. He faltered, torn by her pain, by the words welling in his throat: *Marwen, I didn't mean that! Forgive me, I didn't mean it. . . !*

If he had stayed even for another breath he would have spoken them. He turned away, pulling open the door and closing it behind him without allowing himself to think or to look back.

He rode back to Althen hunched against the wind, raw with loss and black humiliation. What a fool he had been, what an abominable, stupid fool! Well, he told himself, so be it; he had learned better. He would return her gifts, and he would never go to her again.

But when morning came he did not send the cloak back, or the ring. It was over, of course it was over; he had made that quite clear; there was no need to make it any clearer. No need to make such a final, unendurable gesture.

He spent two days drilling recruits to exhaustion. Then he discovered that a caravan of supplies was leaving for Getann, and he volunteered to lead it. It was a task beneath his rank, but he made a joke of it, wolves liked the forest and so on. No one cared much. If he went, someone else did not have to.

It was a slow journey in the wintertime, and he made it slower than need be, stopping twice in villages along the way to rest their heavily burdened horses. In Getann he found other things to do, and when he had done them all he took a handful of men and went deep into the forest to hunt. Game would stretch the garrison's supply of cattle and pigs; that was reason enough to go, but the real reason was the violence of the hunt, and the intense, ancient tranquillity of the forest, which even his violence could not undo, which wrapped itself around him, shoving the world aside and allowing him to think.

The short days passed quickly; the long nights lasted forever. He could come to no decision he could live with. He told himself a thousand times that he would leave her. She was a whore and a liar and he would leave her. He had made many desperate resolutions in his life and always a kind of courage came with them, a defiance which gave him strength. But there was no courage in this resolve, only a void of darkness, and as often as he made it, he unmade it again. Perhaps, he told himself, perhaps she loved him. Why else would she spend time with him at all, why else take so many risks simply to be with him? Suppose she *did* love him and he scorned her, abandoned her in that viper's nest of councillors and priests?

Dear goddess, did it matter if she lay with Borosar, did it really matter, if she loved *him*? What she had told him was true: honour meant whatever those with power said it meant— sexual honour as much as any other kind. He had seen that in Tamri, even as a child. The master's daughter would have been beaten senseless had she accepted a man's caresses, and the slave girl who laughed with her and fixed her hair would have suffered the same punishment for refusing.

No magic, no permanent meaning could be given to an act which could be so many different things—a passionate gift or a playful game or a brutal injury or a mechanical breeding of young; an act as meaningful as the making of the world, as meaningless as a clod falling unnoticed from one's boots. Slaves knew that well enough, even if their masters did not.

I thought you understood, she had said. *I love you. I thought you understood. . . .*

If that was true, he thought, if she truly loved him, if she had not lied, if all the rest was politics and he was the one she wanted. . . ? Gods of all the world, how could he have done it: to wound her so, and walk away and leave her? He ached with regret even to think of it.

But did she love him?

He shook his head. He was a fool to imagine it. What could he possibly mean to her, if she could bed down with his own captain, the man he must follow into battle? If she could marry one lord and seduce another, and use them both with absolute calculation, and then come to him and wrap her soft arms around his neck and say she loved only him?

Steps crunched in the snow behind him. He turned sharply. Tamon paused, made a small gesture of appeasement.

"You be thinkin', captain?"

"No." He shrugged, shifted the bow and quiver over his shoulder, and looked at the woods beyond Tamon's squat frame as though there were something there worth looking at. "Let's go back."

Tamon did not stir. "You be fair unhappy, captain."

"Why do you say that?" he asked evenly, not meeting the man's eyes.

"These woods be fair still and cold."

"I see." He smiled faintly, sadly. "It's that obvious, is it?"

"Aye."

"Well, there is nothing either of us can do about it, Tamon."

"We dies soon, maybe, all of us," Tamon persisted. "Nothing be worth dying over before we dies."

He knew what Tamon was getting at. He should stop brooding, drink, ride over to the next village and find a girl. That was the warrior's answer to everything, even death.

But he could not turn his desire away from her. Last summer, moving in and out of the wilds of Dohann, he had bedded two or three village girls who favoured him. But he had been happy then. Now the loveliest woman in Kamilan could be standing before him naked and he would have no wish to touch her.

Love's last revenge, he reflected bitterly, to make a man chaste. Chaste and cold, like this empty, pristine valley.

They left for Althen in the morning. It was a splendid late winter day. He rode easy, the hood thrown back from his cloak, the sun warm as summer in his hair. They travelled all day, stopping only to sleep in a small village, and left early again the next morning. His spirits rose with every southward mile. He told himself it was the weather. It was the bright sun spilling into the trees, so fierce that they glistened and the water slid from their branches into spears of ice; it was the cheerful bawdy songs his men were singing—that was why his dark mood fell away, and his horse kept wanting to run—it had nothing to do with her. But when a soldier hurried out to meet him in the trampled stableyards of Althen, before they had done more than dismount and ease their legs a little, he knew what the man would say before he spoke, and he could not prevent the leap of excitement in his blood.

"There's a messenger waiting for you, captain." He pointed to a figure lounging by a fence. "Don't know how, but he knew you were on your way before we did."

So she is a witch, too, as well as a wanton; why does that not surprise me?

The messenger was a sturdy fellow, grubby and bearded and strangely familiar.

"You wished to speak with me?" Shadrak said.

There was no one close by. The messenger spoke softly, but in an undisguised woman's voice.

"I have a message from the queen."

He stared at her.

"Don't you know me, captain?" she said, with a trace of amusement.

He laughed then, harshly. "I recall a Drav spy once who looked like you. We nearly shot her."

"Do you mean to shoot me this time?" Kiri asked. "You look as though you might."

"No." He forced himself to smile. *How was it possible to be so torn—so wounded and so happy in the same instant?* "What is your message?"

"The queen is at Medwina's forest house. She would like you to visit her there."

Oh, goddess, to see her again, to hold her. . . ! He was astonished at the sheer, raw force of his hunger, the suddenness of it, the power with which it dissolved anger, resentment, jealousy, everything. For three weeks he had tried to come to some resolution, and had not done so. Now even the wish for a resolution erased itself in longing.

"Is it her wish, minstrel, or her command?"

"She won't command you in this, Shadrak. You know that."

Then I won't go.

The words formed in his mind, but he could not speak them, no more than he could have taken his dagger and cut his own fingers off, one by one, simply to see them fall.

"Is she there now?"

"Yes."

"Is she angry?"

In spite of the beard which hid most of her face, he could sense Kiri's smile.

"No."

She was not angry. She wanted him back, then. She would wrap her arms around him as before, and smile, and call him her black wolf, and melt all his bones with kisses. Nothing else mattered. At least it did not matter enough to hold him, to keep him from shouting for a fresh horse and leaping onto its back with a single bound.

"Come on, then!" he shouted at Kiri, without looking back, and rode headlong across the long sweep of the valley towards the forest.

"I never meant to hurt you, wolf." Her voice was soft as small rain, soft as the kiss of her fingertips across his face. "Whatever you believe, you must believe that. I never meant to hurt you."

He did not know how many times they said it, each of them, over and over, in so many different ways, that they were sorry. That he had not meant it. That she was doing what she thought necessary. That they forgave each other every word. That there was nothing to forgive.

The hours passed unnoticed, dissolving in sweetness. She was so lovely, all sorcery in his arms, all fire. He would never have enough of kissing her, just here in the curve of her throat, where the pulse beat softly against his mouth; or here, on her fingertips, these subtle nailed fingertips which traced such maddening paths across his flesh, but were somehow always gentle. Or anywhere at all, everywhere, ending in this bewitching mound of golden hair, wet with her pleasure and his own, the pretty pink bud flushed with contentment, but like himself still quietly afire, kindling anew to his fingers and his tongue.

He supposed it would all burn out one day, that he would tire of her, or grow calm and passionless, the way men grew towards their wives. He could not imagine it. He could not believe that he would ever look at her with anything except desire.

"Do you mean to have three weeks worth of pleasure in a single night?" she asked lightly.

"Yes!" *Fool that I was for leaving you, even for a single day. . . !*

The hearth burned low; the night was half gone. He left the sweet shelter of her bed to stoke the fire. She poured them each a glass of wine and sat beside him.

"So, wolf," she said softly, "are you happy?"

"Yes."

Her hair was tangled, caught here and there under the cape she had wrapped around her shoulders. She looked sleepy, and utterly enchanting.

"It doesn't take three weeks to ship supplies to Getann," she said. "What were you doing all that time?"

"A lot of things. I went hunting for a while. Mostly I was thinking."

"About what?"

"Leaving you."

He was astonished at the fear which darkened her eyes—astonished, and ashamed, and comforted.

"And do you mean to do so?" she asked, looking at the fire.

"No," he said simply.

She pulled the cape tightly around her shoulders, as though in spite of the brightening fire she was cold.

"It may be a mistake, what I'm doing," she said. Her voice was low, almost desolate. "It's so hard to know. Sometimes things seem very clear to me, and I act on that, and then I find they weren't clear at all—that I misjudged everything. I misjudged Landis. Maybe I'm wrong about this, too. But I did what I thought. . . ." She paused, choosing words. "What I thought might work. And it seemed such a small thing. . . ."

She looked at him then, directly. "I don't know if I have any good choices left, Shadrak. Except to undo myself, and you, and all of us, one way or the other."

"Lady. . . ."

How would he ever sort through the tangle of vulnerability and power in this woman? He did not know, and he thought that finally he did not care, that it did not matter. He had not been aware of reaching a decision in the silent forest of Getann, but he had done so nonetheless—the decision that very little mattered when he balanced it against this woman, and what she meant to him, what she was worth. She had risked so much to have her freedom, her sovereignty. Except for this thing with Borosar she had always been good to him, always. And even that . . . even that was perhaps as much a measure of her courage as anything else, a measure of her determination to survive, aye, and to see that *he* survived.

It might not work; he knew that. She might go down, and if she did there was no question but that he would go down with her, and Cassian would be proven right, all of them would be proven right. . . .

He wanted to laugh then, the way he laughed sometimes when he rode into combat, when fear itself was part of the will to fight, and dissolved into it; when he felt his own daring like wine in his blood, felt his own strength, the perfection of hand and eye and judgment, the certainty of triumph which he carried sometimes like a shield, like a kind of madness, no matter

287

who his enemy was, or how many. *I am a match for you all, aye, and more than a match! I will break your swords to splinters, and send you home in the bellies of the ravens!*

"Lady." He reached, plucking locks of pale hair one by one from the prison of her cape. "I will ride the storm with you. I have no choice. I love you more than my life."

She smiled a little, but her eyes remained troubled. "I'm not treacherous, Shadrak. Whatever men say about me, I don't betray my friends. If we survive this war, you will have land and a lordship, and the highest rank I can dare to give you. I promise you that."

"And is that all I will have?"

A small laugh. "The rest you have already, wolf, don't you? All of it?"

All of it. The pale wanton hair, the soft mouth, the copper-tipped breasts sweet as apples, the laughter which she shared with so few, the love words spoken sometimes in raw passion and sometimes in utter tranquillity: my love, my heart, my beautiful wolf. . . .

She wound her hands in his hair and pressed her face into the curve of his neck. "Don't leave me, Shadrak," she pleaded. "You'll break my heart to splinters if you leave me."

What could Cassian say, what could anyone say? Her love was worth the risk, and so was the promise of land and a life that would be better than the border. To have both he could bear the scorn of these self-satisfied lords. He could keep his feet amidst the snares they set for him—just barely sometimes, but he could do it. And he could take, finally, a kind of dark pleasure in the acknowledgement of her power, and in her willingness to use it all in her own defense and his. She was still the proud queen he had admired so utterly in Dohann, vulnerable and defiant, walking out of the mountains ragged and with bleeding feet.

He felt Tamon tug lightly at his arm, and he pulled himself out of his own thoughts, and walked back into the feast hall, aware of Borosar's wine-glazed pride and Crayfe's relentlessly watching eyes, but more than anything aware of her. She played their perilous game as well as they did, and better, but when the games were put aside she came to him with all her splendid gifts. And that was sweet, dear goddess, that was sweeter than any smile from any sweet-faced virgin.

If the world judged him base for that, and said he was not a man but a slave, and had no honour, then so be it.

28. Crayfe

Like Angmar the Wise, the seneschal Crayfe rarely left the fortress city of Kamilan. He did not need to; the world came to him. It came openly, boisterous with scheming and raucous with gossip. It came secretly through back gates, with cloaked faces and padding feet, trading whispers for gold. It came from every corner of the realm and beyond, and he watched it that winter—the winter before the Great War—with an increasingly bitter and uneasy eye.

It was his habit to sit sometimes for hours, alone except for a servant who saw that he had food and drink, and that his feet were warm. He would lay out his hoard of knowledge as a child might lay out his treasures on the grass, barely glancing at old familiar pieces, frowning over those which had seemed promising and then turned out to be useless, smiling at new discoveries, however trivial they were. Information for its own sake pleased him.

He would go over everything, rearranging and reassessing. He had a prodigious mind for detail; and unlike people who watched others in order to gossip, he never confused a rumour with a fact. He could lie or tell the truth with equal facility, but he never forgot which was which.

He was a powerful man in Kamilan, and much of his power rested on this endless gathering and storing up of knowledge, and on his ability to look at all of it without confusion or a blink of dismay, even when it concerned himself. All the names they called him got back to him, all the cruel jokes: he was Crayfe the Round, he was Prince Porkbelly, he was the Miracle of the Mountains—(for, asked Borosar the warlord, how did a man get a two inch cock past a sixty inch belly even twice, to account for the two pudgy, squint-eyed sons he managed to have?) He was Crayfe the White—the colour of his face, they said, when he heard the sound of a drum. He was Crayfe This and Crayfe That, but the one name they never called him was the one he called himself: Crayfe the Watcher.

All that winter he watched the scattered lords of Council. He watched his hated enemy Borosar. He watched the queen. And he watched the Thyrsian wolf which Borosar occasionally tucked under his arm and took to the palace like a mascot—watched him with meticulous, fascinated attention. He saw what no one else was likely to see until it was too late. Borosar, strutting cock of the mountains that he was, would be the very last to see it.

Shadrak was dangerous.

Not to Kamil honour, or to any other figment of Council's imagination. Talk of honour always made Crayfe smile—as if these lords who plotted and lied and seduced other men's wives had any honour left to damage. It was not that at all. The captain of Belengar was just plain, ordinary, drawn-sword dangerous, a cutthroat adventurer with a gift for popularity and nothing in the world to lose. But none of them were noticing the danger, and when he suggested it, quietly, no one was prepared to listen. Young Favian actually laughed. Shadrak, he said, was rabble—as if that had anything to do with anything.

Crayfe shrugged and let it pass. None of his peers in Council had ever impressed him much. They were all in varying stages of childhood, imagining that their rank or their good looks or their skill with arms were some kind of barrier between themselves and the sinkhole of all human existence, looking up with shock and bewilderment every time they found themselves bitten by yet another rat. He would not have cared in the least to see them all go down, except that if they did, he was likely to go down with them.

The winter broke, and messengers rode everywhere across the land, summoning the lords of Kamilan and their warleaders to a council in the royal city, from whence they would follow Borosar into the field. Even as the first of them were arriving, the caravan of Mercanio the One-Eyed came unlooked-for out of the south, and made its way across the valley to Althen Garrison. In his wagons, amidst other gear of war, were tens of thousands of arrows and over eight hundred Thyrsian-style bows for Shadrak of Belengar and his men.

Then, as if that were not menacing enough, Borosar arrived at the meeting with his pet wolf in tow, and announced that he had been raised to the rank of warleader of Dohann, which was pure nonsense, since Dohann was no lordship but merely a few million hectares of rocks and trees. Favian, outraged, had almost to be shoved into his chair, and thereafter had nothing to contribute to the discussion except puffs of smoke. Theron insisted that the temple of Jana must be razed to the ground and the land purified of sorcery and corruption; only so could they hope for victory against the Dravians. Angmar talked endlessly of Kamil honour. Borosar, arrogant as Harash himself, wanted nothing from his peers except their oaths of loyalty—which, in spite of everything, he got.

"Great Mohr preserve us, what a farce!" Favian sprawled into one of Angmar's wooden chairs, almost sloshing his wine over himself as he did so. He was worn out with anger, and had only snarls left, like a tired dog.

"Do you believe this, Crayfe? Any of it? That gutter-bred Thyrsian a warleader—as though he were a lord of Kamilan, or even an honest soldier! And the queen spending gods know how many thousand ells on a wagonload of toys! Gods, what a farce. . . !"

Favian took a long drink and wiped his mouth. "I would not have believed Borosar could be so besotted," he went on. "She has him by the balls and she drags him where she wants. Theron is right, Crayfe; it's madness to give women power. They have no wits themselves, and can only turn a man's wits upside down."

Really, Favian, you don't have to keep saying it; we know.
But why has Borosar turned witless in this particular fashion,
at this particular time?—that is a question neither you nor
anyone else is asking.

Crayfe could not stop himself from asking that question
now, for his entire perception of Kamilan's political situation
depended on the answer. He knew Shadrak lusted after the
queen. That fact, in itself, would have meant little. More than
one mongrel howled in the streets at night for some sleek-
furred bitch behind a fence. But this mongrel was clearly well-
received inside the gate. He was given men to lead, and arms,
and now a rank absurdly higher than his worth. How had all of
that happened? Was it simply Borosar's wild ambition,
Borosar's determination to stop at nothing to win the war and
hold the queen's favour? Or was Borosar himself a pawn in a
far more dangerous game?

Favian finally noticed that Crayfe had stopped listening to
him, and turned to complain to someone else. Crayfe edged
away to where the prince consort was standing, slightly apart
from the others, saying very little.

"You've grown quiet of late, Landis," Crayfe said. "If I didn't
know you better, I might think you were communing with the
gods."

"I'm no quieter than usual, seneschal. And if I didn't know
you better, I might think you cared."

Crayfe laughed. He did not like Landis. He did not like any
of them, but as he acknowledged Borosar's military skill, he
also acknowledged the lord of Maene's intelligence. Landis
was the brightest of them. He was cold, and single-mindedly
ambitious, and absurdly rigid in his sense of himself and his
rank and his image. Like so many other highborn men, he
imagined that his place in the world was in some way guaran-
teed. He imagined that he was made of something different
than ordinary mortals, and that the stuff he was made of would
somehow protect him from chaos. But, insofar as so dangerous a weakness permitted, he was farsighted, and thoughtful,
and resolute. He was also, unlike his tiresome mentor, a man
not much troubled by fantasies of virtue.

Most men did not recognize that fact. Most men, in this as
in everything, saw only surfaces. The lord of Maene's outward
behaviour was always so unfailingly correct; it took the end-

lessly watchful eye of a man like Crayfe to see that beneath it was only policy.

"I would like a word with you, Lord Landis," Crayfe said, "if you would spare me the time."

Landis gave him a long, penetrating look. Then, with something almost like a shrug, he nodded. "We can go to Angmar's study," he said.

"I would prefer to go outside."

"There are no spies in Angmar's house," Landis said coldly.

"There are spies in everyone's house," Crayfe replied, unruffled. "Shall we walk?"

They went outside. The night air was still cold, but already Angmar's garden smelled of wet earth and fecundity, and of the rot of last year's dead flowers.

"Gardens in the first of spring," Crayfe said, "are like brothels at sunrise. All the prettiness and perfume are stripped away, and you can see what is really underneath: death and corruption. Did you ever notice that?"

"Not really," Landis said. He sounded bored.

"Death and corruption don't concern you, then," Crayfe said. "Well, no doubt life is easier that way." He thought a moment, considering his strategy, and then said simply:

"The weapons which the queen bought aren't toys, you know."

"I never said they were."

"One of my men spent three years in the east, with the Larandav army. He fought against the Thyrsians. He says an iron-tipped arrow fired from a composite bow can pierce common armour at two hundred yards." Crayfe paused, and went on even more quietly:

"With a thousand men and weapons like that, a man could take all of Kamilan, and make himself king."

"He could," Landis said dryly, "if the great god Mohr came down out of the heavens and swallowed up the Dravians first."

Ah, yes, the Dravians. The wolf at the gate, for whose sake the wolf inside the gate is being given more and more space to run. . . .

"Dravians or no Dravians, prince, the man is dangerous. Were I in your place, I would not allow Borosar to make every play he pleases, just because there is a war ahead."

The innuendo in that was deliberate. It was too dark to see Landis's face, but he could hear the chill in the man's response.

"I didn't come out here to be lectured by you, seneschal. If you have something important to say, I wish you would get to the point."

Poor Landis, Crayfe thought, without sympathy. It was difficult to imagine a man in a more impossible position. He had married the queen expecting to multiply his own power and wealth. Everyone, in fact, had expected that. Years before, in the days of Adelmar, Council had blocked his marriage to Marwen for that very reason—they believed it would make Landis king in all but name, and make the house of Maene the absolute power in Kamilan.

Only it did not turn out that way. Though he had gained prestige, Landis had actually *lost* power. He found that he could not draw on the queen's strength to advance his plans and ambitions; instead, she was drawing on his strength to advance her own.

No one, of course, had reckoned with the Dravians, or with that rutting fool Borosar. Still less had they reckoned with Marwen herself. They had all underestimated her, Landis most of all. He had thought of her as just a girl; the word slipped from his lips enough times for Crayfe to notice. Just a girl, and a hurt girl at that, abused and frightened and surely all the more willing to tuck herself under his well-feathered wing. She did not possess any real power in his eyes. She was merely the custodian of the kingship in her blood. Her consort would exercise that power, and she would pass it on to his sons.

Or so the lord of Maene had imagined.

He had done himself in rather nicely, Crayfe thought. The queen did exactly as she pleased, and her husband found himself compelled to support her, or at least be silent, because he dared not risk a break with her until he had a son.

Now he had a son and it was no better, for babies did not grow up to be kings in a moonturn. The child had to be kept safe, and the kingdom with him, and for that they needed a measure of unity in Council, they needed an army which could meet the Dravian threat—and, alas, they needed Borosar. The lord of Maene was now compelled not only to accept his wife's leadership, but to shrug aside her adultery as well.

How he was able to do it bewildered Crayfe. It was not something he would have tolerated from any woman. Queen or not, a whore was a whore, and a man who was a man put a stop to it, one way or another.

Crayfe pressed on.

"Have you never asked yourself why Borosar favours the wolf so much?" he said.

"I think that's obvious," Landis said coldly.

"Oh, it's perfectly obvious. He means to smash the Dravs any way he can, and secure his position with the queen—whatever that position may be. Shadrak is useful to him. Of course. Only. . . ." He paused, purely for effect. "Only when one thinks about it a little, it's no longer so obvious. One wonders if Borosar would really go so far on his own. And one remembers that it wasn't Borosar who spent the queen's dowry on Thyrsian arms."

There was a breath of silence. Even in the dark he could see Landis stiffen.

"What are you suggesting, seneschal?"

"Suggesting?" Crayfe shrugged. "I'm not suggesting anything. I'm only asking questions. I ask why a mere border captain took it upon himself to challenge the prince of Dravia. I ask why that same border captain is given a new command, leave to recruit his own men, and now the rank of warleader and a whole caravan of fine weapons. I'm senseschal, after all; my men guard the city gates and keep the peace. I thought it might be wise to watch such an extraordinarily fortunate man. He comes to the city quite often, usually with a handful of his most trusted men, and spends his nights at the house of one of Lady Medwina's priestesses. Now the gods alone know what he does there. Maybe he prays, maybe he plots, maybe he whores. But the house is close to the palace, and Medwina's people are in the queen's palm—every last one of them. I've seen how he looks at your lady, Landis, and it's not the look of a respectful servant. So when she fawns on Borosar, and Borosar fawns on him, I ask one question more. I ask. . . ." He paused again, this time out of genuine hesitation, wondering how much he dared to say. "I ask which man is really the favourite, and which one the foil."

Silence closed over them—the kind of silence which fell when men knew exactly what had been said, but would not yet admit to either hearing it or saying it.

"You have an extraordinary imagination, Crayfe," Landis said at last. "It will bring you to grief one day."

"Perhaps."

"The man is slaveborn," Landis went on, pointedly.

"Yes, indeed. And alien and bloody and dangerous. You would be surprised how many women find such things alluring. They have a taste for . . . what shall we call it?. . . the lower things in man? Great Mohr knows I've had my own experience of that, prince."

Aye, he added silently, *and they died hard, both of them; I don't put ambition ahead of honour the way you do.*

"Why are you telling all of this to me?" Landis asked. "It's Borosar you should be telling. But you'd never dare, would you? He'd put his sword through your fat belly before you finished speaking. Do you think that I will tell him for you?"

Crayfe did not answer.

"Listen to me, seneschal, and listen well," Landis went on grimly. "All your life you've been a plotter and a trouble-maker. I don't know what you intend by this, and I don't especially care. But be careful. There are words which are dangerous even in the mouth of a friend, and you are not my friend."

"Oh, stop being pompous. I'm not impressed by it, and no one else is listening. If you wish to make a fuss over my words, you will damage no one but yourself. You might be wiser to listen. You're not a fool, and whatever you may think of me, neither am I."

"Shadrak is a savage, a whore's get without name or rank or honour. She would never degrade herself so. It's not possible."

"She's a woman. Anything is possible."

"She is a queen!"

"She's a woman," Crayfe repeated flatly. "A woman who happened to have a king for a father, and unfortunately, no brothers."

There was a long silence.

"Very well, Crayfe," the prince consort said at last, wearily. "You have said your piece. As you say, I'm not a fool; I will remember what you've said. Either way, whether you've lied to me or told the truth, I will remember."

Aye, Crayfe thought, *and if I'm proved wrong you will hate me, and want revenge. And if I'm proved right you will shrug and say you thought as much yourself. Did I not fear for my own future, I would sit back and watch you all get eaten, one by one, and laugh. . . .*

Book Four.
The Witch Queen of Kamilan

They did not falter
or talk like a woman. With one voice,
they threw their votes in the urn of blood.

Aeschylus

Moon, moon, gold-horned moon, blunt the
hunters' knives, cast wild fear upon all men, that
they may not catch the black wolf. . . . My word is
binding, more binding than sleep, more binding
than the promise of a hero.

Old Russian Charm

A free woman never commits adultery.

Hind Bint 'Utba

29. The Mailed Fist of Dravia

All her life, until Marwen came back from Aralev with her Dravian minstrel, Luned had been the favourite of the royal household. Queen Arden had adored the strong-willed, energetic servant. Luned had tended Arden's bedchamber, laid out her clothing, stoked her fire last thing at night and fetched her a hot drink in the morning. Luned had listened to her griefs, shared her confidences, and pampered her child. When Arden died, Luned simply moved into the same role for young Marwen, and Marwen accepted her, having no reason to prefer anyone else.

Now Luned was no longer the favoured one. It had happened quietly; even she had not noticed at first. But one by one her old duties to the queen were replaced with new, less personal ones. When Aran was born she was given charge of his nursery—a duty which kept her close to the queen in a way, but nonetheless removed her from the intimate place which she believed would always be hers.

The minstrel Kiri—a woman of dubious quality, and a foreigner besides—sat at the queen's elbow now, and shared her counsels. Hard-eyed shield women tramped about like soldiers, guarding her chamber, and they blocked Luned's entrance there as readily as they blocked anyone else's. Even Caithland the eunuch appeared to have her absolute trust.

But Luned, in Luned's view, had nothing. Luned been tossed aside like an old coat. So much for gratitude, so much for half a lifetime with the house of Adelmar.

It did no good, Kiri discovered, to remind Luned that the queen was only twenty and she, Luned, was forty-eight. Or to remind her that people were simply different, that it was not fair to demand that Marwen love her just because Arden had. It did even less good to point out that giving her care of the little prince was surely a sign of the greatest trust, more important than tending the queen's fire or whispering secrets in her ear.

Luned scoffed. "She has no time for the poor wee thing; that's why I can care for him."

Kiri stared at her, astonished. People with hurt feelings, she thought, could be extraordinarily silly.

"That's not true, Luned. She adores him."

Luned went on mending and did not answer. She would not argue with Kiri. But among the other servants she sometimes expressed her views, sometimes deliberately in Kiri's hearing, almost as though she hoped her words would somehow get back to the queen, change her, make her more like her mother.

Luned disapproved of many things Marwen did. In particular she resented the queen's relationship with Borosar. She did not know what kind of relationship it was; that was part of her resentment. She also admired the prince consort, and that was the other part.

"It's unworthy of her," Luned would say, whenever the subject came up, as it often did. No matter how loyal they were outside the walls, inside the walls servants talked, and nothing could stop them.

"It's unworthy of her. A man like that, twice her age and a drunk. If they could come by wine on the battlefield, think what kind of general we'd have!"

"He fought the Dravians all those years, against King Algard, and never was defeated," Harad said.

"So? Our men are brave. Anyway that's not the point. She has a splendid husband—"

"Who sits in the fortress of Maene all winter with a slut who's half *his* age, telling his kinsmen not to pay their taxes! A splendid husband indeed."

"So why did she drive him away?"

"Who says she drove him away?" Malia demanded. "I never thought he was so special. It never mattered what you put on his plate; he ate it like he'd just come from a feast somewhere else."

"Some people have manners. Like my lady queen did. She did everything with grace. If only she'd had the raising of the princess, instead of Medwina—!"

"And if wishes were horses, Luned would be queen, and then we'd see things done properly."

"All right for you to laugh. It will all come to no good in the end. Borosar is a lecher, and that black captain of his is nothing but a savage. Gods, how can she favour men like that?"

Luned looked defiantly at Kiri, as if daring her to respond. Kiri said nothing. When the war was over, those questions would answer themselves, even to Luned's satisfaction. Either that, or there would be no more questions asked at all.

They had lived with the threat of that war for so long, yet when it came the suddenness of it seemed overwhelming. It was only a moonturn after Borosar's departure when the first messenger came. He had ridden without stopping from Getann, and he could barely stand. The Dravians, he told them frantically, were in Dohann. Belengar had been taken, and Berend's army was pouring down the Magdal valley—more than five thousand mounted warriors in armour, and four times that many more on foot: spearmen and pikemen and phalanxes of infantry with broadswords; and a train of siege engines and mounted crossbows. Their sutler wagons alone stretched out for leagues.

"Lady, I don't know what hope we have, and nor does Borosar. The wolf harries their flanks, and stalks their camps by night. But they are so many, and they are moving fast. Borosar can only fall back, and fall back again; he slows them down, but. . . ." The messenger wiped his face. "He advises you, lady, to be ready for a siege. They might be at the base of this mountain in as little as a week."

After that the couriers came every day, and sometimes every hour, tracing the relentless progress of Berend's army. Getann was taken, and the villages all around it destroyed. The fortress of Caerne, which belonged to Borosar's own kin, was a smouldering shell. Kiri remembered, painfully, Marwen's words about an earlier time, an earlier war: *I came to dread the sight of messengers. . . .*

Fugitives began pouring out of the north. Most of them fled ahead of Berend's army; a few were survivors who had not fled soon enough. Their faces were blank with horror, like so many she had seen along the caravan roads. Their stories were similar, when they could tell their stories at all: stories of blood and screaming and fire, of children thrown into wells, and captives dragged behind galloping horses until they were torn apart by rocks and trees, and women passed around among hordes of men and raped until they were dead. And under all of it rang the triumph of Berend's warriors, echoing the triumph of their king, a man who was proud to be called Berend the Scourge. He flung out his boasts like the blows of his sword, knowing they could wound. He would crush the witch queen's neck beneath his heel, he said, and he would burn the high city to ash, till even the stones crumbled. In a hundred years, he said, men would not remember that Kamilan had ever been.

An army large enough and sufficiently well armed could conquer a country literally in the time it took to march across it. Kiri knew that, and so did the Kamils. Fear lay over the land like fog. The bright summer sun was a mockery, and the crops waving green in the fields broke their hearts.

You have planted, the land seemed to say, *but Berend will reap. Your barley is his, and your calves and your corn. Your pretty children he will take for slaves. Your daughters will fill his brothels, and your sons will die in his mines. It was for that you all were made, did you not know?*

The queen had memories of Algard's wars, but they were the memories of a child. She had no experience of leadership in war, and she turned without hesitation to Angmar the Wise, and brought him back into the palace. She gave him a measure of authority which astonished everyone who knew them—an authority far exceeding anything she had ever given Landis.

War changed everything in the high city. All day, from dawn till dusk, armed caravans crept up the mountain road with stores of food and fuel, yet everyone, even in the palace, seemed to be living on siege rations. Old nicked swords, unused for years, came down from their walls, and old men sat on their steps until the light failed, honing them anew. The city ramparts were ringed with piles of stones—simple weapons, but terrible ones, when the earth itself pulled them down onto the narrow road below. Long-time enemies embraced in the streets; no Kamil hated another Kamil now. Even Crayfe, huge and sweating as he hurried about the city, trying to keep up with the queen's demands—even he seemed to Kiri less villainous now, just another human being trying to stay alive.

Kiri herself moved into the ranks of the queen's most skilled defenders without a question asked. A few raised eyebrows, perhaps—she was still Dravian, after all—but no questions. She trained with the shield women every day, and when they went wearily to other duties or to their beds, she stayed in the barracks yard with her crossbow. She stayed until her eyes wept from sighting it and her arms screamed from drawing it, stayed until Caithland smiled and said: "You would give the wolf himself a contest now, minstrel."

Minstrel. . . ! What song is this I'm singing now, this song like a beat of blood, so terrible and impersonal?

She did not hate the Dravians. They were, after all, her countrymen. Sometimes she thought about the battles which might lay ahead, and imagined herself doing brave and splendid things. Yet there was no desire in her for those battles. Every time a messenger came, some of the young men would drop whatever they were doing and run to him—*Is Berend coming? Is Berend coming?*— their eyes and their voices eager, hoping the answer would be yes.

She did not want the answer to be yes. And yet she knew she would fight more fiercely than any of those young men. She would never yield, never bargain, never accept the inevitable, as men so often did, laying down their arms and paying their ransoms, scoring it up to the gods or fate or honour, smiling, *it was a good war, we'll have another next year. . . .*

No, none of that. She sought no man's death, but any man who came against her—against her queen—with death in his hand, she would take his death without flinching and drive it back into his own heart: *This is yours, villain; keep it!*

Messengers came again. Berend had left the Magdal valley and turned east towards Tamri.

"It was a wise enough move," Angmar said. "Greedy as the Dravian is to swallow us, he isn't blind with greed. It would have been reckless to leave Favian's great fortress undefeated behind him."

"But it will give us time," Marwen said. "And it will give Borosar time as well."

"Aye, lady," Caithland agreed. "But unless Borosar can fashion a miracle, it's hard to see that it will matter."

They were sitting at the queen's table with a handful of others. The servants quietly removed the remains of a frugal supper. Every day Malia complained bitterly about Harad: *He will give me nothing, lady, except in spoonfuls. How do you expect me to cook?*

Cook what he gives you, Malia, the queen would always reply. *We will not complain.*

Every day Malia threw up her hands, and walked about muttering and sighing, and cooked what Harad gave her from the stores. Lean as it was, it was always good. If the day came when they were eating grass, Marwen said once, Malia would make it taste like bread.

The wine was watered more than usual tonight. Caithland took a long draught, frowned but said nothing, and put his elbows on the table.

"What are we to do about Theron, lady?" he asked. "Today he called on people in the crowd to burn the goddess Jana's temple. If the leaders of Kamilan will not act, he said, then the sons of Mohr must act for them. He says the Dravians are agents of Mohr's vengeance, and will destroy us unless we turn back to the god."

"Ignore him," Marwen said. "Has the seneschal placed guards at the temple?"

"Some, lady, but not enough."

"Then send some of your own men. And let the high priest rant."

"There are many who believe what he says, lady," Caithland said.

"I know that. And if I attack him, they will have still more cause to believe it. Let him be for now."

There was a stir at the door, and one of the shield women rushed in. With her was a youth covered with dust and stumbling with exhaustion. His left sleeve hung in tatters, and there was blood on his tunic. Later, when he had told them everything else, he told them he had ridden so desperately that he had twice been thrown.

Every time before, even with the worst of news, the messengers would be speaking even as they came. This one only fell to his knees before the queen.

"Lady. . . ." he said helplessly, and then again: "Oh, my lady. . . ."

"Speak, lad!" Angmar said sharply. "No one will hurt you. Speak!"

He looked up. Tears were spilling from his eyes. "Lady, we are undone."

Then, having begun, his words spilled out without a pause for breath. "Borosar met the Dravian army two days ago at dawn, and gave battle, and was defeated. He's dead, lady, and I don't know how many others, and the army has been driven into the Gap of Clythe, and there's nowhere for them to go, and Berend's father-in-law has brought another four thousand warriors from the east, the king of Dorath gave them leave to pass through his lands, and Berend is only waiting for them to join him before he attacks again. . . !"

"Wine," the queen said sharply. A servant rushed to bring him some, and helped him to chair, and made him drink it.

"How is this possible?" she demanded, when he had recovered himself a little. "Borosar swore he wouldn't meet them in open battle unless he had no choice! Goddess of the world, what came over him, that he would throw himself on their swords?"

"He had no choice, lady. When the lords of Tamri saw that Berend was turning against their city, they demanded that he fight. 'Shall we run like craven dogs,' Oswin said, 'while they burn our homes before our eyes?' For as you know, lady, the valley of the Niela is broad and rich, and the finest holdings there are Favian's. First they argued, and then they cursed, and then Favian said they would take their men and withdraw to defend Tamri, be damned to their oaths; they owed no faith to a general who ran like a whipped hound. Even Landis counselled him to fight then, saying it was better than seeing their forces split by mutiny."

"Did the warleader of Dohann say nothing to all of this?" the queen demanded.

"He wasn't there. Borosar sent to him only after it was decided, and told him to pull in his men and join them for the battle. Great Harash, lady, he was angry! I think he would willingly have run Favian through where he stood. They called each other names neither will forget, if they live."

The messenger paused, and gulped wine. "The warlord chose his ground as best he could. I don't think he chose badly, but he was hopelessly outnumbered. They say he killed twenty Dravians with his own sword before he went down. . . .

"And so it ended, lady. He was slain, and our men were driven into the Gap of Clythe, and from there they cannot escape, for Shadrak has the cliffs at his back, and Berend's army camped in a half-circle before him. It took me nearly the whole night to crawl through their lines."

"Shadrak?" Angmar demanded harshly. "What do you mean? Does he lead now in Borosar's place?"

"Aye, lord. It was Borosar's command, and he refused to change it. Ah, lady, he was a hero to the end! He wouldn't let them touch his wound, or give him any potions until he'd finished speaking, and by then he was all but gone. He swore at Lord Oswin, and at Favian too. 'You have counselled me to my death,' he said, 'and Kamilan to its knees. But by the gods you will obey me now, or I will walk out of my grave and follow you, and follow your sons and your grandsons to the end of time, if the Dravians let any of you live!' And then he took his chain of rank from his neck, bloodied as it was, and gave it to Shadrak, in front of all of them. 'The army is yours,' he said; 'save it if you can.' And so the wolf leads them now."

"And Oswin accepted this?" the queen asked.

"Aye, lady. It galled him hard, but he accepted it. A dying man's curse is not an easy thing to face. And the gods know it scarcely matters who leads them now."

The tapers burned unsteadily, throwing shadows across the great stone altar, lighting now one and now the other of the goddess-figures standing behind it, carved figures of Jana, who was both one and many and always three: virgin, mother, and crone. Beside the altar, the high priestess of Jana sat in dark thought; the queen of Kamilan knelt at her feet.

For a long time, after the queen finished speaking, the chamber echoed with silence. Medwina rose, paced a little, and responded at last, her voice quiet and stern.

"I can't help you, sister-child. If I had the powers you ask of me now, I could have brought you home from Dravia. You must look to yourself. You are also sorceress."

"Myself?" the queen whispered.

"Yes." Medwina's long fingers closed against her face, lifted it. "You have great power, though you've never tested it. It's different from mine; it always has been. Jana is many goddesses; no priestess can serve them all. You're closer to her her dark side than I am. Use your power, Marwen of Kamilan, for it's her dark side we have need of now! Call forth the wolf who shadows your path! Call forth the darkness and the sea! You are the only one who can!"

The queen sank onto her heels, bewildered and afraid. "Will you help me?" she whispered.

"As much as I can," Medwina said. "I fear it may not be very much."

The queen knelt for a long time, feeding the fire on the stone, carefully, object by object, leaf and grass, branch and stone, shreds of moss, feather and fur and blood, last of all the wolf's tooth. . . .

"From the forest, from the shadows, from the pathways of the moon, twice you have come to me unbidden. Now in Jana's name I bid you. Come!"

She said the words three times, and waited. The tapers burned low, and night closed deep on Kamilan. The altar fire burned out. The wolf moved across the patterned stones without a sound.

The queen glanced eagerly at Medwina, and saw with astonishment that the priestess's gaze still brooded on the goddess-figures, unchanging, while the wolf passed boldly beneath them.

She can't see it . . . oh, goddess, then I truly am alone. . . !

The wolf sat, watching her with restless, hungry eyes.

—Why have you sent for me, Marwen of Kamilan?

—*I have a task for you.*

—*Will you claim your debt now at last, and set me free?*

—*I don't know what debt you speak of.*

—*The debt I owe to the ancient house of Alyth. I have waited many lifetimes, and followed many queens, searching for one who would set me free. Few had the power to do so, and none chose to use it. If you do, I will carry out your task.*

—*You agree without knowing what I will ask?*

—*Aye, lady. As you will give me freedom without knowing what it will cost. Heed me well. I will serve you only once. No matter how desperate your need, I will not come to you again; I will no longer be as you see me now. If I carry out your command—*

—*Successfully.*

—*Agreed. If I carry out your command successfully, my punishment will be over. I will be free to return to the circles of the world, where all things end and begin again. That is my bargain with you.*

—*Well then, I accept it.*

—*Swear it, queen! By the blood of Alyth, swear it!*

She drew her dagger and pressed the point carefully but cruelly into the vein of her wrist. Blood ran down the blade and dripped quietly onto the altar stone.

—*Serve me, Wolf, and be free forever. As Jana has made the world, if it is in my power to grant you this, so shall you have it. I swear!*

—*Command me, then.*

—*Go to Dohann, and find Shadrak of Belengar. Lead him and my army to safety. There must be a path out of the Gap of Clythe. The forest is yours, and every shadow in it; you can find a way!*

—*There is no path out of Clythe except through the Dravian camps. I can pass there without risk, but your soldiers cannot—or have you such power that you can make men invisible?*

—*We shall see, Wolf. Go. Find Shadrak, and do not leave his side until you've led him to safety.*

The wolf rose, began to turn away.

—*Wait! Tell me one thing more! What was your debt to the house of Alyth?*

—*You have sworn, lady. You can't take back your oath.*

—I won't try to take it back. Tell me what you did, to bear so hard a punishment.

—I killed a queen's son. Her only son, in the flower of his youth. He would have been a king. Farewell, Marwen of Kamilan. Farewell.

It was nearly dawn when the queen left the sanctuary. She walked slowly, aware of little except blind exhaustion, and strange sounds around her like muffled cries of terror, and a mist before her eyes. The vestibule, bright-lit and warm, seemed to her like a place of fire, Caithland a mailed shadow rising to greet her, his face bewildered, as though he did not know her.

"Caithland, will you help me? I can't see. . . ."

He reached, but Kiri was faster, her strong arms closing hard around the queen's body as she crumpled. The minstrel knelt, easing Marwen down and cradling her head against her lap.

"Lady, oh gods, lady, what has happened? Marwen, what have you done?"

"Kiri. . . ?" Her eyes opened briefly; closed again. "Kiri, I'm so weary. . . . Come closer; I can hardly see your face. There are riders coming. Send someone, see who they are. . . ."

"There are no riders, lady," Caithland said. "The city sleeps."

"There are; I can hear them. Go see, Caithland, they ride like the wind."

"Fetch Medwina," Kiri whispered.

But there was no need. The high priestess was already shoving through the cluster of guards. She knelt beside Kiri, lifting Marwen's head and holding a small silver cup to her mouth.

"Here," she said. "Here, my dear one, drink this."

The queen obeyed like a child, and collapsed. Kiri looked hard at Medwina.

"What happened?" she asked, not very gently.

Medwina rose. "She will sleep for a long time," she said. "When she wakes, give her broth and some soft bread, and comfort her. She will want your lyre, I think, Kiri. Play for her, and don't leave her alone."

"What happened?" Kiri demanded again, bitterly.

"She tried her strength," the high priestess said. "And she found it greater than either of us knew."

30. The Battle of Tamri

The camp was quiet. For long stretches no one spoke in Shadrak's tent, and no one slept. The warleader sat with his elbows on his knees, brooding. Cassian had fixed the bandage around his leg, and brewed some herbs for him to drink, but the wound still hurt him bitterly.

Worse, far worse, was thinking about the queen. What would become of her, when Berend's armies cut them down, and swept Tamri, and closed around the the heights of Kamilan? Even with the Kamil army defeated, it would be a bitter siege, for the fortress town was built to fight, and the Kamil people would not give up. It would last a year, or even two, but the food would give out, and they would slowly starve.

What would become of her?

"She be witch queen, captain," Tamon said softly. "They has no way to hold her. They tries, but they has no way."

Shadrak looked up. Tamon's face was shadowed in the dim light, and strangely soft.

"Do you believe that?" Shadrak said.

"Aye."

There was no comprehending human creatures, he thought. Cassian was his best-loved friend, yet it was this half-savage, half-articulate soldier, this man who was only a step or two above a paid assassin, who understood his love.

And maybe it was, as Cassian said, that Tamon did not see the danger. To Tamon, the queen was just another village girl—the sexiest, most sought after village girl, hanging her arms about his captain's neck, and to him that was simply the world unfolding as it should.

Maybe that was all Tamon understood. And maybe, Shadrak thought, maybe Tamon understood something which Cassian did not. Maybe that was why he was always there, with his hand on his sword, outside any door they lay behind; why he offered now what few blunt, groping words he could, here at the edge of death.

She be witch queen, captain. They has no way to hold her. . . .

The fog came out of the sea. It gathered along the rugged shores of Dorath, heavy with the cries of seabirds, rolling landward in immense, death-gray clouds. It spilled across the Dorathian plains and over the mountains into the the valley of the Niela, drowning Tamri, slithering up the great peaks of Clythe and across Dohann. Its edges drifted down the valley of the Magdal, wrapping the royal city in choking mist, creeping under the wooden doors of the temple of Mohr where Theron sickened as he slept.

Never in living memory had there been such a fog, even in winter. It stifled men's breath, and chilled them to the bone. When what should have been morning broke on the Dravian camp, men could not see their hands before their faces, or identify a voice a few arms-lengths away. They walked as though blind, feeling their way with sticks. The king gathered his priests and his counsellors into his tent, where a half dozen flaring tapers fought against the unnatural dark. He demanded sacrifices, oracles, answers.

What does this mean?

It was a death knell, the priests said. Those who had brought such bitter grief to Dravia were marked for death. When the fog lifted, a great battle would be joined, and the justice of the gods would be made clear to the world.

The king was satisfied with that answer, and waited. All day long the Dravian soldiers huddled in their tents, hungry and soaked through with cold. Even their cooking fires would not burn. Some cursed, and some prayed, but most of them just shrugged and endured it, wondering perhaps what their king wanted in this fell and miserable land.

The fog lifted in the final hours of the second night. At sunrise they discovered, on the western edge of their encampment, a long swath of silence: the guardposts untended, the sentries dead. Those who found them swore their throats had not been torn by weapons, but by fangs. Beyond them, in the cliff-walled Gap of Clythe, there were no fires, no tents, no living men at all. The Kamil army was gone.

"Ride with me now who can!"

Shadrak's single challenge rang clear through that soft gray morning, and they rode like the wind, bowmen and cavalry, let the rest follow as they might, no one could stop him now and no one tried. He had a wildness in him, a dark fire, and the goddess of that black fog rode by his side. Even the men who hated him followed him now. They swept down the valley of the Niela and onto the broad plain of Tamri, and as the sun rose noonward they saw banners, and massed men advancing grimly across the sodden landscape—the army of Edgard of Heydren.

Then Shadrak's men raised up their own captured banners of the Dravians, and those in the front ranks held before them shields blazoned with the mailed fist of Aralev. Edgard's horns sounded out a welcome, and they answered it, and rode boldly on.

"They be like lambs in a pasture, be they not?" Tamon murmured.

The Dravians rode almost into bowshot before they realized their danger—not that it would have mattered in the end. Nothing short of headlong flight would have saved them. For here, finally, Shadrak had what he had waited for, what he had begged Borosar to wait for: a place where he could unleash his splendid bowmen on horseback. In the mountains he would wear his enemies down with time. Here, on this broad and pitiless plain of Tamri, he would cut them utterly to pieces.

314

"Never have I seen such a carnage, lady," the messenger said. "We were one to four, and Shadrak laughed, and said he wouldn't have cared if we were one to ten. It took only minutes to encircle them. When they held their ground we shot them where they stood, and when they tried to break through in force, we pulled back and shot them as they came. I don't think they ever knew how it was possible. All that armour they were wearing—it might as well have been parchment."

He held out his cup eagerly for more wine.

"And what does Lord Favian say now about my wagonload of toys?" the queen asked wryly.

"Lady, Lord Favian says as little as possible about anything. The warleaders don't know what to do. They are brave men, and glad of the victory, but they don't like it that they have to stand aside and see a slaveborn barbarian—for that's what they call him, lady—to see him honoured like a hero, and cheered everywhere through their camps. His men made him a great banner, with a black wolf on it, and it flies outside his tent now as though he were warlord."

"The man presumes too much," Angmar said.

"He is commander," the queen said. "He has the right to a banner." She turned back to the messenger. "What will Berend do now? Is he still advancing on Tamri?"

"We don't know what he's going to do. He sent scouts out to search for his father-in-law. Well, they found him, lady, though I think by then they didn't know him; for the ravens were there. It must have been a terrible sight, that plain. . . .

"They say when the word was taken back to him he cursed like a madman. For some reason he blamed you, lady, and raged that it was sorcery. He swore he would put all of Tamri to the sword in revenge. Shadrak has already sent men about, through the whole of the Niela, telling the people to take their children, their animals, and their most valuable goods, and go. Berend still has a great army, and wherever it passes he will leave nothing living behind him."

After, when the war was over, Kiri wondered how it was that Berend did not see his danger. He was an intelligent man. He had raised a well-armed, well-disciplined force. He had managed the battle against Borosar with skill. Surely then, he should have looked at that raven-black plain of Tamri and wondered how he might cross it. More desperately still, he should have wondered how, even with sixteen thousand men, he might destroy an enemy who simply would not stand and fight, and how he might take Tamri—much less the royal city itself—until he did so. Most desperately of all, he should have asked himself what would happen if he did not accomplish all of those things before the leaves fell.

But Berend was lord of the great house of Aralev, and his fathers claimed blood descent from Telhiron. He was a warrior, a king, and a man. He had behind him the largest, fiercest army the mountain lands had seen in many lifetimes. Ranged against him were a few thousand Kamil barbarians, a sorceress, and a slave. Nothing less than victory was possible.

It was not the sort of war the bards of the old days would have liked much. More than one messenger told his tales with an uneasy mixture of pride and sidelong glances, as though he were not sure how they would be received. Shadrak fought like a cutpurse in the streets. He attacked Berend's long sutler trains from ambush, fired burning arrows into his tents at night, pitilessly killed and maimed his horses. Every league that Berend marched he left dead men behind, more and always more of them, and still he had no enemy to fight. And his own men did not fight well in such a situation. One captive put it to the Kamils thus: "What's the use?" he said. "We chase you, and you run. We turn away, and you attack. You're no army; you're pieces of fog and packs of wolves." And then he put his head down and wept, and said the gods had abandoned Dravia.

Many of the Dravians would willingly have gone home to lick their wounds and try again in a year or two. But Berend would not yield. Rage consumed him. He struck out at everything: he tortured captives to death, and ordered a tree chopped down and burnt when a branch slashed his face. Again and again he put his own men to the sword for a small blunder or a small impertinence. He was Berend the Scourge indeed, but there were some now who were calling him Berend the Mad.

Finally, all else failing, he tried to bait the Kamil warleader into personal combat. When that story came to the royal city, it would be talked about and argued about for days.

"Berend challenged him?" the queen whispered, disbelieving.

"Himself? No, lady. The king would not fight a freedman, no more than his brother would. They sent one of their great captains, a man called Erland the Red. They sent couriers out to us under a flag of truce, asking for a meeting. Our leaders agreed, and Erland came to our camp the next day with a splendid escort, looking much like a king himself."

"I remember the man," the queen said. "I met him once or twice. Berend liked him. They were two of a kind, I think."

"Aye, lady, they say he is cruel. But Shadrak just laughed at him, and laughed at his challenge. 'How shall I come to meet you, Dravian?' he asked. 'Alone, so you may kill me from ambush? Or with my whole army, so your men may encircle us all, while you and I are fighting? Do you think I'm such a fool? Go tell your master that if he fancies a fine wolf pelt for his feast hall, he shall have to catch me first; I won't come to him!'

"Well, lady, Erland was so angry he could hardly speak, for this was a terrible insult to his honour. And the wolf was not done with him. 'For two moonturns,' he said, 'you've been chasing us up and down the mountains, and you can't defeat us. You can't even *find* us except with a white flag waving over your heads. And this is the best you can think of for strategy? Your country has sore need of a king, Dravian, and your king has sore need of a general!' "

Caithland shook his head in disbelief.

"Such words from someone as baseborn as he," Angmar said, "would make a man draw his sword on the spot."

"Aye," the messenger said. "Erland did so, and swore they would fight then and there, and Shadrak again said no. As leader of the Kamil army he would fight only the leader of his enemies, that is the king. 'Tell your master Berend the Mad to come himself,' he said, 'and I will meet with him. I have no time for his lackeys.'

"And so, lady, after many words were spoken which I won't repeat to you, for they were very rude, the Dravians were compelled to leave without satisfaction, and go back to their king humiliated. Some of our captains spoke after among themselves, saying Shadrak handled the matter badly, that he should have fought, that he shamed them all by refusing. But later we learned from our spies that Erland and the king almost came to blows, each one blaming the other for their

loss of face. So now the king and his great general are at odds—
and that's better, Shadrak says, than if the general merely were
dead. Oh, he's cunning, lady, and wary as a wolf. I myself
think if he'd agreed to fight they would have used some
treachery against him."

"He can blame no one for that except himself," Angmar said
heavily. "He was the first to make this a war without honour."

Marwen gave him a withering look. But Kiri thought the
old man's words had some wisdom. She would not have put it
the way he did—as a statement of blame—but it was nonetheless true: the code of honour protected men from certain kinds
of barbarism. Only highborn men, of course—and sometimes
highborn women. Only in certain ways, according to certain
rigid rules, but it did protect them. Shadrak had scorned that
code, and they would not forgive him for it, not now, and not
ever.

Angmar was growing weary, and on his aging face Kiri saw
often a deepening ambivalence. The queen had many qualities
which he admired, and not the smallest of these was her willingness to learn—to learn, especially, the thousand things
about warfare and defense which, as a woman, she had not
been taught. Angmar admired that, and yet a part of his mind
seemed always to be thinking: *A king would not have had to
ask about this; a king would have known.*

A king would have been in the field against Berend, too,
and all this bitterness among the Kamil captains would not
have been. Take it a step further, she reflected, and the war
itself might not have been, for Held would never have been
killed, and Berend would never have been lord.

Every day Angmar was reminded that the queen was skilful
and brave and strong. Every day he was reminded anew that
there should be no queens at all.

He would break under the weight of the contradiction, she
thought, if he did not find some way to resolve it.

So day by day, messenger by messenger, the summer passed.
Valley by valley the north of Kamilan was trampled and
burned, but the villages were mostly deserted before Berend
got to them: the farmhouses empty, the granaries bare. He had
supplies in plenty, even yet; he did not need their cattle or
their grain, but he needed living enemies to kill. It maddened

him to find most of them gone. He called them rats and dogs and vipers. Let them run, he said; they could run until they fell into the sea. He would burn Tamri to the ground, he said. He would spread the citadel of Kamilan with salt, so that until the end of time nothing would live there.

Kiri was Dravian, and had never thought of herself as anything else; this man who raged across the Kamil valleys was her king. And Edgard of Heydren had been father-in-law not only to Berend, but also to the lord of Ostern, in whose domain was the border village of Vanthala. Among his men, slaughtered on the plain of Tamri, had perhaps been some of the comrades of her youth, perhaps her kinsmen, perhaps even her brothers.

She pitied them—most of all because she knew that she might have been among them. Their own scorn for her sex was the only thing which had prevented it. And yet the pity was distant and empty. Too much had happened. Too much had been learned, and once it had been learned, it could never be brushed aside.

Suppose they *had* accepted her? Would she have become one of them, and died at Tamri? Or would she have learned what she learned just the same, maybe even more quickly? Learned that there was no glory in burning villages and stealing pots and pans and gold-buckled belts, no glory in taking slaves, no glory in killing someone who had never harmed you? Learned that whatever pride and splendour there was in strength and skill—and yes, perhaps even in combat—its place was elsewhere, it had another face than this, another name?

What would have become of me? she wondered. But there was no answer; there never would be.

The end came, like the beginning, with a quickness that bewildered the Kamils. Midsummer came and passed. In the south, where the Dravians had not destroyed them, the green crops were spattered with pale gold, and the gardens were laden with fruit. Here and there in the forests, the odd shrub was turning to red, the odd leaf to yellow. The summer was passing, and even an arrogant king knew he could not winter an army along the edges of Dohann. Tamri had to be taken, and although Berend said it was nothing more than a backwoods fort, it was still a fort; it might take them a month to hammer it down, maybe longer. The Dravians decided that they had wasted too much time chasing Shadrak, and lost too many men. They massed their forces, honed their swords, and marched on Tamri.

"I don't mind telling you, lady," the messenger said, "he still had a fearsome army left, and when it poured down onto the plains of Tamri, it was enough to make me cold with fear."

Shadrak let the army come, let it gobble up Favian's valley holdings one by one, let it spread in a shimmering horde across the plain of Tamri, to within sight of the city's towers. There he attacked them, and there the great battle which never seemed to come, came at last.

The messengers rode through the dead of night, stopping for nothing, shouting at every farmhouse, every wayside town, running their horses to the edge of exhaustion and taking others whenever they wanted. No one begrudged them horses— not with news like this. They came banging on the city gates a few hours before dawn, shouting at the top of their lungs: *Call out the guard! Take us to the queen! By the gods, wake up, and open the gates! We bring news of victory!*

Heads emerged from windows, torches lit, a murmur caught and began to spread, lifting to sudden dazzling shouts, spilling from doorway to doorway, from rooftop to rooftop: *It's over, it's all over, we beat them at Tamri! Berend the Mad is running for his life! We have won. . . !*

People spilled into the streets, running after the messengers, tugging at their boots, *Is it true? Is it true?* The shouting ran ahead of them. By the time they reached the palace, light was already leaping from its windows; and the queen, with a great cape wrapped around her nightdress, ran out to the gates to meet them.

Even by torchlight Kiri could see that the men were drunk with exhaustion and joy. One of them nonetheless managed a hurried bow, and burst out:

"I bring you greetings, lady, from the warleader of Dohann, who sends you word of his great victory at Tamri! The Dravian army is destroyed, lady, and the king is wounded and running like a hare! We've won, lady, we've won!"

They took the messengers into the hall, gave them food and drink, and wore them out with questions. It took hours to get the whole story; the first thing they wanted was news of their captains.

Landis was safe. Shadrak and Oswin were wounded, but were both still on their feet. Favian had taken a sword thrust in his side, and lay in Tamri hovering between life and death.

"Ah, he fought, lady, you should have seen him! There is no braver man in all the world!"

The messenger himself was from Tamri, Kiri noted, and of course held up his own masters for special praise.

"When we had used up all our arrows, finally," he went on, "it was the cavalry that carried the day then, and the lords of Tamri. Berend's army was all bright armour and banners and noise, but no courage. Everywhere we pressed them hard, they broke. I'll wager there are two or three thousand of them scattered over Dohann, hungry and shamed, trying to get home any way they can. The rest are dead or captive. We over-ran the king's camp, and all but captured him. We got his gold drinking cups and his bedclothes and all his weapons except his sword and his shield; *and* his two concubines—for he was so sure of victory, lady, that he brought his whores along."

"What became of them?" the queen asked calmly.

The messenger paled slightly, aware that his companion was glaring at him and Angmar looked appalled. He had forgotten himself. He should not have mentioned this to a woman—but no woman, dear gods, should have questioned him further.

"It is the custom, lady. They are prizes of war."

She did not yield. "Whose prizes?"

"Lady—" Angmar began, but she ignored him completely, pinning the messenger with her eyes until he answered her.

"The warleaders drew lots for them, and they were taken by Lord Oswin and. . . ." He hesitated. "And the prince consort, lady. Landis of Maene."

"I see."

"Anyway," the other messenger went on quickly, "we took all the king's treasures, and with them his gold crown, which he brought to wear in triumph through the gates of Kamilan. And Shadrak took it, and carried it to the top of a hill. He drove a stake into the ground, and put a dead man's head upon it, and crowned it with Berend's crown. And there the pride of Dravia sits, lady, on the brow of a grinning skull, and though it's valuable I don't think there's a man of us who'd dare to touch it."

The messenger fell silent, half out of weariness and half out of awe, for although he knew his tale was true, he still did not entirely believe it.

Nor did any of them. Through every window of the palace they could see the Kamil sky shimmering with flame. Bonfires roared in the streets, the taverns had flung open their doors, and carefully hoarded casks of wine were spilling into cup after cup. Here everyone had gathered in the feast hall, servants and guards alike, many still in their night clothes, and many already giddy from wine.

In the brief pause that fell the queen asked again: "The prince consort is well?"

"Aye, lady. He's unhurt."

"And Shadrak of Belengar? You said he was wounded."

"He's weary to death, I think," the messenger said—the one who was not from Tamri—"for he hasn't rested since the war began, and his wound doesn't heal. And although the soldiers worship him, the lords do not. I fear they will find it even harder to accept him now."

"Has the victory earned him nothing in their eyes?" Kiri demanded.

"They're proud men, minstrel," Angmar said. "It's one thing to endure the intolerable in adversity. It's quite another thing to endure it after."

"That is so, lord," said the other messenger. "If Shadrak were wise, he would yield command to Lord Oswin; that's what everyone expects. But he's proud, too, and I fear he won't do it."

"Nor should he," the queen said grimly. "My army is not a trinket to be handed around to whoever thinks he should have it. Caithland, call up your men. I want a guard of thirty, and the fastest mounts we have. Tell them to cover all their insignia, and carry our standards furled. We'll travel like common soldiers."

"To Tamri, lady?"

"Yes, to Tamri. And now, by the sacred goddess, you will see how your queen can ride!"

31. Of Warriors and Women

They searched the field with torches all night, hour by bitter hour, fashioning litters with cloaks and pieces of wood to carry the wounded. Citizens of all ranks came from Tamri to join them, looking for kin and friends among the survivors and the dead. The civilians brought wagons, blankets, and food; they brought barrels of fresh water more welcome than gold.

Shadrak walked most of the time; it was easier than climbing on and off his horse. Tamon protested, sometimes in words, more times with a look: *Captain, you be too bad hurt for this. . . !* But it made no difference. The place held him, and pulled him into its darkness. He knew the war was over, but he did not believe it. Had he gone to his tent, he would have lain in it raw and sleepless, surrounded by dust and screams and clashing iron. He felt triumph when he saw the Dravian king in flight, and he would feel it again in a day or two; he knew that from experience. But now he felt only this driven exhaustion, suffused with pain and battle-fury and bewilderment: was all this done in a day, so much death, so many pain-black eyes staring into the torchlight, begging for help or for release?

For those who might live, a mouthful of water, a litter, a torch waved high to summon bearers or a wagon. For those dying in anguish, a knife wielded quickly and clean, Dravian or Kamil, it made no difference. He would expect as much from an enemy, and whether in the end he got it or not, he would offer it. There were debts one owed to existence itself, rather than merely to individual men.

"Captain. . . ." Tamon's voice was a raw whisper. He never called Shadrak anything but captain, and he never would—not even if his captain rose to be emperor of Larandau.

"Be a girl, this one," he said harshly, pointing.

She was young, and not very big. A war-axe, wielded by a man on horseback, had brought her down from behind. Four Dravians lay dead around her.

"She fought like a man," someone said, admiringly.

Shadrak did not reply; he was too weary. He had long known that there were women in the Kamil army, and probably in every other army in the world. He had stumbled on the first of them as a green youth, when he left a dusty, boring camp to go swimming, and found one of his soldier comrades bathing in the water. They had stared at each other for a full minute. He was foolish enough to be pleased with his discovery, thinking she might lay with him. She was angry and afraid, convinced he would betray her.

Neither outcome followed. She wanted nothing to do with men's beds. And he, having won his freedom and his small place in the world by the sheerest unlikely chance, saw no reason to destroy hers.

Over the years he became aware of others, usually only after they had been wounded: runaways, orphans, lovers, dreamers, adventurers, the occasional criminal. Their hair was lopped short and their bodies shapeless in some older man's clothing; altogether, they were not much different from the men around him. Most were brave, a few were shirkers. Most were skilful, a few were fools. One might well say they fought like men, but having said so, what had one said that mattered? They ate like men, too, and laughed and quarreled and sweated, and cursed the insects and the mud. And they died like men, hard and often unmourned. This one at his feet was younger than his queen.

The sound of horses broke into his thoughts. He turned. A great body of torches was moving towards them. There were perhaps fifty men on foot, four of them carrying a litter. Beside it, grim-faced and exhausted, rode Oswin of Tamri.

The warleader drew rein, staring down at Shadrak. He was wounded himself, and clearly in a foul mood. It was not difficult to guess why—talk of it had swept the ranks. Oswin had assumed that, as lords of Tamri, he and Favian should lead the first victorious Kamils into their city. But Favian had been wounded and could not be found, and the prince consort was not a man to miss a moment. He claimed the right to enter Tamri on the queen's behalf, and marched off in full glory with Ranir and his warband, leaving Oswin to hunt for his kinsman among the ruins of Berend's army. The warleader of Tamri was humiliated and furious.

"So," he said to Shadrak. "You are still here."

He spoke as though the fact irritated him intensely. Nonetheless, Shadrak reflected, if he had gone into Tamri to drink and flaunt his triumph, that would have irritated the warleader even more. It was difficult to please some men.

"I am still here," he said. *In more ways than one.*

The bearers had moved closer, and he saw that the man they carried was Favian. His face was uncovered; he lived then. They all lived, all the men who hated him, even Berend. . . .

"How is your kinsman?" he asked.

"He will wield a sword again before the snow flies."

Aye. And we need not ask for whom he will sharpen it, do we? He swore it loud and clear enough, and more than once.

"I'm told you fought bravely today," Oswin said.

Shadrak did not respond. He knew that Oswin's words were not intended to be generous; they were merely a gesture, a pat on the head to a dog before it was sent back to its kennel. He could have found some appropriate, meaningless response, but reeling with exhaustion as he was, it did not seem worth the effort.

His silence angered Oswin. The lord had made what he no doubt considered an extraordinary gesture, and it was being ignored.

"An honest man can always acknowledge the truth, Shadrak," he said coldly. "Even to those who aren't of his station or his kind."

"An honest man wouldn't find it so painful," Shadrak replied.

"What would you know?" Oswin snarled. He sawed at his horse's reins. "You weren't taught honesty in the gutter where you were bred—nor anything else that I can see."

"I was taught to survive."

The sun rose fierce and burning. With daylight men came incessantly to his tent, and they kept coming long into the night, burdened with problems they wanted him to solve. A quarrel had broken out between the healers from Tamri and the army surgeons. Merchants from the city were already gathering in the camp to buy slaves from among the Dravian prisoners. A soldier had knifed another over a bauble stolen from a corpse. And everyone's reaction to a problem was the same: Go ask the wolf. He will know what to do.

Tell the army surgeons to shut their mouths and be glad they have help; if they tend my men as badly as they tended me, we'd be better off without them. Sell no slaves; it's for the queen to decide what becomes of the prisoners. Put the murderer in irons; he will be tried. . . .

"Cass . . . goddess of the world, Cass, I'm tired. Help me with this cursed thing, will you?"

Cassian eased him out of his clothing and into a chair, propping his foot up on a wooden block. The wound stank when he unwrapped it; the flesh around it was pulpy and aflame. Cassian frowned darkly.

"You must have this looked at, Shadrak."

"I did. That was when it turned bad. Bathe it, and put a compress on it, and let it be. I've survived worse."

Hoofbeats approached outside—not a messenger this time, or someone needing orders, but a large body of mounted men. Before Shadrak could send someone to investigate, Tamon burst into the tent.

"Captain, Oswin be comin' with half his warband! And they be armed like they's riding to battle!"

Goddess, I don't know if I have the strength to lift my sword. . . .

He stood up; pain shot through his leg like sharp, slender nails.

"How many men are outside, Tamon? Our own men?"

"Two hundred, maybe. Enough. Always enough, captain; we makes sure of that."

Shadrak looked around for a cloak, but he could not see one; everything in the tent was scattered and in disarray.

"I will see the warleader, if that's what he has come for. Greet him politely, and ask him to wait."

But Oswin would not wait. Horses clattered to a stop outside, and seconds later the tent flap was swung wide and the warleader of Tamri stormed through, three of Shadrak's protesting guardsmen at his heels.

He paused abruptly, though, seeing Shadrak naked except for a cloth wrapped around his loins. His hard gaze took careful note of the wolf's bandaged ribs, of the suppurating wound above his knee.

"How dare you—?" Cassian began fiercely, but Shadrak gestured him to silence.

"Have the Dravians returned, warleader?" he asked quietly.

"What in Mohr's name are you talking about?"

Shadrak sat down again, carefully, trying to show Oswin neither his weakness nor his pain. He lifted his foot onto the block where it had rested before, and motioned Cassian to continue his work.

"You barge into my tent without permission, armed for battle and in too much of a hurry to even let me put my clothes on. What else am I to think?"

"I'm done asking your permission for anything, wolfspawn."

Tamon bristled like a dog about to lunge, but Shadrak and Oswin both ignored him.

"Then why are you here?" Shadrak asked.

"I'm on my way to Kamilan. I've come for Borosar's sword and chain of rank, so I can return them to the Council and the queen. He is dead, and as his next in rank and in command, that duty falls to me."

"He is dead, Oswin. I am not. His badges of rank I will return to the queen myself, when she asks for them. Until then, warleader, I still command this army."

Oswin's hand moved instinctively towards his sword-hilt; then with great effort, he curbed himself, and let it fall again.

"You don't command me, Shadrak," he said grimly. "Not any more. Keep your pretender's trinkets for a few more days;

you will yield them in the end. And then look to your wolf's throat, for there will be more than one man waiting to cut it!"

"On the first campaign I was ever on," Cassian said, "I had a good friend who ran afoul of a bully in the company, a real scoundrel, who baited him until they finally came to blows. My friend got beaten senseless. I was surprised by that; I had seen him fight before. He knew all kinds of tricks. He could have left the brute in small pieces.

"After, when I was patching him up, I asked him why. 'You chose to lose that fight,' I said; 'are you out of your mind?' 'No,' he said. 'My mind is just fine. This way, the scoundrel's satisfied. If I had beaten him, he'd kill me the first time my back was turned. . . .' "

Cassian frowned, and said nothing more.

Tamon glared at him. "What for you be telling stories like that?" he demanded bitterly.

"Sorry," Cassian said. "I couldn't help thinking about it, that's all."

"It was the queen's fight, Cass," Shadrak said. "I could hardly choose to lose it."

Nonetheless, the point of the story was well taken, he thought. His triumph had made him infinitely more vulnerable than before. He was nothing, not even a peasant. He was sword-fodder born of a Thyrsian slave, a man who did not even know his father's name, and he had just led the Kamil army, the Kamil lords themselves, to victory against an enemy four times their strength. The very fact raised questions about the lords' power, their inherited right to land and wealth and privilege, their superior sacred blood.

Had be been a man of at least a little substance, they might have shifted the boundaries of rank and let him in, and so maintained the illusion of aristocratic merit. All lines, after all, had a founder. All lords had an ancestor who, in the beginning, was not a lord.

But the gap was too immense, the implications too shattering—more shattering still if they learned that he had dared to bed the queen.

They had no reason now to tolerate him; he himself had removed it. And he was desperately unsure as to what they might do next.

In battle his judgment was instinctive and quick. Even the politics of commanding this fractious group of lords had been within his grasp while they all faced a common enemy. But it was different now, and he was dazed with fever and exhausted; no course of action seemed safe. If he remained in the field with his men, it was tantamount to acknowledging his insignificance. If he gathered them, wounded as he was, and marched into Tamri to claim his place among the victors. . .? They might insist on a fight now, the fight they had so often and so reluctantly refrained from provoking. Usually it was Landis who had argued for restraint. Would he do so now? Or would he lean back and sip his wine and smile, happy to see his rivals at each other's throats?

And what of the queen? The situation had changed for her, too, and she would have to adapt, find new strategies for dealing with men who were finally her enemies as much as they were his.

You're in a maelstrom, Cassian had said, *and you will drown there. She will discard you in the end, even if she doesn't want to. She will have no choice. . . .*

He laid his head back, spent. He did not know any longer what to do, neither how to shield her, nor how to shield himself. He did not know if either was still possible.

The war is over, and we won it. We won it splendidly. We should be drowning in wine and laughter, with garlands in our hair. Instead I crouch like a cornered wolf in my tent, surrounded by armed men, as though we were not victorious but under siege; and I dare not even send for a healer because any healer worth hiring would have me flat on my back for days, and who can say what would pass in the meantime? Maybe they will do nothing; maybe all they care about now is scrambling for Borosar's place. . . . Maybe, and maybe not . . . goddess of the world, I'm so tired I can't think. . . .

A soldier stuck his head into the tent.

"My pardon, warleader, but there's something I think you might like to see."

Shadrak stood up, discovering that he was no longer steady on his feet, and went outside. The light of the brilliant noonday sun speared into his eyes. He squinted against it, staring across the plain of Tamri. A great shimmering of horses and flags moved there: the queen's flags. Her couriers had come then, thanks be to Jana. He would at least have orders, and could direct his actions accordingly. But why such an escort?—couriers rode fast and light. . . .

"Marwen. . . ." He did not know that he spoke. He did not know any more if he saw or imagined, but she was there with them, surely she was there? No one else had that moonwild hair, that grace. He stared as the column approached. Even in soldier's garments she was the loveliest creature in the world—queen, goddess, witch of that dark and desperate fog, there and not there, blurring in the cruel light.

"Cass, am I delirious?"

Cassian's hand closed on his shoulder, hard. "No, my friend. She's quite real."

She dismounted, came towards him; her face was drawn with weariness, her high boots gray with dust. He considered the time which had passed since the battle, barely time enough for their couriers to have gone to the royal city and returned again. She must have ridden headlong and without rest, to come to him.

Marwen. Marwen, my brave and faithful love.

Kiri would scarcely have known Shadrak except for his black hair and the wolf-crested banner which flew defiantly outside his tent. He was on his feet, as the messenger had said, but that was all. The fluid grace of his body had become rough-edged, almost clumsy with pain; his face was ravaged with exhaustion and his eyes muddy with fever. His tent itself had an air of siege about it, encircled with soldiers whom she recognized from Belengar. Tamon stood almost in arm's reach of his leader, a permanent warning snarl etched around his mouth.

Shadrak stared at the approaching queen as he would have stared at the goddess herself. Then, overwhelmed, he did not simply bow to her, but dropped to one knee.

"Lady. . . ."

She paused in front of him. It took every thread of will she had, Kiri knew, not to simply gather his dark head against her body and weep. Instead she reached out one hand and raised him to his feet, and said strongly, so that everyone present could hear her:

"There are no words to thank you, warleader, or to tell you in how much honour you are held."

330

There was food in Shadrak's tent, good venison which his men had fetched for him, and which he had barely touched. Kiri had not realized how hungry and thirsty she was until it was offered to them, along with great cups of clean, cool water.

"Lord Oswin left for Kamilan this morning," Shadrak said. "Did you meet him on the road?"

The queen's mouth was full of food, so Caithland answered dryly:

"Aye, we did. Surly as a stepped-on cat he was, and threatening to draw swords and run us off the road—for we rode without flags until we reached Tamri. He was commander of the Kamil army, he said, and he had business with the queen."

Marwen drank deeply of the water Cassian handed her, wiped her mouth, and went on with the account:

"I flung back my hood, so he could recognize me, and asked him by what right he claimed that title. In truth, I didn't think he'd do so publicly unless you were dead, and I was cold with fear. But there is no limit to some men's arrogance. He said when Borosar gave you the command it was only a strategy for the moment. It was the queen and Council, he said, and not Lord Borosar, who would name the new warlord of Kamilan."

"The queen looked at him," Caithland said, "cool as can be, and asked: 'And have we done so?' To which he could only admit we had not. 'Then Shadrak still commands,' she said. And that, although it all but killed him to swallow it, was that."

"Did he return with you?" Cassian asked.

"He tried," the queen said. "He couldn't keep up."

"Do you have horses that fly, lady?" Shadrak said.

"It depends where they are going."

There were no people in the tent now who were not trusted friends. She touched his face in a brief caress, then laid her palm across his forehead.

"You are sorely hurt, wolf—more than they said. I was afraid that might be so."

"It wasn't so to start with," Cassian said. "But he was tended badly, and he refuses to rest. I've done my best, but I'm no healer. If you would use your authority, lady, and send for one whether he wishes it or not—"

"I will do better than that. I will tend him myself."

He protested at first, aware only of the danger around them, ignoring the danger he carried in his body. She let him talk but did not heed a word of it. She brewed a heavy narcotic to make him sleep and then, with great care, she unwrapped the deep, festering wound above his knee, bathed it, and wrapped it in poultices.

The second injury, fresh from the last battle, was clean but very painful. A javelin thrust had struck him full in the left side; with its last force it had pierced through his armour, leaving a shallow but ugly wound. All around it Kiri could see the marks where the ring mail had been driven into his flesh. Two ribs were broken and his entire side was bruised as though it had been smashed with a club.

It must have hurt even to breathe, she thought, but he did not flinch as the queen tended him. He was half asleep when she finished. She ordered his bed made up fresh, with clean linen from her own stores, and then, when he was lain in it, she knelt beside him, ending her ministrations with a scattering of kisses wisped across his face.

"Sleep, wolf," she murmured, brushing his hair. "Sleep. You're safe now. Sleep."

She stood up and looked at Cassian. "If I'm not here when he wakes, encourage him to eat, and give him another sleeping draught. Don't let him get up, no matter what he says. He must regain his strength; he's going to need it."

She paused, and added simply: "I don't need to tell you to guard him well."

"We will do so, lady," he said. "We can't thank you enough for your kindness."

She wiped strands of damp hair away from her face, wearily. "I suppose Lord Oswin has returned by now, and is chafing to see me."

They went outside, Cassian following respectfully, pausing to stare in disbelief at the sight of the royal tents, set up in full glory on the battlefield next to their own.

"Lady . . . lady, you're not meaning to lodge here. . .?"

"Of course." She smiled. "Why should I not?"

"You're the queen. You are expected in Tamri. They will give you royal lodgings in Favian's palace—"

"That would be the usual thing, Cassian. But I will stay here, and though they'll be offended and dismayed, what can they say? The city is full of refugees and wounded. Favian's own palace is sheltering more than a hundred of them. Whatever they may think, they can hardly condemn their queen for refusing to throw the injured and the homeless out of their beds to make a place for her.

"And where the queen is, Cassian, the court is—and so are the places of honour."

The implications were clear enough to Cassian, as they would be to the whole valley of the Niela before the sun rose again.

"You are a most extraordinary woman, lady," he said.

Bonfires roared all night in Tamri, and in the sprawling camps outside the walls. It seemed to Kiri that every soldier who was not wounded was drunk. They talked endlessly about the victory, and who had done what, swordthrust by swordthrust. Despite the tension among the Kamil leaders, morale in the battle had been very high. It seemed every man there had outdone himself. Before he was wounded, they said, Favian had left a swath of fallen Dravians behind him the way a reaper left swaths of grain. Landis of Maene had brought down no less a man than Erland the Red, who had raged about the battlefield looking for the wolf. *Why hunt wolves?* Landis had asked him. *Are you afraid to fight men?* Oswin had been everywhere, as Oswin always was. And as for Shadrak of Belengar, well, it would take more than one night's storytelling to recount every deed of his. . . .

Kiri listened quietly, saying nothing and staying out of the light; everyone was too engrossed in talk to notice her. This group, like all the others, would eventually get around to discussing the new warlord.

—*Be Oswin of Tamri, I expect. He's a great warrior.*

—*Aye, no question; and he's in line for it.*

—*Well, maybe. But the queen is no fool. Was it me, I would keep the command closer to home, and give it to Ranir.*

—*Ranir be no leader.*

—*He's a brave soldier, and steady.*

—*So is my horse.*

—*Mind your tongue, friend. There are Maene men over there.*

—*What of it? We got a better captain than they got. We got the wolf. That's who ought to be warlord.*

—*You're drunk, Falan. And daft, too.*

—Drunk he is, but he's not so daft. There's no better man in the field than Shadrak of Belengar—with a bow or with a sword.

—Aye, or with a plan. And that's what counts. Glory is fine, but myself, I like to walk into a battle knowing my chief has given some thought to keeping me alive.

—He's good. We all know that. But he's slaveborn.

—So? Don't matter to me.

—I thought you said this man wasn't daft.

—Look, blockhead, he can't be warlord. You know that. A freedman can't ever be named chieftain of a clan, or sit on a tribunal, or be a priest, or marry a freeborn woman—

—I know all that. But he was captain at Belengar.

—A border post! Men send their sons there when they're in disgrace! The warlordship is a bit different, lad.

—Well, the boy is right, just the same. A man like that should lead, slaveborn or not. He never left the field all night, looking for wounded lads, and seeing they were cared for. I been soldiering for twenty-three years, and I never saw any finebred lord do that. They fetch their own kin to safety, and then they head for the wine casks, and the rest of us can rot. The wolf is worth the lot of them, twice over.

—It's true. He should be warlord. But it's not possible.

—If the queen would ask us what we thought—

—Aye, and if fish could fly, and rivers run uphill, and tavern girls be made virgins again. . . !

They laughed and went on arguing, and did not even notice the Drav spy, bonnet pulled low over downcast eyes, stagger to her feet and leave the fire.

The naming of the warlord was on everyone's mind; it was for that reason Oswin had been riding headlong to Kamilan— to pursuade the queen to name the new commander at once, so he could reorganize the army, and replenish its supplies, and lead it into Dravia.

"So he could do *what?*" Kiri whispered.

"You heard me," Marwen said bitterly. "For Favian's sake I agreed to meet with them in his great hall in Tamri. The lord himself was there—he's nowhere near being dead. And they pressed me to send for Angmar and Crayfe, or better yet, to make a decision without them, so the army could march. We had the upper hand now, they said. There were two good

moonturns of fighting weather left; we could sweep Dravia in
that time, border to border!

"Do you believe it, Kiri? After what we've suffered, and
what we've seen, they would begin it all again? Oswin was
like a boy, like a lover going to his mistress; he couldn't sit
still for eagerness. All they talked about was honour—honour
and glory and tribute and power. Look at the wealth of Dravia,
they said, look at how much we can conquer, look at how
feared we'll be! By Great Harash, no one will ever spit on Kamil
pride again!

"What's the matter with them, Kiri? They're all men of the
world; they're not stupid. Even if we won as easily as they
said, we'd have to go on fighting forever to keep it. Everything we took from the Dravians we'd have to spend again on
arms, just to keep them from taking it back."

She sat down, pouring herself a large cup of wine, ignoring
the embarassed servant who rushed over, too late, to attend her.

"I hate them," she said softly, darkly. "As much as I ever
hated Held. They will go on forever, generation after generation, riding gloriously to war over the bodies of uncounted, gloriously slaughtered men. Wasting the harvests of their people,
filling the world with slaves, trading women off like cattle. All
the while insisting that they have no choice, that it's all for the
good of the kingdom, that everyone should make the sacrifices they need for their power. The young girls should bow
their heads and open their legs, and the young men should
pick up their swords and go die in someone else's barley.

"Do you know what Oswin said to me, when I told them that
no army of mine would march across my borders, ever—he
said he understood that women were soft, and wished to keep
their husbands by their sides, but we simply had to understand
that there were more important things in life!

"It didn't matter what I said to them, Kiri. They listened, but
it had no effect. And angry as they were, they didn't say much
to me. They didn't know what to say. You can't argue with a
woman. She simply doesn't see; she doesn't grasp the world
the way it is. . . ."

She fell silent. Kiri, half undressed, sat dazed on her bed. She
had imagined herself ready for any insanity, but the thought of
invading Dravia had frankly never occurred to her. Now, considering it, she realized that in military terms it was perhaps

quite feasible. No doubt they stood a very good chance of conquering the land against a shattered army, a hated king, an already submissive population.

But for what?

Dead men, burned houses, children who could not speak for the horror of what they had seen, women made into booty and men into animals, and for what?

Even to ask the question was to fail to understand the world. To achieve mastery was its own justification; it needed no other. That was what being a warrior, being a favoured son of Mohr, being a lord and a man, *meant*.

She sighed, and pulled off her other boot. It was late; one small oil lamp filled the queen's tent with muddy light.

"Did even Landis approve of this invasion?" she asked.

"Yes," the queen said. "He put it in terms of protecting ourselves. Berend would raise another army, he said; we could forestall that by conquering him first. And when I said I didn't care a fig if Berend raised another army—we had defended ourselves once and we would do it again, as many times as need be—he looked at me, Kiri, I swear to you, he looked at me as though I were a child, an impossible, babbling *child*."

Slowly, clumsy with weariness, she began to undress.

"We survived this war against all the odds," she said softly. "I thought perhaps they would give me some credit for that. But they never will. I'm just . . . just *there*, like the peasants and the trees—sometimes useful, sometimes in the way. I don't think they even *see* the world any more; they just ride across it."

There was a small silence.

"You told them you would never send an army of yours beyond your borders, ever?" Kiri asked.

"Yes. And I told them if any man chose to do so on his own authority, he had best stay there, for he would have neither lands nor lordship when he returned."

Dear gods. . . .

"Why didn't you just say it was too late in the year?"

"What?"

Kiri faltered. She had not meant to be quite so crisp.

"It's only a suggestion, lady. But perhaps you could have put them off. It *is* late in the year, and the army is battered, and by the time they were re-supplied and ready to march it would be later still. Next year you could find another excuse, and the year after that another one."

The queen said nothing for a time. Then:

"That would have been wiser, I suppose?"

"It might have been."

She put her face in her hands. When she looked up again, her expression was harsh and exhausted.

"You're right, Kiri, I know that. But how can I pander to people I can't even respect?"

The queen was not finished causing havoc in Tamri. When the sun rose, she went to Shadrak's tent, kissed his groggy face and made him drink more potions, and sent Kiri with a large escort to fetch King Berend's captured concubines.

"If anyone argues with you," she said, "remind them that it's the sovereign's absolute right to question prisoners of war."

Remembering Berend's wives, Kiri was not surprised that the girls were exceptionally beautiful, although one of them was so battered and sullen that one noticed her beauty only later. At first one saw merely a trapped, cringing animal with vacant eyes.

It was difficult to speak with her, even in her own language. Except for a few frightened glances around the queen's tent, she scarcely moved or spoke, responding to nothing because she had learned, horribly, that all responses were dangerous.

It took a long time to draw out her story. She was a country girl. Her father was cruel. She ran away with a soldier. The king saw her among the camp followers, and took her. He was cruel. She did not want to go home. She did not want to stay with Lord Oswin.

Kiri spoke to her very slowly, as though, like the queen, she were using a foreign language:

"The queen asks what you would like to do. She will take you into her household, or send you elsewhere if you wish, perhaps to the country. She has many kinswomen there who would give you a place. What do you want to do?"

The girl did not speak at once; when she did her voice was no more than a whisper. "Will you . . . will you . . . give me something to drink?"

"Yes, of course," Kiri said, rising, and then, seeing the expression on the girl's face, freezing utterly still.

"I tried," the girl said dully. "With a knife. I tried, but I couldn't. It hurt too much. Please."

The queen still spoke Dravian well enough to follow this exchange. Her face paled to soft ash. Unexpectedly, she rose and walked around the tent, making small, empty motions with her hands. When she spoke at last, her voice was harsh with emotion, and there was ice in her eyes.

"I swear to you, Kiri, the next man who preaches to me about honour, I will put a dagger in his bowels!"

The girl, seeing the queen angry, was terrified. After that she would say nothing more, only nod numbly as Kiri explained that she would stay with the queen's household, at least for the time being; that she would be safe, that no one would hurt her. She did not believe it. She did not want to believe it. She did not want to heal, and risk being savaged again. She wanted to dissolve, to cease.

What kind of man was Lord Oswin, that he could thrust himself upon a girl as dazed and damaged as this, and find pleasure in it? Or did he not even notice it, not see her state of mind as meaningful at all? He had a wife of his own, he had daughters; he did not have a reputation as a brute. What sleight-of-mind made it possible to do this—or to come after, angry as baited bear, demanding that the girl be given back?

The concubine Landis had taken was afraid, too, but for very different reasons. She had the kind of splendid, voluptuous beauty which could make men limp with hunger, and women limp with jealousy. Kiri wondered idly whether the pretty things she was wearing had somehow survived Berend's long campaign, or whether Landis had bought them for her in Tamri.

She gave the queen one long sweeping look, a look which was both sly and harshly perceptive. She would have heard many bitter things against the witch queen of Kamilan from Berend, and perhaps a different set of bitter things here—not from Landis himself; the prince had too keen a sense of propriety for that, but from the people around him. And the girl, although young, was no innocent. She could draw a few conclusions for herself, looking at the queen, noting the thin body whose not very remarkable curves were hidden utterly in soldier's garb; noting the cool grey eyes, the toughness, the will.

The wife.

For a full minute neither spoke, they merely looked at each other, and when they had finished both were certain they knew exactly what they were dealing with.

The girl was polite. She was too aware of her vulnerability to be otherwise, yet the odd gesture, the odd look, made it quite clear that she thought little of the queen, and felt superior to her in every way except rank. She felt superior above all as a woman: *she* was pretty, *she* knew how to please a man, *she* would never play the whore against him.

And the cold, scheming queen, of course, would try to punish her, would try to come between her and the splendid, wealthy, powerful man who liked her so much.

They did not speak long. When Kiri asked her what she wished to do, she glanced once towards the queen, and did not answer.

"It's not a trap," Kiri said simply. "Whatever you ask for, you will get."

Such an offer, of course, could be the nastiest kind of trap, and Kiri could almost see the girl's mind searching out the treachery. If she asked to go back to Landis, would the queen smile and send her back with her face slashed? With a dagger in her heart?

"The prince consort has been kind to me," she said, with a trace of defiance.

Why should he not be, Kiri thought, *when you are willing to do and say and be anything he wishes?*

"Do you want to stay with him?"

The concubine looked at the queen. Marwen smiled. It was a smile without warmth and without malice.

"You are fond of him?" the queen said.

More defiance. "Yes."

"Well, I hope he's fond of you, because I'm going to put you in one of those big kettles out there, and make you into broth, and invite him to supper."

Incredible as it seemed, for one long second the girl seemed to believe her, and went utterly white. Then she understood that she was being mocked, and flushed deeply.

The queen summoned the guards to take her back to the prince consort's lodgings.

"Dear goddess," she said when they were gone, "that creature and Landis deserve each other."

32. Confrontation

Despite Angmar's many warnings on the subject, Landis of Maene never believed in sorcery, neither as a power of darkness nor as any other kind of power. He did not believe that any human being could shapeshift or fly or turn others into stone, or compel love or death or anything else with a potion or an incantation. But the power which a *belief* in sorcery possessed was becoming very obvious to him.

Awe followed the queen of Kamilan everywhere she went. In Tamri hundreds, maybe thousands of men—sane men with wounds and bloodied swords in their hands—acted as though it were she who had earned the victory. How else had the fog come, they asked? How else had the Dravian sentries died? How else could arrows pierce armour? How else did the fouling wounds she tended heal so quickly? She was a witch, they said, and they looked at her with gratitude and wonder.

Had they credited Shadrak with the powers of sorcery, it would have made a little sense. At least he had found his way out of the Gap of Clythe, however he had done it. But sense clearly had nothing to do with the matter. It was all rooted in wild stories, and in their belief in some ancient, deep-rooted, compelling female power. They did not ask *how* she could have done any of those things—how anyone could, least of all a girl who was not twenty and whose best talents were those a man could buy in any tavern for a handful of coin.

A witch she was not, he thought bitterly. But the more they believed it, the less they noticed what she really was—wilful, capricious, and without judgment. She had sat in Favian's feast hall, with a victorious army at her fingertips and a demoralized enemy just across a few leagues of mountains, ready to fall into their hands like a ripe peach—she had had all of that, and had flung it away with a few haughty words. *No. We are done fighting. The goddess kept safe our borders; we will not insult her by violating them ourselves!*

Dear gods, what kind of sovereign had so little daring, and so little sense?

"Borders!" Oswin had said scornfully, long after, when she was gone and the wine had poured freely for a while. "Damn the borders. A border which can't be defended is a border which doesn't exist." He shook his head. "I don't understand it, Landis. She seemed courageous; I thought she had something of a taste for a war."

Landis said nothing, although he understood it quite well. She had fought because she was cornered. There was nothing very brave in that; any trapped creature would do the same. The courage and resolve it took to go willingly into danger, not merely to save oneself, but to achieve something splendid, to make one's country renowned—that was a very different thing.

The journey back to Kamilan took forever. They travelled slowly, for they had many wounded with them, even Favian of Tamri, who swore he would not stay behind in his bed while others decided the future of Kamilan. Every league they travelled they were met by triumphant Kamils. And once they left the ravaged northern valleys, every camp became a feast. The people came out from the farms and villages by the hundreds, bringing them chickens and fat pigs, great rounds of cheese, and fresh fruits from their gardens. They spoke of nothing but the victory. And they credited the victory entirely to the goddess and the queen—and to the queen's baseborn warleader, whom she placed as stubbornly at her left hand as she placed Landis himself at her right.

He found it unspeakably tawdry. More than once, in the midst of those feasts, he wanted nothing so much as to get to his feet and tell them all exactly what he thought of this Thyrsian cut-throat and his royal whore.

That she *was* Shadrak's whore he no longer seriously doubted. He had thought a lot about the seneschal's words, even in the midst of the war, and he found that he was persuaded less by the logic of Crayfe's arguments than by his own memories of the Field of Fire. Sometimes, looking at Shadrak in some battle-weary camp, he simply could not bring himself to believe any of it. The man was rabble. He could fight, yes. He had a certain instinctive and remarkable cunning, and he had somehow learned to speak well. And that was all. Absolutely everything else about him reflected his origins, his utter lack of quality. He gobbled food like a wild animal; he cursed as foully as the worst of his rough-hewn soldiers; and, like any baseborn man thrust suddenly into a position of power, he was both arrogant and defensive. He expected to be treated as though he were a lord, but he would neither dress nor act nor think like one. He was not handsome. He owned nothing except his horse and his bow and a few ragged furs and wolf's teeth and trophies plundered from dead enemies.

No woman of rank and breeding would take such a man for a lover.

Part of the prince consort's mind clung to that, and part of his mind acknowledged frankly that women did in fact take such men for lovers, and worse ones. The creature he had whored with at the Field of Fire might well take anyone.

Still, until Tamri, he had wavered, believing one day, doubting the next. Now it was no longer possible to doubt. She had rushed to Shadrak's side the moment the war was over. She tended his wounds with her own hands, and used her own guard as a buffer between him and the lords of Tamri. She made certain the army could not march by refusing to name a warlord until they returned to Kamilan. It was clear enough now. Not only was the slaveborn Thyrsian in her bed, but her political decisions were being shaped by her eagerness to keep him there.

Landis chafed bitterly, but he said nothing. The new war-lord had yet to be chosen, and he meant to influence that decision as much as he could.

He was almost never alone with the queen until they reached the fortress of Maene. There he asked to discuss the matter, and they met in a small quiet room where he often sat with his advisors. Wine was brought, and they toasted each other. He recalled the day she had asked him to marry her.

"Shall we speak frankly, lady?" he asked, echoing her words.

"Of course," she said.

He sat, looked at the wine cup, then at her. "We have become . . . estranged, lady. Whatever the reasons for it, it should not blind us to our political realities. Do you agree with that?"

"Yes. I agree completely."

"You must appoint a man to lead your army. It's the most critical decision you will ever make. I know you want to discuss it with Angmar, but I can tell you exactly what he'll say, and why he'll say it. You must appoint Ranir, lady, if you are ever to have peace in this realm."

"I've thought about it," she said. "But the lords of Tamri would take it very badly. 'Landis of Maene is prince consort,' they will say, 'and Angmar of Maene is chief of Council. When Ranir of Maene is warlord, we will be nothing but servants in Kamilan.' "

"And if you appoint Oswin of Tamri," he said grimly, "you will go through life the way your father did—with a divided Council, a divided country, and endless argument over everything. Only it's going to be worse now, for Borosar at least was loyal to the king. The lords of Tamri have never been loyal to anyone but themselves.

"Lady, think of it! We have now a chance to make our power complete! We can control Council and the army as well. Let the lords of Tamri grumble; that's all they ever do. You must name Ranir, lady. You must!"

He paused, and added quietly: "I'm not trying to command you. When I say must, I speak simply of necessity—sheer political necessity."

"And if I do appoint Ranir, how should I appease the lords of Tamri?—for they will be angry, you may be sure of that."

"There are many ways. Give them more land. Give them the Dravian prisoners. Give Oswin his concubine back—you

343

offended him terribly by taking her, you know. Find Favian another wife with a good dowry. There are ways."

It was her turn to stare into her wine cup. "I will consider what you've said," she told him. "But I don't intend to make any decision until I've spoken to Angmar."

"He will give you the same advice."

"Perhaps." She looked up, smiled faintly. "There is something I want to ask you, since we're alone. When you captured Berend's camp, and took his concubines, the four of you drew lots for them. Why did you take part in that?"

He stared at her. He could not imagine a more unexpected question—or a more irrelevant one.

"Lady?"

"Why did you take part?"

"I thought we were talking about the appointment of a warlord."

"We were. Now we're talking about this. Unless of course you are ashamed to talk about it, in which case I won't press you."

"I'm not ashamed to talk about it."

"Then explain it to me."

"There's nothing to explain. We married according to the Laws of Kind, you will recall. You insisted on it. You have no grounds to fault me for taking concubines."

"Are you that blind?" she whispered. "You think I'm jealous? You think I'm asking you about this because I'm *jealous?* Goddess of the world, I was a captive, too, have you forgotten that? The same age, almost, in a foreign country, surrounded by men with swords in their hands. They didn't draw lots for me, but nothing else was different. Now I ask you again, Landis of Maene, why did you take part in that?"

"It's the way of war. She likes me well enough, as you took the trouble to discover. If I had refused, someone else would have her. Berend should have left his women home."

"And I should have stayed in my father's castle, with my pillow over my head. Yes, I see. Well, we are estranged indeed, Landis, more than I knew."

She stood up. "I am weary. I bid you good night."

"Lady, we've barely touched on the matter of Ranir's appointment! Please! Stay a little, and let's talk about it some more. I know you have doubts. I can answer them. Or we can both answer them; let me send for him now."

Her eyes were cold. She had said she was not jealous. Perhaps that was true, he thought, and perhaps it was not. Perhaps a political discussion was not what she had been hoping for tonight.

They had never lain together here in the fortress of Maene. He thought about it now, deliberately, and discovered that his desire for her was still alive, still keen and sharp. But it had changed profoundly, just as he had. It had grown cooler, sterner, less animal. He had made many painful choices in these last two years, and each of them had strengthened him. The final proof of his strength was that he could still desire her, and it did not matter. He would take her if she let him, and it would not matter. The boundaries were in place; he could admire her smooth body as he would admire any passing harlot, and enjoy himself with her, and walk away.

"You *are* tired," he said quietly. "Let's meet with Ranir in the morning, then."

"If you wish."

He moved towards her. She did not react at all, except to watch him with a kind of icy curiosity, as if her only interest was to see what he might do next.

"The warlordship," he said softly, "was not the only thing I wished to speak with you about."

She waited. She was not going to do anything to make it easier. But that did not matter, either. He could play whatever games were necessary. He wondered what games she made Borosar play. *Kneel down, there's a good doggie, say woof-woof, make friends with the nice wolf for me, won't you?*

How satisfying it would be to turn the game around!

"Marwen, whatever you may have thought, it's you who are my wife, and no one else. And this is my ancestral home. It would please me if you would share my bed here tonight."

Nothing changed in her face. There was no pleasure there, no anger, not a flicker of interest or even of scorn, neither real nor pretended. There was nothing at all.

"I'm weary, Landis," she said again. "Good night."

She did not look back. She did not bother to close the door. She walked away from him as though the room were empty.

So that's how it is, then. You whore all winter with Borosar to buy favours for your slaveborn hound. You run to Shadrak like a bitch in heat the moment the war is over, and tuck him under your arm and drag him back with us to make him a hero, and tell us all to smile on it—and I'll wager you had your twat in his face before he could stand on his feet! Gods know even a wounded dog can lick. And then you scorn me in my own house, after I've backed you in everything, aye, and lost both friends and honour doing it. . . ! Dear Mohr, by what folly is the likes of you made queen?

He poured himself a small glass of wine, sat again, and tried to quell his anger. Anger was unwise now; he dared not offend her. And he needed to think. Somehow, she still had to be persuaded to give the warlordship to Ranir. His reasoning, sound though it was, did not seem to have made much impact. Ranir himself had not made much impact, either. He was a good soldier, but he did not have the kind of presence, the aura of leadership which Borosar had had, or even Oswin of Tamri.

Landis shook his head, taut with frustration. The woman was unpredictable. She might well give Borosar's place to Oswin, hoping to mend the damage she had done in Tamri. She might even try to choose a captain from a lesser house, hoping to find another Borosar. And he, Landis, would have to manoevre for the gods knew how many more years through fields full of petty but dangerous snares, and rooms full of quarrelsome fools, building his future as before—in small, careful ways. And if he had to, he supposed he could. Oswin could be kept happy, and out of the way; all he needed was a war. And there was no other Borosar; there was not even another Oswin. The warbands of the smaller clans were all led by very ordinary men; none of them were a match for the lord of Maene. In time he would still be king, in fact if not in name.

But if Ranir were given the army—if once, just once, the world unfolded as it should, then he would not have to spend his life manipulating events every day, every hour, just to keep what power he had. He could use his power to acquire more. He could make Kamilan great, and forge a kingdom the world would have to reckon with—a kingdom worthy to pass on to his son. He smiled faintly, thinking of Aran. Already he was such a splendid little boy, with the high forehead of the house of Maene, and the strong limbs, and the serious eyes. What

Landis made great, Aran would make greater, and the name of Maene would pass into legend. Their daughters would marry kings, their sons and grandsons would conquer all the mountain lands. Theirs would be a time of greatness, when the Kamils were proud, and reached out into the world, and left their mark upon it. And afterwards, for generations and even for centuries, they would be remembered and admired, even by their enemies: *Aye, by the gods, those were men!*

But no. Instead he must ask, persuade, dear gods of all the earth, *beg* this trifling harlot who called herself a queen to give him what should be his by right, without debate. It was his by rank and birth, by experience and ability, and not least by the marriage which she herself had sought and then betrayed.

He drained the wine, and stared into the empty cup. They would see, that was all; they would have to wait and see. There was still Angmar, and she seemed to respect the old man. If anyone could persuade her to choose Ranir, it would probably have to be him.

But if Angmar persuaded her of anything, during their long meeting in the royal city two days later, she gave no sign. The sage, as they both expected, offered the same arguments for Ranir's appointment, although he warned them not to underestimate the outrage it would create in Tamri. The queen left the meeting without making a decision—indeed without indicating at all the direction of her thoughts.

"She has no idea what to do," Landis said, after she was gone. He was aware of the scorn in his voice, but he no longer cared to hide it—at least not from Angmar. "I'll wager she decides anew every time she hears another argument. She may finish by picking a name out of a bucket."

Angmar said nothing for a time. The war had aged him. There was more gray in his hair than Landis remembered.

"Have you quarrelled with her?" he asked finally.

"No. I've been careful not to. Why do you ask?"

"She looks at you so. . . . " He paused, searching for a word. "So coldly."

"Well," Landis said bitterly, "even she can keep only so many fires going at once."

Angmar met his eyes briefly, and looked away. "You believe Borosar was her lover, then?"

"Yes. Don't you?"

Angmar made a vague, bewildered gesture. "I never could make up my mind. Sometimes I think she's capable of almost any folly. Other times . . . other times it's hard not to admire her."

"You should have been with us in Tamri. She did nothing but make enemies, and offend everyone. And then, when even she could see that she would need to mend the damage a little, do you know what she did? She told Favian she would take only half tribute from him for the next five years; the rest of Kamilan would make up the difference! Who do you think is going to pay the most for her wonderful generosity? It will be the lordship of Maene!"

"The north has always borne the brunt of the wars with Dravia, Landis. I told Adelmar more than once to take account of that. He never did."

"She was taking account of the fact that she made too many people angry, and she tried to buy back their good will. And now the rest of us can pay for it."

"That's called politics. Don't look so shocked, Landis; I'm not saying I entirely approve. For one thing, the decision should have been made in Council. She acts impulsively, and I would be the last to suggest that she always knows what she's doing. Nonetheless. . . . " He paused thoughtfully. "What I'm saying, my friend, is that things haven't worked out all that badly. We survived. She has learned, I think, from some of her mistakes. Borosar is dead, and is best left so. We have a prince, and whatever else, she loves him dearly. She re-opened the tunnel, you know, to try and save him if the city was taken—"

"What tunnel are you talking about?"

"The one Medwina made years ago, when the Dravians were almost at our gates. Mohr knows what good it would have done, in the end. When a city falls, one house is as defense-less as the next. The queen never told anyone, of course; I discovered it by chance. The guard outside the door told me it was a storage room for valuables, and I think he believes that himself. But I was there when the masons walled it shut."

"Do you know where it leads?" Landis asked softly.

"To a priestess's house; I forget her name. She's one of Medwina's kin." He looked earnestly at his cousin. "The queen isn't always unwise, Landis."

The prince consort said nothing, aware that Angmar was watching him curiously. He had known, of course—known for certain since Tamri—yet it was astonishing how much impact Angmar's words carried, how much more certain his certain knowledge could suddenly become. How much more bitterly the wound could hurt.

All winter, he thought. In that house. *The wolf comes to the city quite often, and spends his nights there. . . .* How often was quite often? And did he spend his nights as Landis had spent his at the Field of Fire?

He looked at Angmar. *You old fool, you pass a little time with her and already you have cobwebs in your eyes. Well, gods know I might have them too, if I had stayed.*

"Angmar," he began quietly, "the tunnel wasn't opened for the benefit of the prince."

And then he laid it out, quietly and clearly, as Crayfe had laid it out for him. The old man listened until he was done, saying nothing while he spoke, or for some time after. Then he said only one word, softly, half curse and still half question.

"Shadrak. . .?"

"Yes," Landis said. "Shadrak."

"I wondered why you were so . . . so taut. So bitter." He fell silent again for a time. He looked utterly defeated. "Her father used to say to me: the one thing he was hopeful for was that she might be chaste. It was the pretty ones who always fell."

"Her father," Landis said dryly, "was not the wisest man in the world. I'll wager she was a whore before she was grown— before the Dravians made her a better one."

"Is that why you left her?"

"Yes."

"I blamed you for that."

Landis shrugged.

"What do you mean to do?" the sage asked finally, uneasily.

"At the moment, nothing. She'll soon be done playing king. Whoever she chooses for warlord, he's not likely to cater to her the way Borosar did. The Dravian threat is broken for years. Without that, and with no allies in Council, she will have less and less room to manoeuvre, and she will have to act accordingly. It's all a question of power. One day she will be grateful to live quietly in her palace, looking after her children.

"As for the wolf, I've no doubt she means to reward him with land and trinkets, and keep him close at hand. He will find himself one quiet night with an arrow in his back, and that should not surprise him; he has despatched enough other men the same way."

Angmar stared at the fire.

"You underestimate her," he said softly.

"No, I don't! She did nothing but huddle in her fortress until the Dravs were gone; she isn't going to do anything different now. You believe too many old stories, Angmar—you and all the other fools who think she's a witch and a goddess and I don't know what else! I can't tell you how sick of it I was by the time we got here, watching them wave their bonnets and howl as though she'd won the war herself—she and her damned bloody wolf! If you say one word about sorcery, I swear I'll lose my patience! The only sorcery that woman knows is the sort that is taught in a brothel."

"And how did the fog come then, do you think?"

"I don't know how it came, and I don't care. I don't know why it rained yesterday, either, and until I have a reason to think the queen waved her arms around and pulled the water out of the sky, I'm going to act like a man with a mind!"

The dark chill in Angmar's eyes did not soften. "That's good, Landis, because it wasn't sorcery I was speaking of when I said you underestimate her. It was politics."

Landis stared at him a moment, and then laughed.

"You're not making any sense at all." He stood up. "I must go, cousin. I will see you tomorrow. No, sit; I can find my own way out." He paused at the door, and looked back. "She's a whore, Angmar. Nothing else. Just a whore."

The city was too small to feast an army. Every man who fought, the queen said, would be honoured; what better place than at the Field of Fire? There were mountains of food, and great wagonloads of wine and ale; there was music and joyful chaos everywhere. Yet when the queen stood finally on her dais to speak, the valley fell so still that those who were at the edges of the field could hear the birds twitter.

She could speak well to crowds, Landis thought; there was no denying that. She had a way of seeming to address each person as though no one else was there. She knew how to flatter.

And she did have a presence, a kind of grace which riveted men's attention, even his. It was still full day; the sun glinted on her gold bracelets, on the gold circlet around her head. It was one he had not seen before, but he paid no particular attention until she spoke of it.

She honoured the fallen, and thanked the victors. Then she reached, taking the little coronet from her head.

"This was made for me in Belengar, by some men in the border guard, common soldiers like most of you, who wanted to welcome me home from Dravia. They had no gold, they had nothing very much. They made this out of yew and leaves, so I could sit at their welcome feast wearing a crown. When I returned to the royal city, I took it to a smith, who made it fast, and sealed it with gold so it would last forever.

"This is what you fought for. The woods and leaves and fields and living things of Kamilan. Not for power. Not even for glory, though there is a glory in what you did that will last as long as these mountains.

"We're going to keep what we've won. I will raise no army to go adventuring into other people's lands, but I will maintain the army I have—and it's army to make any king tremble before he crosses our borders to make war!

"And I will give it into the hands of a captain who knows how to fight!"

The field had been quiet while she was speaking. Now it went utterly, breathlessly still. The lords looked at each other in blank astonishment. Council had not even met. She could not possibly be thinking of naming the man *here. . . ?*

Landis felt cold all through, his body knotting with a fear his mind had not yet even fashioned into words. *Not that,* he thought numbly. *She won't, she can't, it isn't possible. . . !* But of course it was possible. She was capable of anything, and he more than anyone should have known that.

"Soldiers of Kamilan," she went on in a ringing voice, "children of Jana, people of the land of Alyth, when our great warrior Borosar was dying in the field, he gave command of his armies to Shadrak, warleader of Dohann. Borosar was a great general, a great hero, a man of courage and judgment and absolute loyalty. I can't better his choice. He gave the command to Shadrak, and Shadrak led you to victory. He will go on leading you."

351

She turned her head and gestured faintly. Shadrak rose, moving like a panther to her side. She flung her gold-bangled arm high.

"The warlord of Kamilan!"

There was a breath of absolute silence; then the valley exploded in deafening cheers.

Oswin looked at Landis. Never, not even in battle, had the warleader of Tamri looked so ready to kill, and the look seemed to include everyone, even the prince consort.

"Your Council had better meet," he gritted. "And I mean now, Landis, with her or without her, but by the gods you'd better meet!"

They met with her. It was a small Council, lacking both the warlord and the high priest, who was too ill to leave his bed. The queen was surprisingly calm. She did not seem to think that anything was wrong.

"Lady." Angmar knotted his hands. "Lady, I hardly know where to begin. How could you do such a thing without consulting us?"

"But I did consult you. I asked every one of you for your opinions. You all put forward your own candidates, and I considered them very carefully. They're all good men. But Borosar himself gave Shadrak command in the field, and you all accepted it."

"Borosar was wounded and dying," Favian said bitterly. "He scarcely knew what he was doing. We chose to honour his deathbed wish; that certainly doesn't mean that we should—"

"May Jana send us more such men who scarcely know what they're doing," she said grimly. "We seem to prosper from it."

"Lady," Angmar said, "you can't make a slaveborn border guard warlord of Kamilan. You simply can't."

"He was a slaveborn border guard in the Gap of Clythe. It didn't matter so much then, did it?"

The claws were out again, Landis noted. It never took long.

She went on: "With the Dravians howling at your throats his origins were quickly forgotten. What was a clan then, or the lack of one? What was a strange-sounding foreign name? What was a slave brand, even, if he could find a way out of there? If he could wipe out Edgard's army before it even got to you? If he could turn the rocks and the trees and the hills themselves into weapons, and break an army sixteen thousand strong to fragments on the plains of Tamri?

"You followed him willingly enough, and I don't believe it was just because of Borosar. Perhaps at the very first, but not after Edgard was destroyed. After that you saw what he could do, and you were glad enough that he could do it. Now the Dravians are beaten, and there are honours to be had, and you would send the finest warleader in the kingdom back to Belengar to mind the pass like a good lad, while you and all of us prosper from the victory.

"Well, it's not going to be. I have listened to your recommendations, and I have made my choice. In five days time Shadrak will be named captain-general and warlord of Kamilan, with all the honours and powers that office confers, *including his place in this Council.*"

The silence was chilling. The lords looked at each other, and looked at her. None of them had expected this. It was too far beyond reason, too utterly outrageous for any of them to have expected it, to have prepared an argument. How did men argue against the unthinkable?

Landis looked briefly at Crayfe. The seneschal had not said a word. His face was pasty with dismay, but there was a vaguely knowing look in his eyes. He had not expected it, either; but of them all he was the only one who was not overwhelmed with surprise.

You underestimate her, Angmar had said. And it was true, Landis reflected; he had. But Crayfe had not. Unlike the lord of Maene, Crayfe did not consider any folly or corruption too improbable to contemplate.

I will learn from you, seneschal; give me a little time. I promise you I'll learn!

"Shadrak is the finest warleader in the kingdom?" Favian cried, outraged. "By the gods, lady, now I've heard everything!"

"No, you haven't," Crayfe said. "We have yet to be told how he was fathered by Harash himself, and born of a virgin, and miraculously suckled by a she-wolf."

That brought a faint smile even to Angmar's face—but not to Favian's; he was already too angry.

"Other men fought in this war!" he went on bitterly. "We fought hard and bravely, and we've been slighted as though we weren't even there! Since the day we left Tamri we've heard nothing but how clever this wolf is, how he saved everyone at the Gap of Clythe, how he's such a marvellous archer, and how he can do this and how he can do that! Well, if he hadn't found a way out of Clythe, I'm sure someone else would have done so. As for his fancy archers, lady, they served well enough against Edgard's little army, but in the battle of Tamri, where everything was decided, they ran out of arrows long before the fight was won. And it was better men than Shadrak of Belengar who wielded their swords then, for all the rest of the day, and rallied our fighters, and won the ground! My kinsman Oswin was one of them, and the prince consort himself was another—!"

"And how many Dravians were dead by then?" the queen demanded.

"Believe me, lady, enough were still alive," Landis said. "You can't credit Shadrak's archers with the victory."

"Nor his leadership? Nor his strategy of running the Dravians ragged around the whole of Dohann, until he could lure them into the open?"

"That strategy was Borosar's," Landis replied. "Shadrak merely continued what the warlord began. And as for his leadership, lady, the truth is he held it by a thread—thanks only to the Dravians, and thanks to me. I can't count the times I had to keep the peace in our camps, and come between him and Favian, or Oswin, or some other man, before they could run each other through!"

"Why did you do so," she asked, "if he were so unworthy as a leader?"

"A battle camp, when men's lives and their very country is at stake, is not a place for duels."

To that she had no answer; she looked at her hands.

"I think you have misjudged the matter, lady," Angmar said quietly. "I'm sure you will reconsider."

She looked up, her expression bitter.

"What I have misjudged, lords of Kamilan, is your capacity to perceive reality in any form that suits you. Men like Shadrak can't do what this man did, and therefore he never did it.

"Well, I'm sorry. You may see it so, but it changes nothing. He's a brilliant captain all the same, and he will be warlord."

Just like that. I decide. Facts don't matter, fairness doesn't matter. I will simply do what pleases me. . . .

"We're all united in opposing this," Landis said grimly. "You can't go against the entire Council. You can't do something which will outrage every honest man in the kingdom."

"I won't outrage nearly as many people as you think. Go out into the streets, lords, and listen. You spend too little time there. You may be united against me; the whole of Kamilan is united behind me."

"Lady," Angmar said. He paused. He seemed to be finding it harder and harder to remain discreet, to speak about this as though it were a serious political decision, and not the self-indulgence of an infatuated girl. "Lady, this is reckless beyond all our power to imagine. You must reconsider. You're right in saying the warleader should not be slighted. There are many honours you can give him short of this one. Think again, lady, I beg you, before you utterly destroy the unity of our kingdom, and the integrity of our traditions."

"There is more to unity in the kingdom than smiles in the Council room. As for our traditions, it was the way of the Kamils since the earliest times to choose their best captain as warleader, no matter who he was. It was the new kings who changed that, the ones who were always at war, who had to name their brothers and their cousins and their sons to every post of importance, because they lived in terror of mutiny.

"Tradition is on my side, Angmar. And the matter is decided. Shadrak will be warlord, and that's the end of it."

Favian was on his feet.

"I can speak for no one else," he said savagely, "but for myself, be he warlord or not, I refuse to sit in this Council with a slave!"

"Then you may resign, and be replaced," the queen replied. "That's the right of any Councillor." She rose. "I wish you good day, lords. I am going to the temple to order the preparations."

She turned, paused, looked back. "I can prevent no one from falling ill, so as to avoid his duty to his commander and to me. But if you remain in Council, and if you're not in your appointed place that day, any of you, I will remember."

For two days she refused to meet with any of them, either privately or in Council. By then the word was all over Kamilan, and her people were already building a dais outside the temple of Jana and gathering flowers to festoon the streets.

The second night Landis was finally admitted. He was led by two fiercely armed women through a hall filled with staring servants, and taken to the shield room. The queen stood by the fire. She greeted him graciously, but she did not smile. The minstrel Kiri stood nearby.

"I would like to speak with you alone, lady," he said.

She motioned to the shield women to leave. When he saw that Kiri was not following them, he repeated the request.

"You're armed and you're angry, Landis," she said. "I prefer that Kiri stays."

He stared at her. "Do you think I would attack you, lady?" he said, disbelieving.

"Truthfully, no. But you have twice done things I never believed you would do. I don't know you very well, Landis, and that's how you wanted it." She motioned him towards a chair, but she did not sit, and neither would he. "I will order some wine, if you wish," she offered.

"Thank you, no. After you hear what I have to say, lady, you may wish that you'd heard it in private."

"And what is it you've come to say?"

"Quite frankly this: that neither I nor the lords of Council will stand aside, and allow you to name Shadrak as warlord of Kamilan. You must choose another. And please don't tell us again that he's the finest warleader in the kingdom. We've heard all that before. You're not a warrior, lady, and the warriors of the kingdom do not agree with you. You must appoint someone else."

"I will not, Landis, however much you disapprove. I think he's a splendid choice."

"A splendid choice?" He laughed, but the laugh ended in a snarl of outrage. "A Thyrsian savage without name or lineage or honour—"

"He is Kamil," she cut in flatly.

He ignored that. "A mongrel? A whore's bastard with a slave's brand on his back? Gods of the world, woman, you've never had a sense of shame, but I can scarcely believe you'd give such power to such a man simply because he's your lover!"

"Why do you say he's my lover?" she flung back. "Because a woman can't think beyond her bedroom door? She can't

356

reward a man simply because he has deserved it? She can't name her best captain to command her army simply because he's the best? Great Mohr, no! That would require more good sense than any woman possesses! Of course, the man has to be her lover!"

"Do you think that's a clever answer, Marwen? No doubt you do. It's astonishing what you seem to think is clever. Your little tunnel to the house of Dania the priestess—that was clever, too. Did you really think you'd get away with it? Your Thyrsian dog could not so much as pad through the city gates without Crayfe knowing. Did that never occur to you? And how long did you think it would be until Angmar discovered that the masonry had been cleared away, and the tunnel re-opened? He admired you for that, the poor old fool. He thought you did it to protect the prince. He knows better now.

"I say again Shadrak is your lover. Were he not, even you would blush to set him above the noblest blood in Kamilan. And even you would see the danger in it."

"There's no danger in it," she said haughtily.

Children stood thus, he thought, feet planted, reaching their hands into pretty-coloured flames.

"You think not? Oh, he's slavishly loyal to you, no doubt! Loyalty, after all, is what slaves are taught—along with cunning, and duplicity, and shamelessness. Why shouldn't he be loyal while you whore with him, and whore with his liege to buy him favours, until he has them all, weapons and lordship and the army, too? In Mohr's name, lady, if you give him Borosar's command you place him in reach of your crown!"

"And if I named Ranir, who is nothing but your servant and your sword arm, where would that place you? Do you fear that I'll lose my power, Landis, or that I'll keep it?"

"You wrong me, lady," he said bitterly.

"Do I? You married me intending to be king. Do you think I didn't know that? You've never seen me as your sovereign. Oh, you say the words, you call me lady, but in your heart you've never called me anything but a girl. You believe that as your wife I should just naturally make the choices which would ease you into kingship. And when I act differently, and shield my own power instead, you call me stupid, and tell me that I'm thinking with my cunt! Well, I have never done so, Landis, and never less than now! You're so insufferably arrogant—

when will it occur to you that you've been outmatched? I never meant you to be king, and you never will be! Kamilan can do better for a sovereign, and I can do better for a man!"

"Then why don't you go and set up court in a brothel?" he cried savagely. "There might be a few men left you haven't tried!"

Something changed in her eyes then, sharply; the ice snapped into fire.

"So. That's always a man's last word in an argument, isn't it? To call a woman a whore!"

"Not my last word, lady. Rather my first. You're no queen, Marwen; no queen worthy of her name would soil her house and her lineage by rutting with a slave. That's a whore's deed, and no one else's!"

"And where all have you rutted in your life, my unsullied prince? We married by the Laws of Kind. You never failed to take advantage of that, but still you think I'm your possession.

"You have no further claim on me, Landis. You have everything I promised you, and what you have is all you're going to get. If Shadrak is my lover, it's no concern of yours, and no concern of Council. And you can tell them that. I don't command my people in their bed chambers, and by the goddess I will not be commanded in mine!"

He stood rigid, his voice raw with outrage.

"And what about your children?"

"What about yours?" she flung back. "Every daughter I bear will be a princess, and every son a prince. I don't care who fathers them; they will be mine, and they will have a place. Can you say the same? What will the lordship of Maene offer to the children of your goat girls and your tavern wenches and your Dravian concubine? Will they all have a piece of land, or a trade, and money for a bride gift or a dowry—?"

"Don't be stupid, Marwen; a man can't begin to—"

"Then leave children to their mothers, as the goddess intended, and lodge your honour somewhere else than in your seed!"

"You would breed bastards to that slaveborn cur, and raise them in the house of Adelmar?"

"If I choose to," she said. Her eyes were murderous. "What do you care about children, prince? You or any of your peers? You march your sons away to die in one stupid war after another. You shove your daughters into the bed of any brute around who'll trade you a piece of land, or send you another legion when you're up to your necks in enemies! And then you tell your wives they have to live in cages for the welfare of their children. . . !

"Well, not in Kamilan. I'm not your mare, Landis of Maene! I'm a free woman, and a daughter of the hill queens. I will bed where I please, and have whatever children I choose. And if you can't endure that, then undo our marriage. That is your right. Pack up your pride and go. But leave your title behind, prince, and your honours, and every other thing you've received from my hand. Either that, or acknowledge that you have them from a queen!"

His mind was spinning, barely registering the challenge, the raw defiance. In all of her contemptuous and contemptible outburst one sentence stood alone, distinct and numbing:

Every son I bear will be a prince. . .!

That slave's get in the ancient house of Kamilan, as royal as his own son, and greedy as vipers for his place. . .?

You bitch! You worthless, irresponsible, despicable bitch!

He threw out his arms in a curse, the motion a barely stifled blow. It took all his will not to strike her hard mouth, not to smash her across the room. His pride alone restrained him. He would not strike her, and have her call her guard, and be dragged from the room like a criminal. The lord of Maene would not be reduced to that.

"Listen to me, Marwen, and listen well. The lords of Kamilan won't tolerate this travesty, and neither will I. We won't have that bloodspattered wolfspawn made our master, just because you fancy him in bed. Nor will we stand by and see your father's house disgraced with every litter of rabble you choose to breed there. By the gods, woman, you're courting mutiny!"

"And you are courting ruin," she cried. "Go! You've said enough!"

"Truth has a sharp tongue, lady. Do you hope to silence it by throwing me out? You will be the sport of every brothel and barracks hall from Vianon to Sardas. They will call you queen indeed—the queen of fools and harlots!"

She swept past him and wrenched open the door.

"Get out!"

Her face was twisted, almost ugly in its anger. She was like an animal, he thought, or like some backwoods slut who hitched up her skirts one minute and screamed curses the next, a creature without morals or sense, only appetites and blind emotions.

Gods of the world, we will not be ruled by this, we will not. . . !

"Well, Kiri, I've done it now, I suppose, haven't I?"

Kiri shoved wood into the fire and did not answer. That Marwen had pushed the power struggle with the lords of Council to the very brink, as she tended to push most things, was true.

Yet it was also true that this moment was, unavoidably, a watershed. At the high tide of victory after Tamri she had only two choices: to consolidate her power by giving Shadrak the warlordship, whatever the risk, or to see her power quietly unravel. To confront, or to back away from confrontation and accept a slow surrender in return for life and a few pleasures and a bit of hope—a surrender she could have made in Dravia, and would not.

If the lords mutinied, they would say she had provoked it, and in a certain sense they would be right. She had defied them as a sovereign and as a woman, and it was the woman more than sovereign whom they would not forgive. Kings and lords quarrelled often over power, sometimes to the death, but she was challenging their power in a way no king would ever do. She was denying them what their fathergod himself had given them—mastery of both the political and the personal world.

The kings of Telhiron's blood were different from the queens of Alyth's—not because they were men, but because they had chosen to follow Mohr. Embittered with life because it had to end one day, Mohr dreamed of immortality, and for its sake he gave men privileges which Jana had never given anyone, neither her daughters nor her sons. He took from men their right to their own lives—their lives as flesh and blood, as creatures of the earth—and gave them instead rights to the lives of others, as many other lives as they could master. Lords were not leaders of their people now, they were owners. And the more they owned, the more armies and slaves and concubines and sons, the more immortal they would be.

At the foundation of all this mastery, all this ownership of lives, was their mastery over women. It served for much more than to assure a man of his lineage, important as that was to them. It also caged pleasure, and that perhaps was more important. It caged the flesh of other men, making them both harsh and obedient, useful servants of dynasty and power. It forged a pattern: if even love was rooted in command and submission, then all things were rooted so, and ought to be. It kept everyone powerless in relation to someone, and the powerless could easily be baited or bribed or seduced—even against their own interests—in the hope of small rewards. And for men, the most precious reward of all was the bartered flesh of women.

Marwen was cutting to the core of their power, and in doing so she was changing the concept of sovereignty itself, and the meaning of war, and the very soul and substance of love.

Would the lords of Kamilan endure it?

Kiri sighed, and hugged her knees, watching the queen. Anger had spent Marwen's strength; she was sad now, and afraid.

"I've made a lot of mistakes, Kiri, haven't I? I shouldn't quarrel with them so much. . . ." She paused, picking at her sleeve. "I never thought they'd find out about the tunnel; that was stupid. But what else could I have done? I couldn't meet with him in the palace; that would have been far more dangerous.

"Why shouldn't I have a lover if I choose? They can take their concubines openly into their feast halls, and embrace them in front of their friends. They can take women by force; they can draw straws and pass out captured girls like sacks of meal!"

"That's all different," Kiri said dryly. " 'Since it's the woman who receives seed, nature itself has ordained that she must be chaste, or she will defile both herself and her house. A man, since he merely gives in sexual congress, and does not receive, cannot be defiled.' "

Marwen stared at her.

"Pardalus of Rosh," Kiri explained. "The great philosopher of Larandau, from the Scroll of Life. He didn't invent the idea, of course. He merely phrased it so marvellously well."

"I see," Marwen said grimly. She dropped her face into her hands. "Medwina was right, Kiri. It's Mohr's world."

"Not all of it, lady. Not yet."

Not yet, she repeated silently, bitterly. *Not quite yet. And may Jana throw him back into the sea!*

33. Conspiracy

There should have been omens. For all his years and wisdom, Angmar could not help but think so. There should have been thunder and lightning, or one of those foul and numbing rains which chilled the world down to its bones. But it was a clear and quiet night when the men came, and the air was soft with flowers. Except for their secrecy it might have seemed like a gathering of old friends.

I am too old for this. . . .

They were five: Oswin and Favian of Tamri, Crayfe the seneschal, Ranir the warleader of Maene, and the prince consort. Five unexpected guests, dressed so that darkness itself could not see them, gathering in his garden in the dead of night. Conspiracy, he reflected, had a smell about it like a brothel; as soon as a man was close to one, he knew.

But there should have been omens. The sky should not have been so innocent, or the rising crescent moon so utterly brilliant and clear.

He could not see Oswin's face clearly. The man's solid warrior body was restless with menace, and his voice was clipped with hate.

"Shadrak must die. We will not accept this folly, Angmar. He must die."

Yes, of course. That had to be the reason for their coming. But not the reason they insisted on speaking here, in the garden, without lights, without wine, without so much as a chair for his old bones.

Shadrak must die. Would to all the gods he had died twenty years ago, with his slave's tunic on his shoulders and his wolf's fangs still uncut. It is too late now.

"We're all united in this, Angmar," Landis said. "Will you stand with us?"

"You can't kill him," Angmar said simply. "He is warlord of Kamilan."

"No," Oswin said grimly. "By the gods, he is not!"

"And you're going to kill him, I suppose, with your own hands?" Angmar said scornfully. "His men would build a wall of corpses around him twenty feet deep before you'd get to him. And even then he might be a match for you." He paused, and concluded simply: "Whether I'm with you or not, it doesn't matter. He is out of reach."

"An arrow travels far and fast, cousin," Landis said grimly. "As the wolf himself has taught us."

Such silence. Such a clean, star-brittle silence.

"The queen has ordered a triumphal procession to the temple of Jana," Landis went on. "They will ride through the whole city, so he can flaunt his power to the mob, sitting at her elbow as though he were already the king he means to be. A well-placed arrow will end his ambitions, Angmar."

A moving target on a bouncing chariot, sitting at the elbow of the queen. . . .

"And if your marksman should miss?"

"He won't."

Angmar was silent for a time. Then he said calmly: "Let's go into the house."

A ripple of alarm went through the group.

"Angmar, don't be foolish—!"

"I'm going into the house," he said. "I'm cold. You may follow me, or you may remain here. It's entirely up to you."

They followed him. He sent the one groggy servant who had wakened back to bed, poured the wine himself, and sat down. Now at least he could send all his energy to his mind, instead of to his legs. Now at least he could see their faces—faces which he knew and had never known. Faces he would never know at all.

I misjudged you, Landis. All these years I saw a man who wasn't there; you are someone else entirely. What did I miss?

"You risk the queen's life," he said simply.

Landis regarded him with bitterness.

"Is that the only risk you see?" he demanded. "What of the risk to my son's future, to his life? The queen is Shadrak's whore. When he is lord of Kamilan, and she has borne *him* a son, how long do you think the prince will live?"

"You can't believe that," Angmar whispered. But even as he spoke, his own certainty faltered. Was there a king in all the world who would not kill the sons of a rival, and so ensure that his own sons followed him to power?

He dropped his face into his hands.

"We have no wish to harm the queen," Oswin said. "But the good of Kamilan must come before everything, even her."

Angmar looked up. "Suppose you succeed, and kill the wolf. Have you thought about the consequences? Marwen will stop at nothing to find you out. She will avenge her captain, you may be sure of that. And while she's not a wise woman, neither is she a fool. She will know where all of this began, and she'll have blood for it."

The unease in the room was physical. The men tried not to look at one another, and did so nonetheless.

So, Angmar thought, there was more to this than Shadrak. Of course there was. The slave warrior could simply be marked for death. They did not need to come to Angmar to decide that.

The queen was another matter.

I am too old for this.

"Angmar." Landis spoke quietly, almost gently. "Angmar, you yourself have said many times that she is reckless, that she understands nothing. That she's a child. That alone would be reason enough to ask why she should rule us. And that's the least of it. She's a plotter and a whore. Borosar would never have named this wolfspawn to captain our forces—he would never have brought us to this pass—if she hadn't seduced him into it. Her one claim to wear Adelmar's crown was that she should mother us a king, and now she has imperilled even that, simply for the sake of her lust. She is unfit to rule."

"She is the queen."

"No. She is the queen mother. My son is king of Kamilan. And the gods know that, as they know that slaves are slaves and dogs are dogs. Shadrak will be struck down at the steps of Jana's temple, and the world will see that he was nothing but a usurper, and his goddess nothing but a fraud.

"It's all planned, Angmar. We will leap to the aid of the queen, as indeed we would be expected to do. In the uproar and confusion we will rush her to safety, and she will quietly be shut away where she can do no more harm.

"I don't hate her, Angmar. Don't misjudge me. It's not her fault that she's a woman. It's the fault of those who allowed her to think she was something more. We're all responsible for that, cousin, and you not the least of us."

"Aye," Angmar said, the word more a sigh than a word. "And if it happens as you intend, who will rule then?"

"I will act as regent until my son is grown."

Angmar looked at his hands, at his feet, at the fire, and everywhere he looked he saw blood. He looked at the five men, holding their gaze one by one, finishing with Landis.

"When you first came," he said, "I was sure this mutiny was bred in Tamri. But it wasn't. You have instigated it, Landis, haven't you?"

"We're all united," Oswin said grimly. "And no one has persuaded anyone against his will."

"Perhaps not. But one of you spoke first. One of you said: We must do this, and this is how it should be done. Is that not so, cousin?"

"Yes," Landis said simply. "And I don't flinch from saying it. I will not stand aside and see my son murdered by a harlot and a slave."

"Then take him, and go into exile. This is not the time to strike. The people love the queen, Landis, and they honour Shadrak, and the army is loyal to a man. You may well find some even in your own warbands who would stand with him. Dear gods, my friends, have you seen nothing in these last weeks? I wasn't in Tamri, nor did I march back with you, but I've heard stories enough. I saw how they were greeted here.

"There will be mutiny."

He paused, and spoke again, his voice taking on the intensity he was renowned for in his youth, in the days when men had marvelled at his eloquence.

"There will be outrage such as this land has never seen. You don't know what you do, my friends. You will be hated beyond words, and even if they can't raise up anyone to replace you, they will bring you down. Shadrak has a thousand men under his personal command. Whatever credit we give them or don't give them for our victory, they wiped out Edgard's army, and he had greater numbers than your warbands combined. Do you think they will stand aside, when they have seen their captain killed, and not avenge him—not turn on you like wolves? Do you think the people will accept the loss of their queen, now above all, when they are drunk with victory, and see her almost as their goddess? You will tear Kamilan to pieces."

"I've thought about that," Landis said. "It will be spread about, in various places and in various ways, that Shadrak was plotting against the queen, that he meant to usurp her and make himself king. That will be easy enough for most men to believe. She discovered his intentions, and ordered his assassination—and then his followers killed her. Each side will come to blame the other. As for the ordinary folk, there will be so many stories that no one can be sure anything, and the simple fact of my son's legitimacy will be the only solid thing they can hold onto."

"I see," Angmar said. "You have indeed thought about it."

All these years, Landis, I taught you to put the kingdom first— not rank, not glory or advantage, not pleasure or desire, not even love, nothing before the king. What happened to you, and why didn't I see it happening?

"Landis, don't do this. You have planned very carefully, perhaps, but you haven't judged well. You underestimate the temper of the country. Bide your time. I don't admire her; it's not possible any more. But she *is* the queen, and because of the victory over Dravia she is honoured by everyone. You will pull your own house down around your head. Give it time, Landis; she will falter. She will make enemies. She may well make an enemy of the wolf himself. Wait, I beg you. If you fear for the child—and probably you should—take him and go abroad. Raise him to be a king, and wait."

"My task is to assure my son's future, not to be his nurse-maid," Landis said coldly.

"Aye," Oswin added. "And what of the rest of us? We are warriors, Angmar. Shall we live out our days like old women, knitting by the fire, while the whole world laughs at us? By the time those two are done with Kamilan, there will be nothing left for the young king to claim!"

"Your minds are made up," Angmar said. "You have it all planned. You don't need me. Why did you come to me at all?"

"We do need you," Landis said. "You're respected. You're Angmar the Wise. And there *are* people to whom we must answer, people who know that what the mob believes is not the truth. If you're with us, they will be satisfied. If you're not, they will be uneasy. They will say: Why didn't you go to Angmar the Wise? If your purpose was right and just, why couldn't you trust him with it?

"Our purpose is right and just, Angmar. You know that. And because it is, we need you with us."

Angmar let his eyes pass across the group. Both Crayfe and Favian looked away. They did not believe they needed him. They would not have come here tonight. That decision was clearly the prince consort's. A bold decision. A risk. But not a great risk. Landis understood the bonds of rank and family and blood, and he knew that Angmar understood them. At worst the sage would walk away and say: *I heard nothing. I want nothing to do with this. Leave me alone.*

Crayfe rose suddenly from his chair. "I told you it was useless to come here."

"Be quiet, Crayfe," Landis snapped.

"I will not be quiet. When has this man ever made anything resembling a decision? He babbles and blathers, and turns a thing this way and that, and then he puts it back and does nothing. He should have silenced Medwina years ago, but he didn't. He should have insisted the queen marry while Adelmar lived, but he didn't. I'll wager he lies in bed with a woman all night long without mounting her, trying to decide where he should begin!"

"That's enough! You have no wits, seneschal; you never have had."

"Indeed? Who warned you about Shadrak? Two years ago at the Feast of Harash I told you the wolf was dangerous, and you laughed at me. When he wiped out Berend's advance attack in Dohann I warned you again. I told you we should send him back to Belengar while we still could, but you said no, he might be useful. You said whatever danger he might pose to us, we could handle it. Well, curse you, handle it now!"

"And so we will," Landis replied calmly. He turned back to the sage. "Don't listen to Crayfe. Even when he's happy he has a sharp tongue; when he's worried it grows sharper. He doesn't mean to disparage you."

"Yes," Angmar said simply. "He does. And he's right. I have never made a decision when it mattered. Nonetheless, in spite of you, Crayfe, I will think before I answer this. Come back tomorrow night. I will give you my decision then."

"May I say one thing more?"

"Yes. One thing, Landis, and then go."

"We need you, Angmar. Without you we'll still succeed, although it will be harder. But we need you to lessen the bloodshed. Every word you say about the right of it will save a thousand lives."

"You're wrong, Landis. With me, it will be hard. Without me, it will be impossible. I think you all know that, or you wouldn't be here." He bowed faintly. "Forgive me if I don't see you out. I am . . . weary."

"Of course, cousin. Good night."

Good night, good night, good night. Great Mohr, my very walls stink of treachery. Is it come to this, Adelmar? I should have died beside you.

They were gone, as dark and silent as they had come. And still there were no omens. Through his window the stars glittered like maidens at a festival, and the cool moon passed among them like a goddess, and moved on.

Kamilan was dying.

It did not matter if they succeeded or if they failed, chaos would be unleashed; and chaos, once unleashed, would answer to none of them again. The land would be torn apart: trusts betrayed, friendships undone, kinsman turned against kinsman. And the eyes of the world would turn, and watch, and be ready: the greedy eyes of Larandau lusting for empire, the bitter eyes of King Berend lusting for revenge.

Angmar's fire burned out. The wine turned stale and sour in his cup. The moon passed beyond the mountains and fell into the sea.

If they failed, the conspirators would all go down, and all the great houses of Kamilan would go down with them.

And the prince? Great Mohr, what of the prince?

There was no solution. There was no escape. They had fallen from dishonour to dishonour, and now they were drowning in it, and there was no escape. Despair washed over him, and with it a consuming bitterness. Gods, he thought, if men needed proof that there should be no queens, they had it now.

He had thought well of her. A hundred times he had acknowledged her courage and her skill and her willingness to work. Yet in the end, in the things which mattered most, she had proven no wiser than a wilful child, and no more moral than a woods cat.

And for that, Kamilan would be undone.

Landis returned by night alone, very late. They faced each other across a small space of shifting light. Angmar saw the uncertainty in his cousin's eyes, the need for support and reassurance, and he felt an odd, unexpected flash of pride.

So. They still think I count.

"Well, Angmar, have you considered? Are you with us?"

"Is there nothing I can say to make you change your mind? It's still not too late."

"There's nothing you can say. Don't waste your breath. I would kill Shadrak myself, without anyone to back me, if it came to that. What is your decision, Angmar?"

"Well, then."

Odd, he thought, how hard the words were to say. He had been the man he was for so long. How did he now become a different man?

"If it must be, then I am with you, Landis."

The prince consort smiled, and gripped him hard by the shoulders. "I knew you'd see it our way! Crayfe doubted you, but I never did. I am glad, Angmar."

The sage drew him to a chair. "Listen to me, then. I trust your good sense, but I don't trust Oswin's much, and Favian's even less. I'll wager there are twenty things they haven't thought about. Caithland, for example, and the palace guard. They're going to be there in force, and so are Shadrak's men. How do you mean to deal with them?"

"By surprise, Angmar. Surprise and deception. We will have a hundred of our own men dressed in the uniforms of the palace guard—"

"And you think Caithland won't notice?" Angmar interrupted.

"No. He'll die without ever knowing they were there. They will be in place just outside the temple, with capes to hid their insignia, looking like ordinary soldiers. When I give the signal, the archers will fire from the roof, killing Shadrak and the escort around the chariot. Our men will rush out and surround the queen, and everyone will think they are her guards. She herself will think so, and allow them to rush her away. By the time anyone knows better, she'll be out of reach, and I will be in command of the palace—for I'll go there at once to defend it, as of course I should.

"As for those who must be killed, they must be killed at once, before they can organize a counterattack. We are agreed on that. It will all happen quickly, Angmar. It has to. In an enterprise like this, everything depends on surprise. "

Angmar considered before he replied.

"And what of the queen?" he asked. "Surely you know that while she lives every hotheaded youth in the country will fancy himself her champion. There will be no end of plots to free her and put her back on her throne."

"I'm quite aware of that, Angmar, and I'm glad you are. Oswin is not. The chivalrous old fool really believes we can put her in a garden somewhere with her embroidery, and that will be the end of it."

Landis stood up, and fetched a cup of wine. "Here. You look weary and spent. Don't worry about us. You don't need to do anything until it's over, and then you need only to speak."

"I don't need to do anything?" Angmar said bitterly. "I need to stand beside you on the dais, and see it all happen. That is enough."

"She's not Adelmar, cousin. I think you keep forgetting that. We're not betraying a monarch; we are protecting one. And that is right and just; everyone will see it so."

No, Landis, everyone will not. Whatever the outcome, some will see it as unjust. We are mired in injustice now.

"There's something I want you to know, Landis," he said, "and to remember no matter what comes to pass. What I am doing now, I am doing for the sake of the prince—that he should live and be a king, and restore the honour we have lost in Kamilan. Not for any other cause on earth would I be moved to this."

But there was another cause, a shadow barely glimpsed in the deepest places of his mind, a memory, a bond. Medwina's words, spoken more than thirty years before, spoken in malice or in warning or in love, he never knew which, he never cared. But he never was able to forget.

I do not stand between you and Kamilan. But if it ever comes to pass one day that another does, you will make this choice again. You will choose Kamilan, though you tear your own heart out doing it. . . !

34. The Sorceress Queen

The chariot was full of flowers. Flowers lay scattered across the queen's lap, and clung to her sleeves and her hair; flowers were snagged in Shadrak's mail, and tumbled in mounds around his feet. Still the crowd flung them more, flung them rainbows of flowers. Trampled petals filled the air with fragrance, and everything that lived in Kamilan was filling it with noise.

Before the chariot, and behind it, wound a long and colourful procession. From her high vantage point, Kiri could see most of it. First had come the advance guard, then the statue of the goddess borne high on a bier. Medwina and her chief priestesses followed, dressed all in red and black in honour of the warlord.

Behind the priestesses came soldiers in bands of fifty—how many Kiri could not begin to count: Shadrak's splendid archers with their perilous bows; Favian's cavalry, and then Ranir's; all of Borosar's men who had come with the queen from Tamri, sweeping into arcs around the front of the temple, each to their assigned place, until the altar and the royal dais were ringed with row upon row of armed men.

All of the great lords were gathered now on that dais, watching the procession. They had by no means accepted the queen's decision, but they had grown calmer about it, at least in their public statements. She had warned them all to be present, and present they were, although Crayfe looked as though he might not survive the morning. Twice Kiri had seen him bend as if in pain, and once he left the dais briefly, and came back wiping his mouth.

Choke on it, you filthy little viper, she thought bitterly. Then she turned again to watch the long and clamourous street, on which the queen and the wolf of Dohann made their slow and triumphant passage towards the square.

Landis was calm, but his eyes never stopped searching the streets, the roofs beyond, the gathering men of war. Everything was in place. His men filled the roof of the merchant's house directly across from him, anonymous and seemingly unarmed, dressed like commoners and cheering at everything. The crossbowmen were kneeling out of sight, waiting for his signal. Below, just where the street ended and the square began, the false palace guards waited quietly behind their shields.

There were more soldiers. There were fife-players and dancers, youths and young women both, their half-naked bodies supple and gleaming in the sun. There were lovely, white-clad girls bringing flowers, heaping them around the altar of the goddess. All of it took forever. Sweat ran down Landis's face; sweat soaked his hair and his tunic. Everything was in place. Why did that cursed procession move so slowly?

But he knew why. They were drunk with vainglory, both of them, drunk with the adulation of the crowd, wanting it to last as long as possible.

The sound of drums drew closer, and then a great roar swept across the square, rattling the rooftops and echoing off the temple walls. The queen's chariot. Shadrak. Caithland's men rode before and behind, carrying shields and glinting with armour; more of them marched on foot alongside. More of them than he had expected. Too many of them, great Mohr, far too many. . . !

For one unbearable moment Landis faltered, feeling everything dissolve in an absolute failure of nerve. They had no chance, he thought numbly. No chance at all. The street spun before his eyes, filled with enemies, filled with clamour and lunacy and death. Everywhere he looked he saw Shadrak's soldiers, he saw the queen's soldiers, he saw that great howling mob of fools. And he stood reeling, devastated by the enormity of his folly. Angmar had been right. They could never hope to succeed in this. He would be utterly destroyed, and he had nothing to shield himself with, nothing at all.

Except will.

The world steadied and fell still, fell into place. His men were where they were supposed to be. Everything was ready. Of course the queen's chariot would be ferociously guarded; what did he expect? He himself had threatened her with mutiny.

Sweat ran from his face and his limbs, but he was calm again, seeing that black terror for what it really was: a darkness inside himself. It was not rational. It was an animal thing which his mind could take by the throat and silence and cast away, leaving him a man again—the man he was supposed to be: a leader and a king.

He stood straight, and waited as his enemies drew nearer. The clatter of hooves, the grind of the chariot wheels against the cobbled street were lost in the shouting, in the proud chant of drums. The crowd was a sea of waving banners. People were packed hundreds deep outside the square, they were on the roofs and in the trees, they were climbing onto each others' shoulders. Then even their cries were drowned out by the crash of metal as the soldiers began to bang their shields and chant, their voices powerful as a pounding sea:

"Mar-wen! Shad-rak! Mar-wen! Shad-rak!"

It echoed to the bottom of the world.

Crayfe's face turned gray. He turned and stumbled from his place. Gods, Landis thought, what cowards men were, undone by every little thing. Let the fools chant; what did it matter, what did it mean? A drunken clown could dance a jig in a tavern and get the same applause, aye, and for as good a reason. His hands clenched. He was astonished at his bitterness, at his outrage. It was all so despicable, so unworthy. They were nothing, just usurpers, just a gutterbred savage and a royal whore.

The chariot advanced. Slowly. So unbearably slowly. Flowers clung to everything, even the horses' backs. The cheering hammered in Landis's brain.

It's over, Shadrak. Enjoy the glory. You have another moment or two of it, and then it will be done. You will go back to your slave ancestors without so much as a grave. As for you, Marwen queen of harlots, I think you will be chaste from this day on.

He did not look at Angmar. He no longer cared what Angmar thought or felt He waited, poised, very calm.

"Landis."

The voice was an enemy, an intruder. He shut it out. It spoke again.

"Landis, don't! It's not too late. Let them be. Don't give the signal, Landis, I beg you, let them be. . . !"

Landis did not answer. He reached out, roughly and without looking, shoving Angmar aside as he would have shoved aside a branch in his path. Then, in the same gesture, he swept off his plumed cap and began to wave it.

The archer rose, took steady aim, and fired. The arrow struck true, piercing rib-cage and lung. A great volley of arrows followed; it was impossible to say how many. Men were falling everywhere, tumbling over the parapets across the square, crashing onto the dais beside him, all of it happening between a breath and a breath, all of it happening before he felt his own pain, eternities before he believed that the bolt plunged into his chest was real. He clutched at it, seeing without comprehension that the fletchings on it were not Kamil, but Dravian. Panic was exploding around him, the screams of wounded men, the crash of overturned benches and falling debris.

"Angmar?" His knees were giving way and he reached out blindly, tasting blood. *"Angmar!"*

Angmar held him and eased him down. The old man's face was gray and dissolving, his voice a distant sob.

"Forgive me, Landis."

"You?" Landis whispered. "You did this? You . . . betrayed us?"

"Yes."

"Why? It's not possible. In the name of Mohr, Angmar, *why?*"

"To keep Kamilan for your son. You could never have held power. Never! Look!"

It was hard to see, even as Angmar lifted his head and held him steady. In the square below them the queen's chariot had disappeared; her warriors kneeling and standing and mounted had closed around it in a pyramid of shields. Beyond it, there was fighting everywhere, the fake palace guards going down under horses and phalanxes of men—Borosar's men, the wolf's men; even dying Landis could see their colours swirling like the sky. He saw Kiri among them, on a roof, and he understood why the arrow which brought him down was Dravian. Then he saw Shadrak himself, mounted and sword in hand, his ceremonial cape flung over one shoulder, shouting commands. The pyramid around the queen began to move, a great iron-backed animal inching towards the temple steps, the wolf and his hirelings slashing their way through anything which came in its path. The great banner of Favian's warband tumbled. Their lord was already dead, lying on the dais speared with arrows. Oswin, his face twisted in a howl of rage, lunged his horse through a line of men to get to Shadrak, but never reached him. Twenty more were between them, around him, behind; in a moment both horse and man were gone.

Tears ran quietly down Angmar's lined face.

"They would have cut you to pieces, Landis. And there would have been nothing then, no sovereign, no general, no army, nothing, only blind anarchy—every fool, every madman, every scoundrel in the land scrambling for power. Do you think your son would have survived that, and grown up to be a king?"

He pulled a cloth from his pouch and wiped Landis's face.

"They won't live forever, and I will keep the prince safe. I promise you, I'll keep him safe!"

"You. . ." It was growing hard to hear, harder to speak. "You . . . cared more about . . . that slavespawn and his whore . . . than about your own blood. Angmar, why. . .?"

"Not them, Landis," the sage cried desperately. "Kamilan. The future. The king! The king, in Mohr's name, *the king. . . !*"

"I . . . curse you. . . ." Landis whispered, and died.

For a long time Angmar knelt with his cousin's head on his lap, wrapped in a silence so immense that the sounds of combat all around him scarcely reached him. The dais was empty except for himself and the dead. The battle seemed distant and almost meaningless; it would end the only way it could. Once he looked up, noting again, in a kind of bitter self-confirmation, how well the wolf was handling it; noting the extraordinary capacity he had to plan for everything, even when he had very little time to plan. The moment Landis's signal had been given a horn sounded from a roof nearby—one of those great horns they used in the high mountain valleys, which could be heard for leagues. At that signal the temple doors swung wide and soldiers poured out of it, sweeping around the high priestess and her followers, around the flower maidens and the fife-players, so they could flee back into the temple behind a wall of shields and swords. When the queen and her phalanx of guards reached the temple steps they swarmed out again and took her to safety in the same fashion.

It did not take long until she was inside the doors, and out of reach. Through all of it, over the clash of iron and the cries of men, Angmar could hear the alarm signal sounding frantically from Crayfe's barracks at the city gates—frantically, but briefly, too. It fell silent, and soon afterwards the mountain horn sounded again, once, very clear, from across the city. Angmar could easily guess what that signal meant: Shadrak's men now held the garrison and the gates. Not even escape was possible any more. Below, in the war-ringed square, scattered into pockets, the fighting bands of Maene and Tamri were surrendering or being cut to pieces.

I admire skill, Borosar had said. *And he has it. Skill and audacity, like you see once in a lifetime.*

Borosar, Angmar thought with wrenching bitterness, Borosar should be here to admire him now. . . .

"Landis." He stroked the young man's hair and wiped away the froth of blood that trickled from his mouth. "Landis, I did the only the thing I could. I did the only thing I could."

The night before, when Landis left him, he had gone to the temple of Mohr, and knelt there for hours, cold to shivering although the night was warm. Theron, sick as he was, came to greet him, but Angmar sent him away, repulsed by the hatred in his eyes, by the hissing malice in his ruined voice. Neither malice nor love could have a place in this decision. Wisdom was what Angmar needed, only wisdom. No oracles, no signs, no rituals muddying his brain. Only reason, judgment, sense, those things which he had taught so patiently to Landis and which Landis had, when it mattered most, forgotten.

Nothing he felt for Adelmar or Adelmar's child could matter in this decision. Nor could the painful truth that Shadrak had served them well in the Dravian war—better, perhaps, than any of them were willing to admit.

Likewise, in the final judging it could not matter that the queen had betrayed her rank and her blood, or that her slave-born lover had more than earned his death by whoring with her. They had fallen too deeply into dishonour—all of them—to act now as though they lived in a clean and simple world where a single sword-stroke could erase a single, aberrant wrong.

No. There was only one thing he could judge by, and that was Kamilan and its king. But how to serve them? The night was passing; they were already fixing garlands to the queen's chariot. . . .

The king. Yes, he thought, young Aran was truly king, Landis was right about that. She was only queen mother, only regent. He dropped his head into his hands, paralyzed, wishing he were dead. Nothing, not even the pain of those weeks when he had been dying, had been more terrible than this. There were sounds in the street, although he knew it was still dark. People were already building their fires. Shadrak's servants were laying out his armour, his gold bracelets, the fine ceremonial cape the queen had ordered for him. . . .

When the queen has borne him a son, how long do you think the prince will live?

Angmar the Wise looked up at the stone altar of Mohr and knew what he would do. It was not a sudden illumination. The thought had been with him almost from the start. He had looked at it, put it aside, looked at it again. Each time he was more sure.

Shadrak would almost certainly kill his rival's son. Landis had been right about that, too, as he would have been about many better men. But it would not happen quickly. The wolf was wary. He would wait. He would consolidate his power. He would hope the child died naturally; many did. Later, five years hence, or ten if need be, he would find a way to do it so that no one would ever know. Princes, after all, had to learn many things: to use arms, to hunt, to ride; there would simply be a fall, or a runaway, or a hunting accident.

But if Shadrak and the queen were killed, now, at the height of their power and popularity, there would be only chaos in Kamilan, chaos and death, and everything undone, and the little king trampled in the ruins. . . .

Angmar rose and left the temple. First light was breaking softly in the east. In the west the last thin wedge of moon paled as it fell towards the dark, distant lands of the Almedes. The queen's army, garrisoned at Althen, was already on the mountain road, riding proud to honour their new warlord.

Angmar began to walk. He was old, but he was still strong. He had twenty good years still in him, and he had a task to do for his king.

The dais was scattered with death. The lords of Kamilan lay where they had fallen, among overturned ceremonial benches, among broken garlands and fallen banners. They were less than a bowshot from the sanctuary doors, less than a stone's throw from Jana's abandoned, temporary altar where Shadrak would have knelt for his honours. Here and there small pools of blood spread and trickled down the temple steps.

Kiri stood silent, her crossbow dangling from her hand. The sun was at noon, and the mutiny all but finished. A few handfuls of men from the warbands of Maene and Tamri were still fighting their way towards the gates, hoping to escape. She doubted that any of them would manage it.

In the square it had been over for some time. She looked at Marwen. The queen's face was taut and bitter.

Kiri thought back to their brief, desperate council of war after Angmar had come to them, remembering Marwen's one unrelenting demand:

"I want them all!"

It was Marwen who had insisted they carry on with the ceremony. What better moment could they have, she said, than the one the conspirators themselves had chosen, when they would be all together, brazen and sure on their traitors' dais, easy targets from those same perilous roofs, their warbands there, too, encircled on all sides? *We will have them all,* she said, *and we will end it!*

Shadrak sat with his elbows on the table, staring at his hands; it was she who paced like a caged animal. His own instincts, Kiri knew, would strain the same way as hers, and for the same reasons. But, oh goddess, the risk to her. . . !

"You're not going to end it, Marwen," Medwina said quietly. "They have brothers and nephews and sons. You can never end it. Don't risk your life for this. Let Shadrak take his men and move on them now."

"No," the queen said. "We will go on with the ceremony."

Shadrak would not look at her.

"Lady," he said, anguished, "don't ask this of me—"

"I don't ask it, Shadrak. I command it." She paused, and said again, savagely:

"I want them all!"

But she did not get them all. Crayfe the seneschal was gone. No one knew how. It was one of those things which should never have happened, but somehow did. The guards around the dais had known there was danger; they had been warned to let no one through. But this man was a lord of Council and he was obviously ill; and besides, he was *leaving* the dais, not entering it, surely there could be no danger in that. . .?

They never found a trace of him, and they never learned how he got away. Probably, Kiri thought, he had set up an escape route long before, perhaps years before, fearing that the country would fall to the Dravians. Years later, caravaners from Larandau would swear they had seen him in the court at Vianon, as fat and as devious as ever, toadying to the emperor.

Kiri and the queen picked their way through the ruins, weary, aware finally of the weight of the armour they wore, of the day's intense heat.

"Lady."

They stopped, turning as Angmar the Wise approached them. He bowed faintly. His face was gray with suffering.

"I have been waiting for you, lady."

Kiri's hand closed on her dagger.

"Keep your blade sheathed, minstrel," he said coldly. "You've killed enough for one day. Lady, will you ask your men to let me leave here, and go to my own house? I am weary."

"Angmar." She reached to touch his arm, saw his face harden, and let her hand fall. "Angmar, I know you don't believe me, but I grieve for you."

"Why grieve?" he said. "Had you lived as a woman should, there would be no cause for grief."

"Had *I* lived. . . ?" She paused. "Yes, that's at the heart of everything, isn't it? The way I lived? My life was yours to govern—you and Landis and the lords of Council and the priests and the scroll-makers. It was never mine, it was yours, and when I took it for myself I undid the world.

"I'm sorry for all this death, Angmar, and for your sorrow. But I'm not sorry for my actions, and I never will be, no matter how many worlds I undo."

"You will be destroyed one day, lady."

"So be it. You asked for leave to go home. You have it. I thank you for your loyalty, Angmar, and I wish you well."

"It wasn't loyalty to you."

"I thank you nonetheless."

He bowed again, the same icy, scornful bow, and moved past them, stern and upright for all his years and sorrow. The guards drew back to let him go, and closed ranks again; they never saw him after in the world.

The history of Angmar of Maene, as recorded in the Sixth Book of Kingdoms of the Chronicles of Larandau:

Many evils did the Kamil queen visit upon her people, bringing sorcery and wickedness back into the land, and all of this they tolerated. But in the year of the Great War, after the Dravians had been destroyed on the plains of Tamri, she named the Thyrsian warrior Shadrak to be warlord of Kamilan. This they could not tolerate, for the man was slaveborn and known to be her lover. The lords of Council swore they would not serve him, and planned to put him to death.

It is not known how their plan was discovered, whether by treachery or by witchcraft. But when she learned of it the queen turned her fury full against them, killing them all, her husband and consort among them, as they gathered at the gates of the temple of Jana. Only Crayfe the seneschal managed to escape, and Angmar the Wise was spared—some said because of his years and his long service to the land, others because it was he who had betrayed his cousin. But that is not to be believed, for no man hated the sorceress more bitterly than he.

That day died Landis of Maene, and Favian the lord of Tamri, and Oswin the great warrior, and many hundreds of their kinsmen and followers. Of these a number took refuge in the temple of Mohr, where Shadrak pursued them to their deaths, riding even into the sanctuary to find them.

Thereafter the wolf went with armed men across the land, under the queen's banners, and from every great house he took hostages, and all the kinsfolk of Maene and Tamri were compelled to swear an oath of loyalty to the queen or lose their lands. Then happened a thing which had never before been done in any kingdom. The women were made to swear as well as the men, for the queen said no woman could be bound by a man's oath, but must stand on her own honour. Some chose to swear then, and some would not, and by this men were parted from their wives, and children from their fathers.

These and many more outrages Angmar of Maene watched and endured in silence. The queen's warlord lived openly as her lover, and when her belly grew large with his seed, Angmar could bear no more, fearing as he did for the little prince, who alone stood between the wolf's children and the Kamil throne. So it was that in high summer, the year after the Great War, with the help of a servant in the queen's household, he took the prince and fled with him, and after many impossible dangers brought him to safety in Larandau. There he was no longer called Aran, which was a barbarian name, but instead he was called Landor, after the great general of Adelmar who was the founder of his house. There also he was taught the skills of a warrior, and the history of his fathers, and the great destiny which awaited him in Kamilan. . . .

So it ends, Kiri thought, and it does not end.

A thousand times in her bitterness she had cursed Angmar for a madman, but she knew he was not mad at all. His world perhaps was mad, his iron-ordered world of male dominion, which led this most loyal of men to finally betray everyone, even the king he sought to save. But given that world, there was a terrible reasonableness to everything he had done, and worse, a terrible integrity. He was a man the scroll-makers would remember well.

She sighed, and put him from her mind. It was too fine a day to spoil with melancholy. The sun burned pleasantly on her back, and the air was heavy with perfume. It was high summer, and the queen's long journey was all but complete. Day by day, village by village, outpost by outpost, they had crossed the whole of Kamilan. By now it was a blur to Kiri. There had been too many fairs and feasts to remember, too many tribunals, too many pleas and plaints and grumbles, too many faces bright with hope and eagerness. Their queen had come; now, please Jana, things would be made right!

—*Lady, we need a bridge across this river; it's twenty leagues to the next one, and three men have drowned in the ford. . . .*

—*Lady, this wretched woman sold me three barrels of grain, and not one kernel grew. . . .*

—*Lady, my parents have chosen me a husband, and I hate him. Do the Laws of Kind not give me the right to choose. . . ?*

—*Lady, I try to fight these bandits, but every time I want to gather some men to go after them, the villagers find something else they have to do. . . .*

The hill was long. At the top they rested their horses, looking back at the broad valley of the Niela. It spread behind them as far as the eye could see, to the Gap of Clythe and the mountains beyond. The walled city of Tamri was a distant brown speck on the plain.

"I will do this every summer, I think," the queen said. "My father always said if the people need help they should come to the king. But how can they do so, when they have children to tend, and fields and herds to care for? Or when their kinsmen don't want them to go?"

Kiri sighed happily. She would willingly do this every summer for a long time, she thought. It was like caravaning, without the boredom and with plenty of good food.

"The young chieftain at Creyfell was a fascinating man, don't you think?" the queen said. Then, catching Kiri's expression, she laughed. "Don't look at me so, my friend. I'm not going to sleep with him. At least not this year."

Kiri laughed, too, and they rode on. The road was newly cut and rough, and their progress was slow. More than once Caithland drew rein, wiped his arm across his face and looked back at the queen as if to say: *Really, lady, must we. . . ?*

The Niela vanished behind them, and heavy mountains closed around. Sometimes the queen's eyes would rise searchingly towards the peaks ahead, as if, just for a moment, she was trying to see beyond them, to see the roads and the cities and the houses of the world. How many cities were there across those mountains, how many houses, how many small places where a child could be tucked away? Her enemies blamed her because she did not use her gold to send out hundreds of men, or ask any of her loyal friends to undertake the search. She told them she had no right to do either. The Kamil treasury belonged to the kingdom, and her friends' lives belonged to her friends. To which of them should she say: *Go, wander the earth for me; I can't tell you where. Risk fever and shipwreck, aye, and murder if they find you out; I can't tell you for how long— your whole life, perhaps, looking for a child who might already be dead, and whom none of us has seen since he was eighteen months old. . . ?*

She would not ask that of anyone. From her own resources she hired a few men to search, as many as she could, and otherwise she chose to keep the world she had, and cherish it, and live. Men might blame her for that—men who themselves walked away from mates and children and burning cities with barely a backward look, in the name of destiny or honour or their bonds to other men.

She and Kiri did not talk about it much, not since the night when it had all been said, the night Shadrak gave up and returned with his soldiers, drenched and hungry and utterly defeated. They had found nothing. Angmar had covered his tracks so well they could not even discover which border he had crossed, whether into Dorath, or Dravia, or the lands of the Almedes. Where he would go from there no one could begin to guess.

They sat for hours in Kiri's chamber, close to the fire. She played sometimes; the softness of the lyre comforted both of them.

"They will raise him to be my enemy," the queen said. "To hate everything I stand for, and everything I've done. To hate Shadrak most of all, and you as well."

"They may fail," Kiri said.

"Yes," Marwen said. "And because they may fail I must go on loving him, and because they will probably succeed I dare not love him very much. How will both of those things be possible?"

Slowly, tenderly, she ran her hand over the mound of her belly. She was close to her time; had she not been, she would have been out combing the land along with her soldiers.

Already she treasured this child; she had chosen its name. It would be a girl child, she was certain of that: a beautiful black-haired princess, named for Alyth, the hill queen of old. And she would grow up to be like Alyth, strong and skilful and passionate and wise.

"Blood isn't sacred, Kiri," she whispered darkly. "It's the raising of a child which makes it yours, not the breeding. If they make him my enemy, then so be it. He will not be mine. I will never give this land back to Mohr. Never, not even if it's Aran who comes for it in his name."

There was a long silence; then the queen spoke again, her voice still softer and more dark.

"The Wolf warned me, Kiri. The one who followed me to Dravia. I summoned him in the temple, the night the messengers came and told us Borosar was dead and the army was trapped . . . he said it would cost me more than I knew."

Kiri stared at her, taut with fear.

"Lady. . .?"

"He was under bond, Kiri, and I set him free. To go back to the world, where all things end and begin again . . . he who killed a prince in the flower of his youth. . . ."

Neither spoke again. The lyre, too, lay silent, and there were no sounds at all except the sighing of the fire and the rain.

From that night onward, it was as though the queen had closed a door behind her. She could neither mourn her son as dead, nor cherish him as living. And how could she raise her daughter to be a maybe queen?—*maybe your brother will come back and maybe he won't, maybe he will be fit to rule and maybe he won't. . . .*

No, Kiri thought, that was utterly impossible. And it would grow more impossible as the years passed and the princess began to look towards her future, most impossible of all in a land where the Laws of Kind had held sway for so long, where the crown had always passed from mother to daughter. Among a free people, no other line of inheritance was or ever could be certain.

There was shouting ahead, and Kiri looked up sharply. A half dozen or so armed men had appeared out of the rocks, bows slung over their shoulders. They wore leather breastplates with the queen's crest; except for that, they might have been foresters.

"Welcome, lady. You do us great honour," one of them said, bowing low. "The warlord is expecting you. He is beyond, at the fortress."

"Thank you," the queen said. "Is the building going well?"

"Very well, lady. We'll finish before the snow comes. And next year, the wolf says, we'll build another by the lake of Tamri."

He spoke with great pride. A few years earlier, he might well have howled with outrage. More than one man had, swearing that the great god Harash had not made him a warrior to cut rocks and carry wood. But as the ring of forts began to stretch along the borders, the raiding parties from Dravia no longer dared to cross, and Kamilan's own bandits slunk away to find easier prey in other lands. The valleys of Dohann, which for so many years had been left to wild despair, began to fill with fat goats and thatch-roofed houses and young women quick to smile. Thousands of people could live here, and live well, if only it were safe.

Well then, they swore, they would make it safe. They built forts and watchtowers and bridges; they kept endless watch on the cliff-tops with their mirrors and their horns. And if some of the young men looked wistfully into the distance sometimes, and wished they might instead be riding off to a magnificent war somewhere, and be heroes, the wish was fleeting. Life in Kamilan was good—at least for those who were content to live.

Horns rang, echoing from peak to peak as they rode towards the fort. Shadrak did not wait for them to arrive, but rode headlong out to greet them, rearing his mount to a stop alongside the queen, his hand raised in a gesture which was part greeting, part salute, part hunger to touch her.

"Lady!" He steadied the horse and reached for her hand as she was leaning eagerly to offer it, her face bright with pleasure. They kissed long and wantonly—all the more wantonly, Kiri thought, for being on horseback, and unable to embrace as they might have wished. It was Shadrak who broke the kiss at last, drawing back a little, one hand still tangled in her hair. For a moment they only regarded each other, the world around them quite forgotten.

The queen occasionally bedded elsewhere, and so did he, and because of that more than one young fool had imagined he could steal the wolf's place in her heart—only to discover, sadly or angrily, that he might as well have tried to steal the moon.

"Welcome, Marwen," he said. "It's good to see you."

She ran featherlight fingertips down his bearded cheek. "I missed you, wolf. Are you well?"

"I haven't slept for a fortnight, waiting for you to come."

"You're exaggerating."

"Yes," he said, smiling. "But only a little."

"Poor wolf," she said wickedly. "You're not going to get any sleep tonight, either."

He laughed and kissed her again.

"I'm used to hardship, lady. I will suffer through it. You look utterly splendid, my love."

"I look like a gypsy. And I feel like one. It's two moonturns since we left Kamilan. Kiri says I would have made a good caravaner."

The mention of Kiri's name reminded him that there were other people present, some of them his friends, and he had not greeted them. He did so, and they went on towards the fortress then, slowly, the queen riding close at his side.

The fires were high long before the sun fell, and the smells of roasting meat hung richly on the air. Near the tree where Kiri was sitting, a young bagpiper was warming up his instrument—or perhaps his courage, for he played so badly that even he must have been distressed by it.

"Please Jana we won't have to play together," she grumbled to the servant beside her, who was unpacking the queen's trunks and shaking out her bedding. The latter chuckled merrrily.

"When they crack the wine casks and start dancing," she said, "who is going to notice?"

And indeed, no one seemed to. It was like Belengar again, so much like Belengar that she found her sense of present reality occasionally slipping; found herself once, for a fraction of a moment, wondering what had become of Marwen's crown of leaves; found herself reaching out, as the queen leapt up to lead a dance, with a protest already forming on her lips: *But lady, your feet. . . !*

Oh, it was not the same, not really. The black ramparts of the half-finished fortress loomed over them in the falling darkness, five times the size of little Belengar, with a garrison to match. Seven fires fed the night's feasting, instead of one. The fugitive was a strong queen now, and the border captain was warlord of the land.

But the night nonetheless closed deep and threatening. There were ice fields high over the pass of Dorath, and even in summer the east winds were cold after sunset, a cold which even their fires could not entirely subdue. She sensed the same paradox she had at sensed at Belengar: a place of safety in a coil of peril. Shadrak watched his lady with the same hungering protectiveness; he knew better than any of them, perhaps, how fragile their safety was. He would ring the land with fortresses as Jana had ringed it with mountains, but their enemies would come just the same, as Telhiron had come, and the first Adelmar, and Berend. Mohr had almost won this land, and then it had been taken back, wrenched from his grasp by a woman and a slave. He himself had been made god by mutiny, and he would never give up until Kamilan's mutiny had been undone.

The music was wild now, crashing against the mountainsides and wailing eerily into the clefts of valleys. Kiri no longer played. The soft sounds of her lyre would have been utterly lost in this reckless keening of shawms and drums. Nor did she join the dance, although it was merry. The soldiers were happy to have wine and the company of even a small number of women; the servants were as eager as always to have a party. Most times she would have joined them, but tonight her mood was dark. She sat cross-legged, as she used to sit sometimes in Mercanio's camps, watching and yet lost in her own thoughts. The dance swept by her. She saw the queen's hair spinning in the firelight, the booted feet of dancing soldiers, the black wall of mountains . . . and then, very clearly, she saw Mohr. He was just above the skyline, a presence more than a shape, but immense and restless, brooding over his tiny wounds. For a long time she saw him, as real as a man, with a man's face but without a man's heart. There were no dreams in him, no sorrows, no yearning flesh. His seed was cold. He was a god made of words, and the word was Power. . . .

Voices jarred into her consciousness, a laugh, a cheerful insult, one servant calling the other an old crow. She looked up. The dance went on, but the queen was no longer in the circle, and nor was the wolf; Kiri did not need to ask where they had gone. The voices went on, arguing amiably but with conviction.

—*Really! Among all these soldiers. . . !*

—Ah, leave off. Everyone knows he is her lover. When the wine runs out and we've all danced ourselves silly, he will sleep in her tent anyway. So what's the difference?

—There is a difference. She behaves like a tavern wench sometimes, more than like a queen. It's unworthy of her.

Unworthy. That was the word Luned had always used. Luned thought so many things the queen did were unworthy. And then Luned herself took the queen's baby son, and gave him to Angmar to carry off. Did she ever wonder if that was unworthy?

—You're talking rubbish.

—Her mother Queen Arden would never have dreamt of such a thing!

—Aye, and with that dried-up old king for a partner, why ever would she want to?

—I still say it's unworthy.

Unworthy that a queen should love without marriage, that she should take a slaveborn soldier to her bed, warlord or not; unworthier still to do so openly and proudly, laughing out of the circles of music into the circles of darkness and throbbing blood, tumbling together in the wet grass; the revelry would go on for hours, and their hunger was too sweet, too urgent to waste. . . .

It was much later when they returned to the fires, walking slowly, very close, still wrapped in the soft afterglow of pleasure. They knelt close by the fire, perhaps suddenly noticing that the night was chill. They had brushed themselves off, but not very carefully. Bits of grass and leaves still clung to their clothing, and to Marwen's gracefully flaring sleeves. The back of Shadrak's tunic looked soaked with dew, and the queen's hair was tangled as wind had never tangled it.

Of such things her enemies made a legend.

It did not matter that mostly she governed well. Perhaps it would not even have mattered if she had governed badly. They would have blamed her for it more bitterly than they would have blamed a king; nonetheless, the stories they told about her would have been much the same. For all men knew perfectly well that a woman was either pure or she was not, and if she was not, then she was capable of anything.

The stories went everywhere, even as far as Larandau. They were told around the feast tables of Maene and Tamri, relished with laughter in barracks halls and stables, and nursed with cold hatred by the distant campfires of exiles. They were recounted, too, eagerly and cruelly, by women who had lost land or kinsmen, and also by women who had lost nothing at all. Like Berend's wives in Aralev these women could not imagine freedom, only chaos. They knew what was right, and what was decent, and they had known it for so long they had forgotten who taught them all of it. They hated the queen as fiercely as their men did, and sometimes more so.

Inside Kamilan her enemies were not numerous, and they could do nothing against her for the moment. The people and the common soldiers were passionately loyal, and even among the highborn there were some who shrugged and said: *Treason is treason. Any king in the world would have put the plotters to death—what in Mohr's name did they expect?*

But the shadow was there, the coiling hatred, waiting for its moment, and biding the time with tales of lust and folly. She was unnatural, they said, unnatural and false and cruel, a creature of dark powers and darker passions, a witch queen who betrayed her husband, abandoned her child, and shamed the very gods.

The bitterest thing in all of it, Kiri thought, was that much of what they blamed her for was true. It was true that she did not mourn, that she steeled her heart and said: *The child is gone, there's nothing I can do.* It was true that the duties of her rank ate up most of her time, and she lavished the rest on her friends and her dark lover; true that the Kamil palace rang all winter long with feasts and dancing; true that the seasonal festivals were splendorous and wanton. It was true she drained the Kamil treasury to build fortresses and roads, that she bought the slaves out of Getann and set them free—and that after, when they asked her why she did not send more men out looking for her son, she said: *I have no way to pay them.* She was glad, they said, that he was gone; glad to spend her time with Shadrak and raise his wolf-eyed daughter to be queen. It was true she loved her daughter better than she had ever loved the prince.

And all of that was unforgivable. They invented sins, to make the stories better, but the real sin was that she had taken back her life, and having done so, dared to take joy in it. They did not see that sometimes her joy was edged, that there were currents of darkness in her eyes, as in one who knew her days of joy were numbered. They did not see, and if they had seen, they would not have cared. They cared only that she had killed good men, that she was a sorceress and a whore.

Kiri sat until the fires burned low and the wind from the passes left her shivering with cold. She could write a thousand songs about Marwen of Kamilan, she thought bitterly, but those things were the only things the world of Mohr would notice or remember.

Aye, then so be it. Then it's those things I will sing of, all those things they hate. But I will sing them as she lived them, proudly. Not as evil in the eyes of their jealous and blood-hungry god, but as strength and beauty in the eyes of Jana, who knows and who has not forgotten that once the world was different.

About the author

Marie Jakober was born and raised on an isolated farm in northern Alberta. At 13, she won an international literary competition based in India, with her poem "The Fairy Queen." She attended high school in Edmonton, and graduated with distinction from Carleton University in Ottawa.

Her first novel, *The Mind Gods*, was a finalist in the Search For a New Alberta Novelist competition in 1974. She subsequently published two novels based on the revolutionary struggle in Nicaragua: *Sandinista,* which was awarded the Writers Guild of Alberta Novel Award in 1985, and *A People in Arms.*

In 1988, Ms. Jakober was selected to take part in an international panel on "History and Mythology in the Modern World," at the Olympic Arts Festival. She lives and works in Calgary, where she has been active for many years in women's groups, social action, and the city's writing community.

OUT OF THE MISTS OF MEDIEVAL GERMANY
COMES A RIVETING TALE OF SORCERY AND
SEXUAL OBSESSION. . . .

. . . . THE BLACK CHALICE;
Book One of the Reinmark Chronicle;
by Marie Jakober

. . . A worldly and disillusioned Crusader knight . . . a
beautiful pagan sorceress . . . a tormented young squire . . . a
mysterious castle on a road which does not exist . . . a lord
who dreams of power such as no man has ever had . . . and a
proud empire on the brink of civil war. . . .

This is the world of THE REINMARK CHRONICLE, a
world where truth and legend are inseparable, where veelas
haunt the forest and old Nordic gods still ride to battle . . . a
world brought vividly to life in a new magic realist novel.

Available November 1, 1994

Gullveig Books
Box 66023
University of Calgary Post Office
Calgary, AB, CANADA
T2N 4T7